The Raate Road

James   Mullins

Published By: Longinus Publishing

ISBN: 9798859441785

Table of Contents

Chapter 1

Nearly Midnight, Finnish 9th Division HQ, Three Kilometers South of Suomassalmi, Central Finland

January 1st, 1940

Colonel Hjalmar Siilasvuo peered down at the map spread across the campaign table in front of him. The well-worn wooden table, its faded gray paint chipped in places, occupied the central position in the 9th Division's headquarters large tent. He placed his index finger on a small wooden tile that represented Task Force Mandelin on the map. The tile sat just to the north of the village of Hauklia which lay near the Raate Road.

A long string of tiles spread across the Raate road representing the estimated location of the Soviet 44th Division's various units. The line of tiles ended a dozen centimeters shy of the village of Suomassalmi on the map. That precious space, which looked so small on the map, represented the four kilometers that separated the now destroyed Soviet 163rd Division from the force sent to rescue them. A force now in need of rescue itself.

Each of the tiles, which represented a battalion sized formation of the Soviet 44th Motorized Rifle Division, resembled a snake when viewed as a whole. The colonel smiled as he thought about the analogy, *It is indeed a snake come to strike at the heart of our nation and inject the poison of Bolshevism into its healthy body.*

The colonel smiled ruefully as he thought about the cancer that had consumed their large neighbor. Regaining his focus, Siilasvuo's gaze returned to the tile representing Task Force Mandelin. On the opposite side of the Raate road, sat another tile representing a Finnish unit, Task Force Makiniemi.

"I know it looks impossible, but it's not. In fact, these are the best odds we've had against the 44th since Vinogradov crossed the border. Remember what Renning's company alone managed to accomplish while we were finishing off the 163rd." Major Valli asked Siilasvuo.

"Yes, but it nearly destroyed the company." Siilasvuo countered.

"True." Major Valli said, "But it proved how unprepared the Ukrainians that comprise most of the fighting men of the 44th are to fight under these conditions. They are poorly led, lack the proper clothing for the conditions, and are bewildered by the terrain. These men grew up on the vast flatlands of the steppe. They don't know how to deal with trees."

"You're right of course. Our frozen primordial forests are a far cry from the flat steppes just north of the Black Sea. Their homeland enjoys much warmer sunshine and moderate temperatures in January than our humble little slice of the world." Colonel Siilasvuo replied. He turned to the enlisted man, manning the radio set and said, "Corporal Wirta, signal Lieutenant Colonel Mandelin and Makiniemi to attack."

"Immediately, colonel." Wirta replied.

Wirta picked up the microphone that lay on the campaign table. In addition to the mic, the table held a large radio set. Like the radio table's counterpart that sat in the middle of the tent next to the wood-burning stove, its gray coat of paint had seen better days. The corporal keyed the mic, and said, "Mandelin and Makiniemi you may tickle Stalin's balls."

Valli rolled his eyes, "Do all our codes and passwords have to involve perverse statements?"

Siilasvuo smiled and said, "No, but it amuses the men, and therefore increases morale. In addition, I like to imagine the faces of the Soviet radio operators listening in on our conversations turning crimson when they hear the words."

"Can you imagine one of those commissars asking what was just said and the poor bastard manning the radio repeating it?" Valli asked.

"Do you think the operator would tell the truth?" Siilasvuo asked in curiosity.

"Hard to say. I imagine it must be a really tough decision. Lie about what was said and risk getting shot or tell the commissar the truth and risk getting shot." Valli said.

Siilasvuo briefly chuckled then changed the subject, "I wish I could be there on the front lines leading the men."

Major Valli put a hand on the colonel's shoulder and said, "I'm afraid we are long past those days my friend. Fighting is better left to younger men."

Siilasvuo looked down at himself. His trim muscular form was apparent even through the uniform he wore. His gaze then shifted to Major Valli's less than perfect form, which showed evidence of the major's penchant for the good life and said, "Speak for yourself, I'm still the same weight I was during the Great War. Not all of us have overly indulged in the finer things life has to offer."

Valli rubbed his balding head as he smiled and said, "You have to live for today, as you are not guaranteed a tomorrow."

The colonel's gaze shifted to the map, and he sighed wistfully, "I wonder how they are doing?"

"I'm sure they are doing just fine. The 44th would probably be very difficult to deal with out on a flat plain with all those tanks, but here they are confused little ducks to afraid to move." Valli replied.

Siilasvuo opened his mouth to reply when the radio set suddenly crackled to life. The two officer's gaze shifted to the radio which sat in the corner of the tent opposite the entrance flap. Corporal Wirta, the operator, sat in a folding campaign chair as he leaned forward. Wirta held a pencil and notebook in his hands ready to record what was about to be said. The two officers heard, what to them sounded virtually unintelligible, but to a trained ear like Wirta's was as clear as the words being spoken by the officers just a few meters away.

When the transmission ended, Wirta kept scribbling

notes into his notepad, "Well?" Siilasvuo demanded impatiently.

Corporal Wirta stood and turned toward the Colonel, "That was an update from Task Force Mandelin. They have succeeded in capturing a section of the road but have now come under heavy counterattack."

Valli slapped Siilasvuo on the back and said, "There see. Nothing to worry about, Mandelin has already captured his objective."

"Yes, but can he hold it?" Siilasvuo said.

"He'll hold." Valli reassured the colonel.

"I don't share your confidence, major. Let's do what we can to bolster their firepower." Colonel Siilasvuo said, "Corporal Wirta, signal the artillery, I want six of our eight guns, transferred to Task Force Mandelin's section of the road."

"Yes, sir." Corporal Wirta replied.

Siilasvuo's gaze fell to the wooden counter to the south of the village of Hauklia which represented Task Force Makiniemi, "What's going on with you?"

The colonel closed his eyes and imagined what the men of Task Force Makiniemi must be going through. He envisioned Finnish men on skis launching themselves at the Soviets on the road blazing away with their Suomi sub-machine guns. He smiled at the vision of his brave men, pushing their way through the enemy as they battled their way onto the road.

Suddenly, a tremendous explosion tore a large hole in the Finnish line flinging bodies and pieces of bodies in all directions. He looked from his men to an approaching

Soviet KV-1 heavy tank. The barrel of its main gun still smoking from the high explosive shell it had just fired. The other Finnish attackers, turned and launched themselves at the tank, only to be mowed down by the metal monstrosity's coaxial machine gun, *No.* Siilasvuo screamed in his mind.

The colonel was pulled from his vision as the radio once again crackled to life. Wirta dutifully wrote down the transmission. This time Siilasvuo, fearing the worst didn't rush him to make his report. Finally, the corporal turned to Siilasvuo and said, "I have a report from Task Force Makiniemi, colonel."

Siilasvuo looked up at the ceiling of the tent and took a deep breath, *Please God.*

The colonel exhaled sharply, "Go on."

"Makiniemi fought their way onto the road but were then beset upon by enemy tanks." Wirta said.

"And they've been pushed back into the forest with heavy casualties." Siilasvuo finished.

"No, sir. Well, they did take some casualties, but they were able to disable the attacking tanks, and secure the road." Wirta said.

Siilasvuo again looked up at the tent's ceiling and sent a mental, *Thank you.* To God.

The colonel turned to Wirta and said, "Signal Mandelin and Makiniemi to secure their foothold on the road. Once they are dug in, they are to signal us and prepare for phase two, widening the distance between the two Soviet forces they have just torn asunder.

Chapter 2

Dawn, Three Kilometers South of Suomassalmi, Central Finland

January 2nd, 1940

Hale and Leo were awoken by the sound of the train's screeching brakes as it began to slow to a stop. The newly commissioned lieutenant gazed out the window at the gray overcast skies and the snow-covered trees that dotted the land, "The trees are different here." Hale remarked.

"They look smaller." Leo agreed.

"Seems to be a lot more fir trees and fewer birch." Hale said, "I've never been this far from home. I don't know the terrain. Am I going to be any good up here?"

Leo placed a reassuring hand on Hale's shoulder,

"Trees are trees and snow is snow. You'll be fine."

Hale smiled at Leo. The smile did not reach his eyes, *I couldn't beat him on my home turf, how am I going to defeat Kuznetsov in this place. I miss Karelia already*. He thought in dismay.

Hale looked back out the window and saw several figures waiting for the train's arrival. A grizzly bear of a man with sergeant's stripes, stood with his arms folded. His thick skull was framed with short iron gray hair. He scowled at the train as if its mere presence offended him somehow. The air was so frigid, that a faint cloud of steam slowly wafted upward off the top of the man's uncovered head. Nearby, an attractive woman with raven black hair and hazel eyes, obviously a nurse, chatted with a middle-aged major.

The nurse wore a white wool overcoat and a white fur hat. She looked like she belonged on the streets of Helsinki. Not in this remote forest a hundred kilometers away from the nearest settlement that could be called a town.

The major wore a gray uniform cut from the same fabric as Hale's new one. His thinning blond hair, absent of gray, indicated that he was in his forties. His ample midsection hung over his belt suggesting that he lived a little too well before the war.

Hale and Leo rose from their seats, put on their coats, and picked up their packs and slipped them onto their backs. They grabbed their rifles and headed for the passenger car's door. The pair opened the door and stepped outside the train into the icy morning air. The stunningly cold air hit the two men like a physical force, "This place is even colder than home." Hale observed.

Leo shrugged, "Once you get past ten degrees below zero it hardly matters. Your piss will freeze before it hits the ground regardless."

Before Hale could reply the sergeant started screaming at a group of privates that were streaming from a third-class car further back from the train's engine. Hale, now an officer, had been allotted a seat in first class. Upon boarding in Mikkeli, when the conductor tried to send Leo to second class, where the NCO's rode, Hale told the conductor that he required Leo to stay with him so they could plan. The old man had smiled knowingly and moved on.

The pair stopped and observed the sergeant as he screamed at the privates still on the train, "You bunch better start moving your asses off that train. If any of you are still on it in sixty seconds you had best be fast, otherwise I'm going to plant my boot in your ass!"

Leo laughed as the privates hastened their efforts to debark the train, "Damn sure don't miss those days."

The attractive nurse stopped chatting with the major and called to the nurses as they exited the first-class car one by one.

The major glanced over at Hale and asked, "Lieutenant Karhonen?"

Hale snapped to attention and said, "Yes, sir!"

Major Valli chuckled, "No need for that crap here."

"Sir?" Hale said.

"Drop the discipline and stop calling me sir. If that Russian sniper is about, you'll get me killed." Valli said.

"My apologies." Hale said.

Valli slapped Hale's back and said, "Hurry up and kill the bastard so you can stand at attention and kiss my ass all you want."

Leo laughed. The major whirled around to face Leo, "What is so funny?" Valli's eyes fell to Leo's stripes and said, "Sergeant." In an admonished tone.

"You, major." Leo replied.

Valli grinned, "At least one of you has a sense of humor. Come with me. Colonel Siilasvuo would like to speak with you."

"What about our horses?" Hale asked.

"They will be taken care of until you need them." Valli replied.

"How far do we have to go?" Hale asked.

"Not far. Division HQ is just over that rise on the other side of the medical tents." The major replied.

As they walked the major asked, "So how goes the war in Karelia?"

"We're holding at the Mannerheim Line." Hale paused, then added, "For now."

"What kind of casualties are we taking?" The major inquired.

"When we fight them in small groups and use the terrain to our advantage, hardly any. The untrained Soviet conscripts are bewildered by the wilderness. The poor bastards defending the Mannerheim Line have it much tougher." Hale said.

"How so?" Valli asked.

"For starters they can catch artillery shells by the bucket full." Leo said.

"Not only is the Soviet artillery relentless. We watched an entire regiment get smashed in a fruitless counterattack." Hale said.

"Seems odd that we would leave the cover of those very expensive defenses we spent half our annual military budget building for the last ten years to launch an attack." Valli observed.

"Colonel Isakson thought a counterattack would breakthrough after his brigade repulsed and shattered two entire divisions." Leo said.

"What happened to the counterattack?" Valli asked.

"The Soviets had set a trap. We nearly lost the entire regiment in a matter of minutes." Leo replied.

"Summer of cunts." Valli said, then added, "We've suffered nothing like the casualties you've described here."

"Oh? How come?" Leo asked.

"Because the Soviets in this sector are completely daft." Major Valli replied.

"What are they doing that makes you think that?" Hale asked.

"Well first off the brilliant general of the first division they sent in, the 163rd decided to divide his troops." Valli said.

"That's dumb." Leo said.

The major continued, "Oh, that's not the half of it. They were sent in with inadequate gear to deal with the cold and little in the way of food."

"That's crazy." Leo said.

"Oh, it gets better. To rescue the morons that we surrounded in Suomassalmi, they sent in a second division, the 44th. The 44th is a fully mechanized division." Valli said.

"That doesn't sound stupid." Hale said.

"Oh, it would have been the perfect thing to do if we were in some other part of Europe that had roads." The major said.

Surprised, Hale asked, "There aren't any roads in this part of the country?"

Major Valli smiled, "Technically there are roads here, but I wouldn't describe them as such. They're little more than game trails with the occasional piece of gravel that has been swallowed up by the mud and vomited back up. Assuming of course the road isn't so frozen that you would need a pickaxe to breech the surface."

"It never ceases to amaze me how dumb the Russians can be." Leo said.

"Had some prior experience with them?" The major asked.

Leo nodded, "Twenty years ago, when I was young and stupid myself, I had the misfortune of fighting with those idiots in the Great War."

"Against the Germans?" Valli asked.

"Yeah." Leo said.

"You're lucky to be alive. The primary Russian strategy for the Great War was to throw as many bodies at the Germans as possible in the hopes that they had more bodies than the Germans had bullets. The Germans always had more bullets. How did you manage to survive?" Valli said.

"I convinced my lieutenant that he needed a sniper to sit back and pick off targets during attacks. That kept me safe while his other men died in droves conducting stupid and pointless frontal assaults." Leo said.

The major opened his mouth to reply when a man in a half-buttoned uniform who was flanked by a woman, and a man in a lab coat came into view at the top of the rise they were approaching, "Pekka?" Hale asked.

Pekka turned toward Hale and exclaimed, "Hale! My God you're alive!"

The man in the lab coat tugged on Pekka's shoulder, "Let's get moving. You're still recovering, and you can't be out here for long. Especially not without a proper coat." Dr. Mäkinen said.

Pekka ignored the Doctor and threw his arms around Hale, "It's so good to see you. I wasn't sure if you survived Volkov's attack."

"I wouldn't have except for Kuznetsov." Hale said.

Before Pekka had a chance to respond, Dr. Mäkinen got in his face and said, "Captain, I insist you return to your bed this instant. Your immune system will shut down if you get too cold and then you will almost certainly die from an infection!"

"Please dear. Do as the Doctor says. You can keep talking to your friend as soon as you lay back down." Eevi, Pekka's wife, said.

"No he can't. The colonel wishes to see him now!" Major Valli insisted.

"Summer of cunts people! Pekka exclaimed in disgust, "Can't I just have one minute with my friend?"

Hale placed his hands on Pekka's shoulders and said, "Return to your bed so you can heal. I'll come visit you as soon as I am able."

Pekka cast a withering glance, first at Dr. Mäkinen and then at Major Valli, "Very well."

The group parted ways. Hale and Leo, with Major Valli in the lead, resumed their walk to the 9th Division's Headquarters. About halfway to their destination, Hale ran into another familiar face, "I'd recognize that mountain anywhere, "Sergeant Kivi!"

"Hale! You survived." Kivi roared happily, then added, "It's lieutenant now. I'm your superior once again."

Hale unbuttoned the top button on his white coat and flashed his collar at Kivi, "Are you kidding me?" Kivi growled, "You're a senior lieutenant now?"

Hale beamed, "Promoted by General Mannerheim himself."

Kivi smiled and slapped Hale on the back so hard it nearly knocked him over, "That makes two of us. General Mannerheim bumped me to junior lieutenant. Colonel Siilasvuo gave me my second silver circle earlier this morning."

Hale slapped Kivi on his left bicep, "Congratulations! That's great. To tell you the truth it would feel weird to outrank you. You'll have to tell me all about your recent engagements."

"Lieutenant!" Major Valli yelled in a shrill voice, "I must insist that you come with me at once to check in with Colonel Siilasvuo."

Hale whirled around and glared at Valli as he growled, "Fine."

"If you don't mind major, I would like to accompany you to Division HQ." Kivi said.

"Suit yourself lieutenant." Valli replied.

A few minutes later the three men reached the 9th Division's Head Quarters tent. Kivi pulled the entry flap open and Major Valli and Hale went inside. As soon as both men were enclosed within the much warmer interior of the tent, they began to stomp their feet to get the snow off of their boots, before it melted, and remove their gloves.

The inside of the tent was lit by several gas burning lanterns hanging from the ceiling supports of the tent. In the center of the tent, next to a wood burning stove, sat a campaign table. A map was spread out on the table and a single man leaned over the map as he scratched his chin in contemplation. Sensing the newcomer's presence, he turned around, "Welcome back major. I assume this man is Hale Karhonen?"

Valli nodded, "Yes colonel."

Colonel Siilasvuo extended his hand to Hale, "Nice to meet you son. When General Mannerheim informed me that he would be sending an expert sniper to deal with my problem, I didn't realize you would be this young."

"Hale is the most gifted shot with a rifle I ever had the privilege of instructing." Kivi said.

"He was a student of yours?" The colonel asked.

Kivi nodded in response to the colonel's question, "Small world." The colonel said.

Hale, projecting an outward air of confidence that he didn't feel said, "Can you tell me what has been happening colonel?"

Colonel Siilasvuo grinned, "Right down to business. I like that."

The colonel pointed down at the map spread out across the table in the center of the tent and said, "This is the Raate road. The red circles on the map overlay represent the four Mottis that we have chopped the 44th Motorized Rifle Division into. The black ovals surrounding each of the four Mottis represent battalion sized forces. The four regimental sized forces named after their commanders, Lieutenant Colonels Mandelin, and Makiniemi, plus Majors Kari, and Fagernas are comprised of the individual battalions shown on the map."

Siilasvuo pointed at the westernmost black oval, "The force blocking the road, so that the 44th can't move any further west is Task Force Mandelin. They were hit first by the sniper. Mandelin's group sent several squads in pursuit, but the bastard slipped away." The colonel paused to sigh, then added, "He took out one of the pursuing squads in its entirety."

"That sounds like Kuznetsov." Leo suggested.

The colonel turned towards Leo, "You're familiar with

this Soviet sniper?"

"We've tangled with him twice before in Karelia." Hale said.

"Well, you're still alive so you must be pretty good. Better than anyone I've sent against him in fact." Siilasvuo said.

Hale decided not to mention the fact that Kuznetsov saved him from Volkov and then spared him. Instead, he replied, "Perhaps. Many of us didn't make it."

Kivi, sensing that Hale was getting nervous, pointed at the map and said, "Tell us about the other encounters. Perhaps there is a pattern."

"There is none that I can see, but maybe being snipers yourselves, you can puzzle something out that I've missed." Colonel Siilasvuo replied. He pointed at the second black oval and said, "Task force Mandelin is covering three sides of the first motti, Makiniemi has the eastern side. The motti sits just to the west of the village of Hauklia. We believe that General Vinogradov is in that Motti. It is the largest. This force here just to the east of Hauklia is task force Makiniemi. They have the unenviable task of holding the section of road they occupy against two Mottis. Kuznetsov hit them second."

"Am I to assume that the red Xs represent Kuznetsov's points of attack?" Hale asked.

Colonel Siilasvuo smiled, "Correct lieutenant."

Hale whistled, "He's been busy."

"Now you are starting to understand my problem. Despite our recent victories the sniper's successes are sapping morale. I'm afraid if he isn't stopped soon, our men will pull back and the 44th will slip through our fingers." The Colonel replied.

"Tell me about the other two forces." Hale asked.

The Colonel pointed at the map and said, "This one here is task force Kari. Like Makiniemi they have the unfortunate task of being assigned to hold a section of the road against two mottis on either side of them. Kuznetsov skipped over them and hit this task force, Fagernas next. Fagernas is holding a bridge which is preventing the Soviets in the last Motti from escaping. Kuznetsov hit them next. He then circled back and hit Kari."

Suddenly the radio in the corner of the tent came to life. The sergeant seated at the radio listened intently. Hale couldn't understand a word of what was being spoken, "How can anyone understand that?"

As Colonel Siilasvuo walked over to the radio he replied, "You develop an ear for it eventually. Truth be told I've been listening to it for weeks and still don't understand what they are saying. It sounds like gibberish to me."

Hearing the colonel right behind him the sergeant turned and said, "He's hitting Mandelin again."

"This guy keeps disappearing like a fart in the Sahara and then reappearing at will." The colonel said. He took a deep breath and let it out slowly as the radio fell silent, "Tell him we have a special sniper force ready to kill Kuznetsov. See if they can provide you with his last known coordinates sergeant."

The sergeant turned back to his radio as the colonel turned around and told Hale, "I need you in the field now. What do you need to make that happen?"

"Kuznetsov is better than any sniper I have ever encountered. I need more men. Do you have any snipers that can join my team?" Hale asked.

"No, he's managed to kill every sniper we've sent against him except Captain Renning. I think the only thing that saved Renning was the fact that he was blown out of a tank while Kuznetsov was stalking him." the colonel replied. He then turned to Kivi and asked, "Can you join Karhonen's team?"

Kivi's face darkened as he said, "I should be senior to him."

"You said yourself he is the most gifted sniper you have ever taught." The colonel reminded Kivi.

Kivi slowly nodded, "True. I'll go with him. Someone needs to keep his butt covered when the enemy manages to get close."

"Thank you, Lieutenant Kivi. I appreciate you volunteering. Let's be clear. Karhonen is in charge of the group."

Kivi smiled broadly, "Good. I can focus on killing Bolsheviks then."

"Are there any others available?" Hale urged.

"There are the two survivors from Renning's company that fought with him in Karelia." Siilasvuo suggested.

"I'll take them." Hale said.

"Excellent. I suppose he will be long gone before you can get to the spot he just hit. Let's plan to send you out the next time he strikes." Siilasvuo said.

"Can I check in with a friend in the hospital tent before I head out? I promised him I would return." Hale said.

The Colonel pursed his lips, "There's no way you'll be able to intercept him where he is attacking now. Given that fact, I suppose there isn't any harm in it. You are to go nowhere else. If you have to leave the hospital, come directly back here. Clear?"

"Clear, sir, and thank you." Hale replied.

"I'll have the two men report directly to the hospital tent. Who are you going to visit?" Siilasvuo asked.

"Captain Renning." Hale replied.

The colonel laughed, "You seem to know all of my best men, lieutenant. Let us hope that soon I will be able to count you amongst them. Dismissed."

Hale snapped to attention and saluted Colonel Siilasvuo. He turned to Kivi and asked, "Do you know where the hospital tent is?"

"Yes. I've spent some time there myself. I'll show you." Kivi.

"Thank you, lieutenant." Hale replied.

As they started to walk Kivi said, "Reporting to you is going to take some getting used to."

"It is." Hale agreed, "Every time I see you, I get the same nervous flutter in my stomach that I did during my first weeks of training."

Kivi threw his head back and laughed heartily. Hale, used to Kivi communicating by yelling and threatening, was shocked, "I didn't know you could laugh." Hale said.

Kivi grinned at Hale, "Why wouldn't I? You just made my day."

The three men arrived at the hospital tent where Captain Renning was convalescing. Once inside the tent, Kivi led Hale and Leo to Pekka's bed. The captain was eating some piping hot sausage soup. Steam curled upward from the surface of the brown liquid as he happily slurped some of it from his spoon, "That looks good." Hale said.

Pekka set down his spoon and smiled up at Hale, "You came."

"Of course, I came. I always keep my promises." Hale said.

"I know you do, but I was afraid the colonel was going to send you and Leo directly into action against that bastard Kuznetsov." Pekka said.

"Kuznetsov isn't as bad as you make him out to be. He does operate by some sort of honor code. If he didn't, I wouldn't be standing in front of you right now. In regard to the colonel, he's going to send me against Kuznetsov the next time our Soviet sniper friend strikes." Hale said.

"Well hopefully the bastard is sleeping then. I can use some company. Being stuck in this bed is incredibly boring." Pekka said.

Hale grinned, "So tell me how you managed to get yourself blown out of a tank?"

Pekka raised an eyebrow, "You heard about that did you?"

"Yeah. Now give me the details. First of all, how did you manage to get a hold of a tank?" Hale asked.

"Oh, ye of little faith, why the company I brilliantly commanded captured not one, but two tanks." Pekka said.

"Well, pardon me your lordship. I didn't realize we were in the presence of a military genius as brilliant as General Mannerheim." Hale bowed deeply as he said, "You have my sincerest of apologies your lordship. Please forgive my ignorance, my simple peasant mind simply cannot comprehend your greatness." Hale shot back.

The two men stared at each other for nearly a minute. Neither officer refused to lower their eyes and concede defeat to the other, *I thought these two were supposed to be best friends? I'm starting to think I'm going to have to separate them lest a fight break out.* Kivi thought.

Then it happened. The left corner of Pekka's lips turned ever so slightly upward. Seeing his friend's serious countenance start to waiver, Hale burst into laughter.

Pekka immediately joined in. Between chuckles Pekka said, "I've missed you." He thrust a thumb in Kivi's direction and said, "I've been stuck with him for a week now. Absolutely no sense of humor."

Hale gave Kivi a sidelong glance and said, "I agree none whatsoever. I'm not sure how you managed to survive a week of his dreariness without charging into machine gun fire to end your suffering."

"Great, so now you two comedians are going to gang up on me." Kivi complained.

Hale and Pekka turned to Kivi and in unison said, "Yes."

Suddenly Kivi burst into laughter. Hale's eyes widened as he was taken aback by the booming baritone chortle of Kivi's mirth. Seeing Hale's shock Kivi said, "Why should I leave all of the fun to you two?"

Hale started to unsling his rifle from his shoulder as he said, "Who are you and what have you done with Lieutenant Kivi? Are you a Soviet spy?"

All three men burst into laughter as Pekka's wife looked on in bewilderment. Suddenly Dr. Mäkinen appeared and hissed, "Other patients are trying to rest and recover from their wounds. What's with all the damn noise?"

The three men turned towards Mäkinen and started to laugh even harder. Frustrated, Mäkinen turned to Eevi and asked, "How much has this lot had to drink?"

"Not a drop." Eevi replied.

"That can't be possible. Surely nothing without the aid of alcohol is this funny." Mäkinen said.

Pekka stopped laughing long enough to point to Dr. Mäkinen and say, "The look on your face is."

Pekka's observation caused the three men to erupt into fresh peals of laughter. When the laughter started to die down, Hale asked, "You still haven't told me how you got blown out of a tank."

"To tell you the truth I don't really remember. One minute I was fighting my tank and trying not to get blown up. The next moment I remember I was on the ground and on fire." Pekka said.

"What he isn't telling you is that we managed to drive a wedge into the 44th's column." Kivi said.

"We being?" Hale asked.

"E company. The unit I was commanding." Pekka

said.

"They put you in command of an entire company? Man, Siilasvuo must have been really hard up for officers." Hale said.

"He was pretty desperate." Pekka agreed.

"Siilasvuo needed someone absolutely bat shit crazy to distract the 44th, while the rest of the regiment finished off the 163rd." Kivi said.

"You attacked an entire division with a company?" Hale said in awe.

"Well, the colonel thought I did good work down in Karelia using a platoon to defend against a regiment. I guess sending a company against a division seemed like a natural progression." Pekka said.

"I thought all of the Special Operations Group members had fallen to Volkov in Karelia. Where did you manage to find an entire company of them to perform another crazy stunt?" Hale asked.

"Oh, they did." Kivi said, "We led reservists against the 44th."

Hale's eyes widened as he whistled in appreciation, "What sisu! Did they have to cut a hole in the mattress of your hospital bed to make room for your balls?"

Pekka started laughing hysterically at Hale's words, then grimaced in pain, "If you get much funnier, I'm going to rupture my stiches."

"Truth be told, when he told us his plan, we argued between committing suicide, killing Pekka and running away, or ensuring our wills were up to date." Kivi said.

"I voted for killing Pekka." Cunnar said.

"I wanted to just commit suicide." Tomas added.

Hale whirled around, "Cunnar! Tomas! You're alive."

"No thanks to him." Cunnar pointed at Pekka with a smile on his face.

"Hey now, my leadership can't be that bad, you managed to survive all four battles I commanded." Pekka said.

"Yeah, thanks to some twisted plan only known to God." Tomas said.

"I thought Cunnar was supposed to be the whiney one of the pair?" Kivi said.

Cunnar chuckled and said, "I don't have anything to be grumpy about anymore. I should have been killed several times over. I'm grateful for the fact that I'm still drawing breath."

Tomas' eyes fell as he said, "I miss my wife and daughter. I wonder how they are getting along?"

"I'm sure they are both in a warm bed somewhere in Helsinki right now." Pekka said.

Tomas smiled, "We need to hurry up and throw the devils out of our country so I can get back to my family." Tomas started to tear up as he added, "At least what's left of it."

"We do indeed." Cunnar agreed as he put an arm around Tomas' shoulders in support.

"I still haven't heard how Pekka managed to end up in command of a tank." Hale said.

"Capturing a tank was a lot easier than you would imagine. At least one driven by the idiot Russians. Two platoons of tanks were stupid enough to follow a group of my men into the woods. Through creative means we managed to kill five of the tanks and capture another." Pekka said.

"What did you get?" Leo asked.

"A T-26." Pekka said proudly.

"So, what's it like being inside of a tank?" Hale asked.

"It's very cramped, dark and smelly. When the main gun is fired add smoky and reeking of cordite." Pekka replied.

"That doesn't sound comfortable at all." Hale said, "Was it at least warm?"

"Yes, the temperature inside was pretty comfortable as long as you kept the hatches shut. I spent most of my time commanding the tank by standing in the commander's hatch with my torso and head exposed to the outside." Pekka said.

"Why didn't you just command from the inside?" Leo asked.

"Because you can't see shit from inside." Pekka said, then added, "I think that is why a lot of the Soviet tankers are so bad. They rely on the tiny viewports to navigate and fight their tanks."

"The commanders would take many more casualties if they exposed themselves to direct the crew in battle." Kivi observed.

"Instead, they lose the entire crew. It was crazy how

we regularly outmaneuvered groups of enemy tanks."
Pekka said.

"It was pretty impressive." Kivi added, "The Soviet
tankers seemed to be as poorly trained as their infantry.
They didn't seem to know how to fight their tanks in a
forest."

"Compared to what we have the equipment the Soviets
possess borders on the unbelievable. Why are the soldiers
of the Red Army so inept?" Cunnar asked.

"Good question. They seemed much more competent
in Spain." Kivi said.

"I wonder what changed between 1936 and now?"
Hale asked.

"There was a rumor floating around a few years back
that Stalin purged all of his best military officers for fear
that they would try to overthrow him." Kivi said.

"Considering how much warmongering that bastard
likes to engage in, that seems really stupid." Pekka said.

A private entered the tent and asked for Hale. One of
the nurses pointed at the cluster of men around Pekka's
bed and said, "He's the young one with the blond hair."

The private thanked the nurse and rushed up to Hale,
"Lieutenant Karhonen."

"Yes?" Hale responded.

"Colonel Siilasvuo needs to see you immediately.
There are reports of sniper activity from Task Force
Mandelin."

Chapter 3

Noon, One Kilometer Southwest of Hauklia, Central Finland

January 2nd, 1940

Hale, followed by Kivi, Leo, Cunnar, and Tomas led the 9th Division's counter sniper squad through the woods. He was navigating through the unfamiliar forest toward the last known location of Kuznetsov. All four men were mounted on horses so they could make better time across the remote, picturesque snow-covered lands that adjoined the Raate Road.

Hale held up his right arm and formed a fist, signaling those behind him to stop. He dismounted from Liv and while holding her reigns in his hands stepped out in front of the horse and squatted down. Crossing in front of their path was a set of tracks, "This might be something."

Kivi dismounted and walked to Hale. He looked down at the tracks and slowly nodded, "It looks like these were made by one man."

"I agree. These tracks didn't come from a column of men walking in each other's boot prints to hide their numbers. The edges of these prints are well formed and precisely outlined. In addition, the treads of the boots are clearly imprinted into the snow." Hale said.

"Do we follow them toward Task Force Mandelin and look for some shell casings to confirm our suspicion or do we follow now, in the hopes that these tracks belong to Kuznetsov?" Kivi asked.

"A difficult choice. Confirm that this was indeed the enemy responsible for the killing of our man or just follow the tracks which may turn out to be another Finn." Hale said.

"We would lose precious time and he'll likely be able to strike again before we can catch him." Kivi said.

Hale stood and looked around at the surrounding trees as he sighed. The warm air ejected from his lungs formed a large cloud of steam in front of his face, "It may become very difficult to track him once the sun goes down."

"Which is only an hour from now." Kivi said.

"So, we had better not waste time following the tracks back to their source in an attempt to confirm if they belong to a Soviet sniper or not." Hale said.

Without another word Hale and Kivi remounted their horses. Hale gently tapped Liv's sides with his boots and pulled her right reign. The group of five Finns left the game trail they had been following and turned into the primordial wilderness that surrounded them.

Hale followed the tracks for roughly half an hour as they rode without incident. Snow started to fall so he increased their pace, lest the trail disappear before they could catch up to their quarry. Suddenly the sound of a single rifle shot pierced the silence.

Tomas cried out and fell from his horse. The rest of the group jumped out of their saddles and threw themselves into a prone position on the ground, "That sounded like it came from the west. Did anyone see where that shot came from?" Hale asked.

"Oh my God, the blood!" Cunnar's panic laden voice exclaimed.

Tomas held his right hand over the wound in his side. Blood trickled around his fingers as Cunnar looked at him in horror, "It hurts." Tomas gasped.

Cunnar took his pack off and dug through it, desperately searching for his first aid kit, "I'll get you patched up with my first aid kit and then we can get you back to the hospital."

"The pain." Tomas whispered, his voice weakening.

Cunnar finally located his first aid kit. He opened a tin container that held the kit's bandages and gauze, "Move your hand so I can see." Cunnar urged.

Tomas did as he was instructed. Cunnar gasped when he saw the wound, "That bad huh?" Tomas said in a weak voice.

"Just surprised is all. I've never seen a wound that close up before." Cunnar lied.

Tomas' wound gushed dark, nearly black colored blood. Cunnar pressed several pieces of gauze into the wound to try and stop the bleeding. Tomas gasped in pain at the contact and tried to weakly push Cunnar away, "I'm trying to help."

Leo, who had been riding last in the column, searched through the first aid kit until he found the kit's single-use morphine injectors. He quickly jammed the needle into Tomas' leg and dispensed the pain killing drug. A few seconds later Tomas sighed in relief as the drug flowed through his veins. Within two minutes, he stopped trying to push Cunnar away.

"How does it look? Will I survive long enough to see my wife and daughter again?" Tomas asked.

Leo made eye contact with Cunnar and shook his head to indicate that Tomas' wound was mortal. While Cunnar and Leo had been tending Tomas' wound, Hale and Kivi unslung their rifles and were trying to determine where the enemy sniper was. They weren't having any luck.

"See anything?" Hale asked Kivi.

"No." Kivi replied.

"Keep looking. Maybe he'll give us some movement so we can spot him." Hale said. He sounded like he was trying to convince himself.

"Kuznetsov wouldn't be that stupid." Kivi reminded him.

"I can't feel my legs and my eyesight is failing." Tomas said.

"There is nothing wrong with your eyes, it is getting dark." Cunnar said.

Tomas' mind, overwhelmed by pain and addled by a

heavy dose of morphine, nevertheless heard Hale and Kivi converse, "They don't know where the bastard is that shot me." Tomas said.

"Hale and Kivi are the best. They'll figure it out." Cunnar said.

"I'm not going to make it, so I might as well help." Tomas said.

Without warning he sat up. A moment later the sound of a rifle discharging once again pierced the silence of the surrounding forest. "Muzzle flash!" Kivi said with excitement.

"I see it." Hale said as he held in a breath and took aim.

The bullet hit Tomas in the head and killed him instantly. The young sniper centered his iron sights on the location he believed the man that sat behind the rifle that created the muzzle flash lay. He held his breath and then pulled the trigger, "Did you get him?" Kivi asked.

"I'm not." Before Hale could complete his sentence, a bullet slammed into a nearby tree just above his head.

"That seems like a no, unless there were two of them." Kivi said.

"Hale! Tomas gave his life so that you could kill this bastard and you missed!" Cunnar shouted angrily.

"You need to shut up so Hale and Kivi can focus. Can you be quiet for me?" Leo asked the distraught private in a soothing voice.

The location of the second muzzle flash was still imprinted in Hale's mind. He took the time to figure out the best location to place his shot. When he was sure where the body behind the flash lay, he held his breath, lined up the spot in his iron sights, and pulled the trigger, "Did you get him?" Kivi asked in a whisper.

"Very likely, unless he moved after that last shot." Hale said.

As the two Finnish officers tried to figure out if the enemy sniper had been slain, Leo crawled away from the group. Once he was clear of the area, he stood and started to move toward the location of the enemy sniper. He was careful to use the trees and terrain as much as possible to keep himself obscured from the enemy.

Silence descended upon the forest. Once again, the millions of impacts as snowflakes struck the ground was the only thing that could be heard, "Should we do something?" Cunnar asked.

Hale and Kivi shared a look and Kivi, who was closer to Cunnar, hissed, "Would you get that dick off your forehead and shut up already?"

Cunnar fell silent as Hale focused on what to do next, "Did you get him?" Kivi asked.

"I'm not sure." Hale admitted.

"I guess someone needs to present themselves as a nice juicy target so the bastard will fire again." Kivi said.

"I wouldn't recommend that. Kuznetsov doesn't miss." Hale said.

The group of three men fell silent as Hale wallowed in indecision. Meanwhile, Leo drew within a hundred meters of the sniper's suspected location. He went prone and started to pull himself along the ground, careful to be as quiet as possible as he slithered toward his goal.

The veteran sniper paused every ten meters or so and listened for the enemy. Hearing nothing but the sound of the snow falling, he continued to creep forward. Suddenly, he saw a muzzle flash less than thirty meters to his left as the enemy sniper fired his weapon, *Got you.* He thought.

One of the group's horses cried out in pain as the bullet fired by the enemy sniper hit the beast. This time, both Kivi and Hale returned fire. While Cunnar pulled out his pistol to end the injured horse's pain.

Leo unslung his rifle and took careful aim at the location he thought the body behind the muzzle flash would lay. As he took aim, both Hale's and Kivi's bullets passed through the area. Eventually Leo heard the faint sound of the bullets sinking into the bark of a tree, *Sounds like they missed again. Hopefully I'll have more luck from this angle.* Leo thought.

When Leo was confident he would hit, he gently squeezed the trigger. A few moments after he fired his rifle, the target cursed in Russian, *Did I just hit him?* Leo wondered.

A moment later, he heard the sound of a horse galloping away. Leo jumped to his feet and ran to the sniper's former location. He quickly scanned the area and spotted splotches of blood next to the hoof prints in the snow, *I hit him!*

Suddenly a bullet rocketed past. Leo threw himself to the ground. It took him only a few seconds to realize that the bullet had come from the direction of the other Finns, "Cease fire you fuckers nearly killed me!" Leo yelled.

"What happened to the sniper?" Hale shouted back.

"I hit him, and he rode off on a horse." Leo replied.

The sound of a single pistol shot surprised Leo. He threw himself to the ground and asked, "Why are you still shooting?"

"I just put our wounded horse out of its misery." Cunnar replied.

Hale, Kivi, and Cunnar mounted their horses and joined Leo a few minutes later. Hale dismounted, removed a glove, and touched the bloody snow with his index finger, "Any idea where you hit him?"

Leo shook his head as he said, "No."

"We need to move fast. The snow is coming down harder and will soon wipe out the trail left by the enemy. Mark this location on your map so we can return for Tomas' body later then let's go." Kivi said.

The snowfall steadily increased as the four men followed the trail left by the sniper's horse. Wary now, all four hunched down in their saddles as much as they were able. This lowered their profile and would make them harder to hit.

The sun set and darkness shrouded the land. The Finns continued to follow the trail left by the enemy sniper. As time passed it became harder and harder to see the prints as the snowfall filled them in. Eventually the prints disappeared altogether, "We lost him." Hale said somberly.

"Shitty time for a snowstorm." Kivi observed, "The bastard seemed to be heading in a consistent direction though."

"Right towards the motti Colonel Siilasvuo said that the

Soviet's general was trapped in." Hale glanced up into the sky. His vision was filled with falling snowflakes lit by the weak light of the moon. Everyone looked at Hale expectantly as he stalled for time, *What do we do? I really hate being in charge.*

"Let's keep heading in the direction the sniper seemed to be going. With luck he'll pass out from blood loss and fall of his horse." Hale said.

"What if we don't find him." Cunnar asked.

"Then we reach the edge of Vinogradov's motti and get some revenge for Tomas." Kivi said.

Chapter 4

Evening, Two Kilometers Southeast of Hauklia, Central Finland

January 2nd, 1940

The Soviet sniper rubbed the spot where a Finnish bullet came very close to ending his life. The bullet had nicked his side and possibly broken a rib. Every time he inhaled all but the shallowest of breaths, his left side sent fiery bolts of pain to his brain. The bullet that had hit him carved a furrow along his left side, *Another inch to the left and I'd be a frozen corpse right now.* He thought.

He glanced back in the direction he had just come from expecting to see the Finns pursuing him. Seeing no one, and wanting to keep it that way, he kicked the sides of his horse hard. The beast dutifully increased its pace, despite the difficulty of moving through the increasingly deep snow. The sniper shivered from the frigid wind that wormed its way through the new hole in the side of his coat.

It took the sniper's horse an hour to move a single kilometer in the deep snow. Several times along the way, natural contours in the terrain slowed their progress. The constant gale coming out of the north re-distributed the snow, ensuring every depression was filled to the top making the ground look deceptively smooth.

Neither the sniper, nor the horse could see the small gullies and depressions that crisscrossed the land. They only realized they were starting to traverse one when the horse sank into the snow. Several times during the journey, the dry, powdery snow reached the horse's neck. Great gouts of steam emerged from the beast's mouth as it pushed its way through, *Will one of these little valley's simply swallow us up?*

The sniper's thoughts grew darker, If that happened, *Would my body ever be found?* His mind supplied the answer to his thought, *Who am I kidding. If I die here like that, my corpse will be consumed by the first wolf that comes across it next spring when this white crap finally melts. That is of course assuming the snow ever melts in this God forsaken frozen hell.*

Finally, his keen eyes spotted the slightest movement up ahead. He dismounted and sank nearly to his waist in the thin powdery snow. He took his horse's bridal in his hands and started to lead the beast toward the movement he spotted.

The Soviet sentry was desperately trying to stay warm. The gale force winds howling across the land from the north made that task impossible. He stepped behind a tree just in case the sentry decided to shoot first and ask questions later before shouting, "Greetings comrade sentry, today's password is victory for the Motherland."

The sentry snorted in derision and replied, "It is indeed comrade. Sadly, we will not find such an outcome in this horrid place. Show yourself and be recognized."

The sniper stepped into view. The sentry gestured for him to advance, so he complied, "Greetings comrade sergeant. Was the hunting good?"

The sniper slowly nodded, "Yes, at least one Finn will trouble us no further."

The sentry's eyes fell to the tear in the sniper's white overcoat and the red stain that surrounded it, "You only managed to kill a single Finn while getting yourself shot in the process?"

The sniper's hand dropped to the pommel of his sheathed knife, "Is that a problem?"

"No comrade sniper. Sadly, you've probably done better than most today. I'm not sure why comrade Stalin wants to spend our lives on this desolate tract of land populated by an infernal group of demons that are seemingly immune to gunfire." The sentry replied.

"There must be some compelling reason." The sniper replied.

"There is. A line on a map deep within the bowels of the Kremlin." The sentry replied.

"Perhaps your right." The sniper agreed.

The sentry fell silent as the sniper slowly led his horse past him. The sentry licked his lips as the smell of the animal filled his nostrils. A fleeting thought entered his mind, *I could shoot the sergeant in the back. Then take the horse. That beast would feed my entire platoon for a week.*

The sniper, unaware that the value of his life was being weighed against an empty stomach, rode for a hundred meters or so and then dismounted. If the sentry had known what was in the sniper's thoughts, he wouldn't have hesitated to act. The sniper looked around and spotted a tree that may serve the purpose he had in mind. He tied his horse to a different tree in a location that the sentry wouldn't be able to see. This was done to prevent the animal from wandering off or being shot as collateral damage, *If I lose the horse, I'll probably never be able to find the beast again. Especially in this storm.*

He approached the birch tree and looked it up and down, *This tree doesn't look as promising up close. Oh well, there are no other good choices nearby, this will have to do.*

The sniper reached up to the lowest branch and pulled himself upward. Immediately, his wounded side protested in earnest. He ignored the pain and kept climbing until he reached the desired branch, *The snow is deep enough that if I fall out of this tree, I probably won't break anything.*

As he moved out onto the branch, the wind tried to push him off the limb. A blast of the cold air wormed its way into his coat through the hole created by Leo's bullet. He immediately started to shiver as his body tried to maintain its core temperature, *I hope they hurry up and get here before I freeze to death.* He thought.

Chapter 5

Evening, Two Kilometers Southeast of Hauklia, Central Finland

January 2nd, 1940

Hale had lost the sniper's trail nearly an hour before. The steady snowfall erased any sign of the enemy's passing. Now he depended on his internal compass to navigate the snowy wilderness with poor visibility. Luckily his sense of direction had been sharpened by years of navigating the forests of Karelia as a youth.

Being able to find your way through the depths of the Finnish wilderness was a critical survival skill. A necessity for those who hunted for both sustenance and pelts. With the exception of the southern coastal area, Finland's primitive roads made this ability critical for anyone who made a living from the bountiful wildlife that populated the Finnish countryside.

Hale led his group, now one man smaller, through the snowy wilderness. They were virtually blinded by the snowstorm's relentless assault. Up ahead, through momentary breaks in the weather, his keen eyes spotted a shadow that seemed off. Hale, not wanting to take any chances, especially with Kuznetsov in the area, raised his right arm up and formed a fist.

Kivi seeing Hale's signal did the same and the column of four Finns came to a halt. The riders looked more like ghosts than humans. They were covered from head to toe in protective clothing. The group could pass as the four horsemen of the apocalypse except for one characteristic that differed from that legend, they were dressed completely in white. Even their mounts wore a white sheet, to blend in with the icy wilderness.

Hale peered at the location that seemed off to him. Between the darkness and the storm, it was difficult to discern anything beyond a shadowy outline. Even harder still to spot movement amongst the falling snowflakes. The young sniper dismounted from Liv and crept slowly forward.

His lips turned upward slightly as he spotted the Soviet sentry stamping his feet in a vain attempt to keep them warm. Hale drew his pukko blade and started to slowly circle around the lone enemy soldier. He used the trees and the contours in the uneven ground to mask himself from the sentry's view as he moved around him.

A hundred meters away, from his perch on a birch tree, the Soviet sniper's own set of keen eyes, discerned movement, *It's about time.*

The sniper peered intently at the area where he had seen the bit of movement that didn't belong. He strained his eyes to try and focus on the spot, but the storm maintained a steady cascade of snow which obscured his vision, *For a second, when the wind pushed the snow away for a fleeting moment, I thought I saw something.*

Thanks to his elevated position in the tree, the Soviet sniper's body was losing the fight against the cold. He managed, through sheer force of will, to stifle his body's urge to shiver. Instead, he raised his rifle scope up to his eye and centered it on his bait, the sentry. He maintained this rigid posture for nearly five minutes when he finally saw him.

A white figure suddenly rose from the snow, as if materializing out of thin air, with a blade in his hand directly behind the sentry. The sniper smiled and thought, *I've got your ass.*

That was when everything went wrong. A hand suddenly grabbed his left ankle and pulled hard. This caused the sniper to lose his balance and fall to the ground. Suddenly, a huge weight upon his chest crushed the air out of his lungs and made it nearly impossible to draw breath, it was a ghostly figure in white.

Despite the weight on his chest, the sniper managed to draw in a sharp breath of cold air, *I'm dead.* He thought as the Finn tore the rifle from his hands and put the barrel of a pistol up against his head, "If you make a sound, it will be the last thing you do in this life." The man said in Russian.

The sniper raised his hands up to indicate his submission. The Finn released one of his hands from the pistol held to the sniper's head and searched him. He quickly found the sniper's standard issue Red Army knife, and pistol. The Finn pulled the knife from its sheathe and frowned, the blade possessed a wicked serrated edge. This was a violation of the rules stipulated by the 1929 Geneva Convention. An agreement Stalin had refused to sign.

"Perhaps I should use this on you?" The Finn hissed, again in Russian.

The sniper's cheeks, red from the cold, suddenly paled, "I am your prisoner. Please do not murder me. That would also be a violation of the Geneva Convention."

"What did he just say?" Kivi asked Leo in a whisper.

"He declared himself my prisoner and that he shouldn't be murdered as it is against the Geneva Convention." Leo replied.

Kivi drew his pukko blade in full view of the sniper and started to clean his fingernails with it. After a minute of this, with the sniper growing ever more frantic as the realization of what was about to happen to him sank in, he asked, "Why should we spare you? You killed a friend of mine."

The sniper's eyes shifted to Leo who translated the statement into Russian. The sniper smiled at Kivi and said, "You'd be an idiot if you spared me. You should kill me now, before I have the opportunity to slay you. I will not hesitate should our roles reverse, and such a chance comes to pass."

Leo translated and Kivi drew his head back and started to laugh. After a minute of mirth, the big Finn asked, "Do you really believe that bullshit you just spouted? If so, I'll start carving you up right now." Kivi paused for several seconds before he dramatically added, "Slowly."

"No. I do not believe the bullshit, as you put it that I just said. We were told that you Finns are starving and derive joy from torturing your prisoners, right before you eat them. I was hoping that those words would anger you into immediately slaying me so I would not die feeling your teeth upon my flesh. Since it is obvious that my words have failed, there is no point in continuing the subterfuge." The sniper said. Leo's translation followed a few seconds later.

"I'll give you credit Kuznetsov, you sure are a clever bastard." Kivi said.

The prisoner's eyes widened for the briefest of moments before his face became expressionless. The two Finns, failed to notice the momentary look of surprise on the Russian's face. Leo and Kivi each grabbed one of the prisoner's arms and pulled him to his feet. They started to walk in Hale's direction, who was busy checking the sentry's corpse for anything interesting.

"I caught Kuznetsov here trying to shoot you in the back." Leo said.

At the mention of Kuznetsov's name Hale whirled around. For a brief moment, his heart filled with hope. His eyes bored into the prisoner's, who defiantly met his gaze, "That's not Kuznetsov."

"Then who the hell is he?" Cunnar demanded.

Hale frisked the prisoner. His fingers quickly found the blood-stained tear in the prisoner's coat where Leo had shot him, "Here is the wound caused by Leo that created the blood trail."

Hale continued to search the Russian and found three clips of bullets for the sniper's Mosin, but nothing else of interest, "There's nothing on him."

Leo grabbed the sniper's coat with clenched fists and demanded, "Since you are so interested in complying with the Geneva Convention, you will now tell me your name, rank, and serial number."

"My name is—"

The sniper's head jerked forward and a fraction of a second later the sound of a Mosin-Nagant being fired filled their ears, "Down!" Hale said reflexively.

"What the hell? Who shot the sniper? I wanted to kill this bastard, slowly. . ." Cunnar raged.

Hale looked back and Leo and asked, "You have blood all over you, is any of it yours?"

Leo shook his head and said, "No, luckily whoever just shot him was using an explosive bullet, so it didn't penetrate through his skull." Leo turned his lip up in disgust before he added, "It sure did make a mess of his head though."

"That was a Soviet Mosin that fired the bullet, not a Finnish one. We don't use explosive rounds, but the Soviets do." Kivi observed.

Confused, Hale asked, "They shot their own man?"

Kivi nodded, "Why the hell would they do that?" Leo asked.

"I think I understand what is going on now. Do you remember all of those Xs on Siilasvuo's map to indicate where sniper attacks had taken place?" Kivi said.

Hale nodded, "It seemed nearly impossible that one person could attack from so many different locations in so short of a time."

"It is impossible for one person to attack that many times in forty-eight hours. However, if there was more than one sniper, it wouldn't be impossible at all." Kivi said.

"Maybe that is why this man had no identification on

him." Cunnar added.

"Where would the extra snipers come from? According to the radio transmission intercepts decrypted by Siilasvuo's crypto team, the only sniper Vinogradov had was Kuznetsov. The 44th is a motorized rifle division designed to take the fight to the enemy. The Soviets didn't bother to give the division any snipers. When they got stuck here and started to get picked to pieces, Kuznetsov appeared and killed off all of our company's snipers." Kivi said.

"Well, if Vinogradov didn't have any snipers, other than Kuznetsov, there must be a new unit operating in the area." Leo suggested.

"Summer of cunts." Hale cursed, "So if I understand correctly, we could be hunting down numerous snipers, instead of just Kuznetsov?"

Kivi nodded, "As if this wasn't going to be hard enough already just having to deal with Kuznetsov." Hale said.

Without warning, Kivi rolled on top of Hale, "Now you listen." Kivi said in a whisper, "You are in charge so you can't be expressing doubt like that in front of your men. They will lose confidence in you and then you'll be truly fucked."

"I never wanted to be in charge of anything except my rifle. Life is simpler that way." Hale replied.

"Well, you don't have that luxury anymore. Mannerheim saw something in you, so you'd best pull your head out of your ass and get it screwed on straight or you're going to be just one more notch on Kuznetsov's rifle." Kivi snarled.

Kuznetsov cursed the storm. He peered through his scope trying to target the Finns, *Hopefully I got that fool before he talked.*

Kivi rolled off of Hale, who took a deep breath and let it out slowly to calm his nerves. Hale remained laying on his back. He looked up at the steam cloud that hovered over his head for a moment before the wind tore it apart, "All right listen up. There is another enemy sniper out there. Visibility is virtually zero except for the occasional break in the snow fall. Did anyone see a muzzle flash right before the Soviet sniper was hit?"

None of the men replied, "All right then. With the wind twisting sound, we basically have no idea where the enemy is at." Hale said.

Cunnar's voice quavered as he said, "What are we going to do?"

"We are going to crawl back to the horses and get out of here." Hale said.

"Then what?" Leo asked.

"We are going to head for the closest Task Force. From here that will be Makiniemi. Colonel Makiniemi will have a radio. We can use it to contact Siilasvuo and let him know what we've figured out about the snipers. Let's get moving." Hale said.

Kuznetsov watched through his scope for an hour. Seeing no evidence of the Finns, he decided to move toward the place where he last saw them. He unbuckled his feet from his skis and set them down next to his pack, *It makes me nervous to remove the skis as they allow me to make a quick escape, but I can't crawl for shit with them on.*

Kuznetsov started to crawl toward the location where

he had slain his comrade to prevent him from talking to the enemy. He used the cover of darkness, the deluge of snow from the storm, the trees, and the contours in the terrain to keep himself out of sight as much as possible.

As he crawled on the snow-covered earth, the cold started to seep into his body. Before long he started to shiver as his body fought to maintain its core temperature, *What an awful night. How can so many of the Finns operate so effectively in this shit? Most of my weaker comrades are likely glued to their campfires right now trying not to freeze to death. Only those of us that spent time in the vast Arctic wastes of Mother Russia are able to function at all in this place.*

After nearly half an hour of crawling Kuznetsov reached the two bodies of his countrymen. He turned his lip up in disgust at the hollowed out remains of his target's head, *Wow, these new explosive bullets they issued me made a mess of this man's brains. Who are you?*

Kuznetsov rolled the man over. Staring up into the sky was the sightless eyes of Sergeant Romanov, *Too bad, he had some potential.*

Kuznetsov crawled over to the sentry, *This one died by a blade. It's a shame I didn't get here a little sooner. Maybe you would still be alive.*

Not knowing whether the Finns were still in the area, he stayed down on the ground and circled the area looking for tracks. He quickly found several sets of tracks that led off to the southwest, *Should I follow, or seek shelter from the storm before I freeze to death?*

Chapter 6

Just Prior to Midnight, Three Kilometers East of Hauklia, Central Finland

January 2nd, 1940

The fury of the storm intensified as Hale and his three surviving men rode toward Task Force Makiniemi's location. He turned Liv, who was shivering, around to face the rest of the group, "Liv is freezing. I fear she won't be able to continue for much longer. How are your mounts?"

"The same." Kivi said.

"I don't think Heikkinen will make it much further either." Leo said.

"Cunnar?" Hale asked.

"I don't know much about horses, but this one seems on the verge of being hypothermic." Cunnar replied.

"If our beasts are to see the next sunrise, we need to get them out of this wind." Kivi suggested.

"Agreed. Let's find a depression and build a fire. We can cover them up with fir branches to help keep them warm." Hale said.

"Is building a fire wise?" Kivi asked.

"Unless you want to walk from here on out, I don't think we have a choice. If we continue moving in this storm, we are going to lose the horses. If we don't move, without a fire to warm them up, we are going to lose the horses." Hale replied.

Kivi slowly nodded and said, "The risk of discovery by the enemy should be low. I can't imagine they are better able to move through this kind of weather than we are."

"They haven't shown any evidence of being able to thus far. With the exception of Kuznetsov, it would seem." Hale agreed.

"And he can't be everywhere." Leo observed.

Their plan of action decided, the group quickly located a suitable depression. This low point in the land had been gouged out by a glacier during the last ice age. Throughout the two-thousand-year period of the most recent ice age, Finland had been buried in about thirty meters of ice which constantly shifted gouging great furrows across the land.

The depression provided a fair amount of concealment for a campfire as well as protection from the wind. Hale and Leo, being the most familiar with the care of horses, worked on the mounts, while Kivi and Cunnar checked nearby for downed trees that could be used as firewood. Within the hour, a large fire was crackling, snapping, and most importantly radiating life preserving heat in the center of their chosen depression.

The combination of the cover provided by the depression, which removed them from the howling wind out of the north, and the fire started to thaw them out. Over the next several hours, the humans were able to warm up their cores and avoid hypothermia. The horses were bedded down as close as they could manage to get them to the fire. Beds were built for the animals using cut fir tree branches to provide a layer of protection against the snow. In addition, the branches were also draped across the beasts to provide insulation.

Despite all of their efforts, two of the horses, Kivi's and Cunnar's, without the multiple layers of clothing that the humans enjoyed, died during the night. The group awoke to this grisly discovery of frozen equine corpses a few hours before sunrise. Fortunately, Liv and Heikkinen, better rested before they left 9th Division HQ, thanks to their recent travels, survived the night.

Hale looked around at the transformed countryside. By seven AM the storm had blown its course and shrouded the land in a fresh half-meter coating of snow, "The land is always so beautiful the morning after a snowstorm."

"Beautiful? That damn storm cost us two mounts and nearly killed us too." Cunnar snarled.

"I agree with Hale." Leo said, "No matter how deadly the weather was, it doesn't change the fact that this blanket of freshly fallen snow is beautiful."

"Why don't you give me your horse so you can enjoy

the beauty up close?" Cunnar sneered.

"Enough. We can double up." Hale said.

Leo threw Cunnar a hostile glance as he said, "Is that a good idea? It is going to be difficult enough for our mounts to push through this snow. If we give them the extra burden of another rider, it may kill them." Leo said.

"What do you suggest?" Hale asked.

"That we limit the horses to one rider. Kivi and Cunnar can follow in the horse's wake on skis." Leo said.

"Leo is right. If we try to double up on the surviving mounts the combination of the extra weight and deep snow will cause their hearts to burst from the exertion." Kivi said. He turned to Cunnar and slapped him hard on the back. Cunnar, unable to maintain his balance, had to take a step forward after Kivi's slap.

"What was that for?" Cunnar asked.

"For being a whiney little shit." Kivi said.

Cunnar glared at Kivi but wisely chose to keep his mouth shut. "Before we head out the dead horses need to be buried." Hale said to distract the two men from their growing enmity.

All three of Hale's subordinates glared at him as Leo asked, "Why in the hell do we need to do that?"

"To keep their flesh out of Russian bellies." Hale said.

Kivi's face twisted into a smile, "Now you're using your head."

The four men buried the bodies of the two horses using snow. When they finished, the final resting place of the animals just looked like one more mound of snow. Hale and Leo mounted their horses and began pushing their way through the snow as Cunnar and Kivi followed on their skis.

The sniper squad chose to head out around the time the eastern horizon became slightly lighter than the surrounding sky. The group was able to travel like this for two hours. Hale thought he saw something up ahead in the growing light and halted the group. He peered intently at the location where he thought he saw a color that didn't belong in a snow-covered forest.

Leo rode up beside him and asked in a whisper, "See something?"

"I think I saw a patch of gray amidst that copse of fir trees up ahead." Hale pointed.

The young sniper patiently observed for ten minutes before he was able to spot some movement that didn't belong. This time the young sniper's eyes were able to identify the source of the movement, "Friendlies coming in."

"What's the word of the day?" A voice replied in Finnish.

Hale had memorized the word of the day for the next week before leaving camp. He closed his eyes and brought the memory up of the paper Major Valli had handed him with the passwords, "Stalin loves to fornicate with goats."

The sentry gave the expected reply, "Better hide your sheep, lest they suffer the same fate."

"Well met." Hale acknowledged.

"How many coming in?" The sentry asked.

"Four men and two horses." Hale replied.

As Hale neared the location of the sentry he appeared, "You should keep your coat buttoned all the way up, it was your gray tunic underneath that tipped me off that you were there." Hale said.

"I appreciate the advice." The Finnish sentry said as he buttoned up his overcoat.

"Which way to Lieutenant Colonel Makiniemi's command post?" Hale asked.

"Why should you get to speak to the colonel? You should report in to my platoon commander and let him decide if what you have to say is important enough for the colonel's ears." The sentry asked.

Hale unzipped his coat and flashed the two silver circles on his collar, the rank of 1st Lieutenant, "Because I have valuable information about sniper activity to share with the colonel in this sector. If you stand in the way of my report, I'll request you be detailed to my squad. We have already taken losses from the snipers in this area and are shorthanded."

The sentry chose to wisely relent and pointed to the north, "Colonel Makiniemi's command post is about half a kilometer in that direction."

"Thank you private?" Hale asked.

"Kangas, sir."

"I'll be sure to relay your diligence to the colonel." Hale said.

With Hale in the lead, the sniper squad headed in the direction that Kangas indicated. Along the way they ran into the occasional Finnish soldier heading out to relieve one of the sentries. About thirty minutes later Task Force Makiniemi's command post came into view. The command post was a ten-by-ten-meter gray tent. Jutting from a hole in the tent's top was a steel pipe. Smoke lazily curled upwards from the pipe.

When they reached the entrance Hale turned and addressed Leo and Cunnar, "You may come in to warm up, but please stay out of the way and remain silent."

Both men nodded in acknowledgement of the order. Hale turned to Kivi gestured towards the door and said, "Shall we?"

Kivi returned Hale's smile and said, "You're the boss."

Hale pulled the tent flap back and entered. He took two steps forward to enable the other men to enter behind him. He then paused and looked around. The tent was set up very similar to Colonel Siilasvuo's.

The center held a battered campaign table with a map spread out on it. Four smooth gray stones, likely from a creek bed, were being used to hold the map in place. Above the table hung two gas burning lanterns that provided light for the table. Next to the table sat a small black iron wood burning stove. A pot of coffee sat upon the stove happily bubbling and gurgling as it filled the tent with the aroma of brewing coffee.

The fire burning within the stove helped to warm the interior of the tent above the freezing mark. In the back left corner sat a radio set upon another campaign table. Seated in front of the table was a corporal. Lieutenant Colonel Makiniemi was leaning over the map table when the four men entered the tent. He looked up and said, "Can I help you?"

"I need to use your radio to contact Colonel Siilasvuo." Hale replied.

"We have an attack scheduled for this morning and are under strict radio silence." Makiniemi replied.

"By whose orders?" Hale asked.

"What does it matter?" Makiniemi paused expectantly.

"1st Lieutenant Hale Karhonen, sir."

Makinimei looked at Hale's smooth face and said snidely, "Oh good, so there aren't any pre-pubescent general's wandering around my sector that can override my orders."

Hale stiffened as he said, "No, but we are the 9th Division's sniper squad detailed by General Mannerheim himself."

The mention of the General's name caused Makiniemi to visibly flinch, "Let me see your orders."

Hale opened his coat further and pulled General Mannerheim's orders out of his inner coat pocket. He unfolded them and then handed them over to the colonel as requested. Makiniemi spent three minutes reading the orders. When he finished, he looked up at Hale and said, "What is so important that you have to break pre-attack radio silence to report to Colonel Siilasvuo, lieutenant?"

Hale heard the skepticism in Makiniemi's tone, despite having read his orders. He decided to tread carefully, "Have you been having any sniper problems?"

Makiniemi snorted, "You could say that. I've been told that the Soviet's best sniper Kuznetsov is loose in my area."

"What's the effect been on your operations?" Hale asked in a confident voice. Inwardly his mind raced, *I'm not ready for this! Why can't I just be a sniper? How can I make this man believe that I need to speak to the colonel?*

Lieutenant Colonel Makiniemi stared at Hale for several long moments before admitting, "Not good. My officers are overhearing conversations from the men about abandoning their lines and melting away into the forest. The men are brave and willing to face the enemy head on, but they don't want to die for nothing. This sniper Kuznetsov's operations doesn't really move the needle from an operational standpoint, but the damage to morale he's causing can't be ignored."

"Well, I have some bad news. The Soviets aren't hitting you with one really good sniper." Hale said.

"Oh? Then what are they hitting me with?" Makiniemi asked.

"One really good sniper, and a bunch of other snipers." Hale replied.

"How do you know? Are you sure?" Makiniemi asked.

Hale tossed a small plastic cylinder he took from the dead Soviet sniper in the Colonel's direction, "I pulled this from the body of a sniper we killed last night."

Makiniemi caught it. He opened it up and unfolded the tiny slip of paper that was held within it and turned it over so he could read it. His eyes widened as he read the paper out loud, "Sergeant Romanov 3rd NKVD Regiment."

Makiniemi looked back up and met Hale's gaze, "I thought we were only facing off against the 44th. The Soviets have brought in a new unit?"

Hale slowly nodded, "Based on the map of the recorded sniper attacks along the length of the Raate Road, I'd say the enemy is using at least a platoon sized force of snipers to make our task force's lives a living hell."

Makiniemi, glanced over Hale's shoulders at the three other men of his squad and asked, "You don't appear to have much in the way of resources lieutenant. What do you need from me, so you can put an end to these damned snipers?"

"More men." Hale said.

"I can provide that." Makiniemi said.

"Not just any men. Men that are good at moving through the forest undetected and at spotting what doesn't belong." Hale said.

"I have mainly reservists drawn from around Oulu, who are more comfortable on a fishing boat than in the forest, but I think I can provide several men with the skills you describe. Do they need to be good with a rifle?" Makiniemi asked.

"They don't have to be, as myself, Lieutenant Kivi, and Sergeant Virtanen here will be doing most of the shooting, but it would help us solve the problem faster if we had other men that could shoot well." Hale replied.

"I'll provide you with the men you require, but I still won't break radio silence." Makiniemi said.

"You must." Hale insisted, "Based on the map of sniper attacks that Colonel Siilasvuo shared with me, all four of the task forces are experiencing sniper attacks and must be made aware that it is more than one man."

"Even if the Soviets are unable to break our code, I

don't want to increase their readiness by using the radio. They'll think something is up. I would in their shoes. I'll tell you what. I have an attack scheduled to begin at dusk. Once the attack is far enough along, I'll have my radioman call in whatever you need to tell the colonel." Makiniemi conceded.

The two men made eye contact for several long moments before Hale relented, "I guess that will have to do."

"You guess? You're lucky I'm willing to break protocol for you at all lieutenant." Makiniemi said.

"Thank you, sir. I appreciate your assistance." Hale said.

Makiniemi pointed at his radioman, "While I'm busy getting you the men you requested, go ahead and dictate your message to Corporal Erkkila. The mess tent is nearby, your men can get a hot meal."

"Yes, sir, and thank you." Hale replied.

"You can show your appreciation by killing these snipers." Makiniemi replied, then turned away and leaned down on the table to examine the map.

Hale started in the direction of the radio when he noticed Kivi following him. Confused he turned and asked, "You don't want to get some food?"

"I do, but first I want to help you compose this message." Kivi said.

Hale visibly relaxed as he said, "I appreciate that."

Corporal Erkkila had pencil and notebook in hand by the time the two officers reached him, "Just tell me the message and I'll be sure it gets transmitted in its entirety to Division HQ."

"Colonel Siilasvuo, we have made a discovery—." Before Hale could continue Kivi interrupted.

"Tell him who you are first." Kivi suggested.

"Right." Hale said. He cleared his throat and started over, "Colonel Siilasvuo, Lieutenant Karhonen reporting. Discovery made concerning our issue. Our original thought is incorrect. Unit of snipers identified from 3rd NKVD Regiment. Current unit location providing additional men to support us. Continuing original mission. Suggest you increase security at all subordinate units."

"Tell him to consider posting sentries even if Soviet forces are not nearby." Kivi said.

"Did you get that corporal?" Hale asked.

"I got your part sir, but I missed what Lieutenant Kivi said."

"I suggest that sentries are posted even if the Soviets are not nearby. They need to maintain movement, sound, and light discipline, for fear that they become the next victim. If they follow these protocols. With a little luck, they'll be able to pick off a few enemy snipers when they try to infiltrate the sentry line." Hale said. He turned to Kivi and asked, "Do you think we need to add anything else?"

"Yes. Please relay this information to the other task forces." Kivi said.

Hale looked down at Corporal Erkkila, "Did you get all that?"

The corporal nodded, "Good. Read the message back to me." Hale ordered.

The corporal complied with Hale's order. When he was finished reading the message Hale nodded in satisfaction, "Good. Send that as soon as the colonel will allow it."

"Yes, sir." The corporal replied. He opened his mouth to speak but then thought better of it.

"You have something else to say corporal?" Hale asked.

"My brother is manning the barricade surrounding Vinogradov's motti. Do you think you'll be able to stop the snipers?" Erkkila asked.

"Of course." Hale said with confidence that he didn't feel.

Erkkila smiled in relief, "Thank you sir, and good luck."

The two officers turned to leave when Hale remembered the sentry, "One more thing Colonel Makiniemi."

Makiniemi stopped examining a handwritten list of men he was creating and looked up at Hale, "Yes?"

"You should be aware that Private Kangas did an excellent job at concealing himself while on sentry duty. He also executed protocols well." Hale said.

"That's good to know. Thanks." Makiniemi replied.

Kivi and Hale joined the enlisted men in the chow tent. The four men enjoyed a warm meal as they relaxed and traded good natured barbs with each other. The squad was close to finishing their first plate of food when Private Kangas walked into the tent. The Private looked around until he spotted Hale's group. He then walked over to them.

Kangas stood at the end of the table and glowered down at Hale and said, "Thanks a lot."

"For?" Hale inquired.

"Telling the colonel that I had done a good job of concealing myself. Apparently, that put me on a short list of names to get detailed to your sniper squad." Kangas complained.

Hale smiled up at the private while his mind erupted into turmoil, *Why is it so hard to keep everyone happy? Even when you think you are doing someone a favor they get mad at you. I think I'd much rather have a face like a predatory bird's ass, than be an officer.*

Kivi cast a sidelong glance at Hale and then stood. The big lieutenant towered over Kangas. He glared down at him and growled, "You need to show respect to your superiors. Especially those that went out of their way to ensure you were recognized for your skills at concealment."

Kangas flashed an angry glance at Kivi. He opened his mouth to fire off a retort, then thought better of it. Instead, he meekly said, "Yes, sir."

"Private?" Hale asked.

"Yes, sir?" Kangas replied.

Following Kivi's lead Hale said, "In the future I expect you to respect your superior officers. Which includes me."

Kangas' gaze fell and he mumbled, "Yes, sir."

"Do you know when I can expect the other men the colonel promised for my sniper squad?" Hale asked using an authoritative voice that made him feel like a fraud considering how his insides were churning in the moment.

"The other three men are waiting for you outside, lieutenant." Kangas replied.

Kivi and Hale shared a glance, before Hale smiled and said, "Makiniemi seems to be very efficient."

Kivi nodded in agreement, "Indeed."

"Tell them to come on inside and get themselves a hot meal. You do the same and then report to me." Hale said.

"Where will you be at, sir?" Kangas asked.

Hale smiled, "Right here getting seconds."

Suddenly Lieutenant Colonel Makiniemi burst into the chow tent and said, "Karhonen, there's been another sniper incident."

"So much for seconds." Hale said wistfully.

Chapter 7

Two hours before Dawn, Two Kilometers North of Vuokkijarvi, Central Finland

January 3rd, 1940

Major Kari looked through his binoculars at the line of Soviet forces sitting idle on the Raate road. Orange light flickered from dozens of campfires that dotted the road. The enemy soldiers had built the fires in an attempt to keep themselves from freezing to death. During the night the temperature would drop to a lethal forty degrees Fahrenheit below zero.

Up until midnight of the previous day, Kari had his best shots harassing the Soviets on the road with sniper fire. The cry of cuckoo, the Soviet's name for Finnish snipers, had been shouted nearly constantly since the sun had gone down. The Ukrainian soldiers of the 44th, not accustomed to the severe conditions of an Arctic Winter, had no choice but to light the fires. The same fires that enabled the Finnish snipers to see them from a great distance. At midnight, the snipers had been ordered to cease their operations and allow the enemy to become complacent.

The major turned to the man that would be personally leading the attack, Captain Lassila, "Are your men ready?"

Lassila, hailed from the nearby village of Hauklia. The captain came from a large family in the village, many of whom were with him tonight. Lassila turned to the major and gave him a wolfish grin, "Yes major, my boys are good and ready to drive the enemy from our lands."

"I'm glad to hear that captain, you may begin your assault." Kari ordered.

"With pleasure, sir." Lassila said.

Colonel Siilasvuo, standing within the 9th Division's HQ tent, glanced down at his watch. When he looked up, his gaze drifted to the map on the well-worn campaign table that sat in the center of the tent as he said, "0700, time for Major Kari's attack."

Major Valli, the colonel's adjutant, put a reassuring hand on the colonel's shoulder and said, "I'm sure Major Kari's force will meet with the same success that Mandelin and Makiniemi did."

"I pray that you are right. We need each of the task forces to be successful in order to seal our trap." Siilasvuo said.

Siilasvuo started to pace as the minutes slowly ticked by. Every few minutes the colonel would look over at his radioman Corporal Wirta. The corporal would give the colonel's unspoken question a reply by shaking his head to indicate no, there has been no word from Task Force Kari.

Suddenly, the radio crackled to life, "Go ahead, over." Corporal Wirta replied.

An unintelligible voice, at least to the Colonel's ears spoke at length. The Corporal replied, "Understood, thanks for the report. Over and out."

"Kari?" Colonel Siilasvuo's voice nearly pleaded.

"Negative. That was Major Fagernas. His group is currently south of the Raate Road heading northward to get into attack position. His group has spotted several Red Air Force planes heading westward." Corporal Wirta replied.

"Damn, I wonder what they are up to?" Colonel Siilasvuo wondered out loud.

Colonel Siilasvuo looked down at his watch and cursed, "The attack is taking longer than it should have. Do you think those bombers are heading to the fight?"

"After the last pasting our flyboys gave to theirs, I doubt it. More likely fighters with a single bomb, and orders to strafe." Valli reassured him.

Again, the radio crackled to life, "Go ahead." Corporal Wirta said.

The voice on the other side replied, "This is Task Force Kari, over."

"Go ahead Kari. Over." Corporal Wirta replied.

The corporal's words immediately prompted the colonel to turn toward the radio. He slammed his fist down on the table in frustration as the voice on the other side of the transmission was unintelligible, "Roger, Kari. Over and out."

Corporal Wirta came to his feet and turned toward the colonel, "Permission to speak, colonel?"

"Out with-it man!" The colonel exclaimed.

"Task Force Kari has secured a section of the road." Corporal Wirta replied with a smile.

Relief flooded the colonel upon hearing the news. He looked down at the map and stabbed his finger upon a tile that sat just west of the Purasjoki River, and south of the Raate Road, "Can you finish sealing the trap Major Fagernas?"

Chapter 8

Noon, One Kilometer Southeast of Hauklia, Central Finland

January 3rd, 1940

"Is this where you found him? Private?" Hale asked.

"Heino, lieutenant, and yes, we haven't touched him."

"How long ago was he shot?" Hale asked.

"About an hour, sir." Heino replied.

"Was anyone else around to see where the shot came from?" Hale asked.

"No, sir." Heino responded.

Hale examined the gunshot wound in the slain soldier's chest. He then turned and gazed out at the surrounding forest. Leo pointed at a boulder about two hundred and fifty meters away, "From behind that large rock maybe?"

"Good eyes. Yes, that is the most likely spot." Hale

said.

"How is this helpful?" Cunnar demanded.

Hale cast an irritated look in Cunnar's direction before responding, "If we can learn the preferential firing positions the enemy snipers like to use, it will be easier to find them in the future."

"Or eliminate their preferred firing positions from an area we wish to defend," Kivi added.

"Such knowledge could save lives." Hale said.

Suddenly a dull thwack sound erupted from Heino's head. Hale, Kivi, and Leo, recognizing the sound, immediately threw themselves to the ground, "Sniper! The three men said simultaneously.

The other men of the sniper squad, now numbering eight, followed suit in a more desultory fashion. Luckily for them, it takes a soldier roughly four seconds to operate the bolt on their rifle, "What do we do lieutenant?" A panicked Private Kangas asked.

"Did anyone see where the shot came from?" Hale asked.

"I thought I saw a muzzle flash." Private Rinne said.

"At high noon, are you sure?" Kivi asked. Then added, "Describe it."

"It was a sudden circular flash. You know kind of like what a lighter would look like from a distance if it was lit for just a second." Rinne replied.

"That sounds correct. Where did you see it?" Hale asked.

Rinne pointed at a tight grove of fir trees about two hundred meters to the south, "There."

Hale unslung his rifle and quickly fired three rounds into the trees Rinne had indicated. Between rounds, as he operated the bolt, he rolled a few meters to the side to avoid any potential return fire. "Why did you do that, lieutenant? Aren't you afraid of revealing your position?" Rinne asked.

"To keep the bastard pinned down for a little while." Hale replied.

A moment later three bullets smashed into the snow near the previous locations Hale had fired from, "No muzzle flashes this time." Leo observed.

The young Lieutenant turned to Kivi and Leo, "Do you think you two could head out? One east and one west."

"I think I know where you are going with this. You want us to try and circle around and come up behind the enemy." Kivi said.

"Yes." Then added, "While you do that, we'll try to provide some distraction from here. With luck I'll nail him before you get into position." Hale said.

"We'll need a distraction to get out of here." Leo said.

"I'll take care of it." Hale said.

Without warning the young lieutenant stood, dashed three steps to his right, and hurled himself to the ground. A bullet hurtled through the spot Hale had occupied about halfway through his crazy dash. Kivi and Leo were already moving before Hale could yell, "Go!"

Leo and Kivi leaped to their feet and ran in opposite directions. They did this for about four seconds before both men threw themselves into the snow. Simultaneously, Hale readied his rifle to return the enemy's fire. A split-second after Kivi and Leo began to dive earthward, a bullet kicked up snow, where Kivi would have been a moment later.

"There." Hale said as he saw the enemy's muzzle flash.

The momentary burst of light from the enemy sniper's rifle was visible right where Rinne had said he would be. Hale quickly did some mental calculations to determine where the enemy's body would lay behind the muzzle flash and fired his weapon. He was rewarded with a scream as his bullet hit the Soviet sniper.

As Hale worked the action on his rifle, one of the new members of the squad, a Private Ahonen, came to his feet as he shouted, "You got him sir!"

It was the last action he took in this life as a bullet buried itself in his chest. Ahonen looked down in disbelief at the expanding red circle growing on his coat. A second bullet struck him on the left side of his chest spinning him around as he started to fall. He was dead before he hit the ground.

Hale saw the muzzle flash from the second sniper and shouted, "There's two of them in the grove!"

Again, he made a quick mental calculation and adjusted his aim to where he thought the body behind the muzzle flash lay. When he was satisfied, he gently pulled the trigger. His rifle, the same rifle given to him by his now deceased father for his thirteenth birthday, responded to his touch.

A split-second later, Hale saw a muzzle flash from the tightly packed grove of fir trees, two hundred meters to their south. This muzzle flash came from several meters away from the previous one. It was very close to the area of the first muzzle flash. The area, Hale knew he had hit someone, *What the hell?* He wondered as a bullet slammed into the snow a few centimeters from his left elbow.

Before he had a chance to fire, a second bullet slammed into the snow just in front of his face. The impact of the bullet sent powdery snow into his eyes. As Hale blinked the melting snow away, he simultaneously rolled to his right. Yet another sniper, from a third location, put a bullet into the snow, right where he had been laying.

This time, Cunnar returned fire with his rifle, "Cunnar move!" Hale screamed.

Cunnar, immediately rolled to his left. The move saved his life as a bullet plowed into the snow about where his right leg had been, "Did I get him?"

Hale was about to reply when he saw a muzzle flash from the same location, "What's he firing at now?"

Hale swung his rifle in the direction of this latest muzzle flash when he heard a cry of pain come from behind him. He turned and his guts clenched as he saw a bullet hole in the back of one of the new squad members. The man had stood to flee, "Stay down!" He roared.

The momentary silence was abruptly ended by a gunshot that could be heard coming from their southwest. Before the sound of the weapon's discharge faded, they heard someone scream from the grove of trees. Hale smiled and thought, *Great shooting Leo. That's two of them that have been hit.*

The enemy snipers shifted their attention to Leo's location and fired their weapons. The Finnish sergeant was about a hundred meters southwest of Hale's group. Both Hale and Cunnar saw a muzzle flash and fired their rifles at it. They were rewarded with another scream of pain.

Kivi had apparently seen some movement as well from his vantage point. He was presently located about one hundred meters to the southeast of Hale's group. Again, the Finns heard an enemy soldier cry out in pain as Kivi's bullet penetrated flesh.

An eerie silence descended on this patch of Finnish forest as both groups stopped firing. Hale strained to listen with his good right ear for signs of enemy survivors. Behind him, he heard one of the new men draw in breath, and hissed, "Silence!"

After several minutes had passed without further activity, Hale turned to his subordinates and asked, "My hearing isn't what it used to be. Has anyone heard anything?"

Cunnar whispered, "No." While the other two men, afraid to speak, shook their heads to indicate no.

Five more minutes passed without any noticeable activity, "Should we try to do something?" Cunnar asked in a whisper.

"Not yet. We need to stay right here. Kivi and Leo are in a better position. When they feel it is safe to move, they'll start closing in on the enemy." Hale said.

Kangas, a little emboldened by Cunnar's question, decided to ask, "How long do we just lay here on the freezing snow? I have to take a piss."

"We lay here as long as it takes. I don't want to lose anymore of you to inexperience and stupidity." Hale said.

"But what about peeing?" Kangas asked again, with an edge of desperation in his voice.

"Go in your pants." Hale hissed.

"Are you serious?" Kangas replied, aghast.

"Well, you could stand up and piss, but then you'd be running the risk of being shot by the enemy. Would you rather piss yourself or die?" Hale said in a gentler voice.

An audible sigh of relief indicated Kangas' decision as he urinated, "A wise choice. Shame has no meaning on the battlefield, only survival." Hale said.

A stalemate descended upon the combatants for nearly half an hour. Hale could hear Kangas, Cunnar, and the other surviving newcomer Private Saksa start to fidget, "Remain silent!" Hale urged.

"I'm sorry lieutenant. Now I'm cold." Kangas said in a sheepish voice.

Hale stifled the urge to laugh at the young Private's predicament as he said in the sternest voice he could muster, "Better cold, than dead."

Thirty additional minutes passed without a sound coming from the enemy's location. Suddenly, on both sides of the grove, a flash of movement erupted. Cunnar took aim at one of the figures moving towards the fir grove, but Hale slapped his rifle away, "Would you shoot one of our own?"

A moment later the sounds of breaking branches could be heard as Leo and Kivi barreled into the trees. For a few brief moments it seemed as if the entire copse of trees shook from the movement of men. The shaking of tree branches quickly morphed into screams and then silence.

"Don't move." Hale reminded his men.

Finally, Lieutenant Kivi's voice boomed through the forest, "We got the bastards."

"Are you sure that's all of them?" Hale asked cautiously.

"If it wasn't I'd be dead." Kivi observed.

Hale laughed at Kivi's response and said, "True."

"There was a total of three Soviet snipers in here. All three had been shot but still had some fight left in them." Leo shouted.

Hale came to his feet and told his men, "Follow me."

Soon Hale was within the grove of spruce trees. He squatted in front of the first sniper's corpse and located the plastic cylinder around his neck. He carefully unscrewed the cap and pulled out the small piece of paper contained within it. He handed the paper to Leo who glanced at it and said, "Corporal Golubev 3rd NKVD Regiment."

The other two plastic cylinders were located on the dead Soviets. Both of the slain snipers were also from the 3rd NKVD Regiment, "That makes four of these so far." Hale said.

"That definitely confirms that the 44th has been reinforced." Kivi said.

"Have they, or is this just an isolated group of snipers

set loose on our men to break our morale so the 44th can escape?" Hale said.

"What should we do?" Cunnar asked.

"Collect our dead and return to Task Force Makiniemi's camp. Once we are there, we need to find accommodations for our horses. With the snow this deep we'll be much nimbler on skis." Hale said.

It took the group a few minutes to secure the two bodies of their fallen onto the backs of their horses. They turned in the direction of Task Force Makiniemi's HQ and started to ride, *Two more men have been lost. Why am I constantly being put into leadership positions? I'm no good at it and men keep dying as a result.* Hale lamented in his thoughts. Then a new voice spoke in his mind, *Three snipers for two novices isn't a bad trade.* The random thought with little disregard for life made Hale shudder.

Chapter 9

Mid-Afternoon, Two Kilometers Northeast of Hauklia, Central Finland

January 3rd, 1940

Kuznetsov heard them long before he saw them. Though they were well trained in the art of skiing quietly, the Finnish skis occasional scraped against something just below the surface of the snow. He removed his own skis and strapped them to his back. Once the skis were securely in place he cautiously moved toward the sound.

Based on what he was hearing they were moving from left to right in front of him, *One of those supply convoys, or a patrol?* Kuznetsov wondered.

Up ahead his keen eyes registered some movement in the fading light of the dreary overcast day. The Soviet sniper smiled and unslung his rifle. It wasn't long before he spotted the movement again. This time he was able to center his scope on the area of activity and the figure of a Finnish skier was revealed.

Kuznetsov took aim at the man. He was careful to account for the wind. The expert marksman also took into account the pull of gravity on a bullet as it traveled across the nearly four hundred meters of distance that separated him from his target. When he was satisfied, he gave the trigger a gentle squeeze with his right index finger.

The rifle responded to the pull of the trigger by slamming the firing pin into the cartridge's primer. This created a small detonation that ignited the gunpowder within. A split-second later the stock of the rifle pushed into his shoulder as a bullet burst from the Mosin's barrel and hurled toward his target. His aim was slightly low, and the bullet buried itself in the man's right leg. The Finn screamed and went down as blood began to spread across the snow underneath him.

Kuznetsov smiled as he worked the action on his rifle. The other Finns, generally having more common sense than the city raised cannon fodder typical of his own country's army, immediately went to ground. Kuznetsov scanned the area with his rifle looking for another target. While he could see the tops of a few packs, he didn't see any bodies to shoot.

A sudden gust of wind whistled through the trees and pushed the powdery snow across the ground in front of him. Kuznetsov sniffed, then smiled, *I smell snow.*

The Soviet sniper patiently waited for the Finns to make the next move. He panned his scope up and down the small column of seven Finns looking for a mistake that would enable him to trim the squad by another man.

Finally, as darkness began to fall, one of the Finns started to crawl away from the rest of the group, *What are you doing?* Kuznetsov wondered.

He kept switching back and forth between the Finn he had shot, and the one that was crawling away. The only way he was able to tell that the wounded Finn was still alive, was the cloud of steam created by each one of his exhales. In time, the clouds of steam disappeared, *Poor bastard must have bled out. Why didn't his companions try to help him?*

Kuznetsov pushed the question from his mind and glanced up into the sky. He saw the first flakes of snow begin to lazily flutter to the earth. As the falling snow slowly increased in intensity, Kuznetsov kept a close eye on the Finn, who appeared to be moving away from both the group and himself, *Where are you going?*

The Finns appeared to be aware of Kuznetsov's approximate location. The crawling Finn was slowly moving away from the sniper's position, *Do they know where I am at?*

Suddenly movement erupted from the remaining men of the column. As one they stood and started to run westward, or right to left in front of Kuznetsov. The Soviet sergeant quickly took aim at one of the men. He was distracted from his target as the lone Finn also came to his feet and began to run away in a haphazard zig-zagging pattern.

Kuznetsov quickly took aim at the man and fired. He cursed as the bullet missed and the man remained on his feet. The Soviet worked the action on his rifle bringing a fresh bullet into the firing chamber. He raised the rifle back to his shoulder and patiently took the measure of the target.

Kuznetsov was about to squeeze the trigger when his position was suddenly peppered with rifle fire. Startled, the gunfire broke his concentration. He swung his rifle in the direction of the enemy and cursed. The snowstorm had morphed into a blizzard which made it nearly impossible to see anything beyond fifty meters.

Kuznetsov saw several muzzle flashes as the Finns sent another volley in his direction. The light was distorted by the falling snow, making it difficult to determine the enemy's precise location. Again, he cursed, *Got to hand it to them. They figured out how to get away.*

His thought was interrupted by a crashing noise to his right as the lone Finn burst into view. In his right hand was his personal pukko blade. The Russian jumped back as the Finn took a swipe at him with the knife.

The sharp edge of the pukko tore a swath across Kuznetsov's coat but narrowly missed his skin. The Russian brought his rifle up and turned aside the Finn's follow up thrust. He then followed up with a blow to the knife wielder's head with his rifle's stock.

Kuznetsov was distracted by the howling of the other Finns as they ran toward him, *What do they think they are? Wolves?*

The momentary distraction nearly cost the Russian his life as the Finn thrust his blade at him. This time, his rifle was out of position, and he was unable to twist away. Red hot pain caused Kuznetsov to cry out as the pukko bit into his left leg.

The Russian managed to keep his wits about him. He grabbed the Finns outstretched arm and pulled him off balance. The Finn fell forward and stumbled past Kuznetsov as he flailed his arms in a desperate attempt to stay on his feet.

Kuznetsov pivoted on his good leg and fired his rifle from the hip. At this range, he couldn't miss, even without aiming. The bullet slammed into the Finnish soldier's back sending him face forward into the snow. The Soviet sniper kept his barrel trained on the enemy soldier as he quickly worked the action on his rifle. After a few moments of staring at the body, he decided that his target required no additional bullets.

Kuznetsov heard the other Finns closing in on him. To escape, he dashed away into the darkness. His left leg throbbed from the knife wound and he quickly exhausted himself pushing through the deep snow. With his breath now coming in ragged gasps, he located a small copse of fir trees and concealed himself within.

They'll be here at any moment! Kuznetsov's mind shouted in desperation.

He calmed his thoughts and worked to put his skis on. Once the skis were secure to his boots, he came to his feet and pushed himself forward using his poles. Luckily, his injured leg held, and he started to build up speed.

He felt them before he heard them as the hairs on the back of his neck went up. He stole a glance behind him and gasped. Through the nearly white out conditions, he spied the outline of the six Finns, they were less than twenty meters away, *Maybe those idiots stuck on the road are correct. These men are half-human monsters. The result of some foul coupling between a human and a snow beast.*

Kuznetsov shook the thought away and steadied his nerves, *They bleed the same as you. This group hasn't accomplished anything you haven't done yourself.*

The pursuit continued for another hour as Kuznetsov,

now exhausted from both the loss of blood from his leg wound and the effort of fleeing, suddenly found himself in open air. He cried out in surprise, before he crashed back to the earth. Upon landing he lost his balance and fell to the ground.

The Russian tumbled downhill as the Finns suddenly found themselves in the same predicament. Unlike Kuznetsov, they executed picture perfect landings and continued skiing eastward. In moments, using the momentum they gained from the jump, they exited the other side of the depression and were gone.

Kuznetsov spent several minutes trying to catch his breath. As he did so, he looked up at the cascade of snowflakes tumbling from the sky above him and started to laugh, "I survived because I'm not as good a skier as those Finns."

Overcome by mirth he laughed for several minutes before bringing himself under control. The timing saved his life as the Finns reappeared and looked down into the depression. Kuznetsov laid perfectly still as he felt the eyes of the Finns upon him.

Luck was with him once again, as the blizzard had already covered him up. To the Finns, he looked like just one more of the snow-covered lumps that dotted the ground by the millions in this part of Finland. Eventually, the Finns moved on and Kuznetsov was able to examine his injury.

Though he had initially bled like a stuck pig, it was little more than a deep scratch. The blood had long since coagulated, helped along by the freezing temperature, closing the wound. The blood that had seeped into his pants had frozen and created a patch of sorts that sealed out the cold, *If I were a cat, I would be fearful that I have used up many of my nine lives on this single evening.* Kuznetsov thought in amusement.

Chapter 10

Evening, Two Kilometers Northeast of Hauklia, Central Finland

January 3rd, 1940

Hale cursed as he searched the area looking for tracks. After the group had returned to Task Force Makiniemi's HQ, they traded their horses for skis. They left Liv and Heikkinen in good hands.

Hale remembered back to the events that led to him and his squad being sent to track down yet another sniper in this horrid weather. Their evening meal had been interrupted by Lieutenant Colonel Makiniemi as he burst in and shouted, "Karhonen! How can you hope to put an end to the enemy sniper problem, if you are always in my chow hall?"

Irritated, Hale pushed his plate away and came to his feet. He walked over to Makiniemi and slapped the three plastic cylinders with the slain Soviet sniper's information contained within them and growled, "We killed three snipers today." He then slapped the dog tags of the two

Finnish privates that fell to the snipers in his other hand, "And I lost two good men doing it. Why is it that I can't ever get an uninterrupted meal in this chow hall after a hard day of solving your sniper problem? Something none of your men seem to be able to do."

For a moment Makiniemi turned a deep crimson color. Hale's eyes fell to the colonel's right hand which had a slight twitch, *Perhaps I have overdone it a little. Maybe if I'm lucky he'll bust me back to private and put Kivi in charge.*

Makiniemi drew in a deep breath and let it out slowly. As he exhaled his shoulders relaxed and his skin returned to its normal pallor, "My apologies lieutenant I was out of line. You and your men have accomplished the mission you were given today and I'm sorry for your losses. Unfortunately, there's been another sniper attack so I must ask you to immediately head out and see what you can do."

Unlike the previous attack this one was to the north of the Task Force which straddled the Raate Road and ensured that two separate elements of the 44th Motorized Rifle Division, remained that way. The colonel had been informed that an eight-man patrol, sent to the area to ensure the Soviets weren't trying to sneak away from their predicament across the area's many frozen lakes, had been attacked by a lone sniper.

Before leaving the camp, Hale had questioned the survivors of the squad about their encounter with the sniper. As Kivi and Leo listened to the men's responses to Hale's questions, Kivi said, "That sounds like Kuznetsov."

"How did he get away?" Hale asked.

"After shooting Private Jutli he fled on skis. Despite the storm we were able to follow him for some time. We were moving fast to catch up, before we realized it, his tracks had disappeared." Sergeant Huhta said.

"What did you do once you realized that there were no tracks to follow?" Hale asked.

"We doubled back until we picked them up again. Just in time too, the blizzard had nearly erased them. The tracks ended abruptly at the top of a twenty-meter depression. We searched the depression but were unable to find him. It was at that point we gave up and returned to base." Sergeant Huhta said.

"Why didn't you circle to see if you could reacquire his tracks?" Hale asked.

Huhta flashed Hale an irritated look as he said, "The weather was terrible, the temperature was nearly unendurable, and we were tired. Returning to base for further orders seemed like the best option."

"Sergeant, it sounded like up to the point that you lost him, that your men had done everything right. For the first time that I'm aware of, a group of our soldiers were able to flush Kuznetsov from his chosen position. It's a damn shame you lost him." Hale said, his voice filled with frustration.

"You weren't there and even if you had been I doubt you would have done any better." The sergeant fired back.

Hale shrugged his shoulders as he said, "Maybe, maybe not. We'll never know. Now I need someone from your squad to lead me back to the location where these events had taken place."

"Me and my men deserve some time with warm coffee and food in our bellies. Maybe some shuteye too. Why don't you get a map and I'll show you where the encounter took place." Huhta offered.

Kivi was about to interject when Hale said, "Not good enough sergeant. You know as well as I do that landmarks are constantly shifting thanks to the wind. You and your team need to take us back there now."

That's it Hale, keep him boxed in and don't let him out of the corner until he gives you what you want, Kivi thought, *I was worried that you were too nice to be in command but so far you've been just hard enough to get the things we need.*

"My men deserve a meal and some rest. What if I were to show you myself where the encounter took place?" Huhta offered.

"Very well. By the look of your men, I agree that they are in need of some rest. I suppose you will do." Hale said.

An hour of skiing Huhta came to an abrupt stop and pointed, "He used this spot as his firing position."

Hale and the rest of the squad followed Huhta's lead and went to the indicated location. The snow had erased any evidence of Kuznetsov's presence. The young Lieutenant circled around the area until he found an odd shaped lump that didn't belong. Using his gloved hands, he uncovered the frozen corpse of a Finnish Private, "That's Laine. Dumb bastard tried to take the Soviet sniper with his pukko instead of just shooting him. We were going to come back tomorrow with a sleigh to fetch him along with the other man I lost."

"Another opportunity lost." Hale said in disgust, "Why does it always seem like Kuznetsov is able to survive, even when he shouldn't. I swear this bastard must share ancestry with a cat."

Hale kicked a nearby snow drift in frustration which sent a bit of snow into the air, "The snow has covered up all of the tracks. Do you know which direction Kuznetsov fled in?" Hale asked.

Huhta nodded, "He escaped eastward. His tracks are gone, but I think I remember the path we took to chase him, when his tracks were still visible."

Hale squeezed the sergeant's shoulder as he said, "Excellent sergeant. Whenever you are able to get your bearings, please lead on."

Huhta was able to discern the path he and his squad took. When he reached the depression, he pointed downward and said, "This is where we lost him."

"What do you think happened?" Hale asked.

"We didn't see the depression until we were in the air. We were able to land and continue on without a problem, but I'm guessing he wasn't. He must have landed badly and remained here as we sped on past him." Huhta theorized.

"How do you know it was here that you lost him?" Hale asked.

"After this point we saw no more tracks. When I realized our mistake, I turned the squad around and came back here. Which is where I picked up his tracks again." Huhta said.

"If he went to ground here, he must have left some tracks when he left." Hale said.

"That's just it. We didn't find any tracks that led away from this spot. After I had some time to think about it, I figured out what probably happened. The bastard must have been here the whole time. With the way it was snowing, if he just laid on the ground for a few minutes, he probably would have resembled any other buried rock in the snow." Huhta said.

Hale nodded in agreement, "If this was Kuznetsov, and I believe it was, he would have been smart enough to realize that and just lay still as you suggested."

Huhta's shoulders slumped as he said in a resigned voice, "I let the filthy bastard that killed two of my men get away."

Hale put a reassuring hand on Huhta's shoulder and said, "There wasn't anything you could have done. Trust me, Kuznetsov is a crafty one. He wiped out my first command and shot me. Then I was dumb enough to lead him back to our camp which was destroyed by a regiment the following day."

Huhta's eyes widened, "I didn't realize there were Soviet's that are that competent."

Hale laughed, "I can understand why you would have held that opinion given how ridiculously poorly they have fought here. I thought what we managed to accomplish in Karelia was a lot, but what Siilasvuo and you men have done to them here is nothing short of epic."

Huhta nodded in agreement, "Even if we don't bag the 44th, we still managed to destroy the 163rd Division in Suomassalmi. I think these events will be remembered for a long time. What do we do now?"

"Since we don't know precisely where Kuznetsov went from here, we head east." Hale said.

"Why east?" Cunnar questioned, "Why not north or south towards the nearest motti?"

"Because that was the direction, he chose to flee from Sergeant Huhta's squad. So, if we head east, perhaps we will pick up signs of his passage and be able to resume the hunt." Hale said.

Hale turned back to Huhta and said, "You know the area better than any of my men, can you continue to lead us?"

Huhta nodded, "I'm exhausted, but I really want to get this bastard, so yes."

The sniper squad resumed their eastward trek with Huhta in the lead. They traveled for a kilometer without picking up any signs of Kuznetsov's passage. Suddenly, Huhta cried out in pain as a bullet slammed into his chest. He turned toward the rest of the squad. He ripped off his mask and looked at Hale's group in shock.

As the injured sergeant put a hand on the bloody wound in his chest, the blood was already freezing in the fifty below zero nighttime air, a second bullet struck him in the back. The sergeant's eyes locked with Hale's for an instant.

Hale watched the life drain from the sergeant's blue eyes and disappear. Huhta died, standing fully upright. The horrific cold had turned him into a grisly statue. Two more bullets slammed into the sergeant's corpse and the kinetic energy from those impacts finally caused the body to fall forward onto the ground.

While this was happening, Hale and the rest of the squad had gone to ground and spotted the muzzle flashes from the enemy sniper, "That small ridge about five hundred meters ahead." Leo said.

Hale scanned the horizon with his eyes and they noticed the small hill Leo was describing, "You saw muzzle flashes come from that ridge?"

"Yes. Leo said, "At least two."

"So, we are dealing with more than one sniper." Hale said.

"How much you want to bet that neither of them is Kuznetsov?" Kivi said.

"What do you mean? Do you know something that we do not?" Hale wondered.

"This feels similar to what happened before." Kivi said.

"Explain." Hale said.

"One of our men was slain by a sniper. Then Kuznetsov left three snipers behind to ambush the inevitable response." Kivi said.

"You're right, this is the same pattern." Hale said.

"It would be awfully nice lieutenant, sir, if you could stop leading us into ambushes." Cunnar said in a friendly voice.

The words sounded like Cunnar, but not his usual tone of voice, "Found a new way to whine?" Hale asked in amusement.

Despite the situation and the misery of being in direct contact with the snow as they lay on the ground, Cunnar removed his mask briefly and smiled at Hale, "Well the other way wasn't working so I thought I'd try something different."

Hale laughed, "We can always count on you to be a whiney grump."

"It's not a bad question. We should start figuring out how to flush these snipers out without having one of our men shot." Kivi said.

"Not you too." Hale said in exasperation.

"Did everyone forget about the snipers that are trying to kill us?" Leo sharped edged voice interjected.

"No." Hale said.

Hale returned his gaze to the ridgeline the snipers had set themselves up on. The ridge was located beyond a frozen lake. The presence of the lake meant a large amount of open space separated them from the snipers. If anyone entered that open space, they would very likely be slain.

There was an island in the lake about a hundred meters to the north. The presence of the island would afford anyone that tried to cross in that area of the lake some desperately needed cover. Hale's eyes continued to trace the line of the forest until it disappeared over the horizon to the north.

"Shall we try what we did last time? Going right at them is definitely not an option." Hale said.

Cunnar snorted, "Unless your coat needs some new holes. Then going right at them should do you just fine."

The as yet un-slain privates, Korpi and Manni shared a nervous look at each other, "Knock it off Cunnar, your usual bullshit is making Korpi and Manni jumpy." Leo snapped.

"It would seem to be the only strategy available. Given the distance maybe send one of our new members with us this time?" Kivi suggested.

"A wise choice. That way they can start learning how to move." Hale agreed.

"Great that leaves me stuck in the decoy group." Cunnar fumed.

Ignoring Cunnar, Hale said, "Kivi head north with Manni and Leo you go south around the lake with Korpi. Myself and private grumpy will remain here as the decoys."

Kivi, with Private Mani in tow headed back the way they had come for a hundred meters. The pair then turned northward. He was careful to keep them at least two hundred meters from the lake and to use the terrain to limit their vulnerability to enemy snipers.

After another half a kilometer of skiing, near the point where Kivi was going to turn eastward to come up behind the enemy snipers, a bullet flew by Kivi's face, "Down!"

Private Mani obeyed instantly. The move saved his life as a second bullet flew through the space, he had just occupied a split-second prior. Kivi scanned the horizon looking for an enemy. After a minute of the pair being on the ground and the enemy not firing at them Kivi rolled onto his back and tried to walk back through what had just happened in his mind.

The bullet meant for him had rocketed by his left ear, so closely he thought he could feel the breeze from its passage. The second shot, the one meant for Mani, who was about six meters behind Kivi buried itself in a tree about ten meters beyond Mani. The tree was located three or four meters further north from Kivi's position, "I think there are at least two snipers out there. The duration between the shots was too small and the angle of the one meant for you was too different."

"How do you even know that?" Mani said in awe.

Kivi pointed to the bullet that had buried itself in a tree trunk, "Because of where you were and where that bullet hit the tree."

Mani looked back in the direction that Kivi pointed. He concentrated for nearly a minute before his eyes were able to discern the ruptured surface of the birch trunk, where the bullet had come to rest, "I see the bullet now. Given what you just said, what is our next move?"

"We need to get them to shoot at us again, so I can figure out where they are at." Kivi said.

"I was afraid you were going to say that." Mani said.

"Sorry son, if you could shoot like me, we could flip a coin for it." Kivi said.

Mani nodded and took a deep breath. He exhaled slowly to calm the butterflies in his stomach. He did this several more times before he finally said, "I'm ready to try. What do you want me to do?"

"This would be easier if there wasn't so much snow on the ground. Let's try this first, I need you to take off your skis. Then remain laying on your back as you wave them up in the air using each arm. That should create enough movement to evoke a response from our sniper friends." Kivi said.

"Alright." Mani said.

Mani removed his skis and began to wave them around in the air as instructed. He did this for nearly half a minute. Nothing happened. When he was about to give up gunfire suddenly pierced the silence of the forest.

Kivi was nearly looking right at the sniper's position when he saw the muzzle flash. He held his fire, and two seconds later, a second muzzle flashed. Kivi adjusted his aim, took a deep breath, and imagined where the man would be behind that muzzle flash. He then held his breath and pulled the trigger.

A moment later, the two Finns heard a voice cry out in pain, "Got you, swine." Kivi said in satisfaction.

"You're awful quiet Mani. Are your socks full of piss?" Kivi asked.

"That second shot hit my ski." Manni said in irritation.

"Can you still use it?" Kivi asked.

"I think so." Mani responded.

"Then what are you crying about?" Kivi asked.

Private Mani cursed under his breath at Kivi. The big man hearing the young private's voice, but not the words guessed at what he had just said, "Quit playing with your balls back there, we've got to get the other sniper to shoot."

"Didn't you see that one shoot too?" Mani asked.

"I did." Kivi replied.

"Then why can't you use the same trick?" Mani said.

"Because unless our enemy sniper is a complete idiot, he moved after I hit his friend." Kivi said.

"I bet he is still in the same spot." Mani countered.

"This is probably a dumb idea, but I'll try." Kivi said.

Kivi closed his eyes and thought back to the first

muzzle flash. He brought the image up in his mind as if it were a cinema film, frozen in a single moment. He memorized the shadowy landscape surrounding the image. Next, he opened his eyes and found the spot, *He must have been in that birch tree when he took the shot.* Kivi glanced upward and noted the position of the moon, *If he likes playing the part of a bird, with a little patience, if I wait long enough the moon is going to silhouette him.*

"How warm are you?" Kivi asked.

"Why?" Mani replied.

"Just answer the damn question. Could you spend two more hours laying on the ground?" Kivi asked.

"Of course. I'm not one of those idiot Russians who are way underdressed for this weather. I have the proper number of layers for the temperature." Mani replied.

"Good man. I think if we just wait the bastard out, the moon is going to do our work for us." Kivi said.

"What about Lieutenant Karhonen and that disagreeable fellow Cunnar?" Mani asked.

"What about them?" Kivi asked in annoyance.

"Aren't they depending on us to eliminate the snipers on the other side of the lake from them?" Mani asked.

"Yes, but the lieutenant is not going to do anything stupid. He's probably figured out that the exchange of fire that has happened here is coming from the wrong location." Kivi paused, then an idea occurred to him, "Why don't you get on your skis, head back there, and tell him the situation?"

"I'm a fisherman, sir. I'm not sure I can navigate the

forest in the dark." Mani said.

"Nonsense. Thanks to the moon and cloudless sky there is plenty of light to see by. Besides, if you truly don't know how, it will be good practice for you." Kivi said.

Unable to argue with Kivi's logic, Mani glumly said, "Very well."

The young Finn put his skis back on. While he was doing so, he rubbed the spot where a bullet had nicked off about half an inch of the left one. He ran a gloved finger along the jagged edge and cursed when a splinter penetrated his glove.

"Quit dillydallying and go. If you hurry, you can be back here before I take my shot. Make sure you keep the trees between you and the enemy." Kivi said.

Without responding, Mani came to his feet behind a large fir tree. He then started to move directly westward, careful to keep the tree between himself and the last known location of the enemy snipers. A bullet slammed into his back causing him to fall face forward into the snow.

Kivi immediately returned fire and a moment later heard the sniper's body crashing through branches and landing in the snow. Private Mani groaned, "Mani, are you hit?"

"Yes." He gasped.

As Kivi started to crawl in the injured Private's direction he asked, "Where are you hit?"

"Something that felt like a sledgehammer hit me in the back. I'm having trouble breathing." Mani replied.

Kivi reached Mani's location. He helped him remove his pack so he could find the wound. As the unblemished white cloth of his coat became visible, Kivi said, "You're not shot."

"Something hit me." Mani protested, "Hard."

Kivi looked down at Mani's pack. He stretched the pack out and saw a thumb sized hole in it, *Interesting.*

He opened the pack and started to dig through the contents contained within. His hand wrapped around the cold iron of the private's entrenching tool. He pulled the shovel out and looked down at it. Toward the left edge the shovel had a fresh divot in it, "Summer of cunts." Kivi whispered.

Mani snatched the shovel out of Kivi's hand and looked down at it, "He shot my shovel?"

"You are one lucky bastard." Kivi replied.

Together the two men started laughing.

Chapter 11

Evening, Four Kilometers Northeast of Hauklia, Central Finland

January 3rd, 1940

Leo and Private Korpi left Hale. The two men headed in the opposite direction from Kivi and Mani, southward around the lake. Leo, in the lead, was careful to keep them two hundred meters from the edge of the lake. An expert woodsman, he used both the trees and the terrain to mask their presence as much as possible.

After nearly thirty minutes of skiing, Leo stopped. Korpi drew up beside him and asked, "Why did you stop?"

Leo held up a finger to his lips and Korpi fell silent. The veteran sniper scanned the terrain in front of them, "Something feels off and I can't quite put my finger on it."

Korpi sat down on the ground. Surprised at the private's reaction Leo asked, "What are you doing?"

"You've been a sniper in this war and the previous

one. Your experience is much greater than mine, so it seems like the best thing for me to do is to keep my mouth shut and let you concentrate on whatever is bothering you, so you can figure it out." Korpi replied.

Leo snorted in surprise at the wisdom in the young man's words, "That's really perceptive. So why did you sit down?"

"My feet hurt." Korpi replied.

Leo chuckled, "I think you will go far in this world private. Your mind is sharp like Lieutenant Karhonen's, you just happened to grow up a fisherman instead of a woodsman."

"To bad I didn't grow up to be a woodsman. I bet those silver circles on his collar get all the girls." Korpi said.

"They would, but he is already married with a baby on the way." Leo said.

Korpi whistled in appreciation, "I think he is younger than I am. He sure didn't waste any time."

"He married his childhood sweetheart." Leo said.

Korpi with a twinkle in his eye replied, "Oh, he knocked up his childhood sweetheart."

Leo rolled his eyes, "I need to shut up now or you're going to figure out more things you don't need to know about."

Leo returned to trying to figure out what was bothering him. The pair remained where they were, Leo standing and Korpi sitting on the ground for the next thirty minutes. During this time the moon continued to climb into the sky. Over time, this had the effect of slowly shifting the shadows in front of them.

Off to the north, a series of gunshots were exchanged, "What's that all about?" Korpi wondered out loud.

"It's up in the direction that Kivi and Mani headed, but the exchange of rifle fire is not coming from the location of the sniper that we are after." Leo said.

They listened for a few more minutes as several more shots were fired. Silence once again reigned and Leo returned to concentrating on his own problems, "That sounded like they ran into another sniper, or the sniper that killed Huhta, moved."

"Maybe that is what is bothering you?" Korpi suggested.

"Explain." Leo said.

"What if there is an ambush on this side of the lake as well and somehow your subconscious feels it. Even if your eyes do not see it." Korpi said.

"I thought you were a fisherman?" Leo asked.

"Born and raised." Korpi said proudly.

"You sound like a bloody college professor or a philosopher. Fisherman and the way you talk doesn't add up." Leo observed.

"I like to read." Korpi said.

"If that's the case I'd say they probably have to throw you out of the library every night to close." Leo said.

"Something like that." Korpi said in a mischievous voice, "You should figure out where the ambush is, so I'll be able to hurry back to the library."

Leo returned to concentrating on his feeling and trying to figure out what was causing it. After another thirty minutes he startled Korpi, who had nearly fallen asleep when he said, "It's gone now."

Korpi yawned loudly and then asked, "What are we going to do?"

"It doesn't feel right to keep going. Maybe if we move a bit further south and then head east. You know, give the lake a wider birth. Perhaps we'll be able to avoid whatever is out there that gave me the feeling." Leo said.

"Alright then. Shall we get to it?" Korpi asked.

Leo nodded. The two men, with Leo in the lead, turned southward. They traveled for about two hundred meters when Leo came to a stop, "Did you get another feeling?"

Leo nodded. Korpi remained silent as Leo scanned the shadowy forest around them. His eyes fell on a shadow that seemed to be part of a birch tree trunk around a hundred meters away. The Great War veteran loosened his grip on his ski poles as he studied the unusual shadow. Suddenly Leo's heart froze when he figured out what he was looking at.

The veteran sniper hurriedly unslung his rifle and began to raise it up to take aim. He saw a muzzle flash from the suspicious shadow's location. His mind exploded in agony when a sudden burst of blinding pain erupted in his chest as the sound of the rifle firing reached him, *Too late.* Leo thought. As he collapsed, he said, "Tell Hale not to blame himself for this."

"Leo!" Korpi said as he reached for his crumpling companion.

Korpi lowered Leo gently to the ground and looked down at his chest. He was aghast at what he saw. A bullet hole bled freely just below Leo's sternum.

Korpi ripped Leo's coat open to look at the wound. The bullet wound was surrounded by black and purple bruising indicating a horrific amount of internal damage, "I've read about bullets like this. They're called explosive bullets and they are supposed to be illegal!" Korpi exclaimed.

Korpi started to scramble for his medical kit when Leo's raspy voice, barely more than a whisper said, "Don't bother. My insides are all chewed up. Just hold my hand. I'm not going to be here much longer."

Korpi removed both his own and Leo's masks from their faces. He then grasped both of the older man's hands with his own, "You'll soon be in a better place."

Leo smiled and nodded slightly as he whispered, "I already am. My wife and little baby daughter are here. They are gesturing for me to join them in the light."

"Then you must go and be with them. Hurry now, you don't want to be left behind." Korpi urged.

Leo smiled as he whispered, "My dears."

It was the last thing he would ever say. Leo exhaled sharply as his final breath rattled from his lungs and then he breathed no more. Korpi's shoulder's slumped, and he released Leo's hands. He crossed the deceased sergeant's arms across his chest and not thinking, stood.

Suddenly, he felt the sharp edge of a blade at his throat. A voice in broken Finnish asked, "Are you with Karhonen's group?"

Korpi replied in Russian, "Da."

"Good. Tell him, Kuznetsov hunts him." The voice replied in Russian.

Korpi's eyes widened as he realized who it was that had ahold on him. Suddenly the man withdrew the knife and pushed Korpi hard in the back. The young Finn lost his balance and fell face first into the snow. He quickly rolled over and looked back to see if he could get a glimpse of the enemy sniper. Kuznetsov had melted away as quickly as he had appeared. He was alone with Leo's corpse.

Frightened, Korpi came to his feet, he thrust his poles into the snow with purpose and hastily sped away from Leo Virtanen's final resting place. He had hardly had any time to get to know the middle-aged warrior but in those few minutes he had started to feel the bonds of brotherhood forming,

 Korpi was able to retrace their journey by following their tracks in the moonlight. Before long he blundered into Hale and Cunnar's position. A shadow appeared out of the black void that surrounded the soldier and grabbed him. Korpi squawked in surprise as he felt cold steel at his throat once more, "Identify yourself." Hale's voice growled.

 "Private Korpi."

The knife at his throat suddenly disappeared and Hale asked, "Why have you returned? I heard a single gunshot come from your area. Did you get the sniper?"

Korpi let out a single sob as he said, "Kuznetsov killed Leo."

Underneath his mask, Hale's face went white. His knees weakened and he had to fight to remain standing. In a cracking voice he asked, "How did this happen?"

"Leo was leading us in the direction of the enemy sniper across the lake. He was carefully using the trees and terrain to keep us invisible from the enemy. Inexplicably, he stopped and said something to the effect that the way ahead didn't feel right." Korpi said.

"What did Leo do?" Hale asked.

"He observed for a time and wasn't able to put his finger on it, so we headed south with the intention of going around the area that was unnerving Leo. As we turned eastward the feeling returned and he stopped. This time he was able to see what his gut was telling him. As he scrambled to unsling his rifle, Kuznetsov shot him in the chest."

"What happened next? How did you get away?" Hale demanded.

"As Leo collapsed, he said, *Hale don't blame yourself for this.*" Korpi said.

"Go on." Hale urged.

"I opened his coat and examined the wound. He was a mess. There was nothing I could do. I held his hands in my own and tried to comfort him. He whispered that his wife and daughter were calling him into the light. I told him to go to them. He smiled then breathed his last." Korpi said.

"How do you know it was Kuznetsov that fired the shot?" Hale asked.

"Because a minute or so later, he placed a knife blade at my throat, in a very similar manner to what you just did and told me to tell you it was him." Korpi finished.

A fresh wave of weakness slammed into Hale. He fought the urge to sink to the ground and failed as his knees buckled, *Kuznetsov did that on purpose. He is hoping to frighten me so that I keep making mistakes and feeding him more men.*

After a long pause Hale replied, "I see private. Thank you for your report."

Hale felt a hand squeeze his shoulder in support. He turned and saw Cunnar, "We'll all miss him. Leo was a good man."

"Indeed." Hale said.

"What are we going to do?" Korpi said.

"It may already be too late, but we need to stop talking, conceal ourselves, and hope that Kuznetsov followed you." Hale said.

The three men did as Hale instructed. Each found a position of concealment to await Kuznetsov's arrival. Hale inserted himself into a small group of spruce trees. Cunnar secreted himself behind a log and used his hands to shift the snow around to create a clear field of fire. Korpi simply laid down on the ground behind a thick birch trunk to conceal his body and peered around it.

The three men then sat in silence for the next hour. With no Kuznetsov and increasing worry about what happened to Kivi, Hale said, "I guess Kuznetsov isn't coming. He may be out there and nearby waiting for us to make a move so he can take us out. Cunnar stay in position to cover us."

"Where are you going?" Cunnar asked.

"I'm taking Korpi, and we are going to go see what

became of Kivi and Mani. We haven't heard anything from their direction in hours." Hale said.

"Is splitting up a good idea? That's what got us into this mess in the first place." Cunnar said.

"Yes. Someone has to cover us in case Kuznetsov is out there." Hale said.

"Why can't it be Korpi?" Cunnar asked.

"Because I'm not sure Korpi would hit anything if he shot his weapon. You on the other hand, can shoot now."

Cunnar unable to deny Hale's logic when it came in the form of a compliment to his growing abilities as a soldier bowed to his superior's wishes, "Very well. Good luck, lieutenant."

"God go with you." Hale said.

The two men clasped hands in the old way, hand to elbow, and then turned away. Cunnar figuring Hale would always choose the best firing position, elected to use the spot Hale had used amongst the spruce trees. Hale with Korpi in tow, started to follow the trail left by the passage of Kivi and Mani.

Chapter 12

Evening, Four Kilometers Northeast of Hauklia, Central Finland

January 3rd, 1940

Kuznetsov sensed a shift in the area a few hundred meters in front of him, *Someone is out there.*

He stood deathly still waiting for the presumed Finn or Finns to resume moving in his direction. Instead, he heard nothing as he waited impatiently with his rifle ready to put down another of the enemy. Doubt began to creep into his mind as the minutes slowly ticked by, *Did they see me somehow? How is that even possible considering I haven't seen them and I am sitting behind this log remaining absolutely still?*

Ten minutes turned into twenty and still the Finns showed no signs of moving, *Is that you Karhonen?* Kuznetsov wondered.

Another ten minutes passed, and his ears picked up the faint sound of movement roughly where he had heard it before, *They aren't moving toward me. Instead, they have turned toward the south. How the hell did they know I was here?*

The Finn's bizarre actions caused doubt to creep into the pit of his stomach. Pushing it to the side, he decided to take action. Kuznetsov withdrew from his hiding spot behind the fallen tree and headed back the way he had come. When he reached a frozen creek, he turned southward and used the depression caused by the water's passage over the millennia since the Ice Age, to conceal him from the enemy.

He traveled for a few hundred meters and then decided to stop, *If I was a Finn and I was confident that there was someone waiting for me up ahead, I would have turned and moved two or three hundred meters southward.*

Kuznetsov unslung his rifle and laid down against the edge of the creek's gully. He raised his head just enough to peer over the top. It wasn't long before he saw movement in the moonlight, *There you are, right where I figured you would be.*

His confidence restored, Kuznetsov observed for a few minutes. There were two shadowy figures heading his way. The veteran sniper took a deep breath and held it as he centered the cross hairs of his rifle's scope on the center mass of the first shadow.

Whoever it was, continued to head straight at him, *I hope your Karhonen.* He thought as he pulled the trigger.

Two hundred meters away the shadow collapsed to the earth, *Got you.* Kuznetsov thought.

He decided that he would use the second Finn to send a message. Unless of course it was Karhonen, *All of the Finns must know fear.*

Kuznetsov removed his skis and set them down next to

his pack. He kept his rifle in his hands as he slowly crept forward. As he drew closer to his victim, he thought he caught a few snatches of a voice on the faint breeze blowing out of the west.

He reached the two Finns just in time to see the one he had shot die, *Damn, that's not Karhonen.*

Kuznetsov drew his blade and circled around behind the surviving Finn who was busy crossing the dead one's arms on his chest. Once he was in position, he crept forward until he was able to reach out and place his blade on the man's throat, "Are you with Karhonen's group?"

The Finn replied in Russian, "Da."

Kuznetsov smiled, *This one understands Russian. Excellent.*

"Good. Tell him, Kuznetsov hunts him." He released the Finn, withdrew the blade, and pushed him hard in the back.

Kuznetsov faded away into the darkness leaving the Finn to wonder why he still drew breath.

Chapter 13

Late Evening, Five Kilometers Northeast of Hauklia, Central Finland

January 3rd, 1940

"I need you to stay here so the enemy can't slip by us." Kivi ordered.

"Why can't I just come with you?" Mani asked.

"Because I am going to head northward and try to swing around our wounded friends up ahead and come up behind them. If you remain here, then neither they, nor the group across the lake, assuming it isn't the same bunch I've already shot, can get past us and surprise Hale." Kivi said.

"I guess that sort of makes sense. What are you going to do after you finish off the wounded group?" Mani asked.

"I'm going to come back here and pick you up, so we can continue on to the group across the lake from Hale as we were originally ordered. Again, assuming the bunch I shot, isn't the same men that simply changed position while we were enroute to here." Kivi said.

"How will I know it is you that is coming?" Mani asked.

"You won't. Shoot anything that moves." Kivi ordered.

"That doesn't make any sense. What if it is you, I see coming?" Mani asked.

Kivi laughed, "You won't see me until my hand is wrapped around your mouth. Again, if you see movement coming from the north, east, or south, shoot it. Am I clear?" Kivi asked.

"Clear, lieutenant." Mani replied.

Kivi gave Mani a feral grin, "Good. I'm going to be furious with you if I come back here and find your corpse so don't fuck up. Got it?"

Mani nodded and Kivi slapped him on the back, "Good man."

Without another word, Kivi turned and disappeared into the trees. He was headed in a northerly direction when he vanished from sight. Once he was clear of Private Mani, the big man moved along silently.

Having learned from Hale and Leo how best to move through subarctic forests, while avoiding detection, Kivi would periodically pause and listen for pursuers. In addition, during the pauses, he tried to identify any other sound that was out of place in the frozen darkness of this primordial forest. Hearing nothing, he would continue on his way.

In the sky above, the moon continued to ascend casting ever increasing silvery hued light onto the snow. The moon had been joined by a second light source. One that can only be found in the northern latitudes, the dancing green ribbon of the Aurora Borealis. When the two sources of illumination combined, they created a breath-taking spectrum of light that caused the snow to sparkle.

Despite the darkness, this dual source increased the ambient light, which was further magnified by reflecting off the snow. This made it progressively easier for Kivi to see as the night went on, *If it gets much brighter it might as well be daylight out here.* Kivi mused.

After an hour, he decided to turn eastward. The forest that surrounded him, mostly consisting of a mixture of spruce and birch trees, seemed to stretch on for an eternity. He paused for a moment to look up into the sky at the Aurora, *So beautiful.* He thought.

When he lowered his eyes back to the frozen hell that surrounded him, he noticed a bulge up ahead. It was set about five meters off the ground. A height where there shouldn't be anything of concern. The odd shape appeared to be merged with a large birch tree about a hundred meters up ahead, *Unless moose have learned to climb trees that has to be a human.* Kivi smiled, looking forward to the action he was about to take, *Hello you sneaky communist cunt. Guess you idiots still haven't learned that using trees as firing positions is stupid.*

Kivi, careful to not make any sudden movements, lest he draw the attention of the enemy sniper, slowly kneeled down. He then moved at a deliberately glacial pace to unsling his rifle from his back. Once the rifle was in his hands, he raised it to his shoulder and took aim at the strange form. When all was in alignment, he drew in a breath and held it as he pulled the trigger.

The silence of the forest was suddenly interrupted by the booming discharge of Kivi's rifle. His target, without making a sound, toppled from the tree and fell to the ground. Suddenly, out of the corner of his eye he saw movement. He started to turn toward the movement when it slammed into his right side.

The force of the blow, delivered by the enemy's shoulder, knocked the big Finn sideways off his feet. As soon as the two men made contact with the ground, Kivi sat up and smashed his elbow into the man's head. The enemy soldier let out a grunt of pain when Kivi's elbow connected with the side of his head.

Kivi, his elbow stinging, pushed the man that had tackled him away and came to his feet. He turned toward his attacker who had also managed to get to his feet. The Soviet staggered as if he was struggling to keep his balance thanks to Kivi's mighty blow to his head.

Kivi drew his pukko blade and lunged at the Soviet, with the edge of his blade leading. The enemy soldier managed to sidestep the big man. This saved his life and Kivi's blade tore a small swathe of material from his greatcoat as it narrowly missed the target.

The big Finn turned toward the enemy soldier as the Soviet took a step back and tried to draw his pistol from its holster. Luckily for Kivi, his nervous opponent, in his haste to pull it out, forgot to unbutton the clasp that held it in place. Smiling, Kivi hurled himself at the Soviet soldier. As he connected with the man's midsection, he threw an arm around his back and plunged his blade into his chest.

The pukko blade sank to the hilt. The Russian's eyes

widened, and he looked down in horror at the blade buried in his left breast. Kivi withdrew the blade and repeatedly stabbed his opponent until the man went into convulsions and started to spit up blood.

Kivi pushed the dying Russian away and stood. He watched impassively as the man stopped convulsing, went into shock, and died a few minutes later. He used the Soviet's white overcoat to wipe the blood off of his pukko blade before he returned the blade to its sheath.

Kivi searched the body. He found two grenades and the standard issue bottle of vodka, which he pocketed. He pulled the little green tube from the man's neck and withdrew the tiny paper that was rolled up inside. He could not read the Cyrillic letters, but he recognized that the man's unit was again the 3rd NKVD Regiment. The rest of the man's gear consisted of a standard issue Soviet soldier field kit, along with ammo for his rifle.

Kivi found much the same on the body that had been sitting in the tree. He thought about the setup, *They used the man in the tree as bait in the hopes that the hidden man on the ground could get the kill. They must know that the majority of Finns are good shots with their rifles, especially the ones out here in the forest. Which means the bait, was likely to at least get hit. These commies are a cold-hearted group. I thought they had little regard for life. I was wrong. They have no regard for the lives of their men.*

After looting the second body, Kivi went prone and listened for ten minutes. While lying on the ground, he slowly scanned the terrain around him, memorizing every detail. He would then periodically shift his gaze to each section of forest around him to ascertain if anything had changed. Seeing no changes, he decided to resume his mission.

Cautious after running into another enemy sniper, Kivi decided to head northward for a few hundred more meters before trying to head eastward again. As Kivi trekked northward on his skis, the hairs on the back of his neck stood on end as if his subconscious was trying to tell him he was being watched. Each time he gave into the feeling and turned to look, he found nothing.

Another twenty minutes passed and Kivi decided that he had gone far enough and made his turn to the east. He covered about fifty meters and then stopped and went prone on the snowy surface of the forest. He used the memorization trick that he had taught the now mostly deceased members of the special operation group.

Once again, he broke up the surrounding terrain into small quadrants in his mind and memorized each quadrant. With the surrounding terrain memorized, he slowly scanned and compared it to his mental image for any changes. Seeing nothing, he breathed a sigh of relief and laughed off his feelings of being watched as nerves.

Kivi travelled eastward for two hundred meters before he paused again. He repeated the mental scanning procedure until he was satisfied that nothing was amiss. Resuming his journey, he turned southward and traveled until he was roughly east of the wounded Soviets. As he lay prone on the frigid snow, the hairs on the back of his neck went up yet again.

This time he spent nearly thirty minutes trying to find the origin point of that feeling to no avail, *I swear there is something out there stalking me but I never seem to be able to spot it.*

Reluctantly, Kivi resumed moving in on the injured Russians. It didn't take long for him to realize that both of the men he shot were dead. They had become frozen, once living statues, entombed in the moment of death until the spring thaw sets them free.

Kivi searched these men, added to his vodka and grenade reserves, and then pulled their identification cylinders. Again, both men haled from the 3rd NKVD Regiment, *I guess its time to collect Mani and be on our way. I'm sure Hale is wondering what the hell is going on over here that is taking so long.*

Kivi, feeling fairly confident that the north was clear, headed away from the Soviet statues, in that direction. He quickly turned west and moved past Mani. Finally, he turned southward. As he approached the location of the Finnish private, he frowned as he picked up a slight odor of something metallic in the air.

Within his mouth, his tongue tasted almost of copper as he covered the last few meters that separated him from Mani. Then he saw him. The young Finn had been nailed to a large birch tree. The nails had been driven through his outstretched arms attaching him to the tree's lowest branch.

That same someone had sliced open his chest cavity and pulled the skin back until both his ribs and guts were visible, *What have these sick bastards done to you?* Kivi wondered, horrified at what he saw.

Upon closer inspection Kivi saw that each one of the ribs had been severed from the spine and that Mani's lungs had been pulled through the resultant opening in his back. Kivi, collapsed to his knees and vomited on the ground. He wiped his mouth and looked up at the tortured form of Private Mani, *My God, did this sick bastard create a blood eagle?*

Overcome by revulsion, the big man fought the urge to weep. Instead, he unslung his rifle and looked for targets. Seeing none, he returned his eyes to the horror that was once Private Mani. Sickened by the sight, he punched the snow in fury until his anger was diffused.

Through frozen tear-stained eyes, Kivi gazed up at Private Mani's body. He hadn't noticed it at first. In fact, it would have been almost impossible to see while he was standing, since Mani's head was slumped over. Mani's unseeing eyes stared directly down at his feet. If his eyes had still possessed life, they would be looking at the ground. From his vantage point on the ground, Kivi was able to make out a small K, carved into Private Mani's forehead.

Kuznetsov! Enraged, Kivi came to his feet and yelled, "Kuznetsov! I'm coming for you, you sick bastard do you hear me?"

When his yelling was met with silence, Kivi added, "Coward! Come out and fight me like a man."

Kuznetsov paused when he heard the distant voice screaming his name. He turned toward the sound and listened. Hearing nothing further, he smiled, and resumed his course, *Now that they know fear. The stage is set.*

Chapter 14

Midnight, Five Kilometers Northeast of Hauklia, Central Finland

January 4th, 1940

Hale came upon Kivi, still laying in the snow. He looked from his former teacher to the form of Private Mani nailed to a tree, *My God what is this?* Hale wondered.

As Private Korpi bent to assist Lieutenant Kivi, Hale approached the body of Private Mani. He fought down a wave of nausea that threatened to overwhelm him and send the contents of his stomach spewing forth. Instead, he detached his mind from his feelings, ironically something that then Sergeant Kivi had taught him to do during his training and examined the corpse.

Hale dispassionately noted the ribs separated from the spine, and how the lungs had been pulled through to form a ghastly set of wings, "What happened to Mani?" Korpi asked.

"It's called a blood eagle." Kivi said.

Hale nodded sagely, "I've read about this. I thought it was a myth. I didn't think this was physically possible."

"Clearly it is no myth." Kivi said.

Korpi, tried to avoid looking at Mani, as he asked, "What is a blood eagle?"

"It's an excruciating way to kill someone. First, you cut them open with a knife, both front and back. At this point the victim usually passes out. Which is a blessing, because next each one of their ribs is separated from their spine using a cutting tool, usually a small ax, saw, or a very sharp knife. When that is complete the lungs are pulled through this new opening to form a pair of wings." Hale said.

"My God what a horrific way to die. How can anyone be so sick?" Korpi asked.

"People are evil, especially when they don't have any consequences for their actions. Fortunately, I don't think Mani was alive when this was done to him." Kivi observed.

"Why?" Hale asked.

"Sound really carries in this forest at night. I would have heard his screams." Kivi said.

"Then whoever did this must have known exactly what to do and been nearby when he died." Hale said.

"Why?" Korpi asked.

"Because the person that did this would have needed to act quickly, before the lungs froze and became unpliable." Kivi said.

"You were nearby. Did you see anything? Do you

know who did this?" Hale asked.

"It was Kuznetsov. He carved a K into poor Mani's forehead so that we would know it was him." Kivi said.

"What a sick bastard. How can anyone do this?" Korpi asked.

"Look here." Hale said. When Kivi and Korpi looked at where he was pointing, he added, "Mani's throat was slit. Kuznetsov did this after he was dead."

"That doesn't make any sense. Why go through all the time and effort to abuse a corpse like this?" Korpi asked.

"Fear." Kivi said.

Hale nodded in agreement, "Kuznetsov is hoping that this would terrify us."

"What would the point be of doing that?" Korpi asked.

Kivi smiled ruefully, "It's a tactic I taught the young men of the special operations group. If you can make the enemy fear you, then they will make mistakes. Men that make mistakes are easy to defeat."

"Kuznetsov probably already knows that we fear him. With this act of barbarity, he is trying to elevate our fear into terror." Hale said.

"What do we do now?" Korpi asked.

"Did you find any tracks that we could follow?" Hale asked.

"No, I haven't been able to do anything since I came upon Mani." Kivi admitted.

"It seems that Kuznetsov little sick science project succeeded in paralyzing you." Hale observed.

"I was completely vulnerable when I came upon Mani like this. He could have taken me out. Why didn't he?" Kivi wondered.

"How long had you been here, when we arrived?" Hale asked.

"Just a few minutes." Kivi said.

"Summer of cunts." Hale cursed.

"What?" Korpi asked.

"We must have just missed him. Somehow, he knew we were coming and let Kivi live." Hale said.

"Or he just wanted to make sure someone got back to our lines alive to describe this horror. He hasn't shown any past evidence of abusing corpses, so this act appears very intentional. If he killed me and there was no one left to convey this grisly sight, his hard work would have gone to waste." Kivi said.

"Could someone be that calculating?" Korpi asked.

Both Hale and Kivi, experienced with Kuznetsov said in unison, "Yes."

"What do we do now?" Korpi asked.

"We go and collect Cunnar before the blood eagle, or some other act of depravity is performed upon him." Hale said.

"What about the snipers on the other side of the lake?" Kivi asked.

"I think they have either already been dealt with, or that it was Kuznetsov trying to force us into the traps he set for us with the other snipers." Hale said.

"That makes sense." Kivi said, "So now what?"

Must I think of everything? Hale mentally lamented, then said, "We head for the nearest, task force. This far east, that should be Task Force Kari to the south of us. Now let's move before he gets Cunnar."

"I don't really like that whiny bastard, but being annoying is not deserving of getting to wear his lungs as a cape either. Let's move." Kivi said.

They made a note of Mani's location on their map. When they had a chance, they would send the poor bastards working the corpse collection detail to come fetch what was left of him. With Hale in the lead, the party turned southward and headed for the Raate Road.

Cunnar, lying prone, thought he heard something moving in front of him. He scanned the forest looking for the source of the sound that he heard. Seeing nothing, he kept his rifle at the ready.

Ten minutes passed and the hairs on the back of his neck stood on end. He thought he felt something or someone coming up behind him. He whirled around but nothing was there, *What is going on? Am I imagining things?*

Cunnar settled back down and tried to make himself as small as possible. To accomplish his goal, he mentally willed himself to melt into the snow. Simultaneously, he kept his head on a swivel to try and ensure that no one was able to sneak up on him. This task was made easier, thanks to the bright night, the frightened Finn had good visibility all around, *Must stay vigilant to stay alive.* He thought nervously.

Beyond the light cast by the moon and the aurora, the frozen forest seemed like a sinister place of shifting shadows. Though there didn't appear to be anything, or anyone nearby, his mind thought it saw movement in the shadowy world beyond his visibility. Then he saw it, maybe two hundred meters in front of him, *There! That was definitely something.*

Cunnar carefully placed his rifle on the large rock he was using as cover and took aim at the point where he thought he saw the shadow shift. When no further signs of movement occurred, his mind was filled with thoughts of self-doubt, *Did you really see what you thought you saw or was it your imagination? Who are you kidding, you're no good at this sniper nonsense. Why did Hale leave you here alone?* Cunnar's mind, filled with fear, supplied its own answer, *He wants to be rid of you. You've been left out here to die.*

Cunnar, trying to reassert control over his wild emotions, thought back to the orders Hale had given along with their rationale. His mind ignored this reasonable train of thought and instead supplied its own thoughts, *He left you out here all alone because he wants Kuznetsov to get you. Maybe they are in cahoots with each other? That would make sense. It would explain why everyone around Hale falls to Kuznetsov.*

Thoughts of Kuznetsov made Cunnar's resolve begin to buckle, *Settle down Cunnar, your mind is lying to you. Hale is a good man and would not intentionally sacrifice anyone to that monster Kuznetsov. Remember how broken up he's been over each man he lost? Not to mention the guilt he carries around for the men he has killed. Hale wants the killing to stop. There's no way he would be working with Kuznetsov to see us all slain. That means that Kuznetsov must be impossible to kill! If someone like Hale was unable to get the better of him, what chance does someone like me have?*

Cunnar, his spirit breaking, sat bolt upright. His eyes

widened in shock as a hand wrapped around his mouth, "Cunnar, it's me Hale, calm down. What's going on?"

Hale released his hand from Cunnar's mouth, and he turned around. Relief flashed across his face as he saw that it was indeed his commanding officer, "I thought I saw some movement in the shadows about two hundred meters out, but I was afraid my mind was playing tricks on me."

"How long ago did you see the movement?" Kivi asked.

Cunnar thought about the question for several moments as he tried to discern how much time had passed during his frantic state and answered, "About twenty minutes."

"That could have been him then. If he had been nearby me, when Hale and Korpi found me. Then the timing of Cunnar spotting him here is about right." Kivi observed.

This revelation caused Cunnar to visibly shake, "W-w-why do you think he let me be?"

"Maybe he knew we were heading your way and didn't want to risk getting entangled with you?" Hale suggested.

"I'm not a sniper. I haven't received the special operations group training that Lieutenant Kivi here imparted to you, sir. What chance would I have against the likes of Kuznetsov?"

Hale put a comforting hand on Cunnar's shoulder and said, "Kuznetsov wouldn't have known that. Besides, you are better than you give yourself credit for private. From what I heard about your exploits since you arrived with Pekka, you are one of the few survivors of Easy

Company's stand on the road. The sheer amount of shooting you did would have improved your aiming quite a bit."

Cunnar nodded, "I do feel like I've gotten better with the rifle, but I'm still far from being able to call myself a sniper."

"Hale, we need to get going. Task Force Kari needs to know that Kuznetsov is operating in the area." Kivi said.

"Cunnar, if I didn't have confidence in your abilities to fight you wouldn't be here." Hale put a hand on Cunnar's shoulder and said, "When we get a chance, I promise we will talk. Unfortunately, right now, time is of the essence. We've got to get to Task Force Kari and warn them about Kuznetsov being in the area.

Without another word, Hale turned and sped off towards the Raate Road, and Task Force Kari's lines. The surviving members of the sniper squad, Kivi, Korpi, and Cunnar dutifully followed their leader. The young lieutenant set a brisk pace and they came upon a Finnish sentry thirty minutes later. Hale spotted the sentry and shouted, "Four friendlies coming in."

"Show yourselves." The sentry demanded.

Hale, along with Kivi, Cunnar, and Korpi moved out into the sentry's line of sight, "What's the password of the day?"

Hale turned a deep shade of crimson as he said, "Khrushchev loves to suck Stalin's dick."

The sentry gave the expected response, "Yum."

Whoever comes up with these passwords is a disgusting pervert. Hale thought once again.

Hale approached the sentry and asked, "Where is Major Kari's HQ Private?

"Ericsson, sir." The young soldier replied. He then turned and pointed almost directly southward, "You'll come upon a cluster of tents just south of the road set up on a frozen pond."

"Thank you, Ericsson. The sniper Kuznetsov has been operating in the area just north of here, so please be extra vigilant. Keep yourself concealed and ensure that your squad mates are made aware."

The young private swallowed hard at this news, "Yes, sir."

"Why would Major Kari place his headquarters so close to the road?" Hale asked.

"The 44th has shown a complete unwillingness to stray far from the road. The proximity enables the major to better direct the flow of battle should it occur." Kivi replied.

Hale, with his three surviving subordinates following, headed towards Major Kari's Headquarters. The young lieutenant crossed the road and topped a small rise. Pausing, he looked downward. Below them, as Private Ericsson had described, was a cluster of three tents set up within the natural bowl created by a frozen pond. In total, the half-kilometer journey took the four men about twenty minutes.

The smell of fresh food washed over them, and their stomachs growled in desire. There were several men waiting in line outside the tent on the right side of the pond. Hale pointed to the gray colored canvas tent on the right and said, "Cunnar and Korpi, why don't you grab a bite to eat at the chow hall. I'm going to check in with

Major Kari, and then we'll join you."

The two privates smiled and Cunnar replied, "Yes, sir."

As Cunnar and Korpi sped off, Hale turned to Kivi and said, "Shall we?"

"What are you going to tell him?" Kivi asked.

"The truth. When we started this hunt, I never anticipated that we would be fighting more than Kuznetsov. We need more men to continue." Hale said.

"Good. I don't think we should sugar coat what was done to Mani. The men here deserve to know what they are facing." Kivi said.

The tent on the left side of the cluster had a large red cross sewn into the top of it. This left the tent in the middle as Major Kari's HQ. Hale nodded in response and the two officers skied down to the HQ tent. The two lieutenants removed their skis and opened the entry flap to let themselves in.

Just inside the tent stood a large private with a Suomi sub-machine gun. The private, pointed the weapon at Hale and Kivi and interposed himself between the two newcomers and a cluster of men gathered around a map table in the middle of the tent, "I don't recognize you. Identify yourself."

Hale looked up at the private, who towered over him and gave the man a warm smile, "Senior Lieutenant Hale Karhonen, commander of the sniper squad here to see Major Kari."

The private's gaze shifted to Kivi. The big officer met the private's gaze, as the two men sized each other up. Kivi gave the private his most fearsome feral grin and loudly cracked his knuckles. The private was not the least bit intimidated by Kivi's display as they were about the same size. Finally, Kivi relented and stated, "Lieutenant Kivi."

Before the private could reply, a voice from the group said, "It's fine Makela. Colonel Siilasvuo alerted me that Karhonen's squad was operating in our area." said a middle-aged man with one metallic golden circle set within the green rank field on his collar. The rank insignia of a major.

The big private stepped to the side and gestured toward the center of the tent. Hale gave the private a warm smile as he walked past him. He approached the major and stiffened to attention, "Lieutenant Hale Karhonen reporting major. I am the commanding officer of the sniper squad."

The major smiled and said, "Nice to meet you lieutenant, I'm Major Kari. Who is the hulking brute behind you? I believe I've seen him somewhere before."

Kivi stiffened to attention and said, "Lieutenant Kivi, major."

"Nice to see you again, lieutenant. I believe we have met once before." Kari said.

"I don't recall such a meeting major." Kivi replied.

Major Kari gave Kivi a warm smile as he said, "I was with a group of officers last fall that came to learn about your Special Operations Group training techniques."

Kivi smiled, "Right sir, now I remember, mid-October, there were about twenty of you."

"I heard what happened to the group. It's a shame

most the of the men you trained were lost, but I hear they accounted for themselves very well." Kari said.

"Indeed sir, the men I trained, under the command of then Lieutenant Pekka Renning, were able to hold off an entire regiment of the enemy." Kivi said with a hint of pride in his voice.

"Ahhh yes, Captain Renning. I also heard what you and the captain managed to pull off here on the Raate Road. You two seem to be quite the team. Your brilliant bit of defensive diversion really saved our asses in Suomassalmi. If your company hadn't provided such a compelling distraction, the 27th Regiment would have been trapped between the Soviet 163rd and the 44th divisions, it would have been really ugly for us."

Kari turned to Hale and said, "You also seem familiar to me. Have we met before?"

"Not that I can recall major." Hale said.

"Karhonen here, was the trainee that gave your group the long-distance shooting demonstration." Kivi said.

"This young man who was your trainee is now your boss? There must be a great story behind that." Kari said.

"Hale is the most gifted shooter and woodsman I have ever known. He has the utmost confidence of General Mannerheim himself." Kivi said.

"Well don't talk him up too much. Piss might go to his head." Kari said with a chuckle, "Anyways, what can I do for you Lieutenant Karhonen?"

"I'm here to report that the sniper Kuznetsov, along with some others from the 3rd NKVD Regiment, have been operating in your area." Hale replied.

"Where?" Kari asked.

"Just to the north of here." Hale replied.

"I see. Should I be worried?" Kari asked.

"Yes. We managed to kill several of the enemy snipers, but once again Kuznetsov gave us the slip." Hale said.

"And we lost good men doing it." Kivi added.

"Interesting. I can hear the sharp edge of hatred in both of your voices when you say the name Kuznetsov." Kari said.

"The man is a monster. He performed the blood eagle on one of my men Private Mani. Who knows what acts of depravity he is concocting this very moment." Hale said.

Major Kari's eyes widened, "I thought the blood eagle was a Viking myth."

"I wish it had remained so, major. Mani didn't deserve to have his body desecrated in such a horrid fashion." Hale said.

"Sounds like they are getting desperate and trying to give us a little of our own medicine to turn the tables." Kari said.

"What medicine is that Major?" Hale asked.

"Fear." Kari replied, "My men have been keeping the Soviets off balance with constant hit and run attacks to their flanks. Thus far, it has kept the enemy to disorganized to attempt a counterattack to remove us from the road."

Hale opened his mouth to reply when the sound of four large explosions could be heard coming from the direction of the Raate Road, "Summer of cunts." The major cursed.

"It looks like you may have spoken a little prematurely about the enemy's resolve." Kivi said.

Hale grabbed Kivi's arm and started to pull him toward the tent's exit, "Come on, we can help."

"Return to me if we survive this Karhonen and I'll see about finding you a few more bodies to fill out your ranks." Kari shouted over the roar of gunfire being exchanged on the nearby road.

Hale shouted over his shoulder as he departed the tent, "Thanks, major."

Hale and Kivi quickly collected Cunnar and Korpi from the chow hall. The four men hastily put their skis on and headed toward the sound of gunfire. When Hale reached the top of the bowl, he peered out, careful to keep himself mostly concealed. What he saw made him shudder.

The Raate Road was laid out below them. The road lay about twenty meters from their position which sat about five meters above the road level. The trees that surrounded the road had been cleared away to form two roadblocks that lay about one hundred meters apart.

The western side of Task Force Kari's roadblock, which consisted mostly of freshly felled trees was on fire. A tank, Hale didn't know what model, was trying to push its way through the barricade but had failed. A second tank sat slightly behind and to the left of the first. That tank had a machine gun mounted on the turret and the tank's commander was pouring fire into the wavering Finnish line which was attempting to defend from behind the barricade.

Hale unslung his rifle as the other three members of his squad joined him. The young sniper laid down on the ground to minimize his profile. Once on the ground, he quickly lined up his sights on the commander of the second tank, the one using the machine gun, and squeezed the trigger.

The Soviet slumped over and the machine gun fell silent. Suddenly a fearsome war cry erupted, and a force of Soviet infantry appeared. The attackers immediately set about clambering over the barricade, careful to avoid the parts that were on fire.

The sudden target rich environment enabled the four men of the sniper squad to go to work on the attacking Soviet infantry with their rifles. As the enemy started to drop in ones and twos, the broken Finnish defenders of Task Force Kari rallied and began to lay down a withering fire into the attackers from three sides. The brave men of the 44th tried to hold their ground and were simply cut to pieces by the superior firepower of the Finns.

With the Soviets on the run, the sniper squad took the time to fix their bayonets and worked to reload their empty stripper clips. Unfortunately, this was not the end of the attack. The T-26 sitting slightly behind the tank stuck on the barricade fired a high explosive round into the logs. The subsequent blast from the detonation of the shell scattered the logs and freed the stuck tank that was revealed to be a T-28. Kivi screamed, "Someone needs to deal with the T-28 that just broke loose!"

A fresh company of Soviet infantry swarmed around the advancing tanks as the Finnish defenders were sent into full retreat by the metal monstrosities bearing down on them. To make matters even worse, a Soviet attack began against the eastern roadblock. The Soviet attacks were supposed to start simultaneously, but poor communication on the part of the divided enemy forces resulted in the western group attacking first.

Now both groups poured fire into the faltering Finnish defenders who were scattering before the might of the combined arms attack. Hale, and the sniper group, now laying prone on the top of the small ridgeline that separated the road from the pond, resumed firing on the attackers. The four of them did the best they could with their rifles, but they simply couldn't fire fast enough to make a difference.

The two groups of attackers advanced toward each other as they swept the faltering Finnish defenders away who started to break and run into the woods to the north, "The bastards are about to link up!" Kivi shouted.

Hale ignored Kivi's outburst and focused on killing the enemy. He took aim at a Soviet private that was ten meters away and fired. There was a second Soviet soldier less than a meter behind him wielding an SVT-38 rifle. Suddenly, the Soviet with the SVT-38 realized that the man to his immediate front, was shot in the side. The enemy soldier turned toward Hale's group, pointed, and yelled, "Cuckoos on the ridge!"

"That's not good." Cunnar observed as he put a bullet into the yelling man's chest.

The screaming Soviet was suddenly silenced as he dropped his rifle and clutched his chest. He waivered for a few moments, trying to stay on his feet, then collapsed to the ground. Several of his squad mates turned toward Hale's group and clumsily began to take aim with their rifles at the prone Finns. Kivi fired his rifle slaying one of the men. He came to his feet and saw that another was about to shoot.

Unable to stop the enemy soldier from firing his weapon, Kivi threw himself sideways as the rifle was fired. The bullet flew harmlessly through empty air as Kivi's left shoulder slammed into the snow-covered surface of the ridge. He sank into the snow and started to slide sideways down the hill.

Another enemy soldier had the big man in his sights, but he was cut down by Hale before he could shoot. Kivi came to a stop at the bottom of the small hill. At this point, he was buried in the snow and nearly invisible to the enemy. The only part of his anatomy that remained visible was his feet.

Kivi reached up and undid the buckles on the skis that held them to his boots and pulled his feet under the snow completing his concealment. Several bullets peppered the snow around the big lieutenant, but none found him. The Soviet squad started to move toward the buried Finn as they operated the bolts on their rifles to reload their weapons.

A few more Soviets were cut down by rifle fire from Hale, Cunnar, and Korpi. Suddenly, the big lieutenant erupted from the snow like some kind of abominable snowman. He fired his rifle and hit one of the Soviets. As the nearest enemy swung the barrel of his gun in Kivi's direction, the big Finn hurled his rifle at the enemy soldier as if it were a spear.

The bayonet smashed into the target's chest knocking him off of his feet and onto his back. Kivi took a step forward and snatched the man's rifle out of his hands as he fell. The three surviving members of the enemy squad, shocked at the snow-covered demon that was tearing through them, started to back pedal as they raised up their rifles to shoot.

Kivi shot one, with his newly acquired rifle, and threw himself at the next. While he was flying through the air, he dropped his rifle and drew his pukko blade. A split second later, he slammed into the nearest enemy soldier's chest. The impact of Kivi's body sent the Ukrainian man falling backwards and his helmet tumbling from his head. Before the enemy soldier's back hit the ground, Kivi plunged his pukko blade into his head.

Kivi's blood boiled as he was overcome by battle rage. Screaming, he ripped the pukko blade out of his slain opponent sending blood and brains into the air. This broke the resolve of the final two enemy soldiers, who threw down their rifles and started to turn and run. This didn't save them as Hale and Cunnar shot them in the back with their rifles.

Kivi, now out of breath, leaned forward and put his hands on his knees as he tried to catch it. As he did so, his eyes fell on a PPD-34 with the large seventy round drum style magazine sitting in the snow a few meters away. His fatigue suddenly forgotten, the big man grinned as he dashed forward and snatched up the weapon.

He turned it on the backs of the advancing Soviet force that had swept by him and poured bullets into them. The big Finn screamed in jubilation as he swept the barrel of the weapon back and forth like it was a hose, and he were a fireman fighting a fire. Using this technique, he cut down dozens of enemies. Simultaneously, Hale and Cunnar came to their feet and hurled grenades into the main body of the attackers.

A loud boom-boom erupted in the middle of the enemy group. The explosion killed several of them and hit a dozen more with deadly shrapnel. This broke the will of the attackers who turned and ran toward the two tanks seeking cover. The two metal beasts, unable to go through the barricade, were slowly pushing forward in the deep snow flanking the road.

Both tanks fired high explosive rounds into two nearby squads of Finns decimating them. Kivi threw his now empty PPD-34 down and looked for something to use on the tanks. His eyes fell on a 37mm Bofors anti-tank gun that had been abandoned by its Finnish crew when the enemy attack swept past the area. Kivi pointed at the gun and shouted to Hale, "Cover me!"

"This is not how he taught us to fight at all. His training emphasized stealth and long-range shooting. Only when we had no other choice were we to fall back on direct confrontation. Is Kivi always like this in a fight?" Hale asked as he shot an enemy soldier that was taking aim at Kivi's back with a rifle.

Cunnar laughed at Hale's question and said, "I guess he doesn't do a good job of practicing what he preaches. I've never seen Kivi try to stand back and use a rifle when he had the opportunity to get into the thick of things. In fact, if it wasn't for his special kind of crazy, we would never have been able to hold the road a few days ago against everything Vinogradov threw at us."

Kivi reached the Bofors and began to turn it toward the nearest tank, the T-28. His arm muscles bulged as he single handedly performed a job that was meant for two men. Hale, Cunnar, and Korpi continued to lay down fire to keep the big man safe as he checked to verify the gun was loaded.

Kivi hunched down behind the protective steel plate of the gun and lined up the weapon's sight on the rear of the T-28 and fired. The well-aimed round smashed into the aft side panel of the tank and penetrated the engine compartment. It's engine now disabled, the T-28 ground to a halt as clouds of black smoke billowed upward from the engine deck.

Kivi opened the breech on the Bofors, and loaded an armored piercing round, identified by the painted gray stripe into the gun. He slammed the breech shut and adjusted the aim of the gun. Simultaneously, the T-28's commander opened the top hatch and looked for the source of the shot that disabled his tank.

Seeing Kivi working on loading another round into the Bofors, he swung the T-28's turret mounted heavy machine gun around toward the big man. Hale, seeing the danger to Kivi, quickly lined up the two iron sights on his rifle and put a bullet into the enemy tank commander a moment before Kivi pulled the lever that fired the gun.

Kivi's shot smashed into the back of the T-28's turret penetrating the thin rear armor. The armored piercing round, entered the crew compartment and bounced around inside the tank cutting the crew to ribbons, "He got one!" Korpi exclaimed.

Kivi immediately started to swing the weapon toward the T-26 on the northern side of the road. The T-26's turret was turning in his direction as it sought to slay the man that had killed the T-28. After creating a few examples to inspire the soldiers of the Red Army, the commissars were able to rally the remnants of the first company of attackers. These men suddenly burst through the breach in the western barricade.

Hale, seeing the danger to Kivi, shouted, "Concentrate your fire on the newcomers."

Hale, Cunnar, and Korpi poured fire into the advancing mass of Soviets as they yelled and charged toward Kivi. Every time one of the Soviet soldiers stopped to take aim at the big man, one of the snipers in Hale's group dropped the offending enemy soldier with a well-placed shot. Despite the accurate fire of the sniper squad, more and more of the attacking force noticed Kivi and his effort to swing the Bofors around toward the T-26.

Giving up on shooting Hale yelled, "Grenades, now!"

All three Finns ripped grenades off their belts and pulled the pins as they came to their feet and hurled them at the enemy. Simultaneously, the T-26 gunner fired a high explosive round at Kivi as the tank won the race to take aim at its opponent. Fortunately for the big lieutenant, the tank gunner's aim was high and the shell sailed past his position. Unfortunately, it struck the base of the hill right in front of Hale and the other snipers.

The subsequent explosion briefly blinded Kivi's guardian angels. With the sniper group temporarily out of action bullets began to fly around Kivi as he worked to position the gun. The Soviets, poorly trained in the firing of their weapons, struggled to hit the big man. Several of the bullets ricochet off the Bofors as Kivi sited the gun.

Kivi's attempt to aim the gun was disrupted as the enemy fire intensified. This forced the big Finn to move around to the front side of the gun and use it as cover. He positioned himself behind the steel plates that were meant to protect the gun's crew from enemy fire. Bullets continued to ping as they hit the gun and ricocheted away as Kivi pondered what to do next.

Finally, he reached down to his belt and felt the comforting shape of several grenades. The grenades had been looted off of the snipers that he had slain earlier in the day, and he smiled as he thought, *This might solve my problem.*

He pulled the pin on several of the devices as he said, "I should be a good neighbor and return these to their proper owners."

He waited for the fire directed at him to diminish. Once enough of the enemy soldiers were busy working the bolts on their rifles, he hurled the grenades into three separate clusters of the enemy. A moment later he was lifted into the air as a high explosive round fired from the T-26 tank slammed into the ground behind him.

Luckily for Kivi the tank gunners received the same amount of weapons training as the infantry. As a result, the shell fired by the T-26 had been aimed too low, causing the projectile to hit the ground about two meters in front of the Bofors anti-tank gun. The error saved the Finn's life as he felt heat upon his back a split second before the kinetic force slammed him into the steel plates of the Bofors.

Kivi spent a moment shaking his head as he tried to clear the cobwebs from his mind caused by the blast. Before he could get back to his feet, the three grenades he had hurled detonated. With an ear-splitting BOOM, BOOM, BOOM noise the grenades detonated in sequence. This stopped the enemy infantry cold as nearly a dozen of them went down screaming as metal fragments ripped into them.

Kivi picked himself up off the ground and dashed around the gun. He quickly re-checked his aim to ensure the explosion hadn't altered the position of the gun. Satisfied that the gunsight was still trained on the side of the T-26, he fired the gun.

The 37mm shell hurtled out of the Bofors' barrel and slammed into the side of the T-26. At this close range, the shell easily penetrated the Soviet tank's side armor and entered the crew compartment. The T-26's gunner felt a brief moment of pain as he was cut in half at the waist by the shell.

Fortunately, the shell ricocheted off the opposite side of the tank from its entry point at an upward angle. A fraction of a second later the twisted remnants of the shell removed the gunner's head. The remains of the armor piercing projectile shattered upon impact with the inside of the turret. The individual pieces that ricocheted off the turret bounced around inside the tank until all of the crew members had been shredded by the shrapnel.

Given a moment of respite from Kivi as the big Finn concentrated on taking out the T-26, several of the enemy infantry had recovered from Kivi's grenade barrage. The Soviets were furious and wanted revenge upon their tormentor. Fortunately Hale, Cunnar, and Korpi were able to rejoin the fight after being briefly blinded by the exploding tank shell. The trio began to fire as Kivi dashed around to the front of the anti-tank gun once again seeking cover from the enemy soldier's fire.

The surviving Soviets, now all in the prone position to minimize their profiles, turned their attention to the three Finns that were firing at them, *There's to many for Hale, Cunnar, and Kopi to kill. One, if not all of them are going to get shot. I've got to help.* Kivi thought.

Kivi's arm muscles again bulged with strain as he turned the Bofors once again on his own. For the second time, Kivi accomplished a feat meant for two men. He had to nearly turn the gun completely around so that the weapon once again faced west. This brought the gun barrel to bear on the enemy infantry firing at Hale and the others. When he completed his herculean task, he selected a shell with a red stripe, a high explosive round, and loaded it into the Bofors. As bullets began to chew up the snow around the three snipers, Kivi fired the Bofors at the largest concentration of enemy soldiers.

The resultant explosion shredded at least a half-dozen Soviets. Their torn bodies cast a red mist onto the nearby snow. The fire from the detonation burned another dozen. Those that were burned began to scream as their clothing was set on fire.

With so many of the enemy slain at once, the survivor's morale broke, and they turned tail and ran westward toward the remnants of the barricade. Kivi, lacking a rifle to use against the enemy, loaded another high explosive shell into the Bofors as Hale and the other two men of the sniper squad fired into the backs of the retreating soldiers.

As quickly as the assault had begun, the surviving enemy soldiers melted away leaving a one-hundred-meter section of the road strewn with over a hundred corpses from both sides. In addition to the human remains, two tanks burned sending large black clouds of smoke billowing into the sky. When the wind shifted, Hale picked up the scent of cooking meat. His stomach growled reminding him that he hadn't eaten in a while. The young sniper shuddered as he realized what the source must be for the cooking meat smell.

The three snipers maintained their positions until they were sure that the enemy was not going to return. Simultaneously, Kivi retrieved the PPD-34 he had used earlier. He then searched enemy bodies until he located the man the weapon originally belonged to. The original owner was recognized because he had a second drum style magazine for the PPD-34 clipped to his belt.

Kivi took the magazine, checked it to ensure it was full, removed the empty magazine from his Soviet sub-machine gun, and slammed the full drum home. Next, he pulled the bolt back to chamber a round and took cover behind the Bofors, waiting for the next group of attackers to materialize from the west. The four men waited for several minutes as the attack on the eastern barricade continued to rage.

After five minutes, Kivi was convinced that the enemy was not going to resume the attack on the western barricade. He turned to see what was transpiring behind him. Just under a hundred meters away dozens of Finns and Soviets grappled with one another in hand-to-hand combat.

Several dozen more stood off and exchanged shots with each other and at the men engaged in the melee. Hale joined Kivi behind and asked, "You planning on more crazy?"

Kivi laughed and slapped Hale on the back, "Of course. This is how I fight. In your face, up close and personal." As the two men talked, Kivi sat down on the frozen surface of the road and started to reload his empty magazine with the bullets he looted off of the gun's original owner.

"Why on earth did you train us to be snipers if you don't even like to fight that way?" Hale asked. He had to yell over the sound of the nearby gunfire to be heard.

"That's what I was ordered to do. The Special Operations Group needed to be guerrilla style snipers to maximize survivability against a foe that vastly outnumbered the group. The entire purpose of the group was to whittle away at the enemy's numbers and keep them looking over their shoulders. Screwing with the enemy's heads like that theoretically would make them both slow and mistake prone. I gained experience in the style of fighting that I taught you during the Spanish Civil

War. This was why I was appointed to train you despite it not being my preferred way to fight." Kivi said.

"How do you prefer to fight?" Hale asked.

"I want to see the fear in my opponent's eyes when he realizes his doom is at hand. The last thing the bastard should smell is my choice of breakfast upon my breath. I love experiencing the joy of my blade sinking into my opponent's flesh, or my knuckles breaking an enemy's nose." Kivi replied.

"Once a bruiser always a bruiser, eh?" Hale asked.

Kivi laughed, "Something like that. Now how about we stop standing around and gossiping like a bunch of old women and figure out how we can get back into the fight? If we're not careful Task Force Kari is going to lose this section of the road."

Hale turned his attention to the battle that raged a hundred meters away. He took stock of the resources that was available to his team, *Four rifles, one PPD-34, and an anti-tank gun.*

"Seeing that you seem to enjoy getting up close and personal with the enemy, would you like to take your PPD-34 and go raise some hell?" Hale asked.

Kivi grinned, "Of course. I'd love to fill those Russian bastards' boots with piss."

"All right then, you go do what you do and the three of us will remain here with the Bofors and provide supporting fire." Hale said.

"Do you mind if I go with him?" Cunnar asked.

Everyone's jaw dropped in surprise at Cunnar's request,

"Since when did you become the volunteering type?" Hale asked.

"Since I experienced how much of a rush it is to fight hand to hand during our last crazy battle on this road. Besides, I'm not that great of a shot with the rifle. Getting closer helps a lot." Cunnar said.

Hale gestured toward the chaos of the fight and said, "Very well then. Feel free to go with Lieutenant Kivi."

Cunnar smiled at Hale and said, "Thanks boss."

Cunnar's words felt as good as warm sunlight from a June day upon Hale's skin as he thought, *He called me boss! Maybe I can lead after all?*

Hale turned to Korpi and said, "Let's use this gun as cover and start killing the enemy. You focus on keeping Cunnar out of trouble and I'll keep an eye on Kivi."

"Yes, sir." Korpi replied.

Kivi, PPD-34 in hand, angled himself toward a group of Soviets that surrounded a lone Finn. The Finn was trying to keep the enemy at bay with the bayonet on his rifle. As Kivi closed the distance to assist, one of the Russians stabbed the Finn in the back with his bayonet. The Finn cried out in pain and sank to his knees. This gave Kivi the opening he needed.

The big Lieutenant mowed down the six Soviets with his submachine gun. Cunnar, shot a seventh enemy soldier that was taking aim at Kivi with his rifle. Kivi turned to Cunnar and said, "See what you can do for him."

As soon as Kivi was clear of the chaos created by the melee between the two sides, he took aim at a group of Soviets providing supporting fire. This group of the enemy was attempting to provide the same kind of support that Hale and Korpi were providing for Kivi and Cunnar to their comrades engaged in the hand-to-hand fighting. Before the enemy squad could react, Kivi's PPD-34 spewed death and cut them down.

This attracted the attention of another squad, that was also providing fire support using their rifles. Seeing the enemy just in time, Kivi lunged toward the ground just as the Soviet soldiers fired at him. All but one of the bullets missed as they sailed overhead. Kivi felt a tug on his pants but no pain. He ignored the feeling and hit the ground hard, PPD-34 still in hand.

"Die you commie bastards!" He screamed as he hosed down the enemy squad with a wall of led.

Kivi, an excellent shot with close range weapons, fired a short burst at each individual enemy soldier. He was able to stretch out the magazine ensuring that each Soviet received two or three bullets while rarely missing. Some of the enemy was slain outright. Others still drew in ragged breaths of the sub-zero air as they fought to live.

Those that initially survived their wounds shrieked from the pain of their injuries in between those hard-fought breaths. This small piece of the Raate Road had become a microcosm of a frozen hell on earth. Dozens of men were locked in hand-to-hand struggle surrounded by the dead and the moans of the dying.

As soon as Kivi stopped firing, the big man's ears picked up a familiar sound. The squeaks and groans of metal caused the pit of his stomach to fill with dread, *Don't these bolshevik bastard ever run out of tanks?* He wondered.

Fearing what he was about to see, he ground his teeth as he turned toward the source of the noise. The road beyond the burning barricade was strewn with enemy vehicles and didn't provide enough room for a tank to maneuver between the vehicles and the trees. Kivi saw branches on a cluster of fir trees a few meters away on the southern side of the road begin to shimmy just enough for his eyes to take notice. As the sounds of the metal monstrosities drew closer, snowflakes began to stream to the ground from the snow laden branches.

Suddenly a T-28 burst through the trees into view. The sound of cracking and splintering wood could be heard as the tank's tracks crushed a few of the smaller trees. A moment later, two other tanks, both T-26s, emerged from the forest behind the T-28. The T-26s were a few meters off the lead tank's rear quarters. Together, the three-tank formation formed a V shape.

The T-28 immediately began to turn leftward toward Kivi and the barricade, *Time to go.* Kivi thought as he ran for the cover of the forest.

Despite protests from his still tender knee, he made it into the trees a fraction of a second before the T-28 completed its turn. The tank ground to a halt as the gunner took aim at a target and fired. The barricade was hit by a high explosive shell. Logs were ripped apart and thrown into the air as the flaming cloud created by the shell detonation expanded outward.

The T-28 started to move forward and the two trailing T-26s fell in behind the lead tank as there wasn't enough room to form a battle line. Kivi frantically took stock of his resources and tried to figure out how to kill these tanks, *You can't.* He thought, *I need to get back to Hale and show him how to operate the Bofors.*

Cunnar thrust his bayonet into the back of a Soviet soldier. The man cried out in pain and fell to the ground pulling Cunnar's rifle with him. The Finn managed to hang onto his rifle. To remove it from the enemy's body, he placed a foot on the moaning Soviet and pulled the bayonet free. Blood gushed from the open wound as the bayonet was pulled free.

Suddenly, the center of the barricade, which lay about ten meters away from Cunnar, exploded. The blast forced him to the ground beside his bleeding opponent. The Finn's face went blank as confusion over what his eyes were showing him paralyzed his brain.

A T-28 burst through the opening created by the explosion. The tank started to fire its coaxial machine gun at the Finns but with so many of the Soviet soldiers close by the tank killed almost as many friends as enemies, *They don't even care about their own troops.* Cunnar thought in disgust.

Not knowing what else to do, Cunnar turned and ran into the forest. As he disappeared past the trees on the edge of the road he was hit in the side. The force of the blow knocked him to the ground and stole his breath. Fearing the worst, he quickly rolled onto his back and pointed his rifle upward at Kivi's smiling face, "Nice to run into you." The big man quipped.

Kivi extended a hand to Cunnar and pulled the Private to his feet, "Where were you going in such a hurry?" Cunnar asked.

Before Cunnar could finish his question, Kivi had climbed back to his feet and resumed running. He looked back over his shoulder and shouted, "To the Bofors!"

Cunnar slapped his head with his gloved hand as he thought, *Idiot. You should have thought to go there.* Cunnar turned and followed Kivi's trail through the snow.

Hale fired his rifle and dropped a Soviet soldier that was about to fire his weapon at Cunnar's back. Hale noticed the grumpy private pause as if confused, *What's he doing?* Hale wondered.

Suddenly, the eastern barricade was ripped asunder by a large explosion. Hale saw Cunnar go to ground next to the man he had just stabbed with his bayonet. His eyes shifted to the dissipating explosion as a T-28 burst through the breech caused by the detonation. The T-28 started to fire its coaxial machine gun at friend and foe alike cutting down a dozen men.

Korpi lowered his rifle and turned to Hale as he asked, "Kivi and Cunnar have disappeared. What do we do now?"

"Kill the enemy tank!" Hale shouted.

"Do you know how to operate the gun?" Korpi asked.

"No but let's figure it out together." Hale said.

His eyes fell on the gun as he tried to determine how to open the breech. Seeing a handle on the right side of the gun towards the rear, he pulled it toward him. This caused a thin steel plate to drop down revealing the gun's breech. The brass casing from the last shell Kivi fired, slid out and dropped to the ground.

"Find a shell." Hale said as he looked around.

Korpi reached into a box of shells he just located and

pulled one out at random, "Here."

Hale took the shell, it had a red stripe, and pushed it into the open breech. Hale pushed up on the handle that revealed the breech and closed it, "Now we have to figure out how to aim this thing."

Hale looked around for something that looked like a gun sight. He didn't see anything on the barrel itself, but noticed an object that resembled a rifle's scope about a hand span to the left of the gun barrel. There was a small opening in the protective steel plate right in front of the device, "Maybe it's this." Hale said.

He leaned down, closed his left eye, and peered into the scope. He saw a target reticle, "This is it. We need to figure out how to aim the gun."

"What about that wheel?" Korpi suggested.

Hale turned the wheel, and the gun began to move to the left, "Brilliant!" He yelled as he rotated the hand-wheel rightward to move the gun barrel toward the T-28.

As soon as the reticle was centered on the tank Hale pulled back and started to look around again, "What are you looking for?" Korpi asked.

"The bloody trigger." Hale said.

Korpi shrugged, "I don't see anything obvious."

"Pull the lever!" Kivi screamed as he emerged from the forest.

Hale reached down and pulled the lever as Kivi had suggested. A loud BOOM erupted next to Hale's right ear as the Bofors fired at the T-28. The shell, poorly aimed as Hale didn't adjust the gun for elevation, smashed into the front right quadrant of the turret and exploded.

The T-28 completely disappeared from sight as it was engulfed in flames, "You did it!" Korpi cheered.

A moment later the flames dissipated and revealed the T-28 was turning its gun toward the Bofors, "No. We didn't do it and now the tank wants to kill us. We're in the shit now." Korpi said.

"Find another shell!" Hale shouted frantically.

"You want one with a grey stripe." Kivi said as he ran up to the gun.

"Here." Korpi said as he handed a shell with a gray stripe to Hale.

Hale slammed the shell into the breech and closed it, "How do you change the gun's elevation?"

Kivi, pushed past Hale and looked into the gun's sight. He then reached over and turned a wheel to adjust the gun's elevation. As soon as he was satisfied, he pulled the trigger. With a loud BOOM, the gun hurtled a 37mm armored piercing round toward the nearby T-28. A fraction of a second later the shell hit the front of the tank roughly in the center.

The shell penetrated the frontal armor of the tank and entered the crew compartment killing everyone inside. The kinetic energy of the blast sent the turret sailing five meters into the air as a crackling flames erupted from the turret ring, "Reload!"

Kivi yelled as he began aiming the gun at the T-26 immediately behind the burning hulk of the T-28. The commander of the T-26 unbuttoned and frantically looked around for the source of the shot that killed the T-28.

Simultaneously, Korpi slapped another 37mm shell into Hale's outstretched hand.

Hale opened the gun's breech and gave the expended shell a moment to fall to the ground. As soon as the shell fell earthward, he rammed the new one home and shut the breech, "Loaded!"

A moment later Kivi fired. This shot sailed above the flaming wreck of the T-28 through the space the turret would have occupied before it was blown off. Kivi's shot smashed into the T-26's turret next to the main gun and was deflected by the curvature of the metal. Inside the tank's crew groaned as the vibration from the shell impact rippled through the armored vehicle's interior. The sound the shell impact produced inside the tank resembled an immense gong ringing right next to the crewmen's ears.

"Load another armor piercing round!" Kivi roared.

The second T-26 moved around the right side of the burning hulk of the T-28 and the tank's commander immediately noticed the Bofors pointed his direction. He screamed some orders at the crewmen inside and the tank's turret began to turn toward the anti-tank gun. Simultaneously, the tank commander unbuttoned his hatch and started to fire the turret mounted heavy machine gun at the Finnish controlled anti-tank gun.

The blizzard of bullets forced Kivi, Hale, and Korpi to duck down behind the gun's protective steel plate. Bullets pinged and ricocheted off the Bofor's steel plate and gun barrel, "Get another round loaded." Kivi yelled over the din of bullets.

Korpi looked over at the box of shells which lay just outside the protection afforded by the protective steel plates of the gun. Kivi noticed his indecision and yelled,

"If we don't fire soon the main gun will kill us all!"

Steeling himself, Korpi leaned out just enough to snatch a shell out of the box. The tank commander noticed the movement and swung the heavy machine gun in Korpi's direction. Dozens of bullets filled the air between the edge of the steel plate and the box of 37mm shells forcing Korpi back into the protection of the steel plate.

Korpi turned to Kivi and said, "The fire is too thick I can't reach it!"

"Summer of cunts." Kivi cursed.

Kivi shared a look with Hale. Neither man knew what to do. The machine gun fire abruptly stopped as a whooshing sound filled the air. A moment later the tank commander started to scream in agony. Kivi stole a look through the gunsight opening and yelled, "Yes! Someone used a Molotov Cocktail on the bastard. He's on fire. Get me a shell!"

Korpi reached out toward the shell box stealing himself for the bullets he was certain would hit him. None came. He quickly pulled a shell with a grey stripe out of the box and handed it to Hale. Hale slammed the shell into the breech and yelled, "Loaded!"

Kivi, who had already aimed the gun, pulled the trigger lever just as the T-26's turret stopped moving with the barrel now pointed directly at them. The Bofor's shot easily penetrated the frontal armor of the T-26 killing the surviving members of the crew, "We got him!" Hale exclaimed.

Seeing their final tank destroyed, those Soviets infantry still fighting lost heart. They dropped their weapons and raised their hands in surrender. Suddenly a terrible scream erupted from the forest as a dozen Finns in gray uniforms burst from the trees. When the newcomers saw that the battle had been won, they stopped yelling and looked around sheepishly.

Hale stood and saw Major Kari leading the group, "We've won, sir."

"I can see that, lieutenant. Good work." Kari turned to the cooks and officers he had mustered and said, "Men, it looks like your bravery is not needed today. Cooks, return to the chow hall and make something special for the survivors. Leave one of your number here to loot vodka off the enemy dead. The men deserve it. Officers, work together and figure out what we have left. When you have the tally of the dead and wounded bring it to me in the HQ tent."

Kari turned to Hale and Kivi and asked, "What happened?"

"The Soviets attacked the barricades." Hale said.

"I can see that." Kari snapped, "Can you be a little more specific?"

"I think it might have been a timed attack that was supposed to hit both barricades simultaneously, but the enemy had piss poor coordination." Kivi said, Hale looked relieved that he didn't have to answer the major's question, "They hit the western barricade first with tanks and infantry. After the first western attack failed, they conducted an assault on the eastern barricade with just infantry. I believe it was supposed to be a combined arms attack similar to what the western barricade experience, but the eastern side's tanks were late to the party. Then the west regrouped and attacked again. With most of your men that were still alive tied up fending off the attack on the eastern barricade, Hale and I had to get really creative to send them packing. After the second attack on the west side was stopped, the east's tanks showed up."

"It sounds like we got really lucky." Kari observed.

"You damned right we got lucky major, if the Soviets did a better job with their coordination, their attack would have succeeded." Kivi said.

"Through all of this did you notice any enemy sniper activity?" Kari asked.

"None that we could detect, sir. The attacking infantry didn't appear to be very good shots, which is another reason why we are standing here instead of a Russian officer with a pistol to your head." Hale said.

Kari nodded, "We've observed the same thing about their marksmanship. The Red Army is bewildering. They equip their men with the best weapons technology available and in quantity, but they don't train them how to use it."

A Finnish Captain approached Kari and said, "I have the initial casualty report, sir."

Kari took a deep breath, sighed, then said, "Lay it on me Ranta."

"The battalion took roughly fifty percent casualties and both barricades will need to be rebuilt." Captain Ranta said.

Kari shook his head in dismay, "We are going to have to tighten the sentry line."

"That will make the men defending the road vulnerable to the snipers." Ranta said.

"We don't have a choice. If the Soviets hit us again, it will be with twice the force that they just hit us with so we must be prepared. Carry out your orders." Kari said.

Kari turned back to Hale and said, "Circling back to the sniper issue. There haven't been any additional victims with my group, so they likely moved on."

"Task Force Fagernas is the only one that hasn't been hit yet." Hale said.

"I was planning on filling out your squad with six additional men before you moved on, but given the casualties I just suffered, the best I'll be able to manage is two." Kari said.

"I appreciate any help you can give me major. Thought it has been costly, we have slain many of the enemy's snipers." Hale said.

"You and your men go grab yourselves something to eat. The two men I'm providing will look for you in the chow tent." Kari said.

Chapter 15

Finnish 9th Division HQ, Three Kilometers South of Suomassalmi, Central Finland

January 4th, 1940

Colonel Siilasvuo rubbed his aching neck. Ever since the war started, he seemed to spend his days gazing down at the map spread across the rickety campaign table in the center of the 9th Division's Headquarters tent. This time his eyes were centered on the Purasjokki River. The river lay less than ten kilometers from the border of the Soviet Union.

Just south of the river sat the tiles that represented the two battalions of Task Force Fagernas. Major Valli put a reassuring hand on the colonel's shoulder as he said, "They'll do fine."

"But what if they don't? All of our successes to date will be meaningless if we can't complete the task of cutting the 44th off from the possibility of help." Colonel Siilasvuo said.

"Do you trust in Major Fagernas?" Valli asked.

"Yes." Siilasvuo replied.

"Do you trust that his men will get the job done?" Valli asked.

"Yes, but what if they are suddenly surprised by reinforcements coming from the Soviet Union? This is the first attack conducted upon the 44th, where that is a real possibility."

"I agree that ill-timed reinforcements coming from the Soviet Union is possible but look at how the enemy has behaved so far. Did they send help when we blocked the 44th from reaching the 163rd?" Valli asked.

"No." Siilasvuo replied.

"Did they send help when Task Force Makiniemi shut the back door and created the motti that General Vinogradov himself is trapped in?" Valli asked.

"The Red Air Force tried to strafe and bomb both Task Force Makiniemi and Mandelin after the success of Makiniemi's assault." Siilasvuo replied.

"And how successful was the enemy response?" Valli asked.

"Nearly completely unsuccessful. Our forces simply left the road and used the cover provided by the trees to avoid being strafed and bombed by the enemy planes." Siilasvuo observed.

"You said nearly unsuccessful. So, there was something that the Red Airforce did that impacted the situation in their favor?" Valli asked.

Siilasvuo smiled, "They managed to drop a few bags of hardtack into Vinogradov's motti."

"Which probably froze solid before it hit the ground and broke their teeth when they tried to eat it. I'm not sure I would call that a success." Valli said with a chuckle.

Siilasvuo took a deep breath and let it out slowly, "Your point has been made major."

Valli smiled, "Good." The major picked up the pot of coffee that was brewing on the wood burning stove, "Would you like some coffee?"

Siilasvuo returned the major's smile, "Yes."

The colonel and major stood in silence for several minutes as they sipped the hot coffee. Siilasvuo could feel the effects of the caffeine coursing through his veins. He glanced over at Corporal Wirta who sat as always, in front of the division's radio set. Seeing the colonel's eyes upon him, Wirta said, "No news yet."

"Am I going to have to kick you out and send you to the mess tent?" Valli chided the colonel.

"No." Siilasvuo snapped.

Siilasvuo returned his gaze to the map and focused on the red pins representing sniper attacks. Though far fewer there were now several blue pins representing the locations where Karhonen's sniper team killed enemy snipers. Seeing where the colonel's focus had shifted, Valli said, "I think the sniper attacks are starting to slow down."

"I agree. We haven't experienced a single attack, since Karhonen's group eliminated the enemy sniper group near Task Force Kari." Colonel Siilasvuo observed.

"Do you think the snipers are finished?" Valli asked.

Siilasvuo shook his head, "No. Kuznetsov is still out

there somewhere."

"True. And who knows how many men of the 3rd NKVD Regiment are creeping through the woods right now looking to ambush our boys." Valli observed.

"I think Karhonen still has a lot of targets to eliminate before we can rest easy about the enemy sniper situation." Colonel Siilasvuo said.

"Maybe we should find Karhonen more men?" Valli pointed out, "His force has never been larger than squad strength and he has been taking losses in nearly every engagement."

"Men we have. Men that have the shooting skills to be useful to the young lieutenant are in short supply. The Task Force Commanders have given up a few men to Karhonen, but I feel as if they are holding back." Siilasvuo said.

"Aye. It's as if they don't entirely trust the young man to keep the snipers away." Valli said.

"Do you blame them? I know Karhonen came highly recommended from General Mannerheim himself, but the lieutenant is little more than a child. It's asking a lot of our men to trust that Karhonen can get the job done." Siilasvuo observed.

"He seemed knowledgeable enough and we can't argue with positive results." Valli said.

"I don't know. I sensed something under the surface with him. A lack of confidence perhaps?" Siilasvuo said.

"Perhaps but maybe you are being to hard on him? We are asking a lot of him to lead older men against the best sniper the Soviets have."

"Maybe your right." Siilasvuo agreed, "I never thought about what we were asking."

Major Valli opened his mouth to reply when the radio crackled to life. Both of the officers immediately turned their gaze to Corporal Wirta as he wrote down the incoming message on his note pad. The message ended and the corporal continued to write for nearly thirty seconds.

Siilasvuo and Valli waited impatiently as the corporal finally stood and turned toward them, "Permi—"

"Yes, yes. Out with-it man!" Siilasvuo snapped in irritation.

"Major Fagernas reports that his attack was successful. His forces succeeded in seizing the bridge over the Purasjokki River. The major is happy to report that the 44th Division is completely cut off from the Soviet Union."

"Then we are one step closer to dealing the Soviets a major defeat." Siilasvuo said.

Chapter 16

Mid-Morning, Task Force Kari's Chow Tent, Central Finland

January 4th, 1940

Private Korpi pushed his plate away and belched loudly, "I think that was the best meal I've ever had in my life."

"You must have a pretty shitty life if this sausage soup is better than anything you've had before." Cunnar quipped.

"Somehow it just tastes better after nearly being slain half a dozen times in the last twelve hours." Korpi said.

"Being in battle does strange things to your senses. I've heard what Korpi is describing happening before. For some men, their body amplifies their senses whenever they are in battle. The ears become more attuned to sounds, the eyes are able to notice the most subtle of movements that they would normally miss, but taste is a new one." Kivi said.

Korpi nodded, "That's it. Everything I experienced seemed different somehow. I couldn't put my finger on it but after what you said helps the experiences make sense.

I was able to discern distinct rifle shots amongst the cacophony of chaos swirling around me. To my mind it was almost as if the world slowed down. I was able to see and react to things that I shouldn't have even been aware of."

"What was the term the doctor used that I spoke to about it?" Kivi said out loud. He then snapped his fingers and said, "Now I remember. The doctor said it was a mutation of the fight or flight instinct. For some people they perceive the world as moving slower than most people perceive it."

"That sounds maddening." Hale said.

"How so?" Cunnar asked.

"Imagine if this was just how your mind worked all the time. Not a temporary reaction to being in battle or some other traumatic event. If your perception of time's passage is slower than most people, that means that all the best parts of life will flash by faster. It would also mean that all the worst parts of life, you know like waiting for your mom to finish cooking dinner when you are starving would seem to go very slowly." Hale said.

"Interesting Hale, I never thought of it like that before." Kivi said.

"If waiting for your mom to put dinner in front of you was one of the worst aspects of your life, you must have had a really nice life." Cunnar said.

Cunnar's words made Hale think about his parents. An overwhelming wave of despair slammed into him as the image of his dead father lying in a pool of his own blood on the kitchen floor in his childhood home. The victim of a Soviet rifleman. The same kitchen where Hale eagerly awaited his mom's home cooked meals. The vision of his father's corpse faded away as his mind shifted to the image of his mom's lifeless eyes staring up at the sky as she lay dead in the snow.

The other three men looked on with concern as Hale's body tensed up. A single tear slid down his face as the young Lieutenant opened his eyes. He fought back a sob as he said in a cracked voice, "It was."

Before the conversation could continue, two men appeared at the end of the table. The table the group sat on, along with the benches, was roughly hewn from local timber. The freshly cut wood would have permeated the chow tent, if not for the more powerful aroma of the cooking food.

Kivi, who sat on the end of the bench to allow his legs to dangle into the aisle, turned his head to look up at the newcomers as he said, "Yes?"

"Is this Lieutenant Karhonen's sniper group?" The older man of the pair asked.

The older man's skin had the cracked and leathery look of someone who had spent his life outdoors in the merciless elements of a sub-arctic forest. His black hair was speckled gray. In sharp contrast to his skin, he had blue eyes that seemed too large for his head and resembled an infant's. Hale quickly wiped away the tear and met the man's gaze as he said, "I'm Lieutenant Karhonen and you are?"

"Corporal Lassila and Private Lassila." The older man answered.

Hale looked past the older man to the younger private standing behind the corporal. The young private looked away from Hale's gaze. The private looked like a younger version of the middle-aged corporal, "Are you two related?" Hale asked.

Corporal Lassila nodded, "Private Lassila is my son."

"How old are you son?" Kivi asked Private Lassila.

"Sixteen." The boy mumbled.

Cunnar slapped Hale on the back, "Hale! We finally have someone younger than you."

His sorrow forgotten Hale cracked a smile, "So it would seem." Hale shifted his gaze back to the corporal and asked, "So why did Major Kari choose to send you two to me?"

"I live in the nearby village of Hauklia with my wife and son. Me and my boy here have spent our entire life hunting and trapping these lands." Corporal Lassila replied.

"How's your shooting?" Hale asked.

Corporal Lassila snorted, "Better than yours, I'm sure."

Kivi laughed, "If that's the case, then me and Cunnar here can take the rest of the war off as we won't be needed."

Corporal Lassila's face looked confused as he said, "What do you mean by that?"

Cunnar laughed and slapped Hale on the back as he said, "The lieutenant here is the best shot any of us have ever seen."

Hale's pale cheeks turned a ruddy red at the compliment as Corporal Lassila glared down at him as he said, "Is that so? Maybe we can have ourselves a bit of a competition?"

Hale met the elder Lassila's eyes with a steely gaze as he said in a stern voice, "Maybe so."

The elder Lassila turned back to Kivi and asked, "Can we get a bite to eat and join you?"

Kivi smiled and pointed at Hale, "He's the one you should be asking."

"Are you shittin' me?" Corporal Lassila asked, "The boy is in charge?"

Hale unbuttoned the top two buttons of his coat and pulled the garment back to reveal two silver circles set within the green rank field on his uniform shirt. Corporal Lassila's eyes widened as he cracked and grin and said, "How about that an officer that can shoot."

"I didn't start this war off as an officer. This rank was earned. Never forget that corporal." Hale gave the elder Lassila a steely eyed glare for several long seconds before he added, "Yes you can grab a bite to eat before we head out." Hale said.

The two Lassilas stepped in line to get a serving of sausage soup and rye bread. Hale turned to Kivi and asked, "What do you think of those two?"

"My first impression is that they spend to much time in the forest and not enough time around other people. It's also odd that the private only spoke when directly addressed, but giving the fact that the corporal is his father, perhaps he's used to letting his father do all the talking." Kivi replied.

"Thanks for the observation. I've spent a little too much time in the woods myself so I'm not a great judge of character." Hale said.

The group fell silent as the two Lassilas returned. The newcomers seated themselves on the far end of the table next to the canvas wall of the tent. They ate their meal in silence and ignored the other four men of the sniper squad.

"Where do you think Kuznetsov is going to strike next?" Kivi asked.

"If he follows his current pattern, he's going to hit Task Force Fagernas next." Hale said.

"You look doubtful of that." Kivi observed.

"How did you even see that? Did my face give my doubt away?" Hale wondered.

"I've been a drill instructor remember? If I can't see below a man's exterior mask, I wouldn't be a very good one now, would I? You glanced downward when you said the words. Someone that drops their eyes or the position of their head lacks confidence." Kivi said.

"I know what Kuznetsov's pattern says he's going to do next, but you know the man better than any of us here. What does your gut tell you?" Kivi asked.

"Kuznetsov is very intelligent. He would realize that he is on the verge of creating a pattern that we could follow. Couple that with the near success of the recent Soviet attack, he's going to hit here again." Hale said.

"That's exactly what I would do, so I don't create a pattern that my opposition could figure out and anticipate." Kivi said, "Now the question is where around here do you think he is going to hit?"

"He's probably counting on Major Kari strengthening his sentry line north of the road, since that is where we engaged him last. I'd say he is going to come up from the south." Hale said.

"Very good, so we know where we are heading now." Kivi said.

Hale turned to the two Lassilas and asked, "Can you tell me about the terrain south of the road?"

The elder Lassila slowly nodded, "Aye."

Silence hung in the air for nearly thirty seconds before Hale exhaled sharply in frustration and said, "Tell me about the terrain south of the road."

"It starts off a bit hilly and then smooths out some as the land slopes downward toward the lake. My cousin who went to the university, Captain Lassila, says that the glaciers tore great gouges in the land during the last ice age. I personally think he is full of shit, but everyone else seems to believe in the crap that comes out of his mouth." Corporal Lassila replied.

"I read something similar about the glaciers in one of my father's books. Circling back to our situation, I think we should set up on the edge of the last hill." Hale said.

The young lieutenant elicited a glare from the senior Lassila, before Kivi interjected, "That would give us a height advantage."

"Kuznetsov may be moving up from the south already, so we need to move out now." Hale came to his feet and said, "Let's go. We are going to set up on the last ridgeline before the land slopes downward toward the lake. Do you know a good spot Lassila?"

The older man nodded sagely and said, "Aye. I know a place that resembles what you are looking for. There is a ridgeline that runs roughly a hundred meters or so east to west about halfway between the lake and the road. We should set up there." Corporal Lassila replied.

"Excellent corporal. You can lead the way." Hale said.

"Yes, lieutenant." Lassila replied glumly.

The group put their skis on and headed southward. The ridge that Corporal Lassila spoke of was only two kilometers south of the Raate road and was exactly as he described. The ridge, which ran roughly one hundred meters before turning away from the lake, stood about five meters above the surrounding terrain and provided a commanding view when looking southward toward the lake.

The ridgeline was speckled with spruce trees which would provide the Finns with a measure of cover from anyone coming up from the south. To the north, in the direction of the road, the earth descended for roughly ten meters below the top of the hill before quickly rising once again. Hale ordered the group to spread out along the edge of the hill centered on him. Kivi and Cunnar, not being great snipers, set up ten meters on either side of Hale. The junior Lassila chose a spot roughly twenty meters from Kivi and his father, twenty meters beyond that, so that the senior Lassila anchored the western portion of the line.

Korpi set up about twenty meters east of Cunnar, so that the group more or less stretched across the entire ridgeline. The men went to work creating their individual sniper nests using their gloved hands, bayonets, or an entrenching tool if they had it. Each man set up underneath a spruce tree and then shifted the snow to enhance their concealment. This would help them to blend into the shape of the tree and not stick out.

When each man completed their task to their satisfaction, they settled down to wait. As the minutes slowly ticked by Hale's self-doubt grew, *Is this the right location? What if he goes around us and hits Task Force Kari? How are we going to even know if that happens?* Hale wondered, *Is Kuznetsov hitting somewhere else right now while we sit out here doing nothing?*

Hale calmed his mind and pushed away the doubt. Each time one of them reared their head, he reminded himself that he had shown Major Kari where they planned to set up on a map. The nervous Lieutenant turned and looked back toward the Raate Road trying to sense if anything was amiss. The only thing he heard was the sound of the wind gently blowing out of the north and causing the nearby trees to creak as they swayed slightly.

Before Hale could continue his mental self-flagellation, his keen eyes spotted movement several hundred meters away to the south, near the frozen lake. The movement took the form of a gap between two trees becoming dark for a second and then shifting back to the sliver of light that Hale had memorized when he first set up his firing position. He checked his rifle for the twentieth time to ensure it was ready. Recently oiled, the action responded easily to Hale's touch.

Hale again saw movement. This time it was about four hundred meters distance. The movement looked odd for a human being, *Unless there are two men walking near each other? Would they be that careless?*

Hale peered across the iron sights of his weapon hoping to spot the movement for a third time. He wasn't sure if it was a target yet. After about ten minutes Cunnar whispered to Hale, "I see something moving down there."

Hale's gaze shifted to Cunnar's sector, and he smiled.

The source of the movement had been traveling in a west to east direction and he now had a good angle to see it through the trees. Standing roughly three hundred meters to Hale's southeast, was a bull moose.

The enormous moose's nearly twenty-point antler rack stretched for a half meter on either side of the mighty animal's head, "Hold your fire, it's a moose." Hale hissed.

Cunnar peered back at the movement. He squinted his eyes against the glare of the sunlight off the snow then replied, "I see it now. It would sure be nice to take down that monster. We'd be able to feed all of Task Force Kari a nice meal with the meat from that beast."

"If we try, we'll give away our position to anyone out there. I'm sure the men of Task Force Kari would rather be free of Kuznetsov and his snipers, then have a full stomach and a potentially fatal bullet wound." Hale said.

"But I'm growing tired of sausage soup." Cunnar countered.

"Be thankful for what you do have. The Soviets have far less. I heard reports that some of them are boiling and eating the leather from their boots." Hale said.

Hale's revelation was enough to cow Cunnar's whining. The outspoken private fell silent and time began to slowly slide by. After five minutes, that felt like an hour to Cunnar, the silence of the picturesque snow-covered forest abruptly ended with the sound of a gunshot. A bullet buried itself in the snow in the ridge just below Cunnar's position.

"Someone is shooting at me!" Cunnar yelled. His voice thick with the panic that was welling up inside him.

"Stay down and don't panic!" Hale ordered.

A second gunshot followed a few seconds behind the first. The bullet disturbed a branch just above Cunnar's head. Hale looked around frantically for a source of the gunshots, "I allowed myself to be distracted by the moose, Kivi did you see anything?"

"No." Kivi replied.

"Cunnar, at least two enemy snipers have seen you. Back out of your spot and use the ridge for cover and reposition. Be very careful to remain as flat as possible while you do it. Centimeters matter." Hale said.

Cunnar did as Hale instructed. He was able to slowly back out of the nest he had fashioned for himself. The enemy, having no other targets to shoot, did not fire any additional shots. An hour passed as Hale's group remained completely still and scanned the terrain in front of them for the enemy.

Hale was startled when he heard a gunshot to his right, *That must have come from one of the Lassilas.* Hale thought.

Thirty seconds later, Kivi hissed, "Corporal Lassila is reporting that he hit a target approximately three hundred meters to his southwest."

"The bastards must have been trying to flank us after they failed to kill Cunnar." Hale said.

"Orders?" Kivi asked.

"Tell Lassila to back out of his nest and shift position twenty meters westward. We don't want the enemy to figure out where he is at. Plus, that will make it harder to get around us." Hale ordered.

"Understood." Kivi said.

Hale could hear Kivi, whispering Hale's orders to the younger Lassila. Corporal Lassila received the message from his son about a minute later and objected, "You tell Hale, that I haven't been spotted and I'm not moving."

The message was relayed back to Hale. Upon hearing it, his cheeks turned crimson and despite the sub-zero temperature, his blood boiled. He took a deep breath and let it out slowly. This helped to ease the rage he felt from Corporal Lassila's. Not thinking, he created a large cloud of steam in front of him, *Idiot! Hopefully no one saw my cloud.* The young sniper chastised himself.

Suddenly, the sound of two rifles being fired nearly simultaneously washed over them, "Summer of cunts." The elder Lassila snarled loud enough for Kivi and Hale to hear.

"Are you hit?" Hale shouted.

"No, but they nearly hit me." Lassila replied in a clipped tone.

"Then move your ass like I told you. NOW!" Hale demanded.

Without further objection Lassila backed out of his firing position. As he did so, the enemy fired two more shots. One of the shots went high, the other buried itself in the snow, right where Lassila had been laying, *The young pup seems to know what he is about when it comes to the enemy. Perhaps next time I should listen to him.* Corporal Lassila thought.

Hale concentrated his gaze to the southwest as he tried to spot the enemy. Within minutes his effort was rewarded. He spotted several figures darting forward as they tried to use the trees as much as possible for cover. The enemy soldiers would have been hidden by the trees from Corporal Lassila's viewpoint.

Hale swung his rifle toward the nearest one and lined up the target in his sights. He then made a slight adjustment for the range, the target's movement, and the difference in elevation between himself and his intended victim. The target cooperated by continuing in the same direction and maintaining the same gait.

When Hale was satisfied that he had a bead on the target. He took a deep breath, held it, and pulled the trigger. Hale saw his target go down as he worked the bolt on his rifle. Suddenly, a shot boomed from the younger Lassila's location. Private Lassila cheered his own success as his target also went down.

"Don't waste time celebrating when there is still killing to be done." Kivi admonished.

Suddenly everyone on the ridgeline started to take fire. The bullets smacked into nearby tree trunks, zinged when they hit rocks buried in the snow, or ended their journey in silence as the deep snowpack absorbed the impact from several of the bullets, "Cunnar get up here!" Hale ordered.

Hale returned fire, "Missed." He said in disappointment.

Cunnar joined Hale and laid down on his chest in the snow next to his commanding officer, "Start shooting anything that moves. There must be at least twenty of them out there." Hale ordered.

A moment later Kivi fired his rifle, "I don't see anyone. Shall I shift?" Korpi asked.

"Stay where you are in case this platoon is a diversion." Hale said.

Disappointed, Korpi didn't reply. Corporal Lassila, using the deep gorge in the terrain behind the ridgeline, dashed westward until he came upon a small hillock. He got down on his chest and started to crawl six meters to the top. Both Hale and Private Lassila eliminated two more targets and this time, when Kivi fired, he hit his target.

Corporal Lassila pushed his way forward and reached the top of the small hill. Less than two hundred meters in front of him, the surviving members of the Soviet platoon were skiing clumsily toward him. He pointed his rifle at the closest enemy soldier and lined the man up in his rifle's twin sights.

The elder Lassila was about to pull the trigger when the air around him was filled with bullets. Cursing he hastily withdrew from the hill as he shouted insults in Russian at the enemy. Lassila, using the small gorge, came to his feet and began to run back the way he had come.

A few moments later three grenades exploded on and around the hill he had just abandoned with a loud BOOM-BOOM-BOOM. Lassila stopped and looked back, *If I would have stayed, those grenades would have killed me.* He paused for a moment and considered the situation, then realized, *I bet the buggers thought they got me.*

Lassila stopped running away and instead got down on the ground with his rifle pointed westward. The younger Lassila once again shouted in triumph as he brought down another enemy. Hale also dropped another target, but he wisely remained silent.

Suddenly, Corporal Lassila spotted movement. A figure dashed around the hill with his PPD-34 submachinegun at the ready. The man looked around confused for a few seconds before he spotted Lassila laying in the snow. It was the last thing he would ever see. The elder Lassila, a little over ten meters away, put a well-aimed bullet through the man's heart, which killed him instantly.

Lassila operated the action on his rifle and waited. When no one appeared, he relaxed his focus and noticed the PPD-34 laying in the snow. He smiled and made a decision to get the gun. He hastily crawled forward and picked up the gun and quickly checked it to ensure that it was ready to fire.

Satisfied, he put on the slain enemy's jacket and dashed around the small hill. In front of him were over a dozen enemy soldiers moving toward him. He smiled in glee and pulled the trigger on his gun. The PPD-34 rapidly spat death at the approaching Soviets cutting down half of their remaining number.

The other half of the enemy force sought the cover provided by the nearest tree trunk. When Lassila stopped firing, they attempted to emerge from their hiding places and put a bullet in him. He smiled at the first man to emerge and held down the trigger on the PPD-34. Like the weapon Kivi had obtained, this one had the drum style magazine which held seventy rounds.

The recoil from the gun was easily controlled by his firm grip as the bullet ripped through the flesh of the approaching Soviets. He cut down half of the surviving members of the rapidly shrinking Soviet platoon. Blood mist was thrown into the air from the dozens of bullet wounds the elder Lassila inflicted on the enemy. The mist immediately froze and fell to the earth as red ice.

Corporal Lassila saw movement in his peripheral vision. An object flew in from his left. Knowing what the item likely was, he smiled grimly and continued to pour fire into the enemy. A few seconds later the grenade at his feet detonated, tearing his legs off at the knees.

"Papa!" The younger Lassila screamed in dismay when he looked over at the source of the explosion.

Hearing the sound of his son's voice, Corporal Lassila turned his head so that he could see his son's face, "Tell your mother that I love her."

The younger Lassila stood and rushed toward his injured father, seeing a Russian appear, he raised his rifle and shot the man in the chest. As he operated the action on his rifle, he said, "You can tell her yourself."

"I got no legs son. How can a man live like that?" Corporal Lassila said.

"I'll take care of you and mom." Private Lassila argued.

Private Lassila kept moving forward toward his father, when a second grenade landed in the snow next to his father's left arm, "Summer of cunts." Corporal Lassila cursed. He met his son's gaze and said, "Goodb—"

The grenade exploded sending what was left of the elder Lassila into the air. The kinetic force of the explosion ripped his left arm off and filled his head with shrapnel, mercifully ending his life. Private Lassila dashed up the side of the gorge and spotted the man that had thrown the grenade. He raised his rifle and got the revenge his wounded heart was screaming for.

Private Lassila didn't notice the enemy soldier taking aim at him. As the Soviet fired his rifle, a huge weight hit the Private in the back pushing him to the snow-covered ground, "Stay down." Lieutenant Kivi ordered.

The big man quickly came to his feet. In his hands was the PPD-34 he had looted from the recent battle on the Raate Road. He cut down the man that had just tried to kill Private Lassila while the Russian was operating the bolt on his rifle.

Kivi looked past the collapsing corpse at the surviving members of the enemy platoon. The remaining enemy soldiers, fully exposed, suddenly really wanted to be behind cover. Only three of them survived long enough to make it as the big man cut down the rest.

Unfortunately for one of the survivors, his cover, which protected him from Kivi, left him exposed to Hale. He never knew what hit him as Hale's bullet ended his life. The other two Soviets, their willpower shattered by the sudden reversal of fortunes, turned and tried to escape on their skis. Kivi abruptly ended their struggle to survive with a few well-placed bursts from his submachine gun.

As the sounds of battle faded away, they were replaced by Private Lassila's sobs. Hale joined Kivi and the two men looked out over the battlefield. The pristine snow had been torn asunder by the grenade explosions and turned crimson by the blood of their slain enemies. Smoke lazily curled from the end of Kivi's PPD-34 as Hale broke the silence, "He wasn't here."

"It doesn't matter if he was here or not. You figured out what his plan was and you stopped that plan. For the first time, you have led us to victory against Kuznetsov." Kivi said.

The faces of all the men that Hale led and lost to Kuznetsov flashed in his mind as Hale said, "Next time we are going to get that bastard once and for all."

Private Lassila's sobs faded away leaving only the sound

of the wind as it whistled through the branches overhead.

Chapter 17

Mid-Afternoon, Village of Hauklia, Central Finland

January 4th, 1940

The moment Private Aimo Lassila had been dreading for the last two hours had arrived. He gazed at the cheerful red house that he had grown up in. The house, though constructed of simple materials and small had been lovingly maintained by his father. He remembered many summers standing at the foot of a ladder. He would hand supplies up to his father while the older Lassila repaired the damage done to the house by Finland's harsh winters.

There were two windows that faced the main throughfare that cut through the center of the small village of Hauklia. Like the house, the window shudders, currently open to let in the sunlight were painted a bright yellow. Two stairs led to a small landing in front of the door.

Memories of happier times flooded his mind. Though his father was a gruff man of few words, he had a soft place in his heart for his son. In particular there was the moment he returned home from school after being beaten up by the village bully. The elder Lassila had wrapped his arms around his son to comfort him. When the tears faded away, he taught his son the skills he needed to ensure the bully would never be a bother again.

A tear slid down his cheek and quickly froze as he realized that he would never be able to seek his father's wisdom again in this life. Lassila looked down at the bundled remains of his father and his shoulders slumped in resignation as the weight of what he was about to do hit him, *I might as well get this over with. I wish someone else could tell her.*

The rare sunny January day in Central Finland created a cheerful atmosphere in the village. Children, bundled up against the cold that even at this time of the day was beyond the imagination of those who lived in more moderate latitudes, ran around the small-town square playing games. Their mothers, taking a break from toiling in the kitchen, stood in clusters and laughed as they gossiped about the latest happenings in the village. Despite the absence of the village's men, the mood was nearly festive.

A mood that Lassila, along with the other members of the sniper group did not share. Though they had defeated the platoon from the 3rd NKVD Regiment and ensured that Task Force Kari would not be surprised from the south by a band of enemy snipers, the small squad paid a heavy price.

"I really don't want to do this." Lassila said.

Hale placed his hands on Private Lassila's shoulders and said, "I know. I'm not going to lie to you and say this is going to be easy. It isn't. I can remember the painful wails of my own mother when she realized my father had been slain by the Russians. You need to do this for her. It's best that she hears the news coming from someone she loves. Your mother can take heart in the fact that she didn't lose both of the men in her life today. It will be really hard for you to get her to see that but try."

"You lost your father to the Soviets?" Lassila asked.

Hale nodded, "Both parents actually. One of them in the very home that I grew up in, the other as we fled for our lives from a depraved madman Commissar Volkov."

Lassila reached up and squeezed Hale's arm as he said, "Thanks. I didn't realize this war had cost you both of your parents."

Private Lassila took a deep breath and let it out slowly. The warm air being expelled from his lungs created a large steam cloud in front of him that slowly faded away. He took the rope of the small sled with his father's remains from Kivi and turned toward the house.

Lassila left the sled and his father at the bottom of the stairs and knocked on the door. He heard movement as his mother stood up from the kitchen table and walked over to the front door to answer the knock. The door opened. Standing in the doorway was a middle-aged woman. Her dark brown hair was flecked with strands of gray and her blue eyes widened in surprise at the sight of her son, "Aimo? What are you doing here? Aren't you supposed to be with your father?"

The woman's eyes fell to the bundle on the sled, and realization dawned on her face. She collapsed to her knees, "No! Please God, it can't be. . ."

Lassila stepped forward, kneeled, and embraced his mother, "He was slain a few hours ago. I'm so sorry."

Lassila mother started to sob uncontrollably as she grabbed on to her son who had knelt in front of her, "What happened?"

Lassila opened his mouth to reply when his sister appeared behind his mother. Like her mother, she had brown hair, but her eyes were hazel, like her father's had been. She held her infant son in her arms, "Papa?"

Lassila's eyes fell to the sled for a moment before he raised them, met her gaze, and shook his head, "No!" His sister shouted.

She began to sob but managed to remain standing. The baby in her arms, sensing his mother's grief, began crying as well. Unable to bare the sorrow, Lassila began to tear up. Though he tried to remain strong for the two women, he too was soon crying uncontrollably.

Out of respect, Hale, Kivi, Cunnar, and Korpi turned away from the family, "I imagine this scene is playing out over and over again across Finland." Kivi said.

"There has been much loss thanks to the evil of Stalin and the Red Army." Hale said.

"Sometimes I wonder if remaining independent is worth so much pain and loss." Korpi observed.

Hale went rigid as anger flared within his breast, "It is worth every drop of blood that must be spilled to preserve it. If we give up and bow down to the invader, who we are as a people will be forever lost."

"How do you know that?" Korpi asked.

"The magazines and newspapers my father had said it was so. The evil Communists of the Soviet Union are working day and night to wash away the identities of the people that they rule." Hale said.

"Is that even possible? How do you erase the history of a people and their identity?" Korpi asked.

"You forbid them to speak their language, cook their traditional foods, worship as they choose, and celebrate their distinct holidays. You brain wash the children in school with party ideology and Russian culture. In a generation, perhaps two at the most, there won't be any Finns, Lithuanians, Latvians, Estonians, or Ukrainians left living within the USSR. They will all be Russian pawns of the party." Hale replied.

"Why would they want everyone to think and believe the same things?" Korpi asked.

"Because it will be easier to maintain control." Kivi replied, "I've seen this in Spain. The fascist government I fought for had begun this process in the areas that they controlled during the Spanish Civil War. The Republicans were doing the same thing, except to promote Communism. The system was particularly hard on those that were not Spanish by birth. Not only were they being brain washed to become party drones, but their identity as a people was also being swept away."

Lassila's mother's sobs faded away as the sorrow in her heart was replaced by rage. She pounded her fist on the door frame until Private Lassila grasped her arms to stop her from hurting herself. She glared up at him and snarled, "Promise me one thing."

"Anything." Lassila replied.

"That you will not rest until all of the swine that has invaded our country are destroyed." His mother demanded.

"I will mother I promise." Lassila replied.

Lassila's mother stood and looked past her son at the four men waiting in the street, "Are you the men my son fights with?"

"Yes ma'am. My name is Lieutenant Hale Karhonen and your son is a member of my squad."

As Private Lassila came to his feet his mother pushed him in Hale's direction, "Good. Take him and get back to doing the good work that my husband died doing. Do not stop until the last invader is destroyed."

"We won't stop until the enemy has been defeated." Hale said grimly.

"Good." Lassila's mother replied simply.

She then pulled Lassila into an embrace and kissed him on the cheek. She released her son and again pushed him toward the street, "Go. Get back to killing the bastards that did this to my husband."

"But what about Papa?" Lassila asked.

The woman's eyes fell to the bundle of her husband's remains. Tears started to flow once again as she shouted, "We'll take care of him. Now go!"

Chapter 18

Late-Afternoon, Task Force Kari Headquarters, Central Finland

January 4th, 1940

The sniper group traveled in silence as they returned to Task Force Kari's headquarters tent. Hale turned to Korpi, Lassila, and Cunnar, "Go ahead and get some dinner while Kivi and I check in with the major and see if there has been any sniper activity we should investigate."

Korpi smiled, "Thank you, sir. It will be nice to have a full stomach and get out of the cold, if only for a little while."

The three enlisted men parted ways with Hale and Kivi. The two officers strode over to Major Kari's tent and entered. Inside things were much as they had been before. Major Kari, along with Captain Lassila, stood over the map table conversing and a sergeant sat at the radio set.

Major Kari turned around to see who came into his tent, he smiled at Hale and Kivi, "Welcome gentlemen. What can we do for you?"

"I'm here to see if you've gotten word of any new sniper attacks." Hale said.

"None here." Major Kari replied. He gestured towards the radio and said, "Feel free to talk to Sergeant Peura about anything he may have heard come across the wireless."

"Thanks Major." Hale replied.

Hale and Kivi strode over to Sergeant Peura. The sergeant turned his head and looked up at the two officers without getting out of his chair, "What can I do for you lieutenants?"

"Have you heard any reports of new sniper attacks come across the wireless?" Hale asked.

"Aye. Task Force Fagernas is catching holy hell from those bastards." Peura replied.

"Did they give any details?" Kivi asked.

Peura nodded, "They did. It seems the platoon they have guarding the bridge over the Purasjokki is being used for target practice."

"How many have they lost?" Hale asked.

"Oh, I think it was half a dozen or so at last count." Peura replied.

"Did they give a timeframe that they lost the men over?" Kivi asked.

Peura again nodded, "Aye. They said it's been since dawn."

"The sun went down nearly three hours ago. Have any more fallen since then?" Hale asked.

"Oh, aye. Vanhanen, that's Major Fagernas radioman. He said that they lost one about an hour ago. Said it was a bit of a shock to the lieutenant in charge of the platoon holding the bridge. He couldn't understand how someone could see in the dark well enough for long distance shooting." Peura replied.

"It's possible to see a long way after nightfall if the conditions are right." Hale said.

"Vanhanen said the lieutenant, he didn't tell me his name, swears the shot came from some three hundred meters away." Peura said.

Hale turned to Kivi and said, "That sounds like Kuznetsov."

"It would explain why he wasn't with the platoon that tried to hit here." Kivi agreed.

"Sergeant, can you radio Vanhanen and tell him to let that lieutenant know that he must stop exposing men on the bridge. If I'm right, any man that shows himself will be waking up in the afterlife in short order." Hale said.

"Aye, I can make the transmission. Can't say that the lieutenant will listen." Peura replied.

"Tell them that the sniper squad is on the way and that we will be there around midnight." Hale said.

"We can be there sooner than that." Kivi said.

"True, but we're exhausted. We need to get something to eat and then sleep for four hours or so before we head out. If we face off against Kuznetsov in our current condition, we'll lose." Hale argued.

"It doesn't feel right letting men die so that we can get some shut eye." Kivi said.

"Which is why I sent the message to the lieutenant. If he listens, then no one else need die before we get there." Hale said.

"Well let's hope for the sake of his men that he isn't one of those pompous asses that think they know it all because they went to university and got handed a silver circle on a platter for it." Kivi said.

Chapter 19

Midnight, Task Force Fagernas Headquarters, Central Finland

January 5th, 1940

After a short reprieve of four hours to enable the group to sleep, they headed eastward. The squad journeyed in silence using the newly created ice road that ran a few kilometers south and parallel to the Raate Road. The road enabled them to make the journey both quickly and far from potential Soviet entanglements. Each man spent this time alone with their thoughts as they trekked eastward.

Upon arrival at their destination, Hale and Kivi entered Task Force Fagernas' HQ tent. Unlike the other HQ tents that Hale had been in over the last several days, Major Fagernas had set up command center differently. Absent was the campaign table and map in the middle of the room, instead, the major had pinned his maps to the walls of the tent. This enabled him to pace back and forth in front of them. A process that helped him to think.

In the exact center of the tent sat a black iron wood burning stove. The stove had a kettle upon it, but unlike the other headquarters tents, the aroma of coffee did not permeate the space. Next to the stove, on a beaten up gray wooden campaign table sat the task force's wireless.

The seat was empty as the radioman was curled up under the table asleep.

A man, presumably the major, stood directly across from the entrance peering at a map. He wore a rumpled gray officer's uniform. Fagernas was an unimposing figure with thinning brown hair. At just over five feet in height he was substantially shorter than Hale and appeared almost childlike against Kivi's massive frame.

The sound of the radioman's snoring drowned out the noise of Hale opening the tent flap, so the major was unaware of the new arrivals. Hale crossed the space and cleared his throat a few meters away from the major. The major turned around, in his hands he held a teacup and saucer. He looked up at Hale and Kivi with a quizzical expression on his face as he took a sip from the cup.

"Good morning, major, my name is Hale Karhonen, I'm the 9th Division's sniper squad's commander."

"Ahhh yes. The young pup Sergeant Vanhanen said was coming to save us from our little sniper problem. As you've probably already figured out, I'm Major Fagernas."

"Can you tell us a little more about what your men have been experiencing?" Hale asked.

The major took another sip of his tea before replying, "The killings started not long after we secured our primary objective, the bridge over the Purasjokki River. Given the strength of the 44th's force trapped inside the motti, I had to focus most of my strength in the west. The bridge creates a bottle neck. This enables us to defend it with a single platoon.

My thoughts appeared to be confirmed when the platoon managed to hold the bridge against a determined assault by the 3rd NKVD Regiment. After that victory, the surviving members of the platoon started to take random sniper fire."

"Random?" Hale asked.

"Yes, not every man who exposed himself on the bridge was shot. Some stood their post for hours unmolested while others were hit minutes after they were assigned guard duty on the eastern side of the bridge." Fagernas replied.

"It sounds like Kuznetsov was playing with them a bit." Kivi observed.

"How do you know it is a specific person doing this to my men?" Fagernas asked.

"Because if it was any other sniper, they would be taking every opportunity presented to kill our men." Hale replied.

"Kuznetsov is their best sniper, and he likes to employ unusual techniques to achieve the maximum amount of fear. The fear acts as a kind of force multiplier that increases the impact of his activities." Kivi added.

"Interesting. As you can imagine, the men assigned to guard the bridge by Lieutenant Halonen are somewhat anxious about being there. I can't say that I blame them." Fagernas said.

"Tell me about Halonen, what kind of officer is he?" Hale asked.

"He's young. Not so young as you, but based on the questions you have asked me, he lacks the seasoning you seem to have obtained." Fagernas said.

"One of those." Kivi said in a disgusted voice.

"You have experience with those kinds of officers?" Fagernas asked.

Kivi nodded, "Yes. I was a sergeant up until a week ago. I had my fair share of dumb lieutenants during my decades in the military."

"Well maybe you can impart some wisdom onto Halonen while you work on taking care of the sniper problem. I simply can't abandon the bridge to the enemy. It's a natural defensive position." Fagernas said.

"Couldn't you just have your men hunker down on this side of the river and use the trees to stay out of sight?" Hale asked.

"No, the main body of the 3rd NKVD Regiment, lay just out of sight around a bend in the road east of the bridge. As I mentioned before, they tried to take the bridge but were bloodily repulsed by Halonen's men after nearly succeeding. I imagine they will come running if we concede the bridge and simply try to defend it from this side of the river." Fagernas said.

"Hmmmm, it seems you are in a bit of a difficult spot." Hale said.

"Damn right I am, I'm stuck between the western most motti of the 44th, and this fresh regiment of NKVD fanatics that clearly have orders to rescue that idiot Vinogradov." Fagernas said.

"Alright major, we'll see what we can do to eliminate your sniper problem." Hale said.

"I'll hold you to that lieutenant. Where do you plan to start?" Fagernas asked.

"I need to speak to Lieutenant Halonen to figure out

where his men were taking fire from and then we'll go from there." Hale replied.

"Good luck." Fagernas said as he turned away from the two lieutenants, took a sip of tea, and returned to gazing at the maps.

Hale and Kivi left Task Force Fagernas' headquarters tent, collected their three men, and set off towards the bridge. They headed a short distance northward to the Raate Road, and then turned eastward toward the bridge. Within the safety of Fagernas' lines, the group quickly and uneventfully covered the half kilometer that separated them from the bridge.

Hale, leading the group, came around a slight bend in the road. Just ahead, the trees fell away on either side and the bridge came into view. A few meters inside the tree line, several men slept around a campfire.

Hale approached the group, careful to remain quiet so as not to wake them. A single man standing guard over the group turned when he heard the sound of Cunnar's ski scrape across an exposed tree root on the road. The guard whirled around and raised his Suomi submachine gun toward the newcomers but relaxed when he saw that the sound was made by a friendly.

Hale stopped next to the guard and whispered, "I'm looking for Lieutenant Halonen. Do you know where he is?"

The guard nodded and pointed to one of the slumbering forms close to the campfire, "Thanks." Hale said.

Hale moved past the guard to get a better look at the bridge. Kivi joined him and asked, "Don't you want to talk to the lieutenant?"

"Not yet. Since he is asleep, I want to get a look at the bridge and how his men are set up." Hale replied.

Several frozen corpses lay on the bridge. Left where they had fallen. On the east side of the bridge six men sat behind a pile of snow that had been formed into a wall. The wall resembled an upside-down backward L, with the long side facing eastward and the shorter bottom side of the L facing northward, "It looks like they are trying to use snow to stay out of sight." Kivi observed.

The frozen river was a stark contrast to the vast forest that surrounded it. Trees grew right up to the banks of the Purasjoki River, "The men on the bridge are completely exposed to anyone hiding in the surrounding forest." Hale said.

"Where would you shoot from if you were trying to kill our men on the bridge?" Kivi asked.

Hale thought about the question for several moments before replying, "You see that bend in the river about three hundred meters to the north?"

"Yes." Kivi replied.

"You could use that grove of spruce right there on the bank of the river for concealment while enjoying an easy view of the bridge." Hale said.

"That's probably where he has been shooting from then. The idiot lieutenant should have posted some lookouts at the edge of the tree line to see the muzzle flashes." Kivi observed.

"I agree. Let's wake the lieutenant up and get his version of events." Hale said.

Hale turned around and returned to the campfire. He

poked Lieutenant Halonen with the end of his ski. The man muttered something unintelligible and rolled over. Hale poked him again, a little harder this time and Halonen sat bolt upright. He glared up at Hale, whose face was lit by the light of the campfire, noted his age, and said, "What is so important that you needed to wake me private?"

"That's senior lieutenant to you." Hale said.

"Senior lieutenant? Surely you jest, you don't look old enough to have shaved, much less graduated from university." Halonen fired back.

"Unlike you, he earned the rank the hard way. Now pull your skull out of your pompous ass, drain the piss from your head, and answer the question." Kivi growled.

"How dare you speak to me like that. Judging by your crassness you must be the child's sergeant." Halonen said.

Kivi reached down and picked the much shorter and scrawny Halonen up off the ground, "No you little shit, I'm also a senior lieutenant and if you don't start showing us some respect, I'm going to crack you open and dine on your entrails."

Halonen, swallowed hard. His Adam's apple bobbed betraying his nervousness as realization finally dawned on him, "You're from the sniper squad."

Kivi released his grip on Halonen who landed hard on his backside. The frozen, concrete-like surface of the road sent a jolt of pain up his spine from the impact. He winced, and then slowly came to his feet, "My apologies, I didn't realize who you were."

"Good. It looks like the piss is finally draining from that empty head of yours. Considering the predicament, you and your men are in, one would think you would be a little less arrogant." Hale said.

The sentry snorted in derision at Hale's statement and Halonen whirled around, "Do you have something to add, private?"

Halonen's loud voice woke the other men asleep around the fire. The sentry ignored his commanding officer, met Hale's gaze, and said, "More like the predicament that his men are in. He hasn't risked himself once out there on the bridge."

Kivi grabbed Halonen by his coat, picked him up off the ground, and pulled him an inch from his face as he growled, "Is that true?"

Halonen nodded, "You are the worst kind of officer." Kivi snarled.

"Would you put me down or I will have you brought up on charges!" Halonen shouted.

"Bah!" Kivi shouted as he set Halonen on the ground and pushed him as if he was shoving an undesirable piece of refuse out of the way.

Hale turned to the sentry and said, "Can you tell us what has been happening, private?"

"Oja, sir, and yes I can."

Hale and Kivi looked at Oja expectantly, "The lieutenant here ordered us to set up defensive positions on the bridge. Using some snow, we built a half meter tall wall across the eastern side of the bridge to conceal us from any potential attackers."

"The snow would keep you out of sight but wouldn't stop any bullets." Hale observed.

Oja patted his submachine gun affectionately as he spoke, "That's correct sir. Luckily when we were attacked a short time later, the Soviets' aim was high. We were able to send them packing with some concentrated fire from our Suomi's."

"What happened next?" Hale asked.

"About two hours after we stopped the Soviet attack, we started to lose men as we switched them out." Halonen said.

"That explains the bodies on the bridge." Kivi said. He glared down at Halonen and asked, "Why were your men left on the bridge where they fell?"

"I didn't want to lose any additional men retrieving the corpses. Those men are beyond any help I can give them, and in these temperatures, they aren't going anywhere." Halonen said.

Kivi started to open his mouth, when Hale said, "A valid point."

Kivi threw Hale an irritated look but remained quiet. "Do you know the location your men were taking fire from?" Hale asked.

Halonen turned to Oja, who rolled his eyes in disgust as he said, "We believe the shots were coming from about three hundred meters upriver."

"Thank you Private Oja, it's good that someone knows what is happening here." Hale said as he looked down his nose at Halonen.

Halonen opened his mouth to reply, but then thought better of it when he saw Kivi glaring down at him, "Let's head back to the HQ tent and take a look at the maps."

Hale said.

"Aren't you going to go kill the sniper?" Halonen asked.

"Yes, but I need to develop a plan of attack first." Hale replied.

"Can't you do that here and then get moving?" Halonen said.

"I could, but since the major has great maps of the area, it would make more sense to develop the plan using them." Hale said. He turned to Lassila, Cunnar, and Korpi, "You men stay here and warm yourselves up by the campfire. Get some sleep if you can."

Cunnar smiled, "Yes, sir."

Hale and Kivi returned to Major Fagernas' headquarters tent, "What did you find out?" Fagernas asked.

"Other than your Lieutenant Halonen is an idiot?" Kivi asked.

Hale elbowed Kivi in the side to quiet him as he said, "I've got a pretty good idea where Kuznetsov may be set up if he is still in the area. I wanted to check your maps to see if there are any known trails or terrain features that could aid us in our approach, so he doesn't slip away."

"Show me on the main map here, where you think he is." Fagernas replied.

Hale pointed at the bend in the river about three hundred meters north of the bridge, "I think he was shooting from this area."

"Give me a moment." Fagernas walked over to a different map on the opposite side of the tent. He studied the map for nearly a minute before gesturing to the two lieutenants, "Take a look at this." Hale and Kivi joined the major in front of the map. This map showed a detailed view of the area north of the bridge.

"I think you could use this game trail right here. It parallels the west bank of the river and would get you north of him while keeping you out of sight." Fagernas said, the major then pointed at a terrain feature to the north of the river bend, "According to the map, there is a ridgeline that runs east to west just north of Kuznetsov's suspected position. You could cross the river here, and then head east until you reach the ridgeline. This would enable you to come up behind him."

Hale nodded, "That could work sir, thank you." Hale turned to Kivi and asked, "What do you think?"

Kivi pondered the question for several moments before saying, "I think we should leave someone in the tree line just north of the bridge, so they could engage the bastard if he shoots again while we are moving into position to hit him from behind."

"A good idea. I think having a person in the location you suggest would also give us some insurance against him being able to escape once we start pressuring him from the north." Hale said.

"Interesting. If he tries to run across the river to get away, our man will be able to shoot him." Kivi said.

"I think it should be Lassila that remains here in the tree line." Hale said.

"That makes sense. He's the best shooter we have amongst the enlisted men." Kivi said.

Hale turned to the major and said, "Thank you for your assistance, sir."

Major Fagernas smiled, "Your welcome. I can see why you were given this responsibility."

Curious, Hale asked, "Why is that, sir?"

"Because you took advice when it was offered to you and then added your own ideas to it to make it even better. That's the mark of a good leader." Fagernas said.

Hale beamed at the compliment, *Maybe I'm better at this than I think?*

Hale and Kivi returned to the men at the campfire. Everyone, save the sentry, was asleep. Hale and Kivi circled around the fire, quietly waking their three men so as not to disturb the others. As they started to leave a voice, with a snide tone, pierced the night, "Did you two finally come up with a plan?" Halonen said.

Several of the slumbering forms groaned from the voice, which had been much louder than the crackling and snapping fire. Hale whirled around and snapped, "You disgust me. You have no consideration for anyone around you. What kind of ass, wakes up his weary men, because they can't be bothered to whisper?"

"I'll tell you what kind of ass," Kivi chimed in, "The pompous kind. Do you know what happens to officers like you?"

"No, but I'm sure you're going to tell me." Halonen sneered.

Kivi gave the arrogant lieutenant his best feral grin as he said, "They get a bullet in the back from their own men."

The color drained from Halonen's face as he started to sputter in anger. He took a deep breath to reply, but the sniper group had already disappeared into the trees. Halonen noticed Private Oja grinning and snapped, "Wipe that smile off your face!"

Oja stroked his rifle reverently as he acknowledged the order, "At once, lieutenant."

Chapter 20

Early Morning, One Kilometer North of The Raate Road Near the West Bank of the Purasjoki River, Central Finland

January 5th, 1940

The game trail was right where the major's map said it would be. The group headed roughly a hundred meters north before Hale halted and turned to Lassila, "I need you to head east and set yourself up in the tree line at the edge of the river."

"No, I want to be in on killing this bastard. Can't Cunnar or Korpi be left behind? Why does it have to be me?" Lassila argued.

Hale took a deep breath and let it out slowly. As the steam cloud created by his breath dissipated in front of him the anger that welled up in his guts at Lassila's defiance, began to similarly fade away, "Because you are the best shooter we have other than myself. In fact, you may be the one that gets to kill him if he takes a shot at the men on the bridge while we are getting into position."

"Or if he tries to escape." Kivi added.

Lassila's gaze dropped to the snow, "Alright. I'm sorry

to argue. I know I shouldn't, but I can't contain this feeling of rage within me."

Hale slapped Lassila on the back as he said, "I understand. I've also lost my father to this damn war."

"How did you overcome the anger? The desire to kill all of them."

Cunnar snorted, "I don't think he has. Hale here has sent many Soviets to the afterlife."

"My biggest problem now is trying to live with the guilt." Hale said.

"How can you feel guilty for killing the invaders that killed your father?" Lassila asked.

"I loved my father and mother dearly, but every time I look down my rifle sights and squeeze the trigger, I'm ending the hopes, dreams, and aspirations of my target. As angry as I am with the enemy, killing so many weighs on your soul." Hale replied.

A bullet suddenly zipped by followed a fraction of a second later by the sound of a rifle firing, "Down!" Kivi yelled.

The group threw themselves onto the ground as Hale asked, "That sounded like it came from the north. Did anyone see a muzzle flash?"

Hale's question was met with silence. He rolled over and looked at Kivi, "This has a familiar feel to it."

"Aye, the bastard is using the same plan as the lake. Lure us in with the hopes of putting a bullet into him and set up other snipers to shoot us along the likely paths of approach before we get to close." Kivi agreed.

Lassila, unable to contain the fury within, leaped to his feet. A bullet hurtled by the reckless private, missing him by inches, "Muzzle flash!" Kivi shouted.

"I see it." Hale said as he swung his rifle toward the enemy sniper.

The young lieutenant took a deep breath and held it as he imagined in his mind where the body would lay behind the rifle that made the flash. When he had the image in his mind, he adjusted his aim slightly and fired, "Did you get him?" Cunnar asked.

Suddenly a bullet kicked up snowflakes right next to Hale's left elbow as it slammed into the ground, "Does that answer your question?"

The loud boom of a rifle discharging erupted to Hale's right. Surprised, he turned his head and saw Lassila stepping back behind a tree, smoke lazily curling upward from the end of his rifle barrel. A fraction of a second later, a voice with a Russian accent cried out in surprise as the young Finn's bullet slammed into his left shoulder.

The impact spun the enemy soldier around before he lost his footing and collapsed to the ground, "Nice shooting Lassila!" Hale said, then added, "Stay down, there may be more."

Hale's foresight saved their lives as a second shooter, somewhere to their west fired, "I saw a muzzle flash." Cunnar said.

"Imagine a clock face and that you are sitting at its center." Kivi said, "What direction would the muzzle flash be from us?"

"Ten O'clock!" Cunnar exclaimed.

Hale shifted his head so that he was gazing in the direction that Cunnar had indicated, "I don't see anything. Cunnar, can you use your memory and try to take a shot?"

"Sure, I can try." Cunnar replied.

Cunnar adjusted his rifle barrel so that it pointed toward the muzzle flash he witnessed. Seeing Hale go through this process numerous times, he followed the same steps. First, he lined up his rifle's sights with the flash, held his breath, then pulled the trigger.

"I didn't hear anyone cry out?" Kivi said.

"They don't always do that, especially if it was a kill shot." Hale said, "Sit tight until we know if the Soviet swine is still alive."

Lassila, still using a birch tree to conceal himself, saw the direction of Cunnar's shot. He exposed himself and quickly took aim at the same location, then fired. The enemy sniper responded by putting a bullet into the birch trunk right next to Lassila's head as he was returning to his protected position behind the tree.

Everyone saw the muzzle flash of the enemy sniper, as he tried to take out Lassila. Cunnar fired first, then Korpi, Kivi, and finally Hale, "Surely one of us have hit him?" Cunnar asked.

Hale turned back to Lassila and said, "Get to the river now! If Kuznetsov is the sniper upriver, he might be heading across it right now to ambush us."

"Yes, sir." Lassila replied.

As Lassila started to move toward the river, the very much alive enemy fired a shot at him. Luckily for Lassila, the enemy sniper was firing at movement and didn't have clear sight of him. Once again, the bullet slammed into a tree trunk inches from Lassila's body.

"Sit tight. I'm going to flush this bastard out." Kivi growled.

"Don't move!" Hale urged.

Kivi ignored Hale and came to his feet. As he started to move westward on his skis, the enemy fired his weapon. The bullet slammed into Kivi with a dull smack sound and spun him around like a rag doll before he collapsed to the snow.

"Kivi's down!" Korpi yelled.

Hale again saw the muzzle flash from the enemy that Cunnar had tried to shoot, "Cunnar did you see the flash?"

"Yes." Cunnar replied.

"Good. I need you to aim just like we described before. Imagine there is a body behind the flash. Try to hit that body but hold your fire for now." Hale said, "Korpi did you see it?"

"Yes." Korpi responded.

"I need you to aim as if the soldier that created the muzzle flash was left-handed, "Got it?" Hale asked.

"Understood." Korpi said.

Hale took aim about half a meter above the muzzle flash and said, "Fire!"

Cunnar and Korpi both fired their weapons. Hale waited for one second and then he fired his. The enemy, panicked by the two near misses, jumped to his feet. As he rose, Hale's bullet smashed into his gut and caused him to cry out in pain.

"Hale you got him!" Cunnar exclaimed.

Hale, ignored the praise and crawled over to where Kivi lay, "Where are you hit?"

Kivi groaned and said, "The bastard hit me in the arm."

"Let me see." Hale said.

"It's to bloody cold to take my coat off." Kivi said.

"Do you want to be cold for a few minutes or do you want to bleed to death?" Hale snapped.

"I suppose I'd rather be chilly for a few minutes. What's with the attitude?" Kivi asked, "You're not the one that was shot."

"And neither would you have been if you had followed my orders." Hale snarled, then added, "Remember that promise you made to Colonel Siilasvuo?"

"Yes." Kivi said glumly as he realized where this was going.

"You just broke it." Hale said.

Kivi finished removing his white coat, now stained on the upper right sleeve with his blood. Once the coat was off, Hale took hold of his arm. The bullet had buried itself into Kivi's meaty bicep. Luckily for the big man, the bullet avoided hitting the bone. Exposed to the sub-zero air, the blood quickly froze, which stopped the bleeding, "How's it look?" Kivi asked.

"You'll live, but you'll have to have a medic remove the bullet. Does it feel like you can still use the arm?" Hale asked.

Kivi opened and closed his fist a few times to test the arm. He then picked up his PPD 34 and grimaced, "It hurts like hell, but yes I can still use it."

"Good, because I can't afford to send you back to Fagernas' camp right now to get you patched up." Hale said.

"Can I put my coat back on? You know before the entire arm gets frostbitten and has to be amputated." Kivi said.

"Funny." Hale said, "I need to wrap it first."

Hale dug through his pack until he located his first aid kit. He opened the kit and removed both a bandage and a wrap. He placed the bandage on Kivi's gunshot wound and said, "Hold the bandage in place with a finger."

Hale then applied the wrap to the bandage to hold it in place, "Remove your finger."

After Kivi removed his finger from the bandage, Hale finished wrapping the wound and fastened the wrap in place with a safety pin, "How's that?"

Kivi flexed his right hand a few times and formed a fist. He then reached for his PPD 34 and lifted it off the snow, "A bit better. The pressure from the wrap has reduced the pain some."

"Good. Now you can put your coat back on." Hale said.

Kivi quickly put his coat on and buttoned it up. He turned to Hale and said, "Now what?"

"You three stay here. I'm going to go check to see if Lassila has spotted anything on the river." Hale ordered.

"So, you're about to stand up?" Kivi asked.

"I'm not that stupid. I'm going to take my skis off and crawl." Hale said.

Hale quickly unfastened his boots from the skis. As he worked Kivi rolled over and grabbed his left arm, "Hale?"

"Yes?" Hale replied.

"I let my battle lust get the better of me. I'm sorry I ignored your order." Kivi said.

Hale smiled at the big man as he said, "Just don't do it again, we can't afford to lose you."

Kivi returned the smile and said, "Will do boss."

"There is a time and place for what you do. This wasn't the time, but there will be one in the future. No one strikes fear into our more numerous foes like you and your crazy antics do." Hale said.

Hale turned to Cunnar and Korpi, "Maintain your positions. If the enemy fires and you see their muzzle flashes, return fire and then immediately shift position."

Cunnar and Korpi nodded to acknowledge the order. Hale turned away and crawled eastward toward the river's edge. Progress was slow, but after nearly half an hour of crawling he reached Lassila.

Hearing Hale, Lassila whirled around with his rifle at the ready, "Lassila it's Hale." He hissed.

Lassila relaxed and returned his gaze to the river, "To what do I owe the pleasure?"

"Have you seen anything?" Hale asked.

"Nothing. Is everyone alright? I thought I heard someone cry out." Lassila asked.

"Kivi was hit, but it's not serious." Hale responded.

"Good. I was worried." Lassila said.

Suddenly a yellow flash of light appeared in the area where Hale thought Kuznetsov must be, "There!" Lassila said, excited.

A split second later the sound of a rifle being fired washed over them, along with the cry of someone being hit on the bridge. Lassila took careful aim at the location of the muzzle flash and fired, "Did you get him?" Hale asked.

Before Lassila could respond, a bullet buried itself on the riverbank a few inches from his hands, "Summer of cunts!" Lassila exclaimed.

"Move!" Hale urged as he fired his own weapon in the general direction of the enemy sniper to distract him.

Hale rapidly rolled over several times to try and create some distance from the place he fired his own weapon from. The decoy worked, and the enemy sniper fired again. The bullet slammed into the snow where Hale had been lying when he took his own shot. As he rolled, he operated the bolt on his rifle.

Suddenly a heavy machine gun opened fire. Hale flinched at the sound before he realized it was coming from the bridge, "I think someone on the bridge saw that last muzzle flash!" Lassila exclaimed.

"Get ready, if that's Kuznetsov, that machine gunner

has a very short life expectancy." Hale replied.

No sooner had the words emerged from his lips when both men saw a muzzle flash. The flash was a dozen meters from the position of the first one Lassila had observed. A split-second later, the machine gun fell silent, "I was afraid of that." Hale said.

Both Hale and Lassila made quick mental calculations to determine where the man behind the muzzle flash lay. Lassila fired first and a split second later, Hale followed. The two snipers were not rewarded with the cry of the injured enemy but with heavy machine gun fire aimed at them.

Bullets filled the air around the two men, "Withdraw! It's coming from directly across the river." Hale screamed.

The hail of bullets caused snow to trickle down from the spruce trees above as the trees shook from multiple bullet impacts. Snowflakes on the ground were also hurtling upward as dozens of bullets tore across the snow-covered ground. The barrage suddenly ceased as a brave Finn took up the machine gun on the bridge and fired at the Soviet machine gunner directly across from Hale and Lassila.

"On your feet and run!" Hale ordered.

The two men came to their feet and pushed their way through the nearly waste deep snow as best they could to get some distance between themselves and the riverbank as the two machine gunners exchanged fire. A loud roar suddenly erupted to the east as a cacophony of weapons fire was added to the sound of the two machine guns.

"What is that?" Lassila asked, in-between breaths as he pushed through the snow.

"The sound of the 3rd NKVD attacking the bridge." Hale replied grimly, "Let's stop and get our skis on. Then we turn northward. We have to get back to the riverbank before Kuznetsov kills all of the defenders on the bridge."

Lassila, to out of breath to reply, simply nodded. He followed Hale as he changed direction. Suddenly Kivi appeared in front of them brandishing his PPD 34, "Do you need help?"

"No, but I think the men on the bridge could use some. Go do what you do." Hale said with a grin.

Kivi flashed Hale a toothy grin, "It would be my pleasure."

Kivi set off southward through the trees on his skis. Less than a minute later, their skis now fastened to their boots, Hale and Lassila were heading northward on theirs. They traveled for a minute before Hale said, "Let's get back to the riverbank."

As Hale spoke the words the Finnish heavy machine gun fell silent. The sniper had claimed a second victim on the bridge. The gunfire increased as the remainder of Halonen's platoon engaged the enemy from the western edge of the bridge.

Hale and Lassila, both out of breath, reached the bank of the river, "Use the trees for cover and keep yourself out of sight. The next time the enemy sniper fires, "We'll have him."

The two men waited for the enemy sniper to show themselves as the two opposing sides put up a veritable wall of lead south of them at the bridge. Hale's keen ear was able to discern that Finnish fire was starting to drop off. He glanced at the bridge and saw that the men of the 3rd NKVD had nearly reached the eastern edge of the bridge.

The Finnish defenders on the east side of the bridge had been completely wiped out. A handful of men, including Halonen, who was making a good account of himself with a Suomi submachine gun, lay on the ground at the edge of the bridge's west side. Hale watched, as the Soviets continued to press forward into Finnish fire.

Hale's eyes widened as he saw one of the advancing soldiers stop and swing the heavy machine gun around toward the Finnish defenders, "Keep an eye out for the sniper, I need to help the defenders." Hale said.

Lassila ignored this advice and put a bullet into the enemy machine gunner on the other side of the river. He quickly shifted position as the enemy sniper took a shot at him. Once again, the sniper's bullet buried itself in the snow right where Lassila had been lying moments before.

Simultaneously, Hale centered his sights on the head of the enemy soldier that had shown himself just above the snow wall. The wall, now benefiting the attacking Soviets, had been created by the Finnish defenders to obscure themselves from the enemy sniper. Instead of trying to hit the little bit of head he could see, Hale lowered his aim and centered his sights on where the man's torso should be behind the wall.

As the Red Army soldier squeezed the trigger on the machinegun Hale did the same with his rifle. His bullet covered the distance that separated him from his target in a fraction of a second. The bullet cut through the snow like it wasn't even there and plowed into the Soviet machine gunner. The man cried out in surprise as Hale's bullet slammed into his right side.

Simultaneously, Kivi arrived at the bridge. Seeing the

desperate situation, he unclipped three grenades from his belt and threw them in rapid succession at the attackers. The enemy bottlenecked by the bridge were packed together as they pushed forward toward the west bank of the river. With a loud BOOM-BOOM-BOOM, Kivi's grenades exploded.

The combination of the explosions and the deadly metal fragments that whipsawed through the air from the exploding grenades injured nearly two dozen enemy soldiers. It looked as if a giant scythe had suddenly reached out of the sky and cut down all of the attacking Soviets on the bridge. One moment they were a screaming mass advancing toward victory; the next they were all down screaming in agony.

Kivi then gave a throaty roar and ran right at the attackers, his PPD 34 blazing. The sight of the big man coming at them, along with the surviving Finns, was too much. The remaining enemy attackers turned tail and ran, "Come back and fight you cowards!" Kivi yelled.

Kivi continued to pour fire into the backs of the retreating enemy. He was careful to keep moving across the bridge so as not to present an easy target for the enemy sniper. The sniper, seeing his countrymen break and run, took aim at Kivi and fired.

The big Finn chose at that moment to stop and change out his magazine. The sniper's bullet zipped by in the air, where he would have been if he had kept running, *That was close.* Kivi thought.

Kivi slammed the fresh magazine into place and resumed his charge across the bridge. The enemy sniper fired again at him and again he missed. Kivi didn't slow as he cleared the bridge and kept running eastward. He rounded the bend in the road that had concealed the 3rd

NKVD regiment from sight, prior to their attack and now did so again.

The Soviets had stopped and started to turn around to make a stand. Kivi screamed like a banshee and hosed down the defenders with gunfire. He cut down the first row of enemy soldiers and then turned tail and ran back toward the bridge. The Soviets, realizing they had been driven back by a single man, howled in rage and gave chase.

Hale saw Kivi reappear as the big man ran for all he was worth back across the bridge. Halonen and the handful of surviving Finnish defenders, having been given a respite to reload thanks to Kivi, opened fire on the resurgent Red Army forces. The defenders were careful not to hit Kivi as he made his mad dash toward survival. Hale added his fire to the fight, shooting and reloading as quickly as he could manage.

Suddenly a fearsome war cry erupted from a new location, west of the bridge. Dozens of Finns suddenly burst into view and poured fire into the advancing Soviets as they dashed up the road from the west. Finnish reinforcements had arrived.

In addition to the men attacking from west to east down the road, several dozen Finns stood on the riverbank south of the bridge and poured fire into the enemy. The additional Finnish fire quickly became more than the enemy could bear. The men of the Red Army broke and once again retreated eastward.

Kivi, discerning the change in fortune, turned and emptied the rest of his second magazine into the backs of the retreating enemy soldiers. He remained standing for only a few seconds before he threw himself to the surface of the bridge. The move saved his life as the enemy sniper fired.

The sniper, anticipating Kivi's next action, intentionally aimed low. Luckily for the big man it wasn't low enough. The bullet came so close to him, it tore a piece of fabric from his hood as it rocketed by just above his neck.

Kivi immediately scrambled to his feet and ran forward. As his mental count reached four, he threw himself onto the surface of the bridge. He landed within the area concealed by the snow wall that had been built earlier by Halonen's men. Momentarily safe, he removed his gloves and worked quickly to reload his two empty magazines.

The first time the sniper had fired at Kivi, Lassila saw the muzzle flash. Having learned that the sniper shifted positions after each shot, he tried to guess where the man might be as he changed position and fired. Assuming he had missed, Lassila shifted his position as he saw a fresh muzzle flash come from the location of the enemy sniper, some two hundred and fifty meters to the north of his position.

Lassila fired his weapon, again assuming the wily opposing sniper was on the move. This time he made the assumption that the enemy had moved in the opposite direction to shift his position. In his gut, he knew that this was another miss and moved to a new position.

With the Finns now gaining the upper hand on the bridge, they were careful not to offer the enemy sniper any additional targets. All three snipers stopped firing as they resumed the waiting game. In the midst of the chaos swirling around the bridge, Cunnar turned to Korpi and said, "It sounds like everyone else is busy."

"We should try and take out the sniper ourselves."

Korpi urged.

"I'm not sure that is a good idea." Cunnar said, "If this really is Kuznetsov we're dealing with, we wouldn't have much of a chance against him."

"So, you'd rather just lay here in the snow and let our countrymen die by that bastard's hand?" Korpi asked, incredulously.

"We don't know for sure if we can even stand up without getting shot ourselves. What if there is still a sniper or snipers north of us?" Cunnar asked.

"Then we die knowing we at least tried to do our duty." Korpi said.

Cunnar rolled his eyes, "You know the best piece of advice I've heard so far in this pointless war?"

"What's that?" Korpi asked, growing increasingly annoyed.

"Our goal is to not die for our country but to make the other bastard die for theirs." Cunnar replied, "What can we do to ensure that our risk is minimal?"

"Why did I have to get stuck here with you?" Korpi lamented, "I'm surprised your feet haven't become frostbitten since your boots are filled with piss."

"I'm surprised you're still drawing breath considering how eager you are to be stupid." Cunnar fired back.

"Perhaps there is a middle ground we can entertain?" Korpi suggested.

"Perhaps. What did you have in mind?" Cunnar asked.

"What if we removed our skis and crawled a hundred meters west?" Korpi said, "There shouldn't be anyone looking for us over there."

"Do you know how hard it is to crawl through this snow?" Cunnar asked.

"Does it matter if it enables us to avoid what you are worried about, while putting us in a position to take out that sniper?" Korpi asked.

"I really wish I would have had enough sense to flee into the woods before the damned Soviets showed up and captured my entire village." Cunnar lamented.

"Quit crying over spilt milk and focus on what we can do now." Korpi suggested.

Cunnar sighed, which created a large steam cloud, "Fine, but you go first."

The two men removed their skis and began to crawl westward through the snow. As the shooting died down to the southeast, they reached their goal, "Alright, let's stand up and start moving northward." Korpi said.

Cunnar gestured with his outstretched hand to the north as he said, "Again, you go first."

Korpi rolled his eyes but remained silent. With rifle in hand, he came to his feet. When nothing happened, he removed his skis from his pack and put them on. Cunnar quickly followed suit and within two minutes they were skiing northward.

"I think if we keep making progress at this speed, we should be able to turn eastward in five more minutes." Korpi said.

It was the last action he ever took as a bullet smashed into his chest. The bullet pierced his sternum, severed his spine midway between his neck and waist, then burst out of his back. Luckily for Cunnar he had been skiing slightly to Korpi's left, so the bullet just missed his right arm.

Cunnar threw himself to the ground and looked for a target. His heart sank as he saw two dozen enemy soldiers moving toward him, "Summer of cunts. I knew this was a dumb thing to do." Cunnar cursed, "We just blundered into an enemy flanking force."

The lone Finn centered his sights on the first Soviet's chest and fired. The man went down as the bullet split his heart in half. Cunnar rolled to his left while simultaneously operating the bolt on his rifle, just as he had observed Hale doing in the past.

The move saved his life as several bullets slammed into the ground right where he had just been lying. He quickly took aim at the second Soviet of the group and fired. This man, hit in the gut, went down screaming.

Cunnar rolled again while he worked the bolt on his rifle, narrowly avoiding several bullets fired at him. He took aim at another target. This man was less than ten meters away and fired. He smiled as a third enemy soldier went down. Just as he began to hope that he could drive the enemy back single-handedly he felt a searing pain in his back.

Gasping in agony, Cunnar looked over his shoulder and saw that an enemy soldier had come up behind him and plunged his bayonet into his back, *I guess this is it.* He thought in despair.

The blade had him pinned to the ground. Unable to pull free, he chose sisu over despair and decided to take a few more Russians with him into the afterlife. He took aim at another enemy soldier in front of him and fired. The final shot of his life hit his target in the gut sending the man tumbling to the ground screaming.

With no more bullets to fire, he reached down to his belt and plucked a grenade from it and twisted the cap. He turned his head and smiled up at the man that had slain him, baring his blood stained teeth, "Fuck you!" He yelled with his final breath. In the handful of seconds, he had left, he thought, *We should have listened to Hale.* His life abruptly ended as the grenade exploded.

Hale's head whipped around as he heard a grenade go off about two hundred meters to his northwest, "There shouldn't be anyone fighting in that direction."

Hale withdrew from his position at the riverbank and rapidly skied down to the road, "I need someone with me now!"

"Whose asking? A grizzled old sergeant with three days growth of gray facial hair on his face. Weathered skin that had seen many harsh winters outdoors, and icy blue eyes that conveyed steel within his soul.

"Senior Lieutenant Hale Karhonen. Bring your squad now sergeant!"

"What about the bridge?" The sergeant asked.

"The bridge is secure but there is fighting to the north!" Hale exclaimed.

"Hey, you sluggards on me!" The sergeant yelled.

Seven other privates, nearly as unkempt looking as their sergeant appeared from the woods, "Have your men fall in behind me sergeant and follow." Hale ordered.

"You heard the man, move your asses!" The sergeant yelled.

As Hale set off to investigate the explosion he smiled inwardly and thought, *This guy reminds me of Kivi when he was a sergeant.*

Before Hale made it a half dozen meters, Kivi fell in beside him, "Where are you going?"

"I thought I heard a grenade explosion off to the northwest." Hale said.

Kivi pursed his lips then said, "There shouldn't be anything there but empty forest."

"Exactly." Hale replied.

The group proceeded northwest until Hale saw movement up ahead. He raised his right arm and made a fist, signaling the rest of the group to stop. He kneeled and unslung his rifle from his back. His heart sank as he saw at least a dozen Red Army soldiers pass by.

Hale turned to the sergeant and said, "Sergeant?"

"Anttlia."

"Sergeant Anttlia, there appears to be some enemy soldiers up ahead, I want your men to fan out and form a line running north to south centered on me." Hale ordered.

Anttilla turned around and whispered orders to the next man in line behind him. Within sixty seconds Anttilla squad had fanned out and formed a line, "Now follow me." Hale hissed.

Hale moved forward toward the last location he had

seen the enemy moving. He found several sets of ski tracks heading southward toward the Raate Road and turned to follow them. Anttilla shifted the line so that it formed up around Hale's new direction. The line of Finns now ran east to west, still centered on Hale and Kivi.

Hale rapidly caught up to the less skilled Russian skiers. When the first man came into view, he raised his rifle up, took aim, and shot him in the back without slowing down. As he operated the bolt on his rifle, the enemy force turned to engage him.

Before they realized how many soldiers they were dealing with, Kivi opened up with his PPD 34. Anttilla and his men quickly followed suit with their rifles and the Soviets were quickly cut down by the Finnish fire. As soon as the last man had fallen, Hale moved forward, "Shoot any wounded that still draw breath." Anttilla ordered.

"No!" Hale objected, "Take their weapons away. We'll circle back later to collect them. They might have valuable intelligence."

Several of the enemy still drew breath when the group came upon them. As ordered, though they muttered discontentedly, Anttilla and his men disarmed the wounded. Once the task was completed Hale said, "Now center on me. We are heading north. This group may have attacked someone, and they may be wounded."

Hale reversed course and followed the Soviet's tracks northward. A few minutes later he came upon Cunnar. The grenade that Cunnar used to take his killer with him into the afterlife had separated his torso from his legs. The split had occurred roughly where his lower abdomen was a few inches above his waist. Separating the two pieces of Cunnar was a small crater. The crater was partially filled with the remains of Cunnar's innards that hadn't been vaporized when the grenade exploded.

Draped across Cunnar's lower half was the man that had slain him with the bayonet. His rifle had been blown free by the grenade explosion and was no longer in Cunnar's back. The weapon lay in the snow about half a meter away, blackened by the explosion. The rifle's bayonet was covered in Cunnar's frozen blood. The surrounding snow was stained red with blood from both men. A few meters in front of the slain Finn were the corpses of two dead Russians.

Hale knelt down next to Cunnar's remains, "Another life lost to this senseless conflict." He lamented.

"Do you know this man?" Anttilla asked.

Hale nodded, "He was a member of my squad."

"He must have been a warrior with great sisu. It appears that he took three of the bastards with him into the afterlife." Anttilla observed.

Kivi started to laugh but stifled it so that it sounded more like a choke. Anttilla turned to the big Lieutenant and said, "Now is not the time to mourn. Though he has been avenged, there is more yet to do."

"Here's another body." One of the privates shouted.

Kivi ignored Anttilla and went over to the private who found the body. He looked down at it and said, "It's Korpi."

"Summer of cunts." Hale cursed, "Why were they this far west? I ordered them to stay put."

"If they had followed those orders the enemy platoon

would have launched a surprise attack into Fagernas' northern flank. These two saved a lot of lives by putting up enough of a fight to alert you." Kivi observed.

Hale sighed and nodded, "I suppose so, but—"

"But nothing! Men die in war. These two made a decision based on a change in circumstance and lives were saved because of it. They should each be commended." Kivi roared, "Now pull your head out of your ass and let's go get that damn sniper."

Anttilla gave Kivi a sidelong glance as he thought, *I think I'm going to like this fellow.*

"You're right." Hale said.

"Of course, I'm right! Let's go get the bastard that has killed so many of our men and put a stop to this shit once and for all!" Kivi demanded.

Anttilla, delighted, turned to Kivi and said, "Begging your pardon, sir, but you sound more like a sergeant than a lieutenant."

Kivi laughed, "That's because I've spent the last ten years as a sergeant."

"You're my kind of officer, sir. Do you mind if we stick with you?" Anttilla asked.

"We'll we could certainly use the men considering what just happened to Cunnar and Korpi." Hale said.

"Of course, you can stay with us. I wouldn't want a fine sergeant like you getting assigned to that idiot Halonen. At least when we lose men, we have something to show for it!" Kivi said.

"If we had been assigned to Halonen as a replacement for the men lost on the bridge, I fear the lieutenant would not have been long for this world." Anttilla said.

"What makes you say that?" Hale asked in confusion.

"Because I would have put a bullet into his scrawny little ass, the first chance I got, that's why." Anttilla said.

Kivi and the seven privates laughed, "Do you plan on putting a bullet in me?" Hale asked.

Anttilla made a show of thinking the question over before responding, "I'm not sure. So far you seem like you have a decent amount of sense and unlike Halonen you get your hands dirty. You keep doing what you're doing, and I'll follow you through the gates of hell."

"Glad to hear it. Fall in behind me. We're going to hunt down the sniper that has killed so many on the bridge." Hale said.

Hale set off northward. He followed the tracks left by the Soviet skis. After fifty meters or so, the tracks turned eastward, "It looks like they started to head south here. We're roughly two to three hundred meters west of the sniper's suspected location, so we'll continue following the tracks."

Hale, with Kivi, Anttilla and his men following, headed eastward. The group reached the river without incident. The Purasjoki River had been frozen solid since November. The river's ice was buried in nearly a meter of snow.

Hale raised his arm up and formed a fist. He then removed his skis and slid them into the loops on his pack that enabled him to carry them on his back while walking. Next, he got down on his chest, and crawled to the edge of the river. Kivi and Anttilla followed suit.

The ski tracks left by the enemy platoon led to the east bank of the river. From this vantage point, north of the river bend, the bridge was not visible. The trio observed for a time until they were certain there were no enemies hidden on the other side waiting to greet them.

"It looks clear. Let's go ahead and cross." Hale said.

The group crossed the Purasjoki River single file. They reached the other side without incident. Hale turned to Anttilla, "Just south of us is a ridge line that will keep us out of sight of the enemy sniper. I believe he is positioned right where the river turns westward."

"How would you like us to approach?" Anttilla asked.

This man knows his business. Kivi thought.

"When we get to the ridgeline, I want you and your men to form a line on me. Then crawl to the top. If we don't see the sniper at that point, we'll move forward." Hale said.

"What if we flush him out and he flees across the river?" Anttilla asked.

"I have a man positioned to the south that will take him out if he tries that." Hale said.

Anttilla smiled broadly, "An officer that knows his business. Who would have figured?"

"Let's go." Hale ordered.

They found the ridgeline a hundred meters to their south. As ordered, Anttilla's men fanned out, centered on Hale until they formed a line. They then proceeded to crawl up the ridgeline until they were able to see what was on the other side.

The terrain below the ridgeline sloped downward toward the river which lay fifty meters away, but there was no sign of an enemy sniper. Disappointed, Hale started to crawl southward, *Hopefully he's still here and we just need to flush him out.*

As they drew near to the river, Kivi whispered to Hale, "One of Antilla's men found where the bastard was likely firing from. He found some brass shell casings. There are a set of tracks that lead eastward away from the spot."

Hale sighed, "Once again Kuznetsov has given us the slip."

"I wouldn't give up just yet. We should follow the tracks." Kivi suggested.

"Alright." Hale agreed.

The group removed their skis from the loops on their packs designed to hold them and fastened them to their feet. Hale, still in the lead, started to move slowly eastward following the tracks left by the enemy sniper that was presumably Kuznetsov.

Chapter 21

Dusk, Three Hundred Meters North of the bridge over the Purasjoki River, Central Finland

January 4th, 1940

Kuznetsov pulled a map out of his coat pocket. The map, far more accurate than anything issued to the Red Army, had been looted off the corpse of a Finnish soldier. He peered down at the paper in the fading light of the day, *I should be right about here.* He thought.

The map showed him to be a few hundred meters east of the Purasjoki River. He removed a glove and pinched the skin, on his forehead, just above his nose as he thought, *Trying to read this Finnish script makes my head hurt.*

Of interest to him was a bend in the river, about three hundred meters north of the bridge, *If this map is correct, I should be able to look right down the river and have visibility on the bridge the Finns just captured.* Kuznetsov thought gleefully.

The Soviet sniper smiled at the thought of how easy it would be to kill Finns if the map was correct. He changed his direction and started to head southwest, toward the bend in the river indicated on the map. As he neared the location, he came upon a small ridgeline, *This gets better and better. Thanks to this small ridge the only direction the Finns will be able to see me is from the south.*

Kuznetsov started to whistle a jaunty tune he had heard on the radio recently. The music was a tune he heard on the last day he was with his family and made him smile. On that early December day, he had been driving his wife and infant son into town. The Soviet sniper school, where he had been an instructor up until the first week in December was located at a secret location in the Ural Mountains. To keep morale up, the school provided a car and a full tank of gas to each instructor once per month to travel to the nearest town, or anywhere else they desired to go, *A good life ruined by Stalin and his stupidity.*

It was an uncommon privilege in a country where movement was severely restricted. His mind slid back to that day. Kuznetsov's left hand held the steering wheel, his right hand rested on his wife's leg. The car's powerful heater had warmed the interior of the vehicle so much, they had removed their coats and tossed them onto the back seat. His wife, Anna, sat on the bench seat to his right and held their infant son in her arms.

The car was one of the newer Model As that the Ford Plant in Nizhny had built. That plant had been constructed under license in the Soviet Union. The Ford Motor Company had sent engineers and foreman to oversee the construction of the plant and to teach the Soviet workers how to operate the assembly line.

This marvelous car, a product of that assembly line, had its very own wireless, a wonder of technology almost unheard of in the Soviet Union. The shortwave radio receiver had been tuned to a channel playing big band tunes from the United States. Kuznetsov smiled as he remembered how perfect that moment was.

He frowned and his mood turned sour as he thought,

The very next day I was given orders to this frozen hell.

Kuznetsov pushed the memories away and focused on the present. He took a deep breath and exhaled, which created a large cloud of steam that seemed to hover around his head. The steam cloud seemed to hang around his head for a few moments before it faded away.

Using his ski poles he pushed his way to the top of the small ridgeline and looked down. Below him, the land sloped downward towards the bank of the Purasjoki River. This snow-covered piece of Finnish forest looked much like every other piece of forest he had the privilege of navigating through during the last month, *Why on earth is that idiot Stalin trading blood for this desolate land? Don't the people of the Soviet Union have enough frozen forests already? Then there is the matter of the foolish purges. The experienced generals those idiot commissars executed would have never wasted the technologically advanced 44th Division on this backward primordial pit. Even the party hacks promoted into the generalships should have a basic understanding of where to employ a motorized rifle division! Sending the 44th here is simply unforgiveable. We could have used this division to crush the Japanese and wrest Manchuria from them, or even against the Germans when their backs are turned to us. Such a waste.* He thought.

Kuznetsov's eyes fell on a log that lay roughly in the center of this small piece of land next to the river. He smiled and headed over to the log. Using his keen eyes, he peered down river, through the leafless trees, at the bridge, *This spot will do nicely.* He thought.

The veteran sniper dropped his ski poles, removed his skis, and set them aside. The imperfect tree trunk's curvature had created a gap between the ground and the bottom of the log. He went to work on the log pushing snow into the opening between the ground and the bottom of the fallen tree.

There that should do it. He thought.

Using his gloved hands, he then piled snow on top of the log to create a small wall. Again, using his hands, he created several divots in the snow just large enough to hold his rifle. Across the length of the ten-meter log, he was able to create four separate firing positions. Finally, he cleared out the snow immediately behind the log and used it to fashion a second wall, this one facing northward toward the ridge, to conceal him from that direction, *The ridgeline concealing my back is nice, but it never hurts to have a little extra insurance. The few seconds this wall might buy me could be the difference between survival and death.*

Kuznetsov looked over his handwork and smiled, *An excellent firing position.* He thought.

The veteran sniper picked up his rifle, chose the center firing position, and set his rifle within the divot he had created. He observed the bridge until a target presented itself. He didn't have long to wait.

Kuznetsov took a deep breath, held it, and placed the crosshairs of his scope upon the target. He observed the gait of the Finnish soldier for a few seconds before deciding on how much to lead him. The veteran sniper made that adjustment and pulled the trigger.

The peaceful silence of the forest was shattered by the loud boom of his rifle. Three hundred meters away, his target went down. Kuznetsov quickly shifted to another position. As he did so, he spotted a muzzle flash about a hundred meters north of the bridge. A split-second later a bullet slammed into a tree immediately behind where he had just fired from. He paused in mid-move, worked the action on his rifle and fired at the muzzle flash.

Kuznetsov then, finished shifting to his next prepared

position. It wasn't long before another target presented itself. This man wore a white armband around his left arm with a large red cross emblazoned upon it, *A medic.* Kuznetsov thought, *I must not have killed my first target.*

He saw another muzzle flash a few meters from the first on the west bank of the river. A bullet hurtled centimeters from his head, *Whoever that sniper is has some skill. Is Karhonen here?*

Kuznetsov waited nearly a minute while the Finnish medic worked frantically on his first victim, trying to save his life. Deciding it had been long enough, he took careful aim at the medic. Usually, he preferred to aim for center mass as it was harder to miss, but he wanted to make a statement. A message that would instill fear into the Finns holding the bridge. A message to abandon all hope, *This is what I crave. The power of life and death. All that you are now, and all that you could be is mine to take.* He thought.

Kuznetsov carefully centered his scope's crosshairs on the medic's head. When the man stopped moving for a moment, he pulled the trigger, *The decision is made.*

It was the last moment of the man's life. The bullet hit the Finn in the forehead killing him. The medic's corpse collapsed onto Kuznetsov's first victim, *That shot went a little high, I was aiming at his mouth.* Kuznetsov thought.

Again, he shifted position. Then waited for his next opportunity. While he waited the light of the day completely faded away and darkness shrouded the land. Thanks to the low ambient light, he was unable to see what was happening on the bridge. He checked his watch, which read four thirty PM, *The moon should be up in a few hours. I should be able to see again once it rises above the horizon.*

Kuznetsov, using his entrenching tool, shoveled snow

until a small chamber was formed. Task complete, he crawled into the small space that would shelter him from the winds and keep him warm enough so that he could sleep. Within seconds of closing his eyes, his exhausted body surrendered to the bliss of slumber.

He awoke a few hours later to the sound of a wolf howling in the distance. Hearing the wolf, he smiled, *There's more than one predator in the woods tonight.* He thought.

Kuznetsov turned his head to look through the opening in the dugout. The silvery glow of the moonlight reflected off the snow-covered surface, *Time to go to work.* He thought.

He crawled out of his crude dugout and set himself up in one of the two positions he hadn't fired from yet. The moonlight reflected off the snow creating a glittering effect that amplified the light. This effect made it possible to see several hundred meters, despite the lack of sunlight. Kuznetsov peered into the scope and frowned, *It looks like they fashioned a wall made of snow, to obscure my view.* He thought with amusement, *It won't save them.*

The veteran sniper, despite the discomfort of the temperature, remained completely still as he watched and waited. About thirty minutes later he was rewarded when one of the men hiding behind the snow wall stood to stretch. It was the last action the man ever took in this life.

Kuznetsov held his position, confident that no one on the bridge had seen his muzzle flash. The shot stirred up the men hidden behind the snow wall. The men that held the eastern end of the bridge against his countrymen, *The men that needed to die if the Red Army was going to take that bridge.* He thought.

The wily Soviet counted at least five men sheltering behind the barrier as they briefly stuck their heads up one by one in an attempt to see where he was hiding. He ignored the opportunities to take a shot and continued to wait, *Time to let the tension build some.* He thought.

An hour later, six men walked across the bridge toward the defensive position on the east side. During that hour, the five Finns holding the bridge anxiety built as they thought about dying to the hidden sniper, *Shift change?* Kuznetsov wondered.

He decided to let the men change places unmolested. The five surviving men, started to walk toward the western side of the bridge. *Presumably to a warm meal and some sack time*, Kuznetsov thought.

He waited until all, but the last man had disappeared from sight before he pulled the trigger. He hit his target on the right side of his torso causing him to fall to his knees where he swayed unsteadily for several seconds. Kuznetsov finished him off with a second shot that hit his chest.

The second bullet instantly killed the Finn and he collapsed into the snow. Kuznetsov quickly worked the bolt on his rifle suspecting one of the man's companions would risk trying to pull him to safety, he was correct. Again, Kuznetsov's rifle boomed. The new Finn, killed instantly, collapsed onto the man he had risked himself to rescue.

Four hours passed with no Finnish activity on the bridge. As midnight approached, he noticed some activity behind the snow wall, *Getting antsy or is it shift change again?*

Kuznetsov was given his answer when the six Finns behind the snow wall suddenly jumped to their feet and started to run toward the western edge of the bridge. Simultaneously, the six men assigned to relieve them, dashed eastward across the bridge. He quickly chose a target and fired. The man he targeted went down.

Kuznetsov operated the action on his rifle as quickly as he could. Ready to shoot, he chose another target. Again, he didn't miss, and the Finn went down. By the time he worked the action on his rifle a third time, the Finns had finished their shift change.

Kuznetsov panned slowly over the bridge with his scope. The bodies of his four victims were fully visible in the moonlight, *I'm guessing it will be a while before they show themselves again.* He thought in amusement.

He leaned his rifle up against the log, and pulled out a ration tin that he had secreted inside his coat prior to going to sleep. Over time, his body heat had thawed the stew within. He used his can opener and quickly drained the contents of the tin, lest it freeze on him before he finished, *Cold stew sure beats no stew.* He thought.

The thought made him think about the plight of his countrymen trapped within the mottis, *Poor bastards. Sentenced to die in this God forsaken wilderness because our officers are idiots.* He thought.

Several hours passed with no sign of anything moving on the bridge. Suddenly a rifle shot to the southwest startled him. He shifted his gaze in that direction and wondered, *Who is over there? 3rd NKVD? I really wish they would have let me known they were going to be in the area before I left their headquarters.* He thought in annoyance, *I shared my plan with their colonel. Why couldn't they reciprocate? Now we are going to step on each other's toes. Or worse, I could mistake one of them for a Finn.*

Over the next several minutes the veteran sniper observed several muzzle flashes as the two sides exchanged fire. Assuming the Finns were the southernmost group closest to the road, Kuznetsov used his scope to try and identify a target. He thought he heard a voice cry out, but he wasn't sure.

Unfortunately, he was unable to see anyone through the barriers provided by dozens of spruce trees and the trunks of the birch trees intermixed with them. Suddenly, a large amount of weapons fire erupted to the south. Kuznetsov's eyes were drawn back to the bridge as he watched soldiers of the 3rd NKVD Regiment attempt to storm the bridge and capture it.

Fearing that he would reveal his position to the Finnish group to his southwest, he decided to observe the battle without participating. One by one, his countrymen killed the six Finnish defenders on the bridge. After the last one fell, they moved forward onto the structure.

The assault was halted when another group of Finns, not visible to Kuznetsov from his position, opened fire on the attackers. The 3rd NKVD stood their ground for nearly a minute as the two sides exchanged fire. Suddenly three explosions erupted within the ranks of the attackers. This shattered their morale and they fled eastward into the forest.

His fleeing countrymen were pursued by a lone Finn who screamed like a banshee as he ran across the bridge, *I recognize that madman, the one they call Kivi.*

Without breaking stride, the large Finn poured fire into the backs of the 3rd NKVD soldiers. Kuznetsnov, finally seeing a target, peered into his scope and tried to center the man in his crosshairs.

The big Finn proved to be to fast and he disappeared from the bridge as he continued to pursue the fleeing Soviets. A few moments later, the yelling stopped, some automatic weapon's fire ensued, and the man reappeared on the bridge running from east to west. Again, the big Finn proved to be to fast and Kuznetsov was unable to line up a shot.

A few minutes passed and once again rifle fire erupted in the forest to Kuznetsov's southwest, *What the hell is going on?*

He heard someone cry out. A few more shots were exchanged, and then someone else cried out in pain. Then another rifle was fired and finally a grenade exploded before the area fell silent once again. A brief flash of yellow from the exploding grenade illuminated the surrounding trees for a moment and then disappeared.

Kuznetsov again used his scope to try and identify a target in the forest. Again, a combination of the trees and distance defeated his efforts, and he was unable to pick anyone out. He swung his scope back to the bridge to ensure nothing was happening there. A dozen Soviet corpses had joined the Finns that had fallen on the bridge. There was no movement amongst the fallen.

Things remained silent for roughly five minutes before a combination of automatic and rifle fire erupted. This time the exchange was further south close to the road on the Finnish side of the river. This fight was far enough away that he was unable to even see the muzzle flashes from the opposing sides as they poured fire into each other.

The forest around this river is becoming far to busy for my tastes. Time to leave. Kuznetsov thought.

He took one last look at the firing position he had crafted and smiled, *It's a shame to leave it.* He thought as he slung his rifle onto his shoulder. He spent nearly a minute pondering his next move, *I don't think anyone knows precisely where I am at. Should I try heading south down the river?*

Kuznetsov shook his head as he thought about all of the things that could happen if he exposed himself with so many enemy soldiers nearby, *No the best thing for me to do is to head east. Maybe I can circle around the 3rd NKVD and come up from the south?*

Chapter 22

Early Morning, Finnish 9th Division HQ, Three Kilometers South of Suomassalmi, Central Finland,

January 5th, 1940

Colonel Hjalmar Siilasvuo stared at the counters on his map. The four task forces under his command Mandelin, Makiniemi, Kari, and Fagernas were represented on the map by several wooden tiles. Each tile equated to a battalion of Finnish soldiers. The pitifully few tiles of Finns surrounded the much more numerous tiles representing the units of the 44th Division. His mind filled with doubt as Siilasvuo wondered, Will *the attack work?*

The colonel's eyes drifted to the eastern edge of the map where a tile representing a new Soviet force, a battalion of the 3rd NKVD Regiment had come into contact with Task Force Fagernas. According to a report from Major Fagernas, the bridge over the Purasjoki River had first come under harassing sniper fire yesterday afternoon. Then a few hours after sundown, the 3rd NKVD assaulted the bridge and nearly succeeded in taking it.

The loss of the bridge would have been a major blow to their efforts of isolating the 44th from the supplies and reinforcements available from the Soviet Union, *I wonder if the troublesome sniper was Kuznetsov?*

Reports had been trickling in from Hale Karhonen's sniper group. The group had engaged enemy snipers on several occasions in the vicinity of the Raate Road. According to Major Kari, Karhonen's group was responsible for preventing the two separate mottis in his area from successfully linking back up. Though Karhonen's squad was small, they had fearlessly charged into battle and were instrumental in averting defeat, *I had hoped to just keep the 44th surrounded and starve them out but with the appearance of the 3rd NKVD and Fagernas nearly losing that bridge I'm afraid I have to waste lives on more decisive action to eliminate the 44th before the Soviets are able to break through.*

Siilasvuo glanced at his watch and exhaled sharply. Major Valli put a reassuring hand on his shoulder, "It will be fine. The Soviets trapped in the mottis are cold, starving, and running low on ammunition. The attack you have planned will push them over the edge and break them."

Siilasvuo smiled at his portly adjutant, "I hope you are right. I wish I knew I was sending men to their deaths to bring victory and not just wasting them. We have few enough as it is. With no prospect of further reinforcements each man is precious." The colonel glanced down at his watch and said, "It's time."

As if on cue the two men heard the rumble of distant artillery fire. Siilasvuo's eyes fell to the map. Task Force Mandelin, attacking the largest motti from the south was the likely source for the distant fire. On the northern side of the road, Task Force Makiniemi had orders to attack southward. Between the two forces he hoped to crush the largest motti. The motti he believed held General Vinogradov, commander of the 44th Division lay near the village of Hauklia.

To the east, Task Force Kari had divided his men into two attack forces. He had orders to attack both the motti that lay east of the Hauklia sector that sat between his force and Mandelin/Makiniemi and the group of Soviets hemmed in by Major Fagernas. Siilasvuo hoped that this attack would keep that motti from trying to breakthrough to Vinogradov while Mandelin and Makiniemi were attacking, "We could lose it all if this attack goes badly." Siilasvuo observed.

"The attack will succeed. The Soviets are breaking I can feel it." Major Valli said trying to reassure his commanding officer.

Siilasvuo smiled, "I wish I had your confidence."

"Do you trust our soldiers?" Valli asked.

Siilasvuo nodded, "I do."

"Do you trust the officers that lead them?" Valli asked.

"Most definitely." Siilasvuo replied, "Our officers are top notch. Especially when compared to the party hacks commanding the Soviet forces."

"Then you should trust in their ability to bring victory." Valli argued.

"I do trust them, but there are so many Soviets and so few of our men. Even though we are now considered a division by high command, saying it is so doesn't change reality. Vinogradov's division still outnumbers us three to one." Siilasvuo countered.

Valli chuckled, "That may have been true a week ago, but I imagine the ratio is much closer to even now."

"Perhaps." Siilasvuo agreed, a grin tugged at his lips, "We have been slaughtering them."

"And remember, our forces are well equipped and experienced to deal with the cold and the deep snow. Unlike the poor fools of the 44th. The idiot Soviet High Command sent their men to this desolate wilderness without adequate clothing, or provisions for these temperatures. Plus, these Ukrainians are unused to operating in deep snow. The combination of these factors ensures this division has no ability to move off the road. I bet you half of the 44th's men have frozen or starved to death at this point." Valli said.

"What about the recent supply drop by the Red Air Force into Vinogradov's motti?" Siilasvuo argued.

"A pittance. Most of what was dropped fell into the forest and were recovered by our men. The Soviet rations recovered by our forces were disgusting and they discarded them. Surely, the poor bastards will break their teeth on whatever hardtack managed to fall within their lines." Valli said.

Siilasvuo picked up a piece of the hardtack that had been recovered from one of the drops and brought to him. He turned the hard biscuit over in his hands. Seeking an escape, the motion caused a weevil to break the surface of the rock-hard piece of bread, "On that we agree. I'd have to be starving before I would consider eating this disgusting, bug infested biscuit."

Lieutenant Colonel Makiniemi paced nervously around the campaign table and wood burning stove that occupied the center of his command tent. The sound of nearby gunfire filled the air as his men attacked the largest Soviet motti. In-between the nearly constant noise emanating from the battle you could occasionally hear the rumble of artillery fire.

To even the odds against the enemy tanks, Makiniemi had instructed the crews manning his six precious pieces of artillery to take a page from the 19th Century's artillery manual and use them as direct fire weapons on the enemy armor. The necessity of using artillery as direct fire weapons had fallen by the wayside with the advent of the modern French 75mm cannon in the late 19th Century. From that point artillery was kept at a distance from the front lines of the battlefield and fired in arcs at the forces of the opposing army. The 9th Division's lack of anti-tank guns forced them to resurrect the practice.

A runner suddenly appeared in the entryway of the tent, "Report!" Makiniemi snapped.

"Our initial attack has been a success, sir. The Soviets have been pushed out of the forest just to the south of the Raate road." The runner, a nervous young private said.

"Casualties?" Makiniemi demanded.

"Light thus far." The runner replied.

"Then tell Captain Koivisto to continue the attack." Makiniemi ordered.

The private stiffened to attention, saluted, and left the tent. Makiniemi turned to the map on the campaign table in the center of his headquarters tent. He poured himself a cup of coffee and took a sip. He then set the tin cup down and slid several tiles representing Soviet forces onto the road from the forest immediately south of the road. He picked up the cup, took another sip, and then one by one moved the tiles representing his forces to the edge of the road.

General Alexei Ivanovich Vinogradov's head swam in the blissful numbness of alcohol. He gazed at the bottle of vodka which sat on a table in front of him. The bottle swayed back and forth in his vision, and he felt as if he were floating. Feeling at peace he let the bliss of unconsciousness take him.

As Vinogradov slipped towards oblivion, his muddled thoughts were interrupted by nearby gunfire. He groaned at the noise and cracked an eye open. None of his officers were present in his small mobile command post. He exhaled in frustration creating a large steam cloud which floated in the air for a few seconds as he thought, *The heater is off. I guess the truck has exhausted its petrol supply.*

A radio, sitting on a small campaign table wedged in a corner of the small mobile command post, which sat immediately to the general's right, suddenly crackled to life. Corporal Yuki Pavlovich, Vinogradov's radio operator acknowledged the call by transmitting, "Da?"

"This is Lieutenant Koval, commander of the 2nd Regiment 3rd Battalion."

"Go ahead." Pavlovich replied.

"My battalion is under massive attack from both the north and the south. I need reinforcements." Koval replied.

Corporal Pavlovich turned to Vinogradov, who was taking a drink from his nearly empty bottle of vodka, "General, Lieutenant Koval of the 2nd Regiment's 3rd Battalion is requesting reinforcements. What should I tell him?"

Vinogradov slammed the bottle down on the table in front of him and glared at Pavlovich, "Why is a mere lieutenant bothering me?"

"Lieutenant Koval, this is HQ, where is Major Rudenko? Over." Pavlovich said.

"Dead." Koval replied.

"What about the company commanders?" Vinogradov croaked.

"Is there no captain left in the regiment to command? Over." Pavlovich transmitted.

"They're dead too." Koval replied.

Pavlovich turned back to Vinogradov, "Si—"

"Yes, yes, I heard. All dead. Tell Koval he should radio comrade Stalin regarding his request for reinforcements." Vinogradov said with a chuckle.

"I can't tell him that. The commissars will shoot you." Pavlovich warned.

"They would have to be able to reach us first. Besides, at this point they would be doing me a favor." Vinogradov said.

"Lieutenant Koval. The general respectfully requests that you radio Comrade Stalin for reinforcements. Over." Pavlovich transmitted.

"Has the general gone mad? That's his damn job." Koval screamed into the radio. The sound of gunfire could be heard in the background.

Suddenly a series of loud booms mostly drowned out the nearly continuous sound of gunfire. A split second later, several explosions erupted in the trees just south of the Raate Road. The blasts were close enough that Vinogradov was able to feel the vibrations of each individual detonation.

"If you can't send me reinforcements, then I need permission to withdraw from the trees south of the road. The Finns are slaughtering my men!" Koval demanded.

"Permission granted." Vinogradov said, then added, "And tell him to stop bothering me."

Corporal Pavlovich's mouth dropped open at Vinogradov's complete lack of concern at Koval's deteriorating situation, "General, those men out there are dying for the Motherland you should respect their sacrifice and do your damn job!"

Vinogradov's head whipped around. His already flushed cheeks took on a deep crimson hue as his eyes narrowed and his nostrils flared at the corporal's words, "I should do my job? I SHOULD DO MY JOB? How dare you corporal! I did my job and commanded my division to move into this God forsaken frozen hell at the insistence of that hairy mustached gorilla in Moscow! And look what that has gotten me!"

Vinogradov's anger suddenly abandoned him and he started to sob, "Look what it got me." He whispered.

Pavlovich keyed the mic on his radio and said, "Lieutenant Koval, permission to withdraw from the forest granted. Establish a defensive line on the edge of the road and hold."

Vinogradov jumped to his feet. He swayed for several moments trying not to lose his balance. He managed to stay on his feet but was overcome by a wave of nausea. Unable to recover, he started to wretch uncontrollably as he hunched over and vomited onto his boots.

After nearly a minute, he stopped, stood erect, and glared at Corporal Pavlovich, "How dare you give an order as if it came from me!"

The Corporal came to his feet and turned toward Vinogradov, "What choice did you give me? Our men are dying out there and all you want to do is drink vodka and puke on yourself!"

Vinogradov, enraged, started to paw at his holster, "Why you disrespectful little peasant. I'm going to!" Vinogradov looked down in confusion at his pistol holster.

"Looking for this?" Pavlovich asked as he held up Vinogradov's pistol.

"You stole my gun!" Vinogradov shouted in rage, as he took a step forward.

"No, I picked it up off the floor the last time you dropped it and passed out. Drunken buffoons shouldn't have firearms. I think you were debating whether to use it on yourself or not when the vodka overcame you. Clearly you don't remember." Pavlovich countered.

"You little shit! I will kill you with my bare hands!" Vingradov declared.

He started to move toward Pavlovich, but his feet got tangled up in an empty chair. The disoriented general lost his balance, collapsed to the floor, and promptly passed out, "Good riddance." Pavlovich said as he spat on the General's unconscious form.

The radio suddenly crackled to life once more, it was Lieutenant Koval, "Command post this is 2nd Regiment's 3rd Battalion over."

Pavlovich glanced over at the General's unconscious form and rolled his eyes, "Pathetic."

The Corporal sighed and then keyed the mic, "This is Division HQ, go ahead."

"I established a defensive line on the edge of the road, and we are holding but there is another problem. Over." Koval said.

"Please advise the nature of your problem. Over." Pavlovich replied.

"We are now under attack from the north side of the road. My men can't hold a five-meter-wide perimeter against two attacking forces from opposite directions. Over." Koval said.

Again, Pavlovich glanced over at Vinogradov's unconscious form. The General had started to snore, "You must hold Koval. There's nowhere to retreat to. Over." Pavlovich advised.

"You ask the impossible. Over." Koval countered.

"I would think that the lines being so close together would enable your men to fight in both directions. Over." Pavlovich replied.

"Very well HQ. I would suggest locking your door. You're going to have company soon." Koval replied with clear irritation in his voice.

"Understood, lieutenant. Over." Pavlovich replied.

Captain Lassila gazed at the Raate Road through his binoculars. The primitive road, little more than a trail really, was choked with Soviet vehicles of all shapes and sizes that stretched from horizon to horizon. The road was surrounded by a snow covered, frozen forest that provided excellent cover for the Finns.

He frowned as he saw the soldiers of the 44th stand firm against his southward attack, *Why aren't they breaking? They are being attacked from both sides of the road and are literally fighting back-to-back to keep from being overrun.*

Lassila lowered his binoculars and decided to move up and check in with his platoon commanders. As the captain neared the front line, the fighting started to ebb off. He saw a man on a stretcher apparently giving orders to several runners as they came and went.

Lassila walked up to the man and recognized him. It was Sergeant Manner, "Why are you giving orders to all three platoons sergeant?"

"Because the lieutenants are dead, captain." Manner replied.

"I see. It looks like you were wounded yourself. You should report to the aid station and have your injuries tended to." Lassila said.

Manner smiled up at Lassila, his teeth were covered in blood, "There's no need, captain. I find it much easier to breathe with two extra holes in my chest."

"Be that as it may, I wouldn't want you dying on me. Without the lieutenants you're more valuable than ever. I'll take it from here sergeant. Why don't you get the doctors to patch you up and when you come back, I'll make you a lieutenant." Lassila pointed to two nearby privates, "You and you, take the sergeant here to the aid station."

"You don't have to do that, sir but I appreciate the sentiment. Hell, I'd want to come back and kill these bastards even if you busted me down to private and I had to pay you for each Bolshevik I sent to hell." Manner said.

"That man is one of a kind." Lassila said to no one in particular as the sergeant was carried away.

The two men moved quickly to pick up Manner's stretcher and carry him northward away from the conflict. The fighting had subsided as the two sides settled into their new positions. Lassila gazed through his binoculars at the narrow strip of roadway that the Soviets still controlled. He saw a young Red Army lieutenant giving orders, *There's a rare sight in the Red Army, a competent officer. To bad Karhonen isn't here. I could use a sniper right now. That man appears to be the only reason we didn't break through.*

Lassila shifted his gaze to the other side of the road trying to see the other attacking force from Task Force Makiniemi. Not seeing a single Finn visible, he smiled as he thought, *They are well hidden.*

Lassila walked up and down the line, careful to stay low and use the trees to keep himself out of sight, lest he end up like his lieutenants. He ordered the surviving men of his three platoons to dig in and hold. Once he was satisfied that the line was stabilized, he withdrew to the north, *I need to report the failure of our attack to Major Mandelin.*

Lassila covered the kilometer that separated himself from Major Mandelin's command post in ten short minutes. The guard standing in front of the tent recognized him and nodded in respect as saluting was not allowed this close to the enemy. Lassila pushed the entry flap aside and stepped into the tent. The inviting warmth of the interior surrounded him and felt like a loving embrace.

The major looked up from the map table and frowned, "Yes, captain?"

"The attack failed. We were unable to take the road and further divide the enemy forces." Lassila replied.

"That's unfortunate." Mandelin replied.

"The section of the road we attacked, has a competent officer giving orders. As I watched he was able to stabilize the enemy's lines." Lassila said.

"A competent Soviet officer? This would be the first I've heard of such a thing." Mandelin said.

"And unfortunately, he is positioned right where we attacked." Lassila said.

"Good officers have a knack of being in the right place at the right time. So, you think another attack in the same location would be fruitless?" Mandelin asked.

"I do." Lassila replied.

Mandelin slowly nodded as he pondered, "Why don't

you take the reserve company and hit them a hundred meters further to the east. Perhaps they'll be softer there."

"What about Makiniemi's men? If we are going to attack, shouldn't we coordinate with them?" Lassila asked.

"No. Task Force Makiniemi is stretched thin. They barely managed to scrape together a platoon for the last assault. Don't forget they are also manning the roadblock that's preventing the head of the 44th's column from moving forward. I'll radio them and inform them of our intent. With luck the Soviets are busy reinforcing where we just attacked." Mandelin replied.

"Very well, sir." Lassila said as he turned to leave.

"Oh, and captain." Mandelin said.

"Yes, major?"

"Don't fail. This is the last uncommitted company we have between Task Force Makiniemi and our own force. You lose this company, and we are reduced to waiting for the Bolshevik swine to starve to death." Mandelin said.

"Understood major." Captain Lassila replied. He started to leave then turned back and added, "Though I think they would freeze to death before they starved major."

Captain Lassila, at the head of Task Force Mandelin's reserve company, stood a hundred meters north of the Raate Road. Looking through his binoculars, he was able to see that this section of road was inhabited by a long line of Gaz-MM trucks. This area of the 44th's column appeared to be lightly defended, *It seems the major was right. They must have pulled men from this section of the road to reinforce where we attacked an hour ago.* Lassila thought.

Lassila turned to his three platoon commanders and said, "Form a wedge. I want 1st Platoon in the lead, supported by 2nd and 3rd. Everyone in 2nd and 3rd Platoon armed with a Suomi I want you to give them up and turn them over to anyone in 1st Platoon with a rifle.

As the leading edge of the spear, I want the 1st Platoon armed with all the Suomi submachine guns the company has. The bigger the punch they pack, the more likely the enemy will flee instead of standing to fight. Try to get as close to the road as you can without getting spotted. As soon as you are observed, hit them hard and fast. 2nd and 3rd Platoon will provide supporting long-range fire with their rifles, "Questions?"

The three officers stared at Lassila, but didn't speak, "Very well then, get it done."

The three platoons exchanged weapons as instructed. For the men of 2nd and 3rd Platoon, giving up their Suomi submachine guns, an excellent weapon, felt like giving up their right arms. Though reluctant, they followed Lassila's orders.

After the weapons exchange, nearly every man in the 1st Platoon was armed with a Suomi. The company moved into position as Lassila had instructed. Well camouflaged by their white snowsuits, the Finns were completely unobserved by the enemy, some of whom were only five meters away.

Suddenly, the men of 1st platoon emerged from their

places of concealment and charged forward on their skis. The Finnish attackers screamed like banshees and blazed away at the enemy with their machine guns. The handful of visible enemy soldiers were quickly cut down.

A few drivers stumbled out of the cabs of their Gaz-MM trucks. They picked up weapons from fallen men nearby and tried to put up a fight. These brave drivers were quickly cut down as the Finns continued to move forward. Only a handful of the Finnish attackers fell as they moved onto the road.

The Finns quickly checked the bodies of the fallen Soviets to ensure everyone was truly dead. With the immediate area secured, 1st Platoon's sergeants quickly divided the men in half. The two groups began to simultaneously attack both east and westward.

The assault forces were able to widen the Finnish controlled portion of the road by thirty meters before assault group west ran into an enemy squad that put up stiff resistance. The squad, led by a competent sergeant, used the front of a Gaz-MM truck for cover as they fired at the attacking Finns. Several Finns were hit and went down. This caused the attack to stall.

Suddenly, a loud roar erupted in the trees just to the north of the enemy squad and 2nd Platoon charged out of the woods and joined the fray. They fired their rifles, cutting down half of the enemy squad. The Soviets that survived the first volley were quickly skewered on the end of 2nd Platoon's bayonets as the Finns closed to melee range.

2nd Platoon was able to widen the breech by another twenty meters before they ran into stiff resistance organized by Lieutenant Koval. The young Ukrainian lieutenant urged his men to hold firm in the face of the

Finnish attackers. Inspired by the young officer, the Soviets managed to stop the 2nd Platoon's advance.

On the east side of the breech, the 3rd Platoon used similar tactics to expand the area of Finnish control. They charged in, fired their rifles, and then skewered any surviving enemies on the end of their bayonets. 3rd Platoon was able to widen the breech by forty meters, until they were stopped by the co-axial machine guns of a T-28 tank. Though the tank was out of fuel, its machine guns proved to be too much for the advancing Finns. They were forced to halt the attack and seek shelter. In all, the attack led by Captain Lassila created a one-hundred-meter breech in the road that cleaved the largest motti in half.

The men of Task Force Kari, continued to hold the roughly one-hundred-meter section of road they occupied between two 44th Division mottis. This was the same patch of ground that Hale and the sniper group had helped to defend against the Soviet's previous attack. Following that attack, in which Kari's battalion had suffered fifty percent casualties, the major was forced to reorganize his surviving men.

Kari eliminated three of his six companies and concentrated the surviving men into three understrength companies. One company, comprised of fifty soldiers, held the roadblock facing westward. The second company held the eastward facing roadblock. The third company was being held in reserve under direct command of the major. In all Task Force Kari, which once consisted of six understrength companies of infantry totaling three hundred men, had been reduced to three companies of roughly one hundred and fifty.

The reserve company, which was rotated out every four hours, was allowed to partake in a warm meal in the mess tent or seek sleep in another tent set up for that purpose. Men that desired neither sleep nor food, could be found in the hastily erected sauna enjoying some well-earned time out of the bitter cold of the frozen landscape. In contrast the men of the 44th, exhausted and hungry died by the hundreds from exposure to the unforgiving climate.

Starving and freezing the Soviets wanted what the Finns had. The smell of sausage soup, which occasionally wafted across the barricade that separated the two forces drove the starving Soviets mad. Driven to desperation by hunger, they came, not by the dozens, or hundreds, but nearly a thousand and they brought tanks, powered by their last drops of fuel.

On the Finnish side of the roadblock stood fifty men backed up by two Bofors 37mm anti-tank guns. In command of the company manning the western barricade was Lieutenant Salo. Salo, a recent university graduate, like so many other patriotic Finns had heeded his nation's call for volunteers early in the fall.

After a whirlwind version of officer candidate school in which an entire year of training had been crammed into a few short months, the young lieutenant was given command of a platoon. Now, thanks to the heavy casualties suffered by Task Force Kari, Salo found himself in command of a company of soldiers and assigned the vital task of holding a small patch of the Raate Road.

As the time for shift change neared, Salo glanced down at his watch. He inwardly smiled as he thought about how he would spend his four hours of down time, *First I'm going to have several bowls of sausage soup and coffee to warm my insides, and then I'm going to sit in the sauna to warm my outside. Perhaps I'll be able to catch a nap while I bake the cold out of my bones.*

His thoughts were abruptly interrupted by the sound of nearby tanks starting their engines. A few moments later, the rumble of tank engines sputtering to life shifted and became the sound of squeaking tracks and groaning steel as the metal monstrosities approached the roadblock. Salo turned to the two crews manning the Bofors and shouted, "Turn both guns westward we are about to have some company!"

As if to emphasize his point, a loud scream of defiance erupted from the throats of a thousand Soviets as they swarmed around the tanks and charged toward the Finnish roadblock, "There's to many, we've got to withdraw into the forest!" Shouted a nervous Finnish private.

"Pour the piss out of your boots and stand your ground soldier! We've beaten these Bolshevik bastards back before and we will do it again. Now find some sisu and fight!" Salo urged.

The Finns let out a roar of their own as they began firing into the approaching Soviet swarm, "There's so many of them you can't miss!" A young Finnish fishermen shouted.

It quickly became apparent that the Finns simply couldn't pour enough fire into the enemy to stem the tide. Major Kari, dashed into the mess tent and shouted, "Meal's over, everyone on the west wall now!"

Kari then dashed to the tent where those who weren't eating or baking in the sauna slept and repeated the message, "Wake up, I need everyone on the west wall now!"

Finally, the major, burst into the sauna and bade those men to report to the western roadblock. In total it took him less than three minutes to alert the men of the reserve company to bolster those defending the western roadblock. He then skied over to the east wall and ordered half of their number, roughly twenty-five men, to join the defenders on the west wall.

While the major worked to rally reinforcements for Salo's badly outnumbered defenders, the Finns had to hold the line outnumbered twenty to one. In the first minute of the attack, the defenders with machine guns, rifles, and grenades inflicted grievous casualties on the attacking Soviets. Nearly a hundred enemy soldiers joined the frozen corpses that had piled up in front of the Finnish position during the last attack.

The Soviets disregarded their casualties and made up for their lower accuracy with a wall of led that began to thin out the already badly outnumbered Finns. In the second minute of the attack, the approaching T-28 and T-26 tanks blasted apart the roadblock. This roadblock was better built than the first that was destroyed a few days ago when the sniper squad was in the area.

The new roadblock had been rebuilt with trees taken from the nearby forest after the first roadblock suffered the same fate. Lessons that had been learned from that attack had been incorporated into this new barricade. This wall provided firing ports for the Finns and was reinforced with a second layer of timber to resist high explosive tank shells.

While the firing ports, which enabled the Finns to fire from a position of relative protection, provided a force multiplier for the badly outnumbered defenders, the barricade itself was once again blasted into kindling when hit with high explosive tank shells. The destruction of the roadblock sent the surviving Finnish defenders scurrying for cover as the Soviets swarmed around the burning remnants.

The Finnish survivors retreated to the small ridgeline, just south of the road. This was the same ridge where Hale, Cunnar, and Korpi had employed their rifles against the enemy during the previous assault. Several of the Finns were shot in the back as the Soviet infantry paused their advance and fired into the backs of the fleeing Finns. Of the original fifty men that defended the western roadblock only twenty made it to the safety of the ridgeline in the third minute of the attack.

Salo's company, now enjoying the partial cover provided by the ridgeline, poured fire into the advancing horde. Their numbers were quickly bolstered by the men of the reserve company as they trickled into the fight in ones and twos. The twenty-five reinforcements from the eastern barricade set up a line just west of the two Bofors Anti-Tank Guns. This line not only provided a measure of protection for the guns, but it also poured fire into the flank of the Soviets attacking the Finns occupying the ridgeline.

The T-28, larger than the T-26, was able to push through the burning wreckage of the barricade. The tank commander quickly determined where the bulk of the Finnish fire was coming from and ordered his gunner to engage them. Before the gunner could turn the turret enough to bring the T-28's main gun to bear, a 37mm shell smashed through the tank's frontal armor and killed the crew.

The T-26, seeing the danger, fired a shot at the Finnish anti-tank gun. The Soviet gunner didn't take the time to line up his shot and the high explosive round sailed over the Finnish gun and detonated between the Bofors and the eastern barricade. The second Finnish gun crew quickly aimed their weapon and destroyed the T-26 before it could reload and fire again.

Without the support of their armor, and now caught in a crossfire, the Soviet attackers began to waver. Sensing the shift, Major Kari jumped to his feet, fired his pistol into the air three times as he screamed, "Charge!"

With a roar of defiance, the Finns leapt to their feet, fired their weapons, and charged headlong at their much more numerous foes. In the face of Finnish resolve, Soviet morale collapsed. Their will to resist quickly faded and they turned tail and ran. The Finns, turning the tables on the Soviets, gleefully stabbed fleeing enemy soldiers in the back with their bayonets. Those that couldn't catch the enemy, instead fired into them killing dozens.

In total the Soviets lost another hundred men during the rout. This brought the total butcher's bill to over two hundred slain in less than ten minutes. In addition to the casualties inflicted by the Finns, the Soviet motti lost their last two irreplaceable functional tanks. In total, the Finnish defenders lost forty men, nearly a third of their remaining force. Victory once again belonged to the defenders as they stubbornly remained in possession of the road. In addition to the cold and lack of food, the Soviets had a new problem, they were running out of ammunition.

Chapter 23

Noon, One Kilometer Southeast of the Village of Hauklia, Raate Road, Central Finland

January 5th, 1940

Captain Lassila gazed through his binoculars at the Soviet controlled portion of the road that lay beyond the barricade hastily erected by his men. The visible portion of the road outside of his company's control resembled a ghost convoy. Trucks and the occasional tank, stretched out as far as he could see through his binoculars in both directions but no men, *Where did they go?* He wondered.

After Lassila's company successfully seized the section of the Raate road that they now occupied from the 44th Division, he ordered his men to erect defensive barricades. Lassila's men had just finished cobbling together two barricades from the materials on hand, a combination of empty ammo boxes, vehicle wreckage, and trees. With a barricade of sorts now in place the exhausted men had built some fires to warm their lunch.

To construct a barricade, the available materials had been fashioned into a barrier by piling them into a haphazard chest high pile. The crude barriers, essentially piles of junk, were hastily erected on both the eastern and western edges of the Finnish controlled portion of the road. Oddly, the Soviets didn't contest the demarcation of the newly seized Finnish portion of the road.

Why is the enemy so quiet? Lassila mentally asked himself, *I don't understand where they went.*

Upon seizing the road, Lassila had dispatched a runner to request Lieutenant Colonel, Makiniemi provide reinforcements to help them dig in and hold this section of the road. That had been two hours ago, *What happened to you Laine?* Lassila wondered, *You should have been back an hour ago. Did the Soviets leave the road and capture you?* Lassila snorted in derision at the thought of the enemy leaving the road. The men of the 44th had proven unwilling to move into the surrounding forest.

Suddenly Private Laine, out of breath, emerged from the trees on the north side of the road. Laine, on skis paused and looked around for his commanding officer. He quickly spotted Lassila and headed over to him. Lassila, upon seeing that Laine was alone, frowned. As Laine approached, he asked, "What news private?"

"The colonel, sir." Laine's eyes fell.

"Go on private, spit it out." Lassila said as his heart sank.

"Colonel Makiniemi says he can't spare you any men captain." Laine said.

"I don't have enough surviving men to fight off a determined Soviet attack. Did he tell you why he couldn't spare any men? We're standing on priceless real estate that needs to be defended." Lassila countered.

"No sir, I guess he didn't think the likes of me would

much care why captain." Laine replied.

"Well, you need to turn your ass around and go back to the colonel. You tell him that if I don't get reinforcements, I'll be forced to give up this position if attacked." Lassila instructed.

"Begging your pardon captain, but I don't think he'll listen." Laine said.

"And why is that private?" Lassila over emphasized the p in private as he spat out Laine's rank.

Laine visibly wilted under Lassila's growing anger, "Well Laine? I'm waiting." Lassila demanded as he started to tap his boot in the snow to emphasize his impatience.

Laine swallowed hard and then met Lassila's steely eyed gaze, "Because Colonel Makiniemi was busy planning an attack with Colonel Mandelin."

"What kind of attack?" Lassila asked.

Laine shrugged, "They didn't let me hang around long enough to find out, sir."

"It should have only taken you an hour to make the round trip to Colonel Makiniemi's headquarters. Where were you for the other hour?" Lassila demanded.

Laine's pale cheeks turned bright red. "I got lost," he admitted reluctantly , his voice filled with embarrassment.

"What do you mean you got lost? How the hell did you get lost?" Lassila demanded, then added, "Navigating a forest ought to be second nature to any Finn. Are you a Soviet spy? Maybe you didn't really speak with the colonel at all? Perhaps instead you were providing intelligence to the enemy as you all shared a bottle of vodka around a roaring fire and took turns sucking the commissar's cock?"

Laine's cheeks turned crimson as he sheepishly replied, "I'm a fisherman captain. I never spent much time in the forest."

Suddenly, Lassila burst into laughter, "A fisherman?" Lassila turned to the other men and raised his voice, "How many of you men are also fisherman?"

The other men stopped eating their meals, some of them in mid bite, and just stared at the captain. Lassila sighed in frustration and then asked, "Alright, how many of you are not fisherman?"

A single soldier with the platoon assigned to hold the western barricade raised his hand. Lassila looked around and pursed his lips in disappointment at the result of his question, "You there, private?"

"Wuollet."

"Private Wuollet, if you aren't a fisherman, what do you do to make a living?" Lassila asked.

"I buy catches from fisherman, and with the help of my wife and children, gut the fish. We then take them to the station and load them onto the evening train in Oulu bound for the markets of other towns." Wuollet replied.

Lassila started to laugh, "So my only man that isn't a fisherman is a bloody fishmonger?

"That would seem to be correct, sir." Wuollet replied.

"Laine!" Lassila roared.

"Yes, captain?" Laine nervously replied.

"You carry your ass back to Colonel Makiniemi and

tell him we need reinforcements right now. Don't you come back here without more men this time. Understood?" Lassila demanded.

Laine opened his mouth to reply but was interrupted by a cacophony of screaming Soviets as they hurled themselves at the western barricade. Lassila's heart sank as he turned toward the enemy, "To late."

Lassila examined the Soviet attackers through his binoculars and spotted a familiar face. The young Soviet Lieutenant who had rallied the enemy soldiers and stopped the earlier Finnish attack, was leading a battalion sized force straight at them, "You again." Lassila cursed.

Lassila turned back to Laine and shouted over the sound of gunfire, "You go back to the colonel and tell him that if he can't provide reinforcements, then I must have his permission to abandon my position. Now repeat the orders back to me."

"I am to return to Colonel Makiniemi and tell him that if he doesn't provide you with reinforcements then you need permission to abandon this position." Laine said.

Lassila slapped Laine on the backside as he shouted, "Good, now go. Quickly!"

Lassila returned his attention to the battle. For the moment, the Finnish defenders, badly outnumbered, were managing to hold the barricade against the much more numerous Soviets. He turned toward the men defending the eastern side. There appeared to be no activity in that direction. Several of eastern barricade's Finnish defenders had turned westward and were watching their brothers in arms fight for their very survival.

Lassila dashed over to these men and shouted, "I need half of you to reinforce the men on the western barricade right now." He pointed at the nearest man and said, "You." He skipped passed the next man in the group and pointed at the next and said, "and you. Lassila continued this process of divvying up the men of the platoon until every man had been divided up into two groups. Now everyone in the first group go!"

Lassila, along with a dozen or so reinforcements joined the platoon manning the western barricade. The Finnish captain watched the Soviets as the enemy officer, Lieutenant Koval, stood in the front of their line and urged his men to charge, *If the Red Army had more like him, Finland would have been crushed in a week.* Lassila thought.

With a loud roar, the Soviets, who had been worked into a frenzy by Lieutenant Koval, suddenly charged. The badly outnumbered Finnish defenders employed their rifles, Suomi submachine guns, captured PPD 34s, and dozens of grenades to stop the attack. The resultant wall of led and explosions broke up the Soviet advance. Fortunately for the Soviets, Koval was not among those slain.

The young Soviet lieutenant shouted at those that ran away from the Finns. He exhorted them to reform. Within a few minutes he had managed to form his men back into a cohesive force. A few more minutes later, he was once again out front, urging them forward, "To victory!" The Soviet lieutenant shouted.

Again, the Soviets roared in defiance and charged hot on the heels of their leader. This time, they managed to reach the barricade. Several of the Soviets started to climb over the junk pile as the remaining men flowed around it into the forest. Finns began to fall as the advancing Soviets flooded their position.

Laine suddenly appeared out of the forest. He

looked around for a few moments until he spotted Lassila and headed over to him, "Colonel Makiniemi says he can't spare you any men."

"Then I will order the withdrawal. We can't hold against this many attackers with the men we have left." Lassila replied.

"He also forbids you to withdraw. You are to stand and fight to the last man and hold this patch of the Raate Road whatever the cost." Laine added.

Lassila took in a deep breath and exhaled sharply, "Then I guess we die here."

Captain Lassila turned to the remaining men that manned the eastern barricade, "2nd Platoon, join the fight!"

The men of 2nd platoon, eager to help their comrades dashed toward the western barricade. The barricade itself was holding, but the much more numerous Soviets had moved into the forest to go around it. Lassila shouted, "The enemy is flanking the barricade! 2nd Platoon! I want six of you to form a southward facing line and the other six to do the same but facing northward. Hold the edge of the road against the enemy!"

The reinforcements from 2nd platoon did as they were instructed. The sudden appearance of additional defenders surprised the Soviets and their attack faltered. After the lines stabilized, the two sides settled into a rhythm and exchanged fire for nearly half an hour. Thanks to the protection of the barricade, for every Finnish defender that fell, around twenty Soviet attackers lost their lives.

Finally, despite the continued exhortations of young Lieutenant Koval, the Soviet attacker's will to continue collapsed and they melted away. Those that were in the forest did not return to the Soviet motti. Instead, they disappeared into the trees, and started the long trek back to the Soviet Union. Those that disappeared had decided that the risk of an NKVD firing squad was preferable to the certainty of dying in the place the Soviets were beginning to refer to as frozen hell.

Of the roughly fifty men that Captain Lassila had led into combat to seize a section of the Raate Road, only twelve still drew breath when the enemy cracked. After the enemy's will to continue collapsed the surviving Finns stood stunned for several minutes before Captain Lassila shouted, "They might be coming back soon, we need to extend the barricade along the side of the road and get ready for the next attack."

Fortunately for the few Finnish defenders that still drew breath, the men of the 44th, their will to fight completely broken by a combination of the conditions, lack of supplies, and Finnish sisu, never returned.

Chapter 24

Late Evening, One Kilometer South of Lake Kokkojarvi, Central Finland

January 5th, 1940

Major Kari tried to stifle a yawn as he neared his command tent. Failing miserably, he opened his mouth so widely that he swore he could hear his jawbone creak with the effort. Embarrassed, he looked around to see if any of his men had seen him. Seeing no one, relief flooded through him, *The men draw their strength from me. They don't need to see that I am exhausted beyond measure.* He thought.

Kari had just returned from making the rounds of his battalion and checking in with his officers. Each man had reported no Soviet activity in the last several hours. The major opened the flap that led into the warm interior of his command tent. Relief washed over him as the warm air filled his lungs. As he began the process of removing multiple layers of clothing so he wouldn't start to sweat, he looked over at Sergeant Peura, his wireless operator, "Have you heard any reports of enemy activity while I was out?"

"Not a peep since Task Force Makiniemi fended off an assault several hours ago." Sergeant Peura replied.

"Alright then I think I am going to get some sleep. Wake me if something requires my attention." Kari instructed.

"Will do, sir. Where can I find you?" Peura asked.

Major Kari snorted in amusement and said, "Right here."

Kari, using his coat as a pillow, lay down on the floor and immediately passed out. Less than sixty seconds later, the sergeant could hear rhythmic breathing coming from Kari. Peura smiled and thought, *Good. I was starting to worry about you, major.*

While Kari slept, Sergeant Peura received a transmission about the reinforcements shortly after the major had fallen asleep. Peura, nearing sixty and old enough to be the major's father, had decided Kari needed sleep. Instead of waking the major and enabling him to prepare for the arrival of his new battalion of reinforcements, Peura had let him get much needed rest, *You aren't going to do us any good if you are falling asleep standing up.* Peura mused.

A few hours later, Sergeant Peura heard activity outside of the tent, *It sounds like the reinforcements have arrived.*

The sergeant stood up from his chair in front of the radio set and stretched, *My body hates that infernal campaign chair but it beats standing all the time.* He thought.

Peura went over to the slumbering major and shook his shoulder, "Wake up major."

Without bothering to crack an eye open Kari asked,

"What is it? It's still the middle of the night? Have the Soviets started to stir? I don't hear any shooting."

"No, sir, it isn't the Soviets." Sergeant Peura said.

"Well, if it isn't the Soviets, let one of my subordinates deal with it." Kari said as he turned over.

"It's Colonel Siilasvuo." Sergeant Peura said.

"What about the colonel?" Kari asked in a confused voice, he had nearly fallen back asleep in the few seconds that had transpired.

"Colonel Siilasvuo, sir. You see, he has sent a battalion of reinforcements." Peura replied.

Peura, was leaning over with his hands on his knees hovering above Kari. Surprised by the sergeant's words, the major suddenly sat bolt upright. Peura quickly stepped back to avoid a collision.

The four hours of sleep the major had helped to push the fog away from his fatigue addled mind. Given the amount of sleep the major had managed to get since the Raate Road campaign had begun, he was still one step away from total exhaustion. This was evidenced by the black lines below his sunken eyes.

"Excellent news. With a second battalion we should be able to hold our position on the Raate Road without any difficulties." Kari said.

"That's not why the battalion is here, sir." Peura said.

"Then why?" Kari asked, confused.

"The battalion has been sent with orders from Colonel Siilasvuo." Peura said.

"What orders?" Kari snapped.

"They are to be used in an attack to further split the two mottis that we are already in contact with." Peura replied.

"So, we are to take these new men and stretch ourselves further? What madness is this?" Kari fumed.

"I'll let the good captain here explain." Peura.

"Good morning, major. I'm Captain Jokela."

"Good morning." Major Kari said sharply, "The orders."

Captain Jokela handed over a folder, "I have them right here."

Major Kari read the orders, when he finished, he looked up at Jokela and smiled, "Siilasvuo thinks we can crack two more holes into these bastards?"

Captain Jokela shrugged, "He didn't say. The colonel needs you to carry out his orders."

"What's the hurry." Kari asked.

"The Soviets have sent a new regiment to try and salvage the situation." Captain Jokela said.

"The 3rd NKVD? I thought they were just a few snipers. Annoying but hardly the kind of force that can push us out of our positions here on the road." Kari said.

"The 3rd NKVD isn't just snipers. They are a group of Bolshevik zealots who believe that Joseph Stalin is God, communism is the state's holy religion, and that they have been placed on this earth to convert the non-believers. The Soviets took these fanatics and gave them military training.

"They're crusaders?" Kari asked.

Jokela nodded, "In a sense. Instead of heeding God's call to liberate the Holy Land from the infidel, they are here to liberate the workers from the capitalist bourgeoise. In their first engagement, these fanatics nearly took the bridge over the Purasjoki River and pushed Major Fagernas' forces off the road." Jokela replied.

Major Kari's mouth fell open. After a moment he recovered himself and said, "Summer of cunts."

Jokela nodded, "Indeed."

"I understand now. We have to finish off the 44th, before these Soviet fanatics are able to push Fagernas aside and reestablish a supply line with the 44th." Kari observed.

"Now you understand the dilemma." Captain Jokela said, "The 3rd NKVD are highly motivated zealots. Thus far they have fought well. In fact, they have fought much better than anything we've seen from the now destroyed 163rd Division, or the 44th." Jokela said.

"We were lucky the Soviet generals are a pack of idiots. The 44th would have fought a lot better had the morons in their High Command used them in a situation more befitting their purpose. Those poor Ukrainian bastards aren't used to this weather. On top of that they are a mechanized division. They were designed to smash through the enemy and conduct a war of maneuver using the superior road networks found in Central Europe. Thanks to our endless forests, they can hardly move and are limited to the roads." Kari snorted derisively, "If you can call them that. More like dirt paths and game trails. The 44th has virtually no room to maneuver here. If the enemy wanted to use this division, in this war, they should have sent it to Lapland where there are no trees." Kari observed.

Captain Jokela nodded in agreement, "It was shockingly stupid to deploy the 44th in Central Finland."

"Circling back to the reason for your arrival. Just so I'm clear on why Siilasvuo elected to deploy you here captain, you've been sent to give me more problems to manage?" Kari said.

Captain Jokela chuckled, "I suppose we have, sir."

Major Kari, walked over to the campaign table in the center of the tent and gazed down at the map, "So you said that Major Fagernas nearly lost the bridge over the Purasjoki?"

"Yes major, earlier this evening." Jokela replied.

"If we hit the road here and here. We will divide the motti between myself and Major Fagernas in two. In addition, Fagernas, would then be able to concentrate all his forces on holding off the 3rd NKVD Regiment." Major Kari said.

"I think taking the pressure off Major Fagernas' western flank would be much appreciated by both the major and Colonel Siilasvuo." Captain Jokela replied.

"Alright then. Where are the men?" Kari asked.

"Right outside." Jokela replied.

Without another word, Kari picked up his coat and started to put it on as he headed outside. Upon seeing the major suddenly emerge from the command tent, the officers called the battalion to attention.

"Men, at ease. Get some sleep if you can. Officers, with me." Kari ordered.

The enlisted men of Kari's new battalion needed no prompting. They immediately laid down on the ground. To maintain their body heat, so that they could fall asleep instead of lay on the ground shivering they snuggled together for heat. Within a minute or two the sound of snoring reverberated through the air.

Four hours later, at six AM, with an attack plan in hand, Major Kari's new battalion hit the enemy. The bewildered Soviets put up little in the way of resistance, and the Finns easily achieved their objectives. Major Fagernas' western flank had been secured.

Major Fagernas turned toward a soldier bursting into his command tent. Upon seeing the major glaring at him the private stiffened to attention and saluted, "You don't salute inside private."

"Sorry major." The private replied.

"In fact, you shouldn't be saluting anyone. With all the damned sniper activity we've had, you'll just get them killed. I don't really relish the idea of dying because you chose to be an idiot. Perhaps in the future, you can follow battlefield protocols?"

The privates' pale cheeks turned crimson as Major Fagernas dressed him down. Mortified, he became tongue tied and stood in silence at rigid attention. Major Fagernas sighed in annoyance and asked, "So private?"

"Pollari."

"So Private Pollari, what is it that is so urgent that you felt the need to burst into my tent? I don't hear any shooting, so it isn't an attack on the bridge."

"It's Task Force Kari, sir." Pollari said.

Major Fagernas, beginning to lose his temper, snapped, "What about them?"

"They've seized a section of the road just west of our line." Pollari said.

"What?" Private Pollari opened his mouth to repeat when the major held up a hand and said, "So we are no longer in contact with the enemy on our west side?"

"That's correct major." Pollari said.

Fagernas smiled, "That's excellent news."

Private Pollari stood at attention while Fagernas pondered this change in the situation, *I could triple the number of men I have holding the bridge.* He let that thought sit for nearly a minute before another idea occurred to him, *No, I shouldn't leave the initiative in the hands of the enemy. I have a better idea for those two companies.*

Fagernas smiled when he saw that Pollari was still standing at attention in front of him, "I have a message for Captain Kokko. You tell him that if the detachment from Task Force Kari is large enough to hold the road against a potential attack from the fifth motti, then he is to report to me with his entire force. Now go!"

Chapter 25

Mid-Day, Three Kilometers Southeast of the Purasjoki Bridge, Central Finland

January 6th, 1940

Hale decided to gamble that Kuznetsov would return to the bridge over the Purasjoki. The Soviet sniper already had a field day shooting the Finnish defenders. Such an opportunity for easy targets silhouetted against the sky would be hard for him to resist. Hale reasoned that Kuznetsov would find such a juicy target irresistible. Even if the target forced him to break with his pattern of never striking twice in the same location.

Since the first attempt at killing Kuznetsov near the bridge had ended in abject failure, Hale wasn't eager to repeat the same scenario again. He had tired of waiting for the Soviets to strike and then responding to it. It was time to take the initiative and try to stop the enemy from having another opportunity to kill Finns from a distance unopposed.

Hale reasoned that if the bridge would again be Kuznetsov's target, then the enemy sniper would be forced to circle around to the south of the Raate Road. Once south of the road, he would need to head westward at some point. The question was how far south would he go? To solve this dilemma, Hale elected to use the forces available to him to engage in aggressive defense.

Being unfamiliar with the area, Hale did not know exactly what path the Soviet sniper would choose, so he deployed his new squad in a north south line in an effort to create as wide a net as possible. Hale hoped that stretching his available forces out as far as they could reasonably cover each other would increase the chance of contact. In total the sniper squad's line stretched two kilometers from its northern starting point to its southern edge.

The young lieutenant figured that Kuznetsov would put some distance between himself and the Raate road. Therefore, Hale deployed the northernmost member of his team roughly a kilometer to the south of the Raate Road. He then stationed each subsequent man two hundred meters further south of the previous man. The plan had one major vulnerability, should Kuznetsov decide to remain close to the road during his westward trek, he would have a kilometer wide gap to slip through.

Hale dismissed this as unlikely. Given the visibility of roughly three hundred meters for a sniper in this terrain, the northern most man would cut the gap to roughly seven tenths of a kilometer. Kuznetsov would know this and stay at least three hundred meters south of the road. This meant that if the Soviet sniper chose to stay close to the road, that there was only a four tenths of a kilometer gap that he could use to slip by Hale's line.

This deployment kept each of Hale's men within shooting range of both the man to his north and the man to his south. If Kuznetsov was able to kill a member of Hale's team, theoretically, the men to the north and the south of the slain soldier, would still be able to engage him so that he wasn't able to slip through the gap in the line created by the death of a single team member.

Hale elected to position Private Lassila, his second-best shooter, in the northernmost position closest to the road. This would hedge his bet as Lassila would be able to kill a target up to four hundred meters to the north. Lassila anchoring the line would narrow the potential gap further to a mere three tenths of a kilometer between the line and the road.

The next four positions in the line were occupied by three of Sergeant Antilla's privates and then the sergeant himself in the position just north of Hale. Starting at two-hundred-meter intervals to the south of Hale, were four more of Antilla's privates, with Lieutenant Kivi anchoring the southern edge of the line.

As the minutes of their wait stretched into hours Hale began to doubt himself, *Did I get it wrong? Did Kuznetsov decide to stick to his pattern of hitting in different locations each time. What if he decided to head west and start over with Task Force Mandelin? He could be killing Finns right now while we are sitting out here doing nothing.*

Hale's thought was interrupted when his keen eyes caught a bit of movement several hundred meters to his southeast, *What was that?* Hale wondered.

The movement was in the sector that belonged to Private Kemppainen. Thanks to the distance that separated them, Kemppainen was to far away for Hale to signal. Hale elected to concentrate his attention on that area, hoping to see more movement. Dividing his attention increased the risk that Kuznetsov would be able to move in closer to Hale, but the movement shouldn't be ignored just because it wasn't in Hale's sector.

Kuznetsov paused for a moment to catch his breath and thought, *I don't understand how the Finns are able to endlessly ski without wearing themselves out. This is exhausting.*

Since the bridge over the Purasjoki River proved to be such a target rich environment, Kuznetsov decided to break with his previous strategy which entailed rotating to a new target each time he attacked. Thus far, his strategy had been effective, and the Finns hadn't been able to devise an effective counter to his efforts. Kuznetsov decided the bridge was a juicy enough target to risk breaking with his successful strategy which had been working, and hit the same target again, but from a different direction, the south.

While he was catching his breath, his stomach rumbled, *I guess this is as good a location as any for lunch.*

Kuznetsov unbuttoned his white coat and pulled out a ration tin that he had looted from a dead Finn. He looked down at the writing and asked himself, "What are you? Guess I won't find out until I open you up and see what's inside. Hopefully you're not cabbage. I'm so sick of cabbage. You'd think with a country the size of the Soviet Union, they could find something else to make rations out of."

Kuznetsov opened the ration tin and peered down at the contents, "Hmmm looks like more sausage soup. The Finns must really favor this stuff. I can't say that I blame them, this is a hell of a lot tastier than the crap the Red Army gives us. Assuming they give us anything at all."

Kuznetsov, not bothering to use silverware, put the can to his lips and started to slurp the contents into his mouth, "I bet that if our people used spices like the ones in this soup, that cabbage would be more interesting. Communists are so uncreative."

The Soviet sniper paused for a moment and laughed, "Great. I'm spending so much time out in these frozen wastes that I am beginning to have conversations with myself. At least the chance of a commissar suddenly appearing and shooting me in the back of the head because of my treasonous words is minimal."

Kuznetsov shrugged his shoulders and laughed ruefully at the thought of the commissars, the Red Army's dreaded political officers, "I can't believe I'm wasting my thoughts on those fanatics." He mused, "Oh well, I guess I had better drink this before it freezes on me."

Hale had been observing the general location where he had spotted the movement for twenty minutes. Seeing no new movement in the area, the young sniper was growing increasingly frustrated, *Whatever you are move!* He mentally demanded.

Doubt began to cloud his mind as he thought, *Did I imagine seeing something there?*

Hale took a deep breath and let it out slowly to calm his nerves, *Stop second guessing yourself. You definitely saw movement in that area.* To calm his nerves, he started to rationalize explanations for the lack of additional movement, *What would have been moving and then decided to not move for this length of time?*

Hale began to think of the answers to his question, *Perhaps it was a mother wolf returning to her den with a meal for her pups? It couldn't be a moose bedding down for the night.* He pondered that thought and then dismissed it, *No, that can't be the reason, it is still to early in the day for a moose to be bedding down.* He reasoned.

It most certainly couldn't be a bear as they have been in hibernation for several months at this point. A deer or a reindeer would have moved by now. Especially if they were foraging for food. Which is likely given the time of day. This is not helping, he lamented.

Kuznetsov finished the last of his soup, *I wonder what this tastes like warm?* He thought, *I bet it's even better warm.*

The Soviet sniper looked up at the nearly cloudless blue sky above, *I have about two hours of daylight left. Plenty of time to get where I'm going and select a good spot to settle in for the night.*

Kuznetsov stood, strapped his skis to his boots, and slung his rifle onto his back. He jumped up and down a few times to ensure his gear was secure and wouldn't make noise as he moved. Satisfied, he resumed his westward journey.

Hale was about to lose hope and focus on his own sector instead of Kemppainen's when he saw movement, *There!*

The movement reappeared roughly where it had disappeared. Hale swung his rifle in that direction and waited, *Another hundred meters closer and I can take a shot.*

Kuznetsov slowly increased his speed as he hit his stride. Suddenly, a piece of his subconscious screamed at him to stop, *Something doesn't feel right.* He thought.

The Soviet sniper planted his ski poles into the snow to stop his forward momentum. He raised his right hand over his eyes to try and reduce the glare from the sunlight reflecting off the snow and scanned the area in front of him, *I don't see anything. Perhaps it's just nerves? Why would there be anyone out there?*

Whatever it was, Hale couldn't tell whether it was an animal or human at this range. Once again, it had stopped moving. The target was close enough to discern some coloration, *Are you a reindeer with a light coat, or an enemy soldier wearing a white snowsuit?*

Doubt began to flood Hale's mind as he thought, *What if it's another Finn wearing a white snow suit?*

He dismissed the thought, *Whatever that is moving around out there it is very unlikely to be a Finnish soldier. The only Finnish force that I'm aware of in this area is Captain Kokko's company. His force should be long gone by now.*

Hale checked his rifle for what must have been the hundredth time since he settled into this position, *Should I shoot?* Hale asked himself.

At nearly five hundred meters distance through the forest, he couldn't see any of the target's details, *I really wish I had a scope for this shot.* He thought.

Finally coming to a decision, he lined up the two iron sights of his rifle with the target which was little more than a black dot. He paused his shooting process and asked himself, *Maybe I should wait for the target to get closer, so I know for sure what I'm shooting at? No, what if that is Kuznetsov out there and he sees you, or one of your men move? He could be lying in wait for them right now or decide to turn around. He might have even spotted me with that scope of his.*

Hale came to a decision and took a deep breath. He adjusted his aim to account for the wind and the slight difference in elevation between himself and the target. When he was satisfied that he could hit the target, there was no way he could choose which part of the body to target at this range, he squeezed the trigger.

Kuznetsov came to a decision, *There's nothing out there. You're becoming paranoid. There's no way that Karhonen's group is in this area. He's probably on his way to what he thinks my next target will be.* The thought made Kuznetsov smile as he imagined Karhonen skiing all the way to the westernmost group of Finns in a vain attempt to engage him.

Suddenly a sledgehammer struck his left shoulder. Surprised, he lost his balance and collapsed to the ground, *What the hell?* He wondered in pain and confusion.

Kuznetsov looked at his left shoulder, the source of the blow which was now sending fiery bolts of pain into his brain. He began to panic as he realized, *I've been shot!*

Hale lowered his rifle and gazed out at the target's location, *Who or whatever you are must have been hit as you are no longer visible.* He thought.

Hale considered his next move carefully, *Should I sit tight and wait for the target to move again, or should I investigate and figure out what I just shot? With my damn luck, Kuznetsov sent a lackey forward to draw me in so he could shoot me when I approach to investigate.*

Kuznetsov reached into his bag and pulled out a first aid kit, *I never thought I would need to use this on myself.* He lamented.

Once he had the kit in hand, he steeled himself for what came next. Kuznetsov unbuttoned his coat and removed it. One by one, as quickly as he could manage while laying prone on the ground, he removed several layers of clothing. It didn't take long before he lay upon a pile of garments and his shoulder was completely uncovered. He pulled a bandage from the first aid kit and tried to wipe away the blood so he could get a better look at the wound.

He located the bullet's entry point, just above his collar bone, *That's lucky. At least it didn't hit the bone and shatter it.* He then checked to see if he could find an exit wound, *No wonder there is so much blood. There are actually two wounds. I believe I've heard this called a through and through.*

He breathed a sigh of relief as he realized there was no bullet for him to remove, *I just got to stop the bleeding or at least slow it down enough to survive the journey to a doctor.*

Kuznetsov unbuttoned his coat and tore a long piece of fabric from his undershirt. Next, he placed a bandage large enough to cover both wounds and secured it with the piece of fabric then tied a knot to hold it in place, *I'm lucky to have come across this kit on the medic I killed last week. Like the food, these Finnish first aid kits are superior to anything we have.*

The injured sniper quickly got dressed, lest he freeze to

death. With the rare sunny conditions, the temperature had risen to a balmy negative ten degrees Fahrenheit. Though some thirty degrees warmer than the recent weather, it was still cold enough to kill in a short amount of time.

Hale came to a decision, *I'm going to go find whatever it is I shot.*

He removed his hat and waved it back and forth above him. When his hat was not immediately shot out of his hand he decided, *Time to risk it.*

Hale gritted his teeth as he stood up. When a bullet failed to slam into his chest, he immediately put his skis on, slung his rifle on his back, and set off toward whatever it was that he had shot. After he had traveled for a hundred meters, he paused and turned back toward his line, *Good, everyone is obeying my order to remain in position no matter what.* He turned back to the east and resumed skiing.

Kuznetsov was able to bring the bleeding from his gunshot wound under control. He wasn't able to entirely stop the bleeding, but it had slowed down considerably. Enough that he felt confident to move out without putting his life in danger. He came to his feet and slung his rifle onto his good shoulder. The movement sent fresh bolts of pain to his brain. After a minute the pain settled back down to a sharp throb and he was able to find a rhythm, albeit a painful one, to propel himself eastward.

Hale suddenly saw movement approximately where he had hit the unknown target. The movement was roughly three hundred meters away now that he had moved eastward. He skidded to a stop on his skis and quickly pulled his rifle off of his back. Whoever the target was, Hale was close enough now to discern that it was not a moose or a deer. The target was wearing white and moving away in a straight line. He quickly realized, *That's a man and if he was Finnish he would be heading south right now, not east.*

Hale raised his rifle to his shoulder and took aim at the target. He spent several seconds observing the target's movement to determine the amount of lead to give. Once the determination was made, he took a deep breath and held it as he peered down the length of his rifle. The moment he had the target lined up in his sights, he gave it the required amount of lead and pulled the trigger.

A bullet whistled by Kuznetsov's left arm. He craned his neck in an attempt to see the shooter. In the distance he was able to discern the outline of a man. His heart froze as he recognized what the man was doing, *He's about to shoot again!*

Kuznetsov faced forward a moment before he crashed into a fallen tree that was in his path. He lost his balance and fell face forward into the snow. Upon impact, his skis were torn from his feet by the log, and he ended up face down in the snow. The fallen tree saved his life as another bullet rocketed by at a height that would have hit his torso had he still been skiing.

The Soviet sniper rolled up against the log to maximize his cover and pulled the rifle from his right shoulder. He gasped in pain as he brought the rifle up and set it on the log. He was careful not to expose more of his body than he needed to.

Kuznetsov immediately spotted who had been shooting at him. He peered into his scope and lined up the reticle on the man's torso. As he lined up the shot, he recognized his assailant, *Karhonen!*

A moment before Kuznetsov pulled the trigger, Hale fired. In his haste, the Finnish sniper did not account for the slight elevation different between himself and his target. The bullet ripped the Soviet sniper's hat from his head as he fired his rifle. The near miss spoiled Kuznetsov's aim causing him to miss Hale.

A bullet hurtled by, just to Hale's right and he realized, *He's shooting back!*

Hale immediately started to move northward. He looked around desperately for some cover to conceal himself with. The trunks of the birch trees in his immediate area were to thin to provide the cover he craved and there were no spruce trees nearby. A bullet whizzed by just in front of him as the enemy sniper fired at him. The young sniper heard another shot, this time from several hundred meters to his southeast, *Thank you Kemppainen!*

Hale spotted a gully to his left and turned toward it. The move saved his life as a bullet slammed into a birch tree a few meters in front of him with a dull thunk. Hale began his mental count to four seconds, the time it took a skilled shooter to operate the bolt on a rifle, as he desperately pushed himself forward toward the ditch.

Again, Kemppainen fired at the enemy sniper, just as Hale's count reached four. Gambling that Kemppainen momentarily spoiled the enemy's aim, he continued for the single second he needed to reach the ditch. Hale swerved to his right, dropped his poles, and hurled himself into the ditch. A split second later, another bullet narrowly missed him as he crashed into the ditch.

Kuznetsov cursed as he missed Karhonen, again, "This guy has more lives than a cat!" He snarled.

Time to turn my attention to the other shooter, Kuznetsov decided.

With Karhonen temporarily occupied, Kuznetsov

reached back and located his hat with his left hand. A sharp wave of pain washed over him as his left shoulder screamed in protest at the movement. He located the hat with his left hand. He grabbed the fur cap with his fingers and waved it around over his head, being careful, to keep everything but his arm concealed. The ploy worked and the other Finn fired. He missed Kuznetsov's arm by a few scant centimeters, *Now I have an idea where you are at.*

Kuznetsov dropped the hat and swung his rifle in the direction of the sound made from Kemppainen firing his rifle. Using his scope, Kuznetsov began to rapidly scan the possible hiding places for the second shooter. Again, he was careful to expose as little of himself as possible while he looked for the enemy sniper, *There you are!*

Kuznetsov, saw Kemppainen's muzzle flash as he fired a shot. The Soviet sniper immediately ducked down. The move saved his life as Kemppainen's bullet slammed into the log right where Kuznetsov's head had been a moment before as he peered through his scope.

Kuznetsov raised his head and peered into his scope as he quickly took aim at the Finn. Through the scope's magnification, he was able to see the man working the action on his rifle as he lined up his reticle and pulled the trigger, *Got you.* He thought.

The time he spent exposed to eliminate Kemppainen, almost cost Kuznetsov his life as a bullet from Karhonen hurtled through the space Kuznetsov's head had just occupied as he ducked down to operate the bolt on his rifle, "So much for your promise Karhonen!" Kuznetsov shouted in frustration.

"Missed again." Hale growled in frustration.

He reached into his right coat pocket and pulled out a fresh stripper clip of bullets and reloaded his rifle. Hale then took the time to remove his skis and slipped them into the loops on his pack designed to carry them. Finally, he removed the pack to lower his profile and dropped it on the ground. He then crawled twenty meters southward, careful to keep his body below the lip of the gully in order to safely shift to a new firing position, *It'll take the enemy sniper a few seconds to figure out that I've shifted position once I fire. Seconds that could save my life.*

Two shots boomed out, one from the southeast and another from Hale's southwest as Kemppainen and the enemy sniper, likely Kuznetsov, exchanged fire. The young sniper decided it was probably safe to peer over the lip of the ditch he currently occupied as the enemy sniper's attention was likely still on Kemppainen.

Hale quickly located the log, the enemy sniper was using as concealment. Next, he readied his rifle to fire and waited for the enemy to show himself. One minute passed and there was no sign of the enemy sniper. When one minute became five, Hale began to wonder, *Where did you go?*

Kuznetsov cursed as he missed the enemy sniper, again, *Why is every damn Finn a good marksman?*

The Soviet sniper stayed under cover and tried to think the situation through, *I'm injured which is likely affecting my shooting. The enemy knows precisely where I'm at. There is more than one enemy out there trying to kill me.* Kuznetsov thought back to a scenario that he had laid out for his class at the Soviet Sniper school. In the scenario the student sniper was alone and outnumbered. In addition, the enemy knew their precise location, *The correct solution to the situation was disengage if you could do so without being seen.*

Kuznetsov looked around at the surrounding terrain. The ground he lay on was slightly below that of the enemy sniper that had most recently fired at him. The other enemy sniper, Karhonen, had disappeared, *The bastard could be crawling toward me right now.* He thought ruefully.

"I don't see where I have a choice. If I stay here, one of the two enemy snipers out there is likely going to shoot me a second time today. I have to risk moving, so I can disengage." Kuznetsov said out loud as if to convince himself of his chosen course of action.

Decision made, he then started to think through how he was going to do it, *The Finns are better skiers than me, so I need to ditch my pack to lighten up, especially since I am injured and they presumably aren't.*

Kuznetsov dug through his pack and pulled out some extra bandages from the first aid kit. He shoved them in his pocket, *I'll likely need these later.*

He also withdrew a Finnish ration tin, and slipped it inside his coat, *No telling how long I am going to be out here trying to disengage, so I'd best have a little bit of food.*

At the bottom of his pack, he came across his full

bottle of vodka. He pulled the bottle out and gazed at it fondly, *I wish I could bring you with me, but I need to keep a clear head, and you are on the heavy side, so I can't spare the extra weight for you.*

He sighed deeply as he tossed the bottle aside, *Time to crawl.*

Kuznetsov stayed as low to the ground as he could manage and started to crawl away from the log. His injured shoulder immediately started to scream in protest by sending white hot bolts of pain to his brain. Every time he moved it felt as if someone was hamming a nail into his shoulder. He gasped in agony and thought, *Maybe I do need the vodka.*

He paused for a moment and thought about retrieving the bottle. Finally, he shook his head and decided, *No, I must maintain a clear head. Man up and deal with the pain!* He mentally chastised himself.

He continued crawling for about ten meters when a bullet hurtled by in the air just above his head. Kuznetsov immediately stopped crawling and wondered, *Can he see me, or is he just guessing?*

After sixty seconds when no second bullet came, he determined, *That Finn back on the ridge to the west was just guessing. Best get moving again before Karhonen decides its safe to come out of whatever hole he buried himself in and run me down.*

Kuznetsov resumed crawling eastward. After a few more minutes of crawling, he came across a depression, that headed off to the southeast, *This looks like it might be a creek that empties into that lake to the south, but hard to say since the snow is so deep.*

He slipped into the creek bed and followed it southeast. With the cover, he was able to safely get up on his hands and crawl faster.

Hale came to a decision, *He disengaged. I need to follow.*

The young sniper put his skis on and came to his feet. He tentatively moved forward, keeping the trees between himself and the last known location of the enemy sniper as much as possible. When no bullet was fired at him, he started to move toward the last place he saw the enemy sniper.

As Hale neared the last known location of the enemy sniper, he paused, turned toward Kemppainen, and waved his arm back and forth to get the young private's attention. Kemppainen returned Hale's wave, *Good, he knows I'm not an enemy. I don't want to make Nea a widow by getting shot by one of my own men.*

Hale continued southeast until he reached the enemy's previous firing position. His eyes quickly took in the scene, a pair of broken skis, a pack, its contents apparently scattered across the snow, a bottle of vodka, several brass bullet casings, and blood. He smiled in triumph, *I thought I hit you! The question is, are you Kuznetsov, or another sniper?* Hale wondered as he thought back to the promise he was forced to make to Kuznetsov after the enemy sniper saved him from Volkov and then spared him, *A life for a life.*

Hale's mind returned to the immediate task at hand. *Where did you go?* He wondered.

The young Lieutenant looked beyond the mess and saw that the snow's pristine surface had been disturbed.

In addition to the trail, at fairly regular intervals, the snow had been stained red with droplets of blood. He smiled as he thought, *I think even a Soviet conscript that spent his entire life in Moscow could follow this trail.*

Hale looked back at his line and signaled Kemppainen to remain in place via hand signal. He then sent the signal to share the previous signal with the rest of the group. Kemppainen acknowledged both signals and turned to inform the other men in the line.

After he finished with Kemppainen, Hale considered how he should follow the trail left by the enemy, *If he is wounded, he won't be able to go far. He still has his rifle, so he could conceivably find another position and shoot anyone that follows the trail. How can I give chase without exposing myself to being shot?*

Hale quickly realized how he must follow the trail. The way that would offer the least amount of exposure and therefore risk, was to pursue the enemy sniper by crawling, *At least I haven't been shot.* After the thought, he paused for a moment and rubbed what remained of his left ear, *At least recently.*

As Hale started to crawl, his thoughts drifted away from the battlefield to the moment that Nea first saw his ear, *I was so nervous that she would reject me.* As he thought about what happened next his chest felt an inexplicable warmth at the memory her response invoked within him. A response from a place of unconditional love. Despite the sub-zero chill the feeling of Nea's love for him made it feel like a warm spring day.

Mind on the here and now Karhonen! He mentally chastised himself. Hale tucked away the feeling of Nea's love so as not to soil it with the negative emotions associated with battle. His mind now focused on the here and now, he resumed his pursuit of the enemy sniper.

After crawling for a hundred meters, Kuznetsov felt more exhausted than ever. He tried to focus his foggy mind on figuring out if that had been the case during any of his previous experiences to take his mind off the pain. The discomfort, from his wound, threatened to overwhelm and paralyze him. It would not be ignored as the dull throb in his shoulder had once again become a searing pain. He could sense that the wound had opened back up and was bleeding. His breath came in ragged gasps, and he was struggling to keep his eyes open, *You can't give up. Karhonen is coming for you!*

Kuznetsov's mind drifted back to the moment he came upon Karhonen, with Volkov's pistol pointed at his head. After he shot that swine Volkov, he made Karhonen promise him a life for a life, *Would he honor his promise, or gleefully kill the man who has killed so many of his comrades?*

It was not knowing the answer to that question that enabled Kuznetsov to find within himself the strength to continue. He clenched his teeth, cursed himself for not bringing the vodka, and resumed his crawling. He was able to continue for another five minutes before exhaustion once again overtook him. Blood loss and the ever-present cold had combined to sap most of his strength.

As Kuznetsov lay on the snow gasping for air, he thought he heard something behind him. Unable to tell what the sound was, he regulated his breathing. He was able to slow the raspy breaths rattling through his lungs enough that he was able to focus his senses on listening. As a result he heard a faint scraping like noise coming from the direction he had just come from, *I don't recognize that noise. What was that?*

He was about to give up when he heard the sound of skis moving across snow come from up ahead, *They've surrounded me!* He thought in a panic.

He tried to fight the wave of weakness that suddenly slammed into him. Despite his efforts to stay coherent, the edges of Kuznetsov's vision began to darken as he drifted toward unconsciousness. Suddenly blurry forms appeared in front of him. The forms wore white snowsuits, and approached on skis, *They've captured me!* He thought in the moment before he lost consciousness.

Hale thought he heard the voice of a man cry out, maybe fifty meters ahead. He smiled as he thought, *He's still moving. Should I just stand up and run him down?*

Before Hale could decide, he heard several voices up ahead, *Who is that? Did Kokko double back?*

Hale lifted his head in order to see what was going on up ahead. His mouth dropped open, shocked at what he saw.

"He's one of ours comrade sergeant!" Exclaimed Private Dimitri Ivanov.

Sergeant Lenkov frowned as he knelt down next to the prone form, "He is indeed, though there shouldn't be anyone out here. I was told prior to our departure for the patrol that we were the only Soviet forces in the area."

"I've heard stories of a lone sniper. A sniper that has killed dozens of Finns and struck fear into their hearts." another private added.

Sergeant Lenkov snorted in derision at the private's notion. He gently turned over the unconscious form in front of him revealing his scoped rifle, "Perhaps you are right after all Sasha."

Lenkov held a hand over the man's mouth and said, "I can feel the warmth of his breath. He's still alive."

"What should we do?" Ivanov asked.

Lenkov pondered the question for several moments, "Dimitri you and Sasha, carry him back to the medical tent near the regimental headquarters. The rest of us will proceed with the patrol. With luck we'll run across the Finns that shot him and get a little payback."

"Da comrade sergeant!" The two privates said in unison.

Working together the two men, sat Kuznetsov up. He groaned but his eyes remained closed. They each grabbed an arm and with a grunt of effort lifted him up off the ground, "It seems comrade sniper is not going to give us much in the way of assistance for this journey." Sasha observed.

"Don't whine. I'd much rather be doing this

assignment then looking for the Finns that did this." Dimitri said.

As the two men started to drag Kuznetsov away, Sasha asked, "Why? Comrade Stalin said that the Finns would be no problem."

"When did you get here, yesterday?" replied Dimitri, "The Finns we face around this thrice cursed road are the result of some unholy coupling between a snow beast and a woman, likely a witch. Maybe even Baba Yaga herself"

"Come on now comrade. Surely you jest. The party says that there is no such thing as the supernatural. It's all just superstition perpetrated by the elite bourgeoise to keep hard working peasants in line through fear." Sasha said.

Dimitri looked around as if to make sure that the trees, or perhaps something else was not listening in on the conversation, "Then how have these Finns done what they have done? They are either supernatural or the party is incompetent."

"The party is not incompetent." Sasha insisted.

"Exactly," agreed Dimitri. "Therefore, it must be a supernatural explanation. The denizens of this forest should have been left undisturbed and now they hunger for the blood of those that dare to violate their realm. These half-human snow beasts hunger for human flesh. They have already feasted upon the 163rd Division and now they sate their hunger upon the 44th."

"But that is why we are here, is it not? The party has ordered us to rescue our beleaguered comrades that have been led into this situation by that incompetent ape Vinogradov. The fools in the army have failed to accomplish their mission so now it is we, the good party men of the NKVD, who must save the day." Sasha countered.

"Would the party put an incompetent man in charge of one of the new elite motor rifle divisions?" Dimitri asked.

"No. That would mean the party itself is incompetent." Sasha replied.

"If the party is not incompetent and our forces have superior numbers and equipment, then how do you explain what is happening here?" Dimitri asked.

Sasha, backed into a corner, sighed, "That half-human snow beasts are responsible for the destruction of the 163rd and have nearly destroyed the 44th."

Dimitri slapped Sasha on the back and said, "Good comrade I'm glad we are finally seeing things eye to eye."

Kuznetsov groaned and opened his eyes. He turned his head to see who was carrying him. Seeing Sasha and Dimitri, he whispered, "Karhonen."

Before either man could respond, Kuznetsov's eyes rolled into the back of his head and he again, lost consciousness.

Hale saw six men approaching him. From the snatches of conversation, he was able to hear, he realized, *They're Russians.*

They're coming right at me and they are less than fifty meters away. What do I do? He wondered.

He reached down and felt a grenade clipped to his belt and smiled, *You kill the enemy of course.*

He twisted the cap off the grenade and pulled the string to arm it and without rising and therefore announcing his presence to the enemy. Staying prone, he hurled it at the six men. The grenade landed a meter behind the point man, placing it about two meters in front of the next man in the patrol's line, "Granata!" The private yelled.

The point man turned, and his eyes widened as he saw the stick style grenade jutting out of the snow. It was the last thing he ever saw as the grenade exploded. The metal casing of the grenade was ripped apart by the explosion sending metal fragments whistling through the air. The tiny bits of metal were then hurled in a 360-degree arc from the exploding grenade by the kinetic force of the blast and sliced into the point man's body. He was dead before he hit the ground.

The second man in the squad, a little further away from the exploding grenade, went down screaming as he was also peppered with metal fragments. Hale took aim at the third man in line with his rifle and fired. The bullet took the man in his chest, and he fell backwards screaming.

The fourth man in the line, armed with an SVT-38 rifle, saw Hale coming to his feet and fired his rifle quickly from the hip. Hale threw himself into a roll and the bullet whizzed by. Hale came to his feet as he desperately worked the action on his rifle. The Russian raised the SVT-38, the Soviet Union's first semi-automatic rifle, to his shoulder and took careful aim.

As Hale finished chambering a fresh round, he raised his rifle to his shoulder, but it was too late, the Soviet, less than ten meters away had the barrel of his rifle pointed at Hale's chest. The Soviet flashed Hale a smile and pulled the trigger. His rifle failed to fire. The Russian's face began to contort into shock as Hale fired his rifle. The bullet smashed into the Soviet's chest and knocked him off his feet.

The three remaining men in the Soviet patrol, spread out and advanced on Hale. Each man had one of the new SVT-38 rifles pointed at Hale's chest, *At least one of those rifles is going to fire.* Hale realized.

Grasping the hopelessness of his situation, he raised up his left arm in surrender, and with his right hand, he set his rifle on the ground. The middle Soviet barked, "On your knees!" Hale had learned that Russian phrase from Olga, the Special Operations Group language instructor, during his afternoon of Russian language training. During the lesson he had met Pekka in for the first time. During his time with Leo, who was fluent in Russian, Hale picked up many more words.

Hale nodded his understanding and dropped to his knees, "Hands on your head!" The man demanded, again in Russian.

Hale placed his hands on his head and defiantly met the Soviet's gaze. Suddenly the men to either side of him clutched their chests and went down. A split-second later Hale heard the sound of two rifles firing from somewhere behind him. Before the surviving Soviet could react to the sudden change in circumstances, Hale snatched up his rifle and fired.

The Russians eyes went wide as he looked down at the red stain on his coat. Hale dropped his rifle and ran to the man he had just shot. He wrapped his right arm around the Russian and supported him as he gently lowered him to the ground, "I'm sorry but it was you or me friend."

The edge of the enemy soldier's lips turned slightly upward as he tried to smile up at Hale. Suddenly his body convulsed as he tried to take a breath and couldn't. A moment later the light went out of the man's eyes and Hale's shoulders slumped, "I'm so tired of the killing."

Kivi appeared behind Hale and slapped him on the back as the younger man came to his feet, "You owe me one."

Hale turned and smiled up at his taller counterpart, "Let's call it even since you disobeyed orders."

Kivi tilted his head upwards toward the sky and laughed heartily, "Cute."

A look of shock came over Hale's face, "What?" Kivi demanded.

"I'm not used to seeing you with a sense of humor. The Kivi I used to know would have let loose a string of curses ending in something to the effect that I'm an ungrateful pup." Hale said.

"Blame it on Pekka." Kivi said with a smile, "That man is infectious."

"He is indeed." Hale agreed, "He also seems to be a miracle worker. I never would have thought you were capable of smiling, much less laughing."

Hale bent over and took the SVT-38 rifle out of the cold dead fingers of one of the slain Russians, "That's new." Kivi observed.

"There's no bolt." Hale said as he examined the rifle.

Kivi pointed to a lever on the side of the gun, "That looks like the kind of primer you would see on one of our Suomi submachineguns or a Soviet PPD-34."

Hale's eyes widened in realization at what he was holding in his hands, "Is this thing a rifle version of a machine gun?"

"There is only one way to find out." Kivi said.

Hale pointed the rifle at a nearby tree and pulled the trigger. The rifle fired and a bullet slammed into the tree with an audible thunk. Without taking any further action Hale pulled the trigger a second time. The rifle fired again.

A smile spread across Hale's face as realization dawned on him. He centered the rifle's sight on the same tree and pulled the trigger again. Once more the rifle fired. He then repeatedly pulled the trigger six more times. Each time he pulled the trigger, the rifle fired another bullet. Finally on the seventh pull of the trigger, the weapon clicked. The magazine was empty.

"Summer of cunts." Hale whispered.

"This rifle could change everything." Kivi observed.

"If every Red Army soldier was issued one of these, it would create a tenfold increase in their firepower." Hale said.

"I thought I saw a few of these with men of the 44th, but most of the riflemen still used Mosin-Nagants." Kivi said.

"This group all had one. I wonder what the difference is between them?" Hale asked.

Kivi pulled the small plastic cylinder on a string off the

neck of the nearest Russian corpse. He carefully unscrewed the cap and pulled out the little rolled up paper within, "Boris Putin, 3rd NKVD Regiment."

"I've heard of the NKVD. It was my understanding that they are spies and enforcers of the party's will, not soldiers." Hale said.

"Perhaps the party is so paranoid that the army will betray them, that they've created their own military units." Kivi suggested.

"What would be the advantage of that?" Sergeant Anttlia asked.

"If there were enough units like the 3rd NKVD, it would give the party a fighting chance, should the army betray them." Hale said.

"So these aren't real soldiers?" Sergeant Anttlia asked.

"I'm sure these men have been trained to be soldiers, but they are likely more than that. They are members of the party and likely to be trained spies or internal security forces." Hale said.

"Stalin seems obsessed with a large military. Why waste manpower on internal security forces?" Sergeant Anttlia asked.

"Because Stalin is also paranoid that his people will betray him. Therefore, the NKVD, has an entire division dedicated to spying on their own people." Hale said.

"To keep them in line." Kivi added.

"Please don't be offended lieutenant but how did you come to know all of this? It was my understanding that you haven't gone to a university and that you came up through the ranks." Sergeant Anttlia asked.

"My father despised the Bolsheviks. He collected all the books about them that he could get his hands on and encouraged me to read them." Hale said.

"Know thine enemy." Sergeant Antilla nodded in understanding, "Your father sounds like a smart man. He must have known that they would try to take what was ours one day. Is he still alive?"

Hale looked down at the ground as his shoulders slumped and said, "No. He died from a Red Army bullet in his own kitchen."

Antilla put an arm around Hale's shoulders and gave him a hug, "I'm sorry for your loss. It sounds like your father was a good man and prepared you for this day."

A single tear slid down Hale's face as he nodded and said, "He was."

Kivi, changing the subject, asked, "Clearly none of these men were the sniper you were chasing. None of their rifles has a scope. So, what do we do now?"

"Chances are the sniper I engaged, and shot was Kuznetsov. Given that fact, there isn't much point in staying here and maintaining the line." Hale said.

Kivi nodded in agreement, "True. So, what did you have in mind."

Hale pointed to the east and said, "He's somewhere out there. Whether he has help or not, I don't know. If this was a regular single squad patrol, then two men are missing."

"Those two men could be helping this Kuznetsov

fellow escape." Sergeant Antilla added.

Hale, said with finality, "We can't allow that to happen."

Chapter 26

Late Afternoon One Kilometer South of the Village of Raate, Central Finland

January 6th, 1940

Captain Kokko peered through his binoculars at the Village of Raate. The tiny village was the namesake for the road that has become the grave of so many Soviet soldiers. He stood roughly a kilometer to the south of the village upon a path running in a north-south direction. The road he stood upon intersected with the Raate Road in the center of the village.

The small village was home to a handful of wooden houses that straddled the road. The structures were painted cheerful pastel colors and stood in sharp contrast to the gray sky and white ground. He noticed that only a single chimney in the village had smoke wafting upward from it, *The enemy must be using that house.*

Unlike most of this region of Finland, the area around the village had been cleared so that it could be farmed. This created an area of uncharacteristically long visibility. Kokko shifted his gaze eastward along the road. Less than a kilometer from the village in that direction, lay the

315

border of the Soviet Union. He smiled as he saw what he had hoped to see, coming from that direction, absolutely nothing. He turned to his 1st platoon commander and said, "Let's take this village back from the enemy and cut the 3rd NKVD Regiment off from the Soviet Union." Kokko paused and smiled malevolently, "Then we'll have a new fly stuck in our web. The same web that has trapped the 163rd and 44th Divisions."

Lieutenant Couri, the commander of 1st Platoon, asked, "Then what do we do with them?"

Kokko turned to the lieutenant and gave him a feral grin, "We do what any spider does to those trapped in our web. We feed."

Captain Kokko waited until nightfall so that they could approach the Village of Raate unobserved. Once the light had faded away and the land was shrouded in darkness, Kokko ordered his forces forward. The soldiers under his command, all veteran skiers that could ski before they could walk, silently crept forward.

A hundred meters out from the edge of the village Lieutenant Couri's platoon, who had taken point halted. Captain Kokko moved up to the head of the column and asked, "Why did you stop?"

"My point man thought he saw a faint orange point of light." Couri replied.

"A cigarette?" Kokko asked.

Couri nodded, "My man had the same thought."

"Where was the spot?" Kokko asked.

Couri pointed, "Right there, about twenty meters south of the village. It was really low to the ground, and we haven't seen anything else since."

"So, the smoker was either prone, or in a hole." Kokko observed.

"What are your orders, sir? Should we proceed?" Couri asked.

Kokko exhaled sharply in frustration, "No, if there are men there, the rising moon will back light us as we approach."

"Then what do we do?" Couri asked.

"Deploy your men here and form a line. If the map is correct, then the farmers haven't cleared the land to the northwest of the village yet. I'm going to take the other platoon and circle around the village to that point. Using the cover of the trees we'll try and sneak in from the north and take the bastards from behind." Kokko.

"If I hear shooting, what do I do?" Couri asked.

"If they start shooting that means they have spotted us before we could get them all with our knives. If that happens, I want you to move into the village with your platoon. Be sure to verify your targets before shooting. I don't want any incidents of friendly fire." Captain Kokko ordered, "Got it?"

Lieutenant Couri nodded, "Understood, sir. We are to hold our position here unless there is shooting. If there is shooting, we are to move forward into the village."

"When will you shoot?" Kokko prompted him.

"Only when we have verified the target is not a friendly." Couri amended.

"Very good." Kokko glanced down at his watch which read four PM, "I'll move into position with 2nd Platoon, and we will begin our attack at five."

Captain Kokko took command of 2nd platoon. Following his lead, the men of 2nd Platoon turned around and disappeared into the trees to the south of 1st Platoon's line. Using the impenetrable darkness of the forest, they traveled in a half circle around the cleared farmland.

The map wasn't entirely correct and the area to the northwest of the village had started to be cleared by the farmers. Fifty meters of forest had been cleared away from the village. The newly cleared land was riddled with stumps, indicating that the farmers hadn't made much progress before the ground froze.

Captain Kokko cursed, "It looks like the villagers had just started to clear the land."

"What do you want us to do, sir?" Lieutenant Eskola, who commanded 2nd platoon, asked.

"Give me your quietest eight men." Kokko ordered.

As Kokko observed the village from this new vantage point, Lieutenant Eskola, who had been in command of this platoon for less than a week, smartly deferred to his NCOs to select the best men. Within minutes, the sergeants had sorted who the eight quietest men in the platoon were., "Here are my eight quietest men, sir. As you ordered." Lieutenant Eskola whispered.

"Very good." Kokko said. He turned to face the men, seven privates and a corporal and said, "Take my lead and follow me. Corporal?"

"Mantyal, sir."

"Corporal Mantyal, you bring up the rear and make sure everyone is following my lead. I don't want someone's stupid mistake to get us all killed."

"Understood, captain." Mantyal replied.

Kokko turned to Eskola and said, "If there is shooting, I want you to bring the other two squads into the village and engage any hostiles. Be sure the men understand that they are to only fire if they are sure of the identity of their target."

"Understood, sir." Eskola replied.

Kokko turned to the selected men and said, "Let's move out."

Captain Kokko slung his Suomi submachine gun onto his back and laid prone on the ground. He gave the eight men with him a few moments to do the same. Once the noise of the men behind him subsided, he started to crawl southeast toward the village.

The moon was starting to rise in the south casting its silver light down upon the ground. Fortunately, the wanning gibbous moon of the last few days was no more, and the moon provided little light. As he crawled, Kokko used the stumps as much as possible to shield his movement from Soviet eyes in the village.

Progress was slow across the open field and time slowed to a crawl as Kokko worried about being discovered. Every shift in the shadows of the village sent his heart racing. He expected the enemy to discover his group at any moment and to feel bullets tear into his skin and end his life.

Less than twenty meters from the edge of the village he heard voices. He paused and raised an arm with a close fist, which signalled the other men behind him to stop. Kokko turned toward the men following him and saw that they had seen his signal.

The sound of voices grew louder as the men talking drew nearer to him and Kokko was able to discern two distinct voices. Kokko pointed at the closest man to him and signaled for him to crawl up to him. The other man did as he was directed and when he was right next to Kokko, the captain said, "There are two sentries up ahead. It looks like they are patrolling the edge of the village. Let's wait here and see if they use a consistent patrol route."

The private nodded and the nine men lay still. The two Soviets paused when they reached the northernmost point of the village. Kokko glanced down at his watch which read four forty-five PM and he cursed, *Eskola is expecting us to attack soon. Hopefully he has enough sense not to lose his patience and go rushing in.*

The two Soviets started to laugh at a joke shared between them. They then each lit a cigarette using a match, *Those two fools just wrecked their night vision. It's time to get moving.* Kokko thought.

Kokko came to his feet and dashed for the edge of the village. He glanced over his shoulder to ensure the other man was still following, he was. When he reached the cover of the first building on the edge of the village, a chicken coup, he didn't stop. Instead, he kept moving forward deeper into the village.

When Kokko reached the first farmhouse. He stopped. The other man had kept pace with him and was right behind him. They stood there for nearly a minute to allow their breathing to slow, "What's your name private?"

"Pelto, sir."

"Alright Pelto, you've done a great job keeping up so far. We are going to check to see if there are any other enemy soldiers on this side of the village. If there isn't we'll deal with our two friends taking the cigarette break." Kokko said.

"Understood, sir." Pelto replied.

Kokko stayed close to the farmhouse and crept forward toward the center of the village. The village of Raate had a small clearing in the center that was bisected by the road and surrounded by seven houses. The easternmost house had a warm and inviting yellow glow coming from its windows, and smoke emerging from its chimney. There appeared to be no men moving around within or without the house.

"It looks like there aren't any other men outside of the house other than our two sentries. Let's start with them, return to the squad, and then move onto the house." Kokko said.

Private Pelto nodded in acknowledgement of Kokko's orders. Kokko and Pelto moved slowly northward, careful to remain in the shadows cast by the village's houses. When they reached the edge of the northernmost farmhouse, the two Soviet sentries weren't visible.

"Where did they go?" Pelto asked.

"They probably finished their smokes and went back to doing their job. The question is, did their route continue eastward around the village or did they double back?" Kokko said.

Pelto, not knowing the answer to Kokko's question remained silent. Kokko glanced down at his watch.

Standing in the shadow of a farmhouse he was unable to see the hour or minute hand on the watch, *What time is it?* He wondered.

"I really hope Eskola can be patient. This is taking longer than I thought it would." Kokko whispered.

The two men waited for nearly thirty minutes for the sentries to return. Kokko started to lose heart that they would ever return. Finally, he saw movement out of the corner of his eye. He turned his head toward the movement and spotted the Soviet sentries. This time the two men appeared to be silent and much more alert than they had been during their previous round, *Has something got them on edge?* He wondered.

As they drew closer the Finns were able to see that the two men were armed with rifles. The moonlight revealed that they were both dressed in white snowsuits, *Damn. I should have ordered the men to put gray arm bands on so we could quickly tell friend from foe in this light.* Kokko thought.

Suddenly, the two Soviets paused and started to look around. Kokko cursed inwardly, *Did they hear something?*

The sound of a large tree branch breaking in the forest beyond the empty farmland answered Koko's question. The enemy soldiers unslung their rifles and got down on one knee as they peered at the forest. Kokko made a quick decision, "We need to take them out before they decide to shoot whatever is in the forest."

"Let's go then." Pelto replied.

Kokko emerged from the cover of the farmhouse and started to slowly creep forward. He made it halfway to the two Soviets before the sound of another tree branch breaking could be heard. This time it came from the northeast. Both of the enemy soldiers raised their rifles to their shoulders and started to take aim at something, *Shit, they are about to shoot.*

Throwing caution to the wind, Kokko dashed forward and wrapped his left arm around the mouth of the man on the right. He drew his pukko blade and sliced open the man's throat. The other soldier, seeing the movement in his peripheral vision, swung his SVT-38 rifle toward Kokko.

Pelto plunged his own pukko blade into the back of the second soldier's neck. The man let out a gasp of surprise, that was cut off when the young Finn placed his hand over the Russian's mouth. The two Finns kept their victim's mouth covered as their blood fed the hungry Finnish soil. Kokko felt the man's body shudder under him, then twitch, and finally remained still.

He rolled the Russian over and looked down at his unseeing eyes. He gazed up into the clear nigh time sky and whispered, "Please forgive me oh Lord for breaking thy most sacred of commandments."

"Amen." Pelto added.

"Help me move them. We need to conceal these two in case there are other patrollers that we are unaware of." Kokko said.

The two men worked together to move the bodies. They placed them one on top of the other next to a trough. They returned to the location of their first kills a third time and covered the blood-stained snow up using the surrounding snow. Finally, they collected the slain Soviet's two SVT-38 rifles and returned them to their owners.

Kokko and Pelto then returned to their squad, "Alright gather around real close." He hissed.

The men did as instructed, "Pelto and I took out those two sentries. As far as we can tell they were the only ones. There is an occupied house in the village. We need to clear it before we hit the group dug in just south of the road."

"Don't you think going into an occupied house is risky? Shouldn't we just hit the men in the trench and circle back for the soldiers in the house?" Corporal Mantyal asked.

"Yes, but what choice do we have? Odds are someone in the trench is going to get off a shot, and then the men in the house will come running. I don't know about you, but I don't relish the idea of being stuck out in the open between two enemy forces. If we hit the house and it goes bad, we can always retreat into the trees but if we hit the group entrenched by the road first and that goes bad, we're screwed." Kokko replied.

"That's a very good point captain. I guess that is why I am just a corporal." Mantyal replied.

Kokko put a hand on Mantyal's shoulder and gave him a reassuring squeeze, "Don't be to hard on yourself corporal. You're new at this."

"And you're not sir?" Mantyal asked.

"Not entirely. I was too young to see action during the Great War, but I, along with a thousand other young men were sent to train in Germany after Finland broke away from Russia. I then saw some limited action during the civil war, but today is the first day I've ever had to kill anyone." Kokko said.

Mantyal's eyes widened at Kokko's revelation, "You're a Jaeger!"

Kokko nodded, "Now if we're done going over my life's history let's move out. Everyone on me, single file. I want Pelto behind me and Mantyal last."

"Bringing up the rear again." Mantyal said with a chuckle.

Kokko, with the eight enlisted men following him, quietly and cautiously made his way back to the occupied house. When they reached the house, he turned to Pelto and said, "Tell the two men immediately behind you to break off and cover the front entrance."

Pelto, his face visible by the warm light shining through the house's windows, nodded. He turned to the man directly behind him and whispered Kokko's orders into his ear. That man did the same to the soldier behind him and the two men moved around to the front entrance of the house. The first man took a position in a doorway across the street that was roughly a forty-five-degree angle from the occupied house's front door. The other man took a position that would place him behind the door if it opened.

Kokko crept along the north side of the house until he reached the back corner. He peered around the corner for several long moments ensuring that there wasn't any Russians. The back door of the house was roughly five meters to the south. There was an outhouse, roughly five meters from the rear door of the main structure.

Kokko, glanced down at his watch, it was nearly five thirty PM, *Stay patient Eskola.*

After waiting for ten minutes to confirm that no one was in the outhouse, Kokko started to move toward the back door. He was careful to duck down as he passed the window. As he reached the back door, it started to swing open. He quickly sat down on the ground, with his back against the house in the hopes that he would be concealed in the shadows.

A man, wearing a dark green uniform emerged from the house. He paused for a moment to blink the sleep away from his eyes and get his bearings. Simultaneously, Pelto was moving around the corner, trying to conceal himself.

The Soviet saw the movement in the corner of his eye and began to turn in that direction. He drew in a breath to shout a warning, but he never got the chance. Kokko stood and plunged his pukko blade into the man's chest. As the Soviet started to scream, he placed his left hand over the man's mouth.

The Russian's blood sprayed the front of Kokko's white snow suit as he stabbed the man repeatedly. As the enemy soldier lost strength, his knees buckled, and Kokko lowered him to the stairs. His heart froze as he heard the sound of movement within the house.

Thinking quickly, he sheathed his pukko blade and dragged the body to the outhouse. As he turned toward the house, the back door started to open. Kokko quickly closed the outhouse door. He was careful not to slam it as another man emerged from the house, *Please don't look down.* Kokko thought.

"Gregory?" The man said.

Summer of cunts. Kokko inwardly cursed, *Were these guys roommates or something?*

"Gregory?" The man asked again.

Frowning, he approached the outhouse and knocked on the door, "Gregory? Are you in there?" The man asked in

Russian.

Kokko, thinking fast, made a retching noise. The Russian laughed, "Ahhh my friend, having trouble holding your vodka? I didn't think you drank that much."

The Soviet suddenly gasped, as he was stabbed from behind. Pelto wrapped his left arm around the man's chest and covered his mouth with his hand. The private felt the lifeforce of the Russian drain away as he held him. The body convulsed three times, as the enemy soldier's body jerked violently. Finally, the Russian exhaled his last breath, then lay still.

Pelto moved the body out of the way, and then opened the outhouse door. Kokko, seeing Pelto and the Russian corpse smiled in relief, "We are starting to make a habit of this."

Pelto returned Kokko's smile and said, "Yes, sir."

"Let's get these bodies out of view of the back door and this red snow cleaned up before anyone else decides they want to take a shit." Kokko said.

"Why don't we just go inside now?" Pelto asked.

"First, there might be a third man waiting for these two to come back." Kokko replied.

"And second?" Pelto asked.

"It's a hell of a lot less risky to ambush these guys as they come out, then it is for us to go inside the house blindly." Kokko said.

The squad quickly removed the bodies of the two slain Russians from sight and covered up the blood-stained snow with fresh powder. Kokko then placed his ear against one of the back windows of the house and listened. He could hear laughter, interrupted by the occasional snap of a burning birch log, *Great. It sounds like they are all awake. What do we do? Storm the house and hope no one gets off a shot or wait for them to realize they are missing two men and come out here?*

Kokko glanced down at his watch, *Six PM. Eskola has been more than patient, we need to wrap this up. I would have given up on us by now and ordered the attack.*

Kokko, along with Pelto, returned to the northern side of the house and whispered, "Everyone gather around."

With the eight enlisted men surrounding him, Kokko said, "We need to storm the house while Eskola and 1st platoon are still in position."

"I'm sure there is a good reason but captain, I just can't help myself. Why?" Mantyal asked.

"When the men entrenched by the road head this way, 1st Platoon can shoot them in the back. If we wait much longer, Eskola is going to assume we are dead and attack himself." Kokko said.

"Why would that be bad? Couldn't we just shoot the men in the house in the back as they rushed to help their friends?" Mantyal asked.

"Sure, and we would also lose men in the other platoon as they attacked the entrenched Russians. A lot of men." Kokko replied.

"Now, if there aren't any more questions let's get this over with. The two men we killed that emerged from the house, reeked of vodka. When I stuck my ear to the window, I heard laughter. If we put two and two together, I believe the Russians inside are engaging in their national pastime, getting drunk."

Kokko paused a moment to ponder a course of action, "I'm going to kick the door down and hurl two grenades in there. Pelto, you take point with your Suomi followed by me, and two other men." Kokko paused and pointed at two men, "You and you."

"What about the rest of us?" Mantyal asked.

"I want you to circle around to the front of the house and set up across the street. If any Russians come running to help out their comrades. Shoot them." Kokko replied.

"Questions?" Kokko asked.

The eight men stared at him expectantly but no one else spoke, "Let's get to it then." Kokko said.

Mantyal, peeled off four men and crossed the street, while Kokko approached the back door. He unclipped his two grenades from his belt and met Pelto's gaze. The younger man gave him a nod. Kokko returned the nod with a smile and turned toward the back door of the house.

Kokko lifted his leg to deliver a mighty kick to the door, when Pelto grabbed his arm to stop him, "What?" Kokko asked in irritation.

"Why don't you try the door first to see if its locked." Pelto suggested.

Kokko put his right foot back on the ground, shrugged his shoulders, and gave the door handle a gentle tug. The door opened slightly, "Very well then. Ready?"

Pelto gave him a nod. Kokko unscrewed the cap on his two grenades and gently tugged the string inside to arm them. Next, he pulled open the door and hurled them into the house. A Russian, sitting at a table with some playing cards in his hand eye's widened when he saw Kokko.

Kokko slammed the door shut as pandemonium erupted inside the house. A handful of seconds later the grenades detonated with a loud BOOM-BOOM. Kokko pulled the door open and Pelto, his Suomi at the ready, rushed into the room. He needn't have bothered as every Russian in the room was down on the ground, slain by the grenades. The kitchen table the men were sitting at had been reduced to splinters and hurled throughout the room by the blast.

Pelto ran through the kitchen and into the living room which lay beyond. He saw a Russian fleeing out the front door, raised his weapon, and fired. Pelto's bullets slammed into the fleeing man's back and he toppled forward into the clearing outside. Mantyal heard several Russian voices screaming from the direction of the road.

A moment later, gunfire erupted. Lieutenant Eskola hearing gunfire from the northern side of the village said, "Get ready to attack."

A few moments later, every single Russian started to climb out of the trench, "Hold your fire men. Wait until they are all out." Eskola urged.

When the last Russian was fully visible the young lieutenant screamed, "Fire!"

The men of 1st Platoon opened fire on the backs of the Russians. They killed all but two, who managed to survive the hail of bullets and disappear into the village. The two men appeared a few moments later, running toward Mantyal's group, "Open fire!" Mantyal barked.

The Russians, seeing four Finns suddenly appear in front of them raised their rifles simultaneously. The two sides exchanged fire. One of the Finns cried out as he was hit with a bullet, while both Russians were hit and went down. Mantyal's group finished them off with a second salvo. With the last Russian slain, Raate Village was once again in Finnish hands.

Chapter 27

Late Afternoon, Three Kilometers Southwest of Raate Village, Central Finland,

January 6th, 1940

Hale squatted and scooped up a handful of snow. He gazed down at the snow in his left hand and saw a faint red dot. He looked up at Lieutenant Kivi and said, "He's still bleeding."

Still squatting, Hale turned his gaze to the trail. There were two sets of footprints about half a meter apart. Between them were two small indentations gouged out of the snow. Hale pointed to the two lines in the snow that would join together from time to time and said, "It looks like they are still dragging him."

"Then we must be catching up." Sergeant Antilla observed.

Hale nodded and pointed to a location twenty meters ahead, "It looks like they changed direction to the north."

"We'd best be catching them soon. We're only a kilometer or so south of the road. I bet they're making for their headquarters area." Kivi said.

"Why do you say that?" Hale asked.

"Because we are nearly equal distant between the Purasjokki River, which is the eastern edge of Task Force Fagernas and the Village of Raate." Kivi said, "If you recall Fagernas told us that Raate Village was the eastern edge of the 3rd NKVD's zone of control."

"Which is why he sent Captain Kokko's company to retake the village. With Raate Village in our hands, the 3rd NKVD Regiment will also be trapped and cut off from the Soviet Union." Hale added, "Your reasoning makes sense."

Sergeant Antilla rolled his eyes and said, "Officers." he then asked, "Are we going to stand here jawing, or are we going to move our asses and kill some Russians?"

Hale smiled as he turned to Kivi and asked, "Do we really talk that much?"

Kivi gave Sergeant Antilla a side long glance as he said, "I'm afraid so. It used to be that we could barely get two words out of you in training. Now half the time we can't get you to shut up."

"You're one to talk. Why I'd say it has at least been twenty-four hours since you've made an insane charge into the midst of an enemy horde screaming in fury." Hale observed.

Kivi gave Hale a feral grin and said, "Then I am clearly overdue. Let's run these bastards down, put an end to Kuznetsov, and then go attack the 3rd NKVD's headquarters."

"With the ten of us?" Hale asked skeptically.

"Sure, why not?" Kivi asked.

"I guess he's right." Hale said.

"Right about what?" Kivi asked.

"We really do talk to much. The old Kivi would have just got it done. Let's move." Hale said.

The Finns resumed their pursuit of the fleeing Soviets. Ten minutes later, as Hale topped a small ridge, he spotted movement up ahead. He held up his right hand and made a fist to signal for the men behind him to stop. He then turned his hand, so that the palm was facing downward and raised and lowered his hand twice, the signal to get down.

Hale quickly unslung his rifle, as the tracks had indicated there were two enemy soldiers dragging a third between them. He lined up the iron sights with the enemy soldier on the right, made a quick adjustment to his rifle to account for the distance, held his breath, and pulled the trigger.

The rifle's stock slammed into his right shoulder. A split-second later, his target collapsed to the ground. The other soldier, suddenly bearing the full weight of the injured man, presumably Kuznetsov, dropped to his knees.

Hale worked the action on his rifle and quickly took aim at the second enemy soldier. The man had turned his head to the right and had frozen in shock at the sight of his comrade laying prone on the ground as he convulsed and coughed up blood. Before his mind could recover from the shock, a bullet slammed into his back.

The bullet smashed into his mid-back. The kinetic force of the impact knocked him forward a half meter. He staggered for a moment then collapsed to the ground.

The combination of the noise from Hale's rifle firing

and suddenly lying in the cold snow, caused Kuznetsov to regain consciousness. He blinked in confusion for several moments before he slowly looked to his left, then his right. He saw that both of his comrades had fresh bullet wounds in their back, *Fuck.* He thought.

A moment later, a hand grabbed Kuznetsov's wounded shoulder and turned him over. He gasped in surprise and pain as the dull throbbing of his bullet wound suddenly became a fiery spike of agony. Each finger of the grasping hand felt like an individual dagger stabbed into his shoulder.

It took him nearly a minute to recover from the sudden pain. Finally, he looked up at the man that had caused it. Staring daggers down at him was Hale Karhonen. He smiled up at the Finnish sniper and said, "Remember your promise?"

Hale slowly nodded in acknowledgement as Kivi asked, "What promise?"

"Kuznetsov here saved me from being executed by Volkov. In return he made me promise him that I would spare his life should our circumstances ever be reversed." Hale replied.

"That's bullshit. This bastard has earned death ten times over." Kivi fumed.

Hale sighed, "I agree, he deserves the slowest death we could devise for him. He is responsible for killing dozens of Finns."

"So, then you are going to kill him?" Kivi asked.

Hale's shoulders slumped and his gaze fell to the ground as he said, "No, my word is important to me, and I am going to honor it."

"Summer of cunts Hale!" Kivi screamed, "This man shot you and killed everyone in your first command. You can't possibly let him go. If you do, he will probably go right back to killing more of us."

Kuznetsov looked concerned. Though he was unable to understand Kivi's words, he understood the intent of his tone. He reached out and tugged Hale's left pant leg.

Hale's gaze shifted to the enemy sniper, the man who had been responsible for the deaths of so many of his men and asked sharply, "What?"

"You promised." Kuznetsov said in thickly accented Finnish.

"I did." Hale gestured northward and said, "You are free to go."

Kivi grabbed Hale's right shoulder and spun him around, "Hale no! This is bullshit. Fuck your promise. The only thing this bastard deserves is a bullet. Besides you've already broken your promise by shooting him."

"When I shot him. I didn't realize it was Kuznetsov, therefore I didn't break my word. I can't finish him. I promised. A life for a life." Hale said in resignation. Inwardly, Hale's mind raced, *You can't do this. This man is your mission. Remember what Leo said. You are bound by the promise but he wasn't.*

Hale stood in silence as he struggled internally with this decision, *You can walk away right now. Let Kivi do it.* The tight muscles in Hale's back began to relax as he reached a decision that enabled him to honor his word, while completing the mission he was given by General Mannerheim. He turned to walk away then paused, *If you let Kivi or any of your other men kill him, you are going to violate the spirit of what you promised.*

Losing patience, Kivi, started to reach for his pistol holster. Hale grabbed his wrist and said, "No, that's an order!"

Kivi's pupils narrowed, and his nostrils flared as he glared down at Hale, "Don't do this." He hissed.

"It's already done." Hale said as he turned back to Kuznetsov and said, "You're free to go."

Without another word, Kuznetsov unsteadily came to his feet and turned his back to the Finns. He looked down at his two slain companions and spotted his rifle. With effort he bent over and pulled it from the man's left shoulder.

He straightened up and started to sling the rifle onto his right shoulder, "Wait." Hale said.

Kuznetsov stopped moving and stood stiffly, *Did he change his mind?* He wondered.

"Leave the rifle." Hale demanded.

Kuznetsov held out the rifle and Hale snatched it out of his hand, "Now you can go."

Without looking back, Kuznetsov began his northward trek toward the Raate Road and salvation.

Chapter 28

Late Evening, One Kilometer East of the Purasjoki River, Central Finland

January 6th, 1940

It took an hour for the news to travel to the commander of the Soviet 3rd NKVD Regiment, Colonel Ivan Maslennikov that the Village of Raate had fallen to a Finnish attack. The colonel was currently located within his command post. He had chosen the only structure in his operating area as his headquarters. The structure, a cabin, was a small hunting lodge approximately a kilometer east of the bridge over the Purasjoki River.

The colonel's adjutant and battalion commanders, eleven men in total, were crowded into the single room lodge. The air was filled with cigarette smoke and smelled of unwashed bodies. The officers didn't mind sharing such close quarters, as the alternative, a tent, or even worse simply being outside would have been much less comfortable.

In addition to the officers a single enlisted man, Sergeant Yuri Vladovich, manned the Regiment's radio set. The sergeant looked up when the cabin's only door, suddenly swung open. A private, breathing heavily, squeezed into the lodge and exclaimed, "Raate Village has fallen!"

Irritated Colonel Maslennikov turned toward the door and shouted, "What?"

Seeing the colonel's face take on a crimson hue, the private cowered and meekly said, "The Village of Raate has fallen."

"Fallen, how?" Maslennikov demanded.

"A regiment of Finns attacked the village and swept away our garrison." The private replied.

"An entire regiment was able to move around us?" Maslennikov said, perplexed.

A new voice belonging to a man in a white snowsuit who suddenly occupied the open doorway answered Maslennikov's question, "The Finns aren't using roads to move their units around."

Maslennikov glared past the private trying to see the man in the doorway and asked, "Who said that?"

"A sergeant, sir. He says his name is Kuznetsov." The private answered.

"Send this Kuznetsov in. Then get out private." Maslennikov demanded.

The men in the room grumbled as they were forced to shift to allow a twelfth body to squeeze into the confined space. Sergeant Kuznetsov entered the cramped cabin and snapped to attention, elbowing a captain next to him in the process, "Sergeant of Snipers Kuznetsov reporting as ordered comrade colonel!" The captain elbowed him back and Kuznetsov winced as his injured shoulder sent a painful reminder that he was recently injured.

"How are the Finns able to move around without roads?" Maslennikov asked.

"Ice roads and sleighs comrade colonel." Kuznetsov replied.

"What is an ice road?" Maslennikov demanded.

"The Finns have created ice roads to the north of the Raate Road but especially to the south. I was able to observe them creating one. To make a road, they flatten the snow with a reindeer that is dragging a large log behind it. The log evens out the snow and creates a smooth roadway. Next, they pour water onto the flat path to harden it. Their sleighs and even the occasional truck can easily navigate the impromptu road." Kuznetsov replied.

"No wonder they are running circles around that idiot Vinogradov. It sounds like they can make a road wherever they want." Maslennikov said.

"Indeed, sir. It is a clever way to deal with the contours in the terrain and the limitations that creates for modern vehicles." Kuznetsov said.

Maslennikov snapped his fingers and said, "Wait a minute. Now I remember who you are. Aren't you the man High Command put in charge of my snipers?"

"Yes, comrade colonel." Kuznetsov replied.

"How's that going?" Maslennikov demanded.

"We've lost several snipers, but at the same time have slain many of the enemy and sown fear into them." Kuznetsov said.

Maslennikov snorted at Kuznetsov in derision, "You've certainly sown fear into their hearts. In fact, the enemy has become so fearful of you and your snipers that they have conquered a village in response and cut us off from the Motherland." Maslennikov said, his voice dripping with sarcasm, "What are you doing here sergeant? Why aren't you out there continuing to sow fear as you put it?"

"I came to give you an update before heading out comrade colonel. Plus, I need some medical attention. I've been shot." Kuznetsov replied.

"Heading out? Heading out where?" Maslennikov asked.

"I've been ordered to the Kolla front, north of Lake Ladoga by the High Command. Our forces there are having trouble with a sniper they have come to call the White Death." Kuznetsov replied.

"Let me see your orders." Maslennikov demanded.

With a sinking feeling Kuznetsov handed the orders over to the colonel, *Why won't these damned officers here let me go?*

Maslennikov scanned the words on the typed paper and then finally nodded, "So you have. Thank you for the information. Before you depart for Kolla, is there anything else you can tell us about the enemy and their dispositions?"

"Can I see your map?" Kuznetsov asked.

Maslennikov turned and gestured down at a map laid across the lodge's only table. Kuznetsov squeezed through the crowded room until he was standing beside Maslennikov. He scanned the map and said, "It looks like you have an accurate representation of the current situation, with the exception of Raate Village now belonging to the Finns."

"The Finns have divided their forces up into four main groups they call Task Forces. Vinogradov is facing off against three of them, and your regiment is in contact with one." Kuznetsov said.

"The group holding the Purasjoki bridge and the village of Raate belong to the same Task Force?" Maslennikov asked.

Kuznetsov nodded, "I believe so colonel."

"What makes you certain?" Maslennikov asked.

"I was heading southward several hours ago when I encountered a company sized force of the enemy moving eastward, paralleling the Raate Road. They looked like a company I had observed on the road in the area controlled by Task Force Fagneras." Kuznetsov said.

"Did you engage them?" Maslennikov asked.

"No comrade colonel. My objective was to return to the bridge over the Purasjoki River in order to thin out the bridge's defenders." Kuznetsov replied.

"Why didn't you engage the company of Finns?" Maslennikov demanded.

"They were far to alert and numerous for me to risk a confrontation." Kuznetsov said.

"If I wasn't aware of your record I'd call you a coward, but your achievements would indicate otherwise. We're you able to return to the bridge?" Maslennikov asked.

Kuznetsov's shoulders slumped as his eyes fell, "No, comrade colonel."

"Why not?" Maslennikov asked.

"I was halted by the Finnish sniper group." Kuznetsov responded.

Maslennikov pointed to Kuznetsov's injured shoulder, "I see that they gave you a memento to remember them by."

"Yes, I believe that it was a sniper by the name of Hale Karhonen that shot me." Kuznetsov replied.

"But you're not positive?" Maslennikov probed.

"No." Kuznetsov lied.

"If you're not sure, who shot you, how do you know that they belonged to their sniper group?" Maslennikov demanded.

"I have tangled with the group several times over the last few days and have become familiar with their tactics." Kuznetsov again, not revealing the fact that he came face to face with Hale and his men.

Maslennikov frowned, "You were given an entire platoon of my snipers. Why were you unable to eliminate this group?"

"Two reasons. They kept finding replacements for the men we killed, and they are led by Hale Karhonen." Kuznetsov replied.

"You keep mentioning Hale Karhonen. Should I know of him?" Maslennikov asked.

"No. Not really sir. Karhonen is the best sniper the enemy has in this theater." Kuznetsov replied.

"In this theater? So, you think they have an even better sniper?" Maslennikov asked.

Kuznetsov shrugged, "I'm not sure colonel. The one they call the White Death is building quite the reputation on the Kolla River front."

Maslennikov nodded, "So he is. At any rate, I will not hold you up further. Dismissed."

Kuznetsov snapped to attention, saluted Colonel Maslennikov and left the cabin.

The colonel turned to his officers and said, "Now that we are surrounded, we need to become more aggressive before we end up like that idiot Vinogradov."

"How, sir?" A major asked.

Maslennikov gave the major a malevolent smile, "By attacking the enemy that surrounds us in both directions of course. I want the bridge over the Purasjoki taken now and I want the Village of Raate in our hands by dawn, so that our daily supply convoy can get through."

Chapter 29

Just prior to midnight, Bridge over the Purasjoki River, Central Finland

January 6th, 1940

Lieutenant Halonen of the Finnish Army felt that something was off. In an uncharacteristic display of bravery, he decided to join his men guarding the bridge over the Purasjoki River. Thanks to a combination of Kuznetsov's sniping and the 3rd NKVD's attack, Halonen's men refused to step one foot on the bridge.

Instead, they set up a barricade made of downed trees on the western edge of the bridge. This afforded them a measure of cover both from the sniper and the 3rd NKVD troops on the other side of the river. Halonen crawled the last ten meters to the barricade, being very careful to keep himself below the enemy's field of vision, and asked, "Is everything alright?"

Halonen's men, used to their young officer being a pompous arrogant ass, looked at him strangely, "Well, do I need to repeat myself?"

"No, lieutenant," Private Oja replied, "I was thinking that things on the other side of the river seemed off myself."

"What have you noticed?" Halonen asked.

"Do you hear that?" Oja asked.

"I don't hear anything." Halonen replied.

"Exactly. It's completely silent over there. The only thing we can hear is the wind rustling through the frozen tree branches." Oja replied.

"You could hear the Soviets before?" Halonen asked.

Oja nodded, "Yes, lieutenant. We could hear snatches of conversation, and the occasional laugh. Now nothing."

Halonen opened his mouth to reply when a group of Soviet soldiers suddenly appeared on the eastern side of the bridge. Catching sight of several of the Finnish defenders, they screamed a fearsome war cry as they charged across the bridge, "Hear they come! Open fire!" The young lieutenant shouted.

The Finnish defenders, numbering around fifty, opened fire on the attacking Soviets. Halonen's platoon had augmented their firepower with two pre-positioned DP-27 machine guns. The Finns had acquired the machine guns by looting them off slain soldiers of the 44th. In addition, the defenders used an assortment of weapons, PPD-34 submachine guns, also captured from the Russians. Suomi submachine guns, and Mosin Nagant rifles.

To supplement the squad of defenders manning the barricade, Halonen had deployed his other two squads just inside the tree line on the west bank of the river. This deployment maximized the platoon's fire power by enabling every man in his platoon to simultaneously pour fire into the enemy.

Halonen's platoon had been supplemented by the

survivors of several other understrength platoons. These ravaged units had been combined and then assigned to Halonen as Finnish officers, who usually led from the front, were increasingly in short supply. The first few ranks of the attackers were simply swept away by the initial barrage of led fired by the defenders.

Several of the Soviets hit by bullets tumbled over the sides of the bridge onto the ice below. Many more collapsed to the ground where they were hit and died. Others went down but weren't fortunate enough to die immediately. Instead, they lay on the frozen surface of the bridge clutching their wounds and crying out in pain as they slowly froze to death.

Despite the blizzard of fire coming from the Finnish defenders, the 3rd NKVD just kept coming. The NKVD was the Soviet Union's espionage and internal security force. The predecessor to the Cold war era KGB. Thus, the sergeants of the attacking force, in addition to being trained soldiers, were also trained in spy craft. As a result of their dual training, the NKVD troopers were able to improvise in ways that the average Soviet soldier wasn't capable of doing. Instead of continuing to send men blindly over the bridge in a human wave attack, a Soviet specialty, they pulled back and re-organized.

They shifted tactics and followed Halonen's example of deploying troops on the riverbank to increase their firepower. In addition, they brought up a dark green BA-10 armored car. The BA-10 had 15mms of frontal armor and was armed with a 45mm cannon, along with two 7.62mm machine guns.

Though thin by tank standards, the armor was just thick enough to repel machine gun fire. The BA-10 rumbled onto the bridge and laid down fire with its 45mm cannon and machine guns. The Finnish defenders had nothing that could stop it.

Only upon seeing the success of the BA-10 to repel Finnish fire did the Soviet sergeants order their remaining men forward and commit them to the attack. Using high explosive rounds in its 45mm cannon, the BA-10 was able to make short work of the barricade on the western edge of the bridge. Simultaneously, the BA-10s machine guns laid down withering cover fire forcing the Finns to retreat from the river's edge. Thanks to the efforts of the BA-10, the way was clear for the 3rd NKVD Regiment to seize the bridge and gain the west bank of the river.

Halonen, seeing that the situation was hopeless shouted, "Retreat!"

Oja, along with a few other survivors of Halonen's platoon, leapt to their feet and dashed away. With Finnish resistance collapsing, the BA-10 accelerated in pursuit. As it neared the western edge of the bridge, Major Fagernas, who was observing the scene from a spot roughly one hundred meters down river turned to the private beside him and ordered, "Now."

The soldier on his knees at the Major's feet, had a plunger style detonator wedged between his legs. He pushed the metal T-bar down and then turned his attention to the bridge. Precious seconds passed as the BA-10's reached the edge of the bridge, "I said now private."

Private Harju a demolitions expert, looked up at the Major sheepishly and said, "I don't understand why it didn't work."

Fagernas gave Harju a withering glare, "Fi—"

Before the major could finish the word, the charges attached to the bottom of the bridge exploded. Nearly a hundred Soviet soldiers were incinerated by the blast as the bridge was ripped apart by the explosion. The driver of the BA-10, feeling the rear of his vehicle suddenly drop, mashed the vehicle's accelerator to the floor with his foot.

The rear wheel of the vehicle slammed into the riverbank. For a few moments the wheels were able to halt the pull of gravity upon the BA-10 as the wheels dug into the snow. After nearly thirty seconds, its wheels unable to find a solid purchase, the armored car lost its battle with gravity and slid backward down the riverbank.

The BA-10 fell three meters down to the river and crashed through the ice. In less than a minute, the back half of the vehicle sank into the inky black waters and disappeared from sight. The unlucky members of the crew, died in less than a minute to the extremely cold water as they scrambled to escape from their sinking vehicle.

When half of the armored car had become submerged, the strong current beneath the ice ripped the vehicle off the river bank. Sixty seconds later, the entire armored car had sunk below the surface of the water and disappeared. The crew within was forever entombed in a watery grave.

The wooden boards that comprised the bridge were hurled skyward as a large cloud of flames pushed upward toward the heavens. As the fire began to fade away, pieces from the wreckage began to land in a one-hundred-meter radius around the bridge's former location. In addition to the damage inflicted by the blast, the heat from the detonation melted the ice for ten meters on either side of the bridge's former location revealing the dark waters of the Purasjoki River.

The air was filled with the smell of burning meat, as fire from the initial blast greedily consumed the Russian bodies. Those pieces of bodies that weren't incinerated in the blast were scattered over the nearby area. When the smoke cleared, it was as if the attacking company had simply ceased to exist.

Major Fagernas smiled in relief at the destruction of the bridge, "It's now impossible for the Soviets to relieve the 44th using this road. Vinogradov is trapped. All we have to do now, is to keep a relief force from coming through the forest."

Harju laughed, "And we all know how effective these buggers are once you remove them from a road."

"Exactly. Find Halonen and tell him to reform his platoon on the west bank and to come and find me once he has determined his casualty count." Fagernas instructed, "While you are working on that I'm going to return to the headquarters tent and radio Colonel Siilasvuo with an update."

Chapter 30

Early Morning, Finnish 9th Division HQ, Three Kilometers South of Suomassalmi, Central Finland

January 7th, 1940

Colonel Siilasvuo, commander of the Finnish 9th Division awoke. He blinked his eyes several times to focus and glanced at his watch, *Two AM.*

Earlier, his body had refused to function. He had been exhausted by long days spent in the headquarters tent coordinating the various units of the division with very little sleep. The soldiers of the 9th Division were currently strung out along the Raate road between the Village of Suomassalmi and the border of the Soviet Union.

Siilasvuo had been reluctant to leave the headquarters tent before this critical moment in the fight, but his body had given him no choice. Unable to keep his eyes open, he had been forced to use a nearby hunting lodge in order to sleep. He yawned as he threw off several blankets and stood up. He looked down at his uniform, frowned, and tried to smooth the rumples in the heavy gray wool.

Siilasvuo exhaled sharply and felt a chill on his cheek as he realized that the temperature inside the cabin had fallen below the freezing mark. He looked over at the lodge's large stone fireplace. The roaring fire he had built prior to laying down to rest had burned down to a few glowing embers. He quickly put on his heavy gray trench coat and a fleece lined woolen hat. He took a deep breath and let it out slowly as he braced himself for what came next.

The colonel opened the cabin door and was immediately slammed by a wall of cold air nearly beyond imagination. The frosty air, hungry to extinguish all warmth within its reach, swirled into the cabin and plunged the temperature inside by forty degrees Fahrenheit in seconds. Siilasvuo stepped outside and thrust his hands into his pockets as the icy air quickly numbed his cheeks. As he quickly made his way back to the HQ tent, his boots clomped on the wooden boards. The boards had been laid out on top of the snow and functioned as a sidewalk between the tents of the 9th Division's headquarters area. They prevented the necessity of wading through thigh deep snow.

He paused for a moment and looked around. He quickly realized that sometime during his rest, it had snowed. The constant foot traffic between the tents had worn down the fresh powder to the point that it was nearly absent from the wooden path, *Must have stopped a few hours ago.* He thought.

Colonel Siilasvuo let himself into the HQ tent through the entry flap and stomped his black shin high leather boots to get the fresh powdery snow off. Major Valli, looked up and smiled, "How did you sleep Colonel?"

Siilasvuo yawned, "Like the dead. Is there any coffee?"

Valli pointed to the pot on the tent's wood burning stove, "I just made a fresh pot, help yourself."

Siilasvuo picked up the dirty mug he had been using for

the last week. He glanced down into it to make sure there wasn't anything disgusting lurking inside and poured himself some coffee. He turned to Major Valli and asked, "Give me an update."

The major pointed to the counters on the map indicating the position of the 44th Division "As indicated by the latest updates from our task force commanders, the Soviet 44th Division has been subdivided into five Mottis."

Colonel Siilasvuo smiled, "That's the same amount as when I laid down. Can you give me a rundown of the sizes and strengths of the individual mottis?"

"Certainly," replied the major. "We believe General Vinogradov is somewhere within the largest motti located four kilometers east of Suomassalmi."

"What's the estimated strength of that motti?" Siilasvuo asked.

"Roughly a brigade of twenty-five-hundred-men is trapped within Vinogradov's motti." Valli replied.

"The 44th Division is a combined arms unit. Do we have an idea of the composition of those forces trapped with Vinogradov?" Siilasvuo asked.

Valli nodded, "The forces contained within are comprised of a mixture of armor and infantry."

"Have they used the tanks for any attacks recently?" Siilasvuo asked.

Valli shook his head, "No. It is Lieutenant Colonel Makiniemi's belief that they are out of fuel."

"That's good news. Has there been any effort to resupply them since the air drop a few days ago?"

Siilasvuo asked.

Valli shook his head, "No."

"Interesting." Siilasvuo said, "They have the largest air force in the world and could presumably gain air superiority over any point within Finland should they desire, but they haven't. What does that tell you?"

Valli shrugged, "That the Red Airforce could give two shits about the Red Army?"

"Perhaps." Siilasvuo laughed, "Or they have a problem coordinating between the two services." Siilasvuo took a sip from his coffee cup, "Tell me about the second motti."

"The second motti, sits just to the east of the Village of Hauklia. It seems to contain most of their artillery pieces and shells." Major Valli said, "We believe that this motti is roughly regiment sized."

"That should be an easier nut to crack assuming the men trapped with their guns are the artillerymen and not infantry." Siilasvuo observed, "Knowing the Russians, they probably assigned infantry to the artillery, and artillerymen with the tanks, and tankers as infantry.

"Where does that leave the tankers?" Valli asked.

Siilasvuo grinned, "As infantry I suppose. I really shouldn't joke like that. It will make me buy into the whole the Red Army is incompetent narrative."

"Well thus far, they have been." Valli argued.

"True but treating them as a competent force has enabled us to keep our casualties down." Siilasvuo countered, "Please continue."

"The third and fourth mottis are roughly battalion sized." Siilasvuo opened his mouth to speak but Valli quickly added, "We believe they are rifle battalions with a few tanks mixed in."

"Interesting. Something to consider." Siilasvuo said, "What about the fifth motti, the one sitting between Major Kari's group and Fagernas?"

"This one contains another battalion sized unit." Major Valli replied, "Like General Vinogradov's motti, the forces within are a mixed bag of infantry and tanks."

"I see." Siilasvuo said, then pointed at the final motti, "I see that Fagneras is still holding the bridge against the 3rd NKVD regiment."

"No, they are not." Valli said, "Fagneras was forced to destroy the bridge around the time you laid down."

Siilasvuo slammed his fist down on the table in frustration and demanded, "Why wasn't I informed?"

"Because the destruction of the bridge did little to change the tactical situation and you needed the rest. Especially with what I believe is coming next." Valli replied.

"And what is that General Valli?" Siilasvuo asked.

"The 44th has been broken down into five individual mottis. Based on the lack of tank use in the last twenty-four hours, and the half-hearted responses to our recent probing attacks, they are running low on both fuel and ammo." Valli replied.

"So, what would you recommend?" Siilasvuo asked.

Valli glanced nervously down at the map, took a deep

breath and exhaled slowly to buy himself a few more seconds to organize his thoughts, "We should attack everywhere."

Siilasvuo but his hand under his chin as he pondered the major's recommendation, "I agree we should attack, but not everywhere at once. Having an exhausted enemy force trapped in mottis gives us the luxury of choosing when the fighting happens."

"What are your thoughts then?" Valli asked.

Siilasvuo stabbed a finger down between the third and fourth mottis, "These two-battalion sized mottis. Can our surrounding forces finish them off?"

"I don't believe so. Kari only has an understrength battalion himself. He's been barely holding the enemy within the motti." Valli replied.

"Since the bridge was destroyed Fagneras doesn't need as many men to hold the river against the 3rd NKVD." Siilasvuo said, "What if we pulled half of his strength over to the 5th motti to aid in the attack?"

Valli closed his eyes and rubbed his forehead with his right thumb and index finger as he pondered the idea, "That could work."

"Then once the fifth motti is destroyed, we can use the combined force against the fourth." Siilasvuo said.

Valli's eyes widened in understanding, "Then once the fourth has been destroyed, we can use the force against the 3rd, then the second, and finally the first."

"Exactly. How long do you think it would take for Fagneras to get his men in position to aid in Kari's attack?" Sillasvuo asked.

"With Task Force Kari holding the road to the west of the fifth motti, and Fagneras holding the road to the east, I would recommend moving the extra men pulled from the river to the north and south of the road."

"I like it. We'll be able to hit them from all sides simultaneously." Siilasvuo grinned, "How long to get the men into position for the first attack?"

Major Valli said, "Perhaps an hour once we get them moving."

"Send the order." Siilasvuo said as he glanced down at his watch, "I want the first attack to start no later than 0400."

"It's nearly three now." Valli said, "What's the hurry?"

"If this works, I'd like the men freed up by the first assault to participate in the second. Assuming it takes an hour to crush the fifth motti, that will give our surviving forces an hour to get into position for the assault on the fourth. Then they can move onto the third. The idea is to destroy the fourth and third mottis before dawn." Siilasvuo said, "The cover of darkness will help to keep our casualties low."

Understanding dawned on Major Valli, "Then we can spend the daylight hours shifting everyone into positions to attack the first and second motti."

Siilasvuo smiled, "Exactly."

Chapter 31

Early Morning, Task Force Kari, Two Kilometers West of the Purasjoki River, Central Finland

January 7th, 1940

Major Kari glanced down at his watch. Unable to see the watch's two hands in the darkness, he turned his body and angled his arm until he caught enough light to see the face of the watch. The time read 3:55, *Almost time.* He thought.

Kari turned his attention to the eastern barricade currently occupied by one of the two companies under his command. In addition to the defenders, the men of two additional platoon's that had been pulled from the western barricade waited. A palpable cloud of nervous energy hung over the men, *I hope to God the Soviets don't attack the western barricade while we're attacking eastward. The single platoon I left to hold the west won't be able to stop them for long.*

Between Kari and the eastern barricade lay the shadowy outlines of over a hundred men. Some of the men, murmured amongst themselves as a distraction from what was about to happen. Others prayed in silence or kept to their own thoughts. The air was thick with the kind of anxiety that only men who were about to risk their lives in combat felt. Occasionally, a nameless soldier would laugh at a joke told by a comrade to break the tension, *I'm glad they can still laugh.* Kari thought.

Kari turned his body until he was able to once again catch enough light to see the time on his watch. The watch read 3:59. He looked up at the sky and silently prayed, *Please God, let us be successful.*

Suddenly, the minute hand on his watch moved, it was 0400, "Now!" Major Kari whispered.

The word was quickly passed, and the men silently came to their feet and started to move. The soldiers of Kari's assault force dashed around the barricade as they picked up speed. Viewed from above, the men of Task Force Kari, looked like the water of a river flowing around a large rock. In the distance, gunfire erupted as the men of Task Force Fagneras opened fire on the Soviets with their guns from their positions in the surrounding forest.

The men continued to silently move up the road as the Red Army's attention was turned to the force attacking them from the forest. The Soviets, confident of their eventual victory, hadn't bothered to put up a barricade across the road on their side of no man's land. Thanks to the initial attack from Fagneras' men, Kari's lead platoon was able to move nearly fifty meters down the road before the Finns caught site of the enemy.

The outlines of the enemy soldiers were plainly visible thanks to the orange light cast by the fires they had built to stay warm. The same fires that had provided lifesaving warmth, so that they could survive the forty below zero temperatures of the nighttime hours, were turned against them by the attacking Finns. Kari's lead platoon fanned out, finding what cover they could, amongst the abandoned vehicles. Once the lead platoon was positioned behind the available cover, their lieutenant screamed, "Fire!"

Two dozen Finns simultaneously opened fire on the Soviet defenders. Kari's entire lead platoon was armed with Suomi sub-machine guns. They laid down a withering blizzard of lead that cut down all before them. On the eastern edge of the motti, Major Fagneras' defenders, who had also abandoned their barricade, were doing the same. The darkness melted away as muzzles from dozens of guns flashed and tracers lit up the night sky. The nearly constant muzzle flashes pushed back the darkness for a short time as the two sides exchanged fire.

Overwhelmed from all sides, the defenders started to fall back. The men of the 44th, mostly Ukrainian, put-up stiff resistance, but they lacked the physical strength to fight for more than a handful of minutes. Many of the defenders were unaccustomed to an arctic winter and lacked the proper gear to stave off frost bite, were severely weakened by the cold. In addition, they were hungry and running low on ammunition.

The soldiers of the Red Army, over the course of the last week, had wasted most of their ammunition firing into the forest at shadows. At times, baited by the shot from a single sniper, they had fired their weapons for hours. To put a stop to the lack of fire discipline, the officers had organized patrols to scout the surrounding forest.

The goal was to establish a defensive perimeter in the surrounding trees, so that the Finns couldn't come right up to the road and fire on the exposed men. None of the men sent into the trees returned alive. This increased the sense of hopelessness the men of the 44th experienced, as the food ran out and men began to die from exposure.

As the men of Task Force Kari and Fagernas pressed their attack, the Soviets quickly lost hope. It happened slowly at first. A defender here or there would realize the hopelessness of the situation as they were continually pushed back by the Finns. After the initial losses that broke through the weak Soviet defenses, more of the defenders fell by gunfire and grenades. Those that remained were forced to fall back further. Suddenly the Finns emerged from the surrounding forest and were amongst the bewildered defenders.

Once the Finns engaged the enemy in melee, it only took a few moments for the organized defense, orchestrated by the few surviving officers, to collapse. One of the Soviets, out of ammunition, and hope, dropped his weapon and threw his arms up in surrender. Those that were next to him did the same as they too succumbed to the impossibility of their predicament. Hopelessness rippled across the defenders much like a stone thrown into the still waters of a placid lake creates a ripple across the water's surface.

The once thought unconquerable men of the 44th Motorized Rifle Division, one of the most modern divisions in the world, threw up their arms in surrender. As the Finns started to gather up their new prisoners, the flickering firelight revealed the haggard faces of men that had completely lost hope, "Search each man and take all of their weapons and ammunition." Major Kari ordered.

"What do we do with them, once they have been stripped of their weapons?" A nameless private asked.

"Release them to alpha company's 3rd platoon. They are assigned to guard the prisoners." Major Kari turned until he spotted the man he was looking for, "Lieutenant Kallio! You and your men are on guard duty." Major Kari ordered.

Kallio appeared out of the darkness and asked, "What

do you want me to do with the prisoners once they are all secured?"

"March them back to my headquarters. If they are hungry, feed them." Kari ordered.

A nearby Russian asked in broken Finnish, "You're not going to eat us?"

Kari laughed, "You have surrendered. Why would we do that?"

"The commissars, they told us that you Finns were starving. That if we allowed ourselves to be taken prisoner, that you would cut pieces from our bodies and eat us slowly over time." The man said.

Curious, Kari asked, "Did they say why we would eat you in that manner?"

"To keep us alive as long as possible to maintain the freshness of our meat." The man said.

Kari inwardly shuddered at the evil a mind must have to think such thoughts, "We are not starving. As you can see, my men are much better fed than you have been." Kari replied.

The prisoner meekly asked, "So you will not be eating us?"

"Of course not!" Kari snapped.

Relief washed over the enemy soldier's face as he said, "Then the commissars lied to us."

"Yes, about a great many things it would seem." Kari looked the Russian up and down and asked, "Why are you not better dressed for the conditions?"

"What do you mean?" The Russian asked.

"You should be wearing a woolen great coat and several layers of clothing, including a woolen uniform, to stay warm in these conditions. You look like you are wearing uniforms made from cotton." Kari replied.

Confusion painted itself on the face of the Russian as he asked, "What is cotton?" He stumbled over the unfamiliar Finnish word for cotton as he said it for the first time.

"A bush that grows white balls that you make clothes out of." Kari replied.

"I understand now, khlopok." The Russian said, nodding, "Yes, our uniforms are made of cotton."

Kari reached out and squeezed the man's shoulder trying to reassure him, "What's your name?"

The Russian stiffened to the position of attention, "Private Mikhail Pavlovich."

"Once you have had a chance to eat private Mikhail Pavlovich. Have Lieutenant Kallio escort you to me. I'd like to talk further. My name is Major Kari."

The Major turned away from private Pavlovich and shouted, "Brave fighters of Bravo company, I know you are exhausted, but we need more men on the western barricade before the enemy realizes it is thinly guarded. Double time it back to your original post."

Major Fagneras appeared out of the darkness and smiled at Kari. Kari returned the smile, and the two officers shook hands, "Well met Major." Fagneras said.

Kari smiled back at him and said, "Well-met indeed."

Major Kari paused for a few moments and looked around. The surviving Soviets were being led away. The remaining Finns had started to gather up the enemy's discarded weapons. A Finnish private, threw back the canvas on one of the numerous Gaz-MM trucks and shouted, "This one is filled to the brim with tank shells."

A distant voice yelled from somewhere out of sight, "Perfect we'll need those for our new tank!"

The private's voice was soon followed by many others shouting out the contents of the trucks, "Officers! I want a report on the gear we have captured in ten minutes!" Major Kari shouted. He then turned back to Fagneras and asked, "Can you spare your survivors for the next attack?"

Major Fagneras gave Kari a broad smile as he nodded and said, "I can indeed. Let's finish this."

Chapter 32

Three Hours to sunrise, Task Force Kari, Three Kilometers West of the Purasjoki River, Central Finland

January 7th, 1940

As he had done several hours earlier, Major Kari sat behind his men as they awaited the time of the next attack. The defenders of Task Force Kari's western barricade were now joined by the men of the eastern barricade. Thanks to their recent victory against the fifth motti, the men assigned to hold the eastern barricade were out of a job. Together, the two understrength companies combined had just over a hundred men between them. At full strength two Finnish companies would field roughly one hundred and fifty soldiers.

As before the Finnish soldiers sat in silence as the minutes ticked down to the agreed upon attack time. Their voices could be heard murmuring as they tried to allay their anxiety through talking. Many sat in silence writing final letters to loved ones or silently praying that they would live to see the next sunrise.

Others tried to find distraction from their heavy thoughts. Groups of men would laugh as a joke's punchline was delivered, "It's good that the men are able to distract themselves." Kari observed.

Captain Ranta, one of Major Kari's two company commanders, nodded in agreement, "It helps to keep their mind off of what is about to happen."

Earlier, after the successful assault on the fifth motti, Major Kari radioed the success of the operation to Colonel Siilasvuo. With Siilasvuo's blessing, Kari reached out to Lieutenant Colonel Makiniemi using his radio. To avoid giving the enemy a chance to listen in on their battle plan as they developed it, the two officers agreed to meet in person. They chose a location in the forest on one of the ice roads to the south of the Raate Road. The meeting point was roughly halfway between their forces.

Like most Finns, the two officers were expert skiers. The two Finnish officers were able to cover the ground that separated them quickly and met twenty minutes later. There, amidst the trees of the frozen primordial forest, the two officers quickly drew up a battle plan in the snow using sticks they had picked up off the ground. The attack plan called for the participation of units from three of the Task Forces, Fagneras, Kari, and Makiniemi. If the plan succeeded, the fourth motti would be destroyed within the hour.

Major Kari's forces, led by himself and Captain Ranta, would attack westward down the Raate Road. Colonel Makiniemi's forces, led by his best company commander, Captain Lassila, would attack eastward toward the men of Task Force Kari. Between them, Major Fagneras' men would again take up positions in the forest surrounding the road to the north and south. Fagneras would then launch his attack at 0600 hours.

Together the coordination between the three task forces would create a complete encirclement of the Soviet defenders. Major Kari glanced down at his watch, "Should be any moment now."

Roughly thirty seconds later, the attack force led by Major Fagneras opened fire on the enemy. The Soviets soldiers trapped within the fourth motti, mostly asleep, were huddled around campfires, for warmth. Since sunset, dozens of them had succumbed to starvation and hypothermia during the long night. Nearly every squad would awake to the horror of a squad mate's corpse laying amongst them. Their comrade's dead bodies already frozen solid, despite the proximity of the fires.

The hundreds who managed to survive the sub-zero temperatures of the night were sluggish in their response to the attack. The pervasive cold these men had been enduring had a detrimental effect on the human body's systems. The brain focused on trying to maintain the body's temperature, had less capacity for coherent thought. Thus, it took much longer for the sluggish minds of the Soviets to react to the attack.

When their muddled minds finally did react, frost bitten extremities proved to be another hurtle that had to be overcome before responding to the Finnish attack. Men, who were unable to feel their feet stumbled about as if they were drunk in a failed attempt to stand. Others, whose limbs weren't as far along in the process screamed in pain, as their frost burned fingers and toes sent fiery bolts of agony to their brains.

Those with frostbitten fingers struggled to simply pull the trigger on their rifles. Men screamed in horror as pieces of their fingers simply snapped off, when they put pressure on them. Finally, those that were able to function started to resist the attack.

In contrast the Finns were properly attired. They wore

multiple layers of wool, fleece and in several cases furs to maintain their core temperatures, despite the unimaginably cold conditions. They wore facemasks, so that not a single piece of their skin could be touched by the frosty air. Air that could freeze a man's spit before it hit the ground.

Unlike their Soviet counterparts, each Finnish soldier was given time in a hastily constructed front line sauna daily. The time in the sauna gave their bodies a respite from the strain of trying to maintain its core temperature in such difficult conditions. The combination of proper gear and a few hours in the sauna allowed the Finnish fighters to function near normal, despite the horrific cold.

The Soviets, who had been fighting a battle all night to simply stay alive, were bewildered by the sudden attack. Those few men whose brains still functioned, smartly stayed on the ground in defensive positions and readied their weapons. Those whose muddled thoughts made them foolish enough to stand were quickly slain.

Once the Finnish attackers of Task Force Fagneras ran out of standing targets, they quickly adjusted their positioning. Like many roads, overtime the Raate Road had slowly sunk, versus the surrounding terrain as the constant traffic ground down the soil. Thus, the Finns stood on higher ground as they initiated their assault upon the hapless defenders of the fourth motti.

The combination of the Finnish positions ten to twenty meters deep into the trees and the lower road, made it impossible for the attackers to see the road itself. In order to shoot the Soviets laying prone on the ground, the Finns had to move up to the edge of the tree line. As a result, the Finns were forced to trade off concealment, to gain visibility on their prone enemies.

This gave the Soviets a chance. The Ukrainian soldiers

were able to fire up at the muzzle flashes on the edge of the tree line and score some hits. To the east, Major Kari, waited as the first two full minutes of Major Fagneras' attack transpired. He glanced down at his watch, then turned to Ranta and whispered, "Pass the word, we go in three minutes."

The word was quickly spread amongst the men of Task Force Kari's assault force. When Major Kari came to his feet at 0605, his men were all looking in his direction. Seeing their commander rise, they stood, and began to move around the western barricade.

Similar to the assault on the 5th motti, Kari's men advanced fifty meters without meeting any resistance. Those that had gathered around the campfires nearest to Major Kari's forces, had been drawn westward by Major Fagneras' assault. Once again, the Soviets abandoned the edge of the motti to focus on the Finns firing at them from the forest.

The Finns carefully moved forward. They picked their way through the column of vehicles and the garbage strewn about by men who had been stuck in the same location for nine days. The Finns, nervous about the dead bodies, took the time to thrust a bayonet into each of the frozen corpses that lay next to the dying campfires.

Captain Ranta, at the head of the force cautiously approached a line of trucks that had been towing artillery. The Soviets hadn't unlimbered the pieces and readied them to fire. Ranta paused and cautiously raised his Suomi submachine gun, *I thought I saw something move.* He thought.

Ranta raised his right hand up and formed a fist. The signal told the men behind him to stop as he peered through the darkness. He was trying to ascertain if the shift in shadows was a figment of his imagination or a threat that needed to be neutralized.

Before he was able to decide, the artillery piece, less than ten meters in front of him and still attached to the truck that had been towing it, fired. The 122mm high explosive shell slammed into the truck just to Ranta's right and exploded.

The expanding fireball from the shell incinerated Ranta and half the platoon immediately behind him. Those that survived the initial blast turned and fled to avoid the growing conflagration. The flames quickly reached the gas tank of the Gaz-MM truck causing the gasoline within to ignite.

The move to immediately flee, saved the lives of the back half of the platoon. These men were fortunate enough to be far enough away to avoid being incinerated in the initial blast. Unbeknownst to the Finns, the truck's cargo deck was filled with boxes of grenades.

The gunpowder within the grenades quickly heated up and reached their flash point. Thirty seconds after the gasoline in the truck's tank had exploded, the grenades on the cargo deck followed suit. The resultant tertiary explosion ripped the truck apart. The combination of the truck being ripped apart, coupled with the destruction of hundreds of grenade casings sent deadly metal fragments hurtling in all directions.

The combination of flames and fragments killed another half dozen men of the Finnish platoon. The truck immediately behind the flaming wreck absorbed most of the fragments hurtling towards the attacking Finns. A few unfortunates were still struck by the remnants of the truck and went down screaming. In less than a minute Captain Ranta and eighteen men of the lead assault platoon had been slain.

The Soviet that had carefully hidden himself behind the 122mm A19 Artillery Piece, was shielded from the initial blast by the steel plate meant to protect the crew of the mighty gun. Once the immediate danger had passed, he tried to flee westward. He too was ripped to shreds by the tertiary explosion, becoming a victim of his own attack. Unbeknownst to anyone, the nameless private had become the second deadliest Soviet in the entire battle. Only Kuznetsov, had managed to slay more of the Finns than this man.

The trees around the demolished truck, despite being frozen solid, caught fire from the red-hot metal fragments that peppered them. In less than sixty seconds a twenty-meter section of the Raate Road, and the surrounding forest had been transformed into a fiery hellscape. When the smoke cleared, all that remained of the truck was a two-meter-deep crater.

With the destruction of the lead platoon, Major Kari's assault ground to a halt. On the other side of the motti, Captain Lassila pressed forward. The Soviets, focused on the men of Task Force Fagneras shooting at them from the forest, didn't see Lassila coming. Armed with Suomi submachineguns, they easily cut down all who stood in their way as they advanced eastward down the road.

In the face of Captain Lassila's determined assault, the Soviet officers failed to maintain discipline amongst their men. Within minutes, the western flank of the fourth motti collapsed. As a result, several individual squads, surrounded by attackers on three sides, fled down the path of least resistance, eastward.

Major Kari's force was surprised by the sudden appearance of several dozen enemy soldiers. Upon seeing the Finns, the Soviet survivors fired a volley, then scattered into the forest. Five Finns were slain, as the enemy managed to melt away.

Some of these men managed to find their way through the trees and return to the Soviet Union. Most died from starvation and exposure as they stumbled around in circles unable to navigate through the dense forest. Those that survived the travails of the forest, were executed for desertion by the NKVD.

When the edge of Captain Lassila's line appeared on the road, Major Fagneras' men whooped with delight. The men of Task Force Fagneras streamed out of the forest and embraced their brothers in arms from Task Force Makiniemi. After losing nearly a fifth of his men, including his best company commander, Captain Ranta, the victory felt hollow to Major Kari. Nevertheless, once again, the Finns were victorious. The fourth motti had been crushed. Only three mottis remained. The once mighty 44th Motorized Rifle Division was crumbling.

Chapter 33

Twilight, Task Force Makiniemi, Three Kilometers East of the Village of Hauklia, Central Finland

January 7th, 1940

Lieutenant Colonel Makiniemi gazed at the stalled Soviet column through his binoculars. He had set himself up on a ridge that overlooked the third motti to watch the upcoming attack. As he slowly panned his binoculars over the chaotic scene below, he suddenly shouted, "I think that's Colonel Pahomov!"

"Where exactly?" Hale asked.

Makiniemi pointed, "Between the two T-28's."

"I think I see who you are talking about." Hale said, "About two hundred meters, correct?"

Makiniemi slowly nodded, "That seems about right."

"Who is that standing beside him, and which one is the colonel?" Hale asked.

"The colonel is the man on the left." Makiniemi shifted his focus to the man Colonel Pahomov was talking to, "It's hard to make out his rank, maybe one red square. A lieutenant. A nobody."

Makiniemi noticed Hale glowering at him and quickly amended, "That lieutenant is a nobody."

Did I just make him nervous? Hale wondered in amusement, "I'll have to make a standing shot as Pahomov is being partially obscured by one of the T-28's. I won't be able to see him if I lay down."

Hale found a nearby tree branch that he could rest his rifle on and brushed off the snow before setting his rifle on it. The branch enabled him to hold his rifle steady at shoulder level. He centered Colonel Pahomov in his rifle's two iron sights. His eyes shifted to a nearby spruce tree. He focused on the movement of a branch caused by the wind.

With the approximate distance and wind direction noted, he lowered his aim slightly to account for the difference in elevation between himself and Colonel Pahomov, *Down hill shots are tricky.* He thought.

When he was satisfied that he would hit, he drew in a deep breath and held it. He then pulled the trigger as he slowly exhaled. The rifle boomed and the bullet erupted from the weapon's barrel. It hurtled through the air, invisible to the naked eye.

The loud report of the rifle startled Makiniemi and he flinched at the sudden loud sound next to him. A moment later he shouted, "You got him!"

Hale quickly worked the action on his rifle as he shifted his gunsights to the man that had been standing beside Pahomov. Hale drew in a sharp breath and said, "The lieutenant must have gone prone. I can't see him anymore. Did you see where he went?"

Makiniemi quickly scanned the surrounding area with his binoculars, "No. He's disappeared."

Makiniemi watched the stranded column for several minutes before turning to the runner that waited patiently behind him, "The death of their colonel seems to have created chaos amongst the enemy. Tell Captain Lassila to begin his attack at once, even if it is not entirely dark when he receives the message."

The private stiffened to attention and then without saluting, one colonel dying to a sniper was enough for today, he pushed off with his ski poles and catapulted himself down the hill. Kivi, who had been standing nearby slapped Hale on the back and said, "Nice shot."

The big lieutenant turned to Makiniemi, "Do you mind if I join the nearby assault force?"

Makiniemi gave Kivi a warm smiled, "I've heard about your lust for close combat." He gestured in the direction of the nearest attack force and said, "By all means. Just remember you are there as a soldier and not a commander. Do not interfere with my men."

Kivi smiled broadly, "As I prefer. Thank you, colonel."

Kivi turned to Hale and asked, "Will you remain here during the attack with the rest of the squad?"

Hale nodded, "Our job is to snipe, not to mix it up with the enemy. I only winged Kuznetsov in the left shoulder. He may be healthy enough to start causing trouble If he is around, you'll need me here to deal with him."

Kivi's expression soured, "Well if you hadn't let him go, we wouldn't have to worry about that now would we?"

Hale's shoulders slumped as he hissed, "I didn't have a choice. I honor my word."

Makiniemi gave Hale a sidelong glance as he wondered, *Does Siilasvuo know about this?*

The colonel filed away this information as he thought, *No sense in making a stink about it now. I need him at his best during the next hour.*

Kivi departed and quickly darted around the trees as he slid down the small hill on his skis. Ten minutes later as the sun had nearly fully disappeared behind the horizon, the Finnish forces positioned to the north and the south of the stranded column opened fire. The Soviets, their morale nearly at the breaking point due to nearly two weeks of unimaginable cold, constant pressure from the surrounding Finns, and more recently starvation was nearly at their breaking point.

Despite all of the hardships they had endured, and the chaos caused by the sudden death of their commanding officer, they didn't immediately give up. The men of the 44th had been trained as an elite fighting force. They styled themselves as Stalin's hammer. From somewhere deep within themselves they were able to draw on a source of strength to bolster their exhausted bodies, anger.

They were angry at the stupidity of high command for wasting their lives in this Godforsaken primordial forest, a place that was completely unsuitable for their vehicles. They were also angry at the constant pressure exerted upon them by the relentless Finnish attacks over last ten days as they sat stranded on this road. Finally, they were angry because those same idiot commanders had seemingly abandoned them to their fate.

The men of the 44th Division were unaware that the 3rd

NKVD regiment, a unit better suited for combat in this terrain, had been sent to extricate them from their precarious position. From the perspective of the 44th's rank and file the same generals that sent them into this mess had, despite the proximity of the Soviet Union, left them to starve.

The men of the 44th drew upon this fury until it could be contained no longer and burst from their chest. They stood in the face of the attacking Finns and screamed their defiance. For the first time in days, they felt warm as the adrenaline coursed through their veins and their hearts pounded in their chests. Ignoring their own safety, with rifles in hand, they charged the Finns, firing at them as they dashed into the forest.

Despite ten days of having their numbers thinned out by dozens of Finnish attacks, the men of the 44th, still outnumbered their attackers. Dozens of them fell as the Finns poured fire into them. They didn't care, the rage in their mind focused them on one goal, kill the enemy.

The leading edge of the Soviet horde reached the Finnish line. Major Fagneras stood in shock, "I thought for certain they would break before they reached our lines."

"Seems they have their dander up." Kivi said, "Can't say that I blame them. If I was in their situation, having been told that we would eat them if we captured them, I would want to go out fighting."

Fagneras turned to Kivi with pleading eyes and asked, "You have experience dealing with Soviet human wave attacks. What can we do?"

Kivi put a reassuring hand on the smaller man's shoulder and said, "Hold your line together. I'll take care of this."

The big lieutenant unbuckled his skis and left them on the ground. He pulled the two Suomi submachineguns slung on his shoulders off and charged directly into the most chaotic part of the fight. The center of Fagneras' line started to buckle as a dozen Finns were stabbed and beaten to death by the crazed Soviets.

With no one left to kill, the victorious Ukrainians looked around for more Finns to slay. That was when they spotted him, "Hello boys." Kivi said with his lips stretched back in a toothy feral grin that showed his K9s.

Those Soviets that still had weapons in their hands desperately started to work the bolt on their rifles to chamber a fresh round. They never got the chance to finish the action. Kivi opened fire with his guns. Kivi's audacity enraged the enemy and they charged him.

A dozen enemy soldiers fell as Kivi stood his ground and hosed them down with bullets. With a Suomi in each hand, he gritted his teeth and continued firing. Despite this, they kept coming. Major Fagneras drew his revolver as the enemy closed in on their position. The major fired his pistol at the enemy in desperation.

A dozen more Soviets fell to the bullets of the two Finns. Fagneras' pistol clicked when it ran dry. Only three of the attackers remained, two with Mosin Nagant rifles, one with a wicked looking knife. The final rays of the setting sun glinted off their blades as they screamed in triumph and charged at Kivi.

Kivi threw his empty Suomis at the two rifle wielders. This bought him a few precious seconds to draw his pukko blade. The knifeman, blinded by his rage, charged directly at the big man. Kivi stood his ground as he held his blade out in front of him.

A moment before it seemed as if the Soviet blade was going to be buried in the big lieutenant's chest Major Fagneras screamed, "Look out!"

Kivi, with shocking speed for a man his size, stepped to the side and thrust his pukko blade into the enemy soldier's back as he went by. He ripped the knife out and turned just in time to block a thrust from a bayonet. He turned the bayonet aside with his pukko and punched the Ukrainian man in the face with his left hand.

As the Ukrainian staggered back from the big man's mighty blow, Kivi twisted to the right as the second rifleman tried to stab him with his bayonet. The bayonet nicked the edge of the big man's left arm as he twisted away. The two men turned to face each other.

The Soviet, seeing that he had a longer reach with his bayoneted rifle, than the pukko blade armed Finn in front of him smiled. Kivi returned the smile, thew his pukko at the man to buy a few precious seconds, drew his pistol, and pumped two rounds into the enemy soldier's chest. He turned to the other surviving attacker who was trying to blink the stars out of his eyes and fired two rounds into his torso.

Fagneras, stunned, said, "That was incredible."

Kivi turned to the major as the blood of his enemies froze to his face and grinned, "That was a normal day at the office."

Despite the Soviet rally and near break out, the remaining Finnish attackers managed to contain the counterattack and push forward. Half an hour after the first shot was fired, the remaining enemy soldiers, exhausted, and out of ammunition, threw up their arms in surrender. The third motti was no more.

Chapter 34

Evening, 44th Motorized Rifle Division Mobile Command Post, One Kilometer West of the Village of Haukila, Central Finland

January 7th, 1940

General Alexei Ivanovich Vinogradov sat at the table in his small mobile command post. Radio messages poured in from Colonel Pahomov's regiment the 305th. The first message Corporal Yuki Pavlovich had received several hours ago was that Pahomov had fallen to a sniper. After that chaos exploded across the airwaves.

The next message following the assassination of the colonel was from a major. Vinogradov's alcohol addled mind couldn't even recall the man's name despite the fact that he commanded a battalion in the general's division. The major had yelled into the radio that they were under attack.

The major's message was followed by a deluge of chaotic transmissions from the 305th. Vinogradov tried to make sense of the chaos. As near he could figure, the Finns were assaulting the regiment from every direction. Further messages followed begging for help. Help that Vinogradov was powerless to provide. Roughly an hour after the transmission informing them of Colonel

Pahomov's death, the 305th fell silent.

Vinogradov eyed the vodka bottle that sat on the table in front of him. It was his last one. The bottle had been more than half consumed and had around a third of the original contents remaining, *Should I drink the last of my alcohol? What will I do when it is gone? The numbing bliss is the only thing keeping me sane.*

Unable to cope with the present reality, the general's brain shifted to his memory of a training exercise the previous summer. During the exercise, the entire division had been called upon to quickly deploy from a column into a one mile wide front, and then rapidly advance against a simulated enemy force. He smiled as he remembered the warm day, *Will I ever feel the warmth of the summer sun and feel sweat trickling down my back ever again?* He wondered in despair.

Vinogradov's mind shifted to a little later on that same day. As the July sun blazed down upon the flat steppe, his men precisely executed the difficult maneuver required by the exercise. The words from the observer from Moscow, *I'm too drunk to remember the man's name,* had caused his chest to swell with pride.

He tried to push through his drunken haze and remember them. Finally, the words, along with the man's name Kliment Voroshilov came to him. As the words flowed from his memory, he smiled, "General Vinogradov, I have never seen such precision in my decades of military experience. Truly your men are the finest in the Red Army. Their movement reminds me of the dancers in Swan Lake as they twirl around each other in perfect harmony."

The two men watched as the 44th, completed deploying. The second part of the exercise required the division to sprint across the flat terrain of the Ukrainian steppe for a distance of five kilometers while maintaining the line. Vinogradov watched in pride as the tanks, armored cars, and trucks of his division raced across the open plain while successfully fulfilling the exercise's requirements.

The riflemen were transported on the cargo decks of the division's vast array of trucks. Many of the trucks were towing artillery pieces. Together, the entire division rumbled across the open field. The vehicles created a huge cloud of dust as they raced across ground that had been baked by the July sun for weeks. Ground that hadn't seen a single drop of rain in a month. As a result, the individual vehicles, whether they had wheels or tracks, kicked up huge billowing clouds of dust in their wake.

Not a single vehicle broke down and fell out of formation that day, *It was glorious!* Vinogradov mused.

In that moment Vinogradov had seen limitless potential for his ambitions. Promotion, praise, perhaps even a seat on the politburo itself. Now, the future held nothing but darkness, *Do I remain here and wait to be captured, or do I take the only action remaining to me?* He wondered.

Coming to a decision, he reached out and snatched the vodka bottle off the table. He downed the bottle's contents in a single gulp, then hurled it against the wall in front of him. The bottle shattered and the pieces of glass scattered throughout the small space. Vinogradov belched, then turned to Corporal Pavlovich and hissed, "Transmit to the remaining units further resistance is futile, and that everyman should find his own way home."

Pavlovich swallowed hard and dared to ask, "Sir?"

Vinogradov came to his feet. He swayed unsteadily for several long seconds before he stabilized himself and turned to the corporal. He glared at his radioman and shouted, "You heard me. Send the order then abandon your post!"

Without another word Vinogradov whirled around and walked toward the door. He paused in front of the door that led to the frozen hell outside and donned his great coat. He looked down at his rank insignia and frowned. He removed the coat and pulled the two red diamonds from the coat's collar indicating his rank of major general and tossed them aside.

Satisfied that he would not be identifiable, he donned the coat. Vinogradov then buckled a black leather belt that held his sidearm to his waist. He quickly checked over himself then glanced over his shoulder at Pavlovich one last time before opening the door and stepping out into the cold.

Vinogradov turned toward the ominous darkness of the trees on the north side of the road and paused, *Are there Finns in those trees?* He wondered.

He smiled as an idea occurred to him and shouted in a commanding voice, "There is a relief force attempting to rendezvous with us. We have been ordered to abandon our positions and meet this force five kilometers north of here. Every man is to proceed to Erkkilä and meet the relief column there! If we all split up and go as individuals, the Finns won't be able to follow."

The men within the sound of Vinogradov's voice turned toward him in shock. They stared at him for several long seconds as frustration built within him. Realization dawned on the general, *These men can't contemplate moving out on their own recognizance.*

"Stop looking at me and move your asses! Abandon

the road and head north!" Vinogradov roared.

This time a few of the men's eyes drifted to the impenetrable tree line on the north side of the road. They turned their heads back to look at the general, their eyes full of confusion. Frustrated, Vinogradov gestured at the trees and again shouted, "Move!"

Finally, a few of the braver souls turned away from Vinogradov and hesitantly walked into the trees. These men inspired others to follow suit and within a few minutes the general stood alone. Suddenly, gunfire erupted roughly fifty meters north of the road.

The Finns gunned down as many of the enemy soldiers as they could but were too few to hold back the tidal wave of broken humanity fleeing northward. The men of the Finnish skirmish line were shocked when instead of attacking, the Soviets ignored them, and scattered. With orders to prevent the enemy from breaking out, the Finns turned and pursued, shooting dozens of the fleeing enemy soldiers in the backs as they tried to run away. It was through this chaos that General Vinogradov was able to slip away into the darkness.

Chapter 35

Dawn, Former 44th Motorized Rifle Division Mobile Command Post, One Kilometer West of the Village of Haukila, Central Finland

January 8th, 1940

Colonel Siilasvuo stood outside General Vinogradov's former mobile command post. The dark green wooden structure was mounted on the cargo deck of a Gaz-MM truck. The intent of a mobile command post was to enable the division's headquarters staff to keep up during a rapid advance.

For a kilometer in either direction from the command post, the Raate Road was littered with the remains of the largest motti. The road was choked with vehicles, burned out campfires, refuse from thousands of men living in a confined space for nearly two weeks, and hundreds of frozen bodies. When combined, these circumstances created a scene that was pure chaos.

Siilasvuo gazed up at the door to the mobile command post. He smiled as he reflected, *I can't believe how quickly the entire division melted away once we started to apply pressure.*

A set of wooden stairs led to the door of the command post. The stairs were portable and could be quickly removed and transported with the command post. Like the truck and the structure of the command post, the stairs had been painted dark green.

At the bottom of the stairs stood two Finnish guards. They were dressed in white over coats and pants. Both men casually held Suomi submachine guns in their right hands as they stood watch. In addition to the submachine guns each guard had a pukko blade and pistol on his belt.

When the two men caught sight of Siilasvuo's approach they snapped to attention. The colonel paused in front of the two guards and asked, "Is the command post secure?"

The guard on Siilasvuo's right smiled, "Yes, colonel." He wrinkled his nose as he added, "Prepare yourself, the Soviet officers that occupied the space were pigs."

Siilasvuo patted the man on the back as he walked by and said, "Thanks for the warning."

The colonel walked up the three stairs that led to the command post's door. He took a deep breath and steeled himself as he opened the door. He was immediately assailed with the smell of days old vomit and the stink of death. He turned back and asked, "Major Valli did you bring a flashlight?"

The major shook his head to indicate he hadn't, "I have one colonel." Pekka interjected.

Pekka dropped to one knee and fished through his pack until he found what he was looking for. He pulled a flashlight that he had looted off of a slain enemy soldier out of his pack. Once free of his backpack, he twisted the top to activate the light. When nothing happened, he frowned and walked over to the stairs. He proceeded to bang the flashlight against the wooden stairs.

On the third strike the flashlight suddenly flared to life. Smiling sheepishly, he handed the now functional flashlight up to Siilasvuo and said, "Sorry colonel, I got it off a dead Soviet officer. Their quality is shit."

Siilasvuo gave Pekka a warm smile as he took the flashlight and said, "No apology necessary captain."

Siilasvuo turned back to the empty chamber before him and swept the light around. There was no one here, alive or dead. He stepped inside and gasped as the vomit smell grew several degrees in intensity. He slowly panned the flashlight over the interior of the command post. Shards of glass glistened on the floor from the light cast by the flashlight.

His eyes caught a glint of red near his feet and he squatted down to get a better look. Discarded on the floor were two red metal diamond shaped rank insignias, *Vinogradov must have discarded his rank insignia.*

Siilasvuo slipped the two red diamonds into his pocket as he stood and thought, *That's how Vinogradov managed to disappear. Did he escape? Or is his frozen corpse somewhere nearby?* He sighed in frustration as he realized, *We'll never know.*

The small, enclosed space, mounted on the cargo deck of a Gaz-MM truck, was roughly two meters wide and four meters long. In the center of the small space stood a table surrounded by eight folding metal chairs. On the table was a map with a thick plastic sheet on top of it.

Markings in Cyrillic covered the center of the map around what was obviously the Raate Road. The markings were made using red and black grease pencils. Siilasvuo took a step forward to get a better look when he stepped in something squishy. Knowing he was going to regret the action, he looked down at his boot. He had stepped into a pile of vomit, "Barbarians." He hissed.

"Sir?" Major Valli asked from the door.

"These Soviets are disgusting." Siilasvuo said, "Can you find someone that can read Russian? There is a map here that might have some useful intelligence."

"Yes, colonel." Valli replied.

Siilasvuo, wanting to avoid another surprise, lowered the flashlight to the floor. In addition to multiple piles of vomit that surrounded a single chair, he gasped when he saw several blood-stained floorboards, "What the hell did they do in here?" Siilasvuo wondered, "Drink until they vomited, and then shoot each other?"

"Colonel?" Major Valli asked from the door.

"Did you find someone?" Siilasvuo asked.

"A Sergeant Antilla from Karhonen's sniper squad." Valli replied.

"Send him in." Siilasvuo said.

Sergeant Antilla entered the small chamber and snapped to attention, "At ease sergeant. Can you read the writing on this map?"

Antilla glanced down at the map, "Yes colonel. My mother was Russian and taught me how to read and write the language."

Siilasvuo shined the flashlight onto the map, "Starting from left to right, tell me what the handwriting says."

"Clustered around the road, written in black is the location of the various units of the 44th." Antilla replied.

"What about this red writing in the area surrounding the road?" Siilasvuo inquired.

"Those are the positions and estimated strength of our forces." Antilla said.

"Add them up, how many men did Vinogradov think we had?" Siilasvuo asked.

Antilla took nearly a minute to tabulate the numbers in his head, "Around thirty thousand."

Siilasvuo, unable to contain himself, exploded into laughter, "Thirty thousand? Surely you jest?"

"No, sir." Antilla said sternly.

Siilasvuo, noticing Antilla's indignation said, "I didn't mean to say you were reading this incorrectly sergeant." He patted Antilla on the back and said, "What about this force on the eastern edge of the map between the Purasjoki River and Raate Village. This isn't part of the 44th, is this the 3rd NKVD?"

Antilla's eyes fell to the map, and he slowly nodded, "Yes, colonel. The writing indicates the position of the 3rd NKVD Regiment, along with some other independent battalions that appear to be attached to the regiment."

Siilasvuo smiled and ordered, "Major, captain, get in here." Siilasvuo turned back to the sergeant and said, "Take those notebooks sitting next to the radio set in the corner and go outside so you can see to read them. If I get you pen and paper, can you translate them?"

Antilla nodded, "Yes, colonel."

Siilasvuo turned to Major Valli and Pekka, "I want Task Force Makiniemi, Kari, and Fagneras to surround the 3rd

NKVD Regiment and eliminate it immediately."

Before anyone could reply, Major Fagneras burst into the room on the heels of Valli and Pekka and said, "They're gone."

"Who's gone?" Siilasvuo asked in annoyance.

"The 3rd NKVD. I just received word from both Lieutenant Halonen and Captain Kokko that they have lost contact with the enemy." Fagneras replied.

"Where are these men located?" Siilasvuo asked.

Halonen is holding the west bank of the Purasjoki River and Kokko is at Raate Village. The 3rd NKVD was trapped on the road between them." Fagneras replied.

"How did they get out? It sounds like you had them penned in on both the east and the west." Siilasvuo said.

"They apparently melted away into the forest to the north." Fagneras replied.

"Smart. Seems like the Soviets aren't complete dolts. If the 44th had done the same, we wouldn't have been able to stop them." Siilasvuo said in disappointment. "The forest north of the road ranges for hundreds of kilometers in each direction. They'll be able to melt away like a fart in the Sahara."

Siilasvuo turned to Valli and ordered, "Do we have an initial estimate of what we have captured?"

"Yes, colonel. We have preliminary figures." Valli replied.

"Well?" Siilasvuo demanded impatiently, "Out with-it man!"

Valli took a deep breath and started speaking, "Eighty-five tanks, four hundred and thirty-seven trucks, twenty tractors, ten motorcycles, one thousand six hundred and twenty horses that are still breathing, several thousand more that aren't, ninety-two artillery pieces, seventy-eight anti-tank guns, and thirteen anti-aircraft guns."

Siilasvuo, avoiding the vomit on the floor, collapsed into Vinogradov's chair stunned. He met the major's gaze, "You're serious? This isn't a jest?"

Valli shook his head, "No, colonel. In addition, we also captured, thousands of rifles, machine guns, and ammunition."

"I thought they had mostly run out of ammunition?" Siilasvuo questioned.

"They had, sir, but apparently the 4th motti had most of the ammunition trucks." Valli said.

"This is too much to believe." Siilasvuo said, "Do you know what this means for the country?"

"That we have enough arms and ammunition to keep fighting the invader for at least another month." Valli replied.

"And that we quadrupled the number of tanks, and doubled the amount of anti-tank guns that our entire army has." Siilasvuo added.

"Sounds like a great reason to throw a party!" Pekka exclaimed.

Siilasvuo smiled, "It is indeed. Major Valli, see that each man is issued a vodka ration this evening."

"Yes, Colonel." Vallie replied.

Lieutenant Colonel Makiniemi entered the room, "Colonel Siilasvuo."

Siilasvuo turned and gave Makiniemi a warm smile, "Welcome colonel and well done."

"Thank you, sir. This is a great day for our nation." Makiniemi replied.

"It is indeed." Siilasvuo replied, "What brings you to this corner of the woods?"

Makiniemi's eyes fell as he said, "There's something I need to tell you about Lieutenant Karhonen."

Epilogue

NKVD Commissariat, Town of Vazhenvaara, Soviet Union

January 11th, 1940

Former general of the 44th Motorized Rifle Division, Alexi Vinogradov strained to break the ropes that bound his wrists. He stood against the splintered wood of a well-used execution pole. His arms had been pulled behind him and secured to the pole with rope so that he would be forced to face his fate.

On Vinogradov's right, also tied to a wooden pole was Colonel Volkov, the only other high-ranking officer of the 44th, to escape the destruction of the division. On Vinogradov's left stood commissar Pakhomov. Pakhomov was the only commissar to have survived the Raate Road debacle.

Lieutenant Egorov of the NKVD, who stood behind a line of twelve soldiers armed with Mosin-Nagant rifles turned to their sergeant and said, "It seems executing generals has become a regular duty in this miserable outpost."

"Oh?" The sergeant said curiously.

"Why just nine days ago I had the privilege of overseeing General Zelentsov's execution." Egorov said proudly.

"You must be on your way to bigger and better things." The sergeant said, hoping that this is what Egorov wanted to hear.

Egorov smiled, "Indeed comrade."

Egorov turned away from the sergeant and gazed upon his prisoners, "Do you have any final words before I read the charges against you?"

Private Alexi Vinogradov, former commanding general of the 44th Motorized Rifle Division smiled at the young lieutenant. Vinogradov was missing several teeth which had been knocked out during his recent debriefing by the NKVD, "Can I have some vodka?"

"Prisoners do not receive a vodka ration. Is there anything else?" Egorov asked.

The three men remained silent as they stared at Egorov dully, "Very well. For the loss of fifty-four field kitchens, the tribunal has sentenced you to death. Sentence to be carried out immediately."

"Squad, attention!" The sergeant barked.

The twelve soldiers snapped to the position of attention. They held the rifles in their right hands with the stock touching the ground by their right foot, "Order arms!"

The twelve men of the firing squad raised their rifles to their shoulders, "Take aim." Egorov ordered.

Obeying the command, they made a show of aiming at

the three prisoners who stood five meters away. Behind the prisoners loomed a brick wall whose surface was pock marked from the impact of many bullets. The bricks had been stained a deep crimson with the blood of those unfortunates who had been executed here.

"Fire!"

The crash of twelve rifles firing pierced the air. Several bullets slammed into each man. Both Volkov and Pakhomov were slain instantly. Vinogradov, his body hit by three bullets, grunted in pain, then coughed. He lifted his head and met Egorov's stunned gaze. He spat out blood and smiled, revealing bloodstained teeth.

Vinogradov drew in a breath and asked in a whisper, "Since my sentence has been carried out, I am no longer a prisoner." Before he was able to continue a coughing fit overtook him. Again, he spat out blood and asked, "May I have some vodka?"

Without replying Egorov drew his pistol and shot Vinogradov in the head.

Hale's adventure continues in Raid on Russia.

Other Books by James Mullins

Special Military Operation Book I in the Ukraine Invaded series on sale now.

Afterward

The dual Finnish victories of Suomassalmi and The Raate Road shocked the world. Two modern divisions of the Red Army were ordered into the Finnish wilderness to cut the country in half. Success would have eliminated Finland's only two supply links to the outside world. Those links were the rail line that connected Sweden to Oulu Finland, and the arctic port of Toku in the country's far north.

Victory for the Soviets would have isolated the southern half of Finland from the possibility of outside help. In winning at Suomassalmi and The Raate Road, Finland kept their supply lines to the rest of the world open and prolonged the war. In addition, the Finnish Army captured desperately needed weapons to help even the odds-on other battlefields.

During the campaign, Finnish casualties numbered around 2,700 which included 858 killed, 1,518 wounded and 324 cases of frost bite. Soviet casualties numbered 3,735 killed, 1,800 prisoners of war, 3,788 wounded, 2,800 cases of frost bite, for a total of 12,073 or roughly 50% of the total force engaged. Further the Soviets that survived the trek home were executed by the NKVD in the summer of 1940. Thus, in the end, the Soviet Union lost two entire divisions to Colonel Siilasvuo's band of reservists.

The 9th Division never existed until it was declared by Colonel Siilasvuo and General Mannerheim in December of 1939. The 9th Division's disparate units had never trained together. The officers weren't familiar with each other. It was basically a random group of strangers coming together with the belief in a single idea, freedom for their people, punching way above their weight class.

War Material captured by Finland during the battles.

Tanks	85
Artillery Pieces	92
Anti-Tank Guns	78
Anti-Aircraft Guns	13
Trucks	437
Tractors	20
Motorcycles	10
Horses	1,620
Rifles	6,000

The Finnish Army started the Winter War with 38 Swedish Bofors 37mm Anti-Tank Guns. Capturing seventy-eight additional guns, more than doubled their ability to kill Red Army Tanks. This equipment would help Finland continue the fight for three more grueling months.

The twin battles of Suomassalmi and The Raate Road are recognized as textbook examples of how to engage a larger force when outnumbered. The tactics used in the battle are studied and taught by militaries around the world. For instance, the United States Marine Corps Officer Candidate School teaches cadets, the lessons learned from the battle. In part, to ensure that they, as future leaders, will not make the same mistakes, and in part to demonstrate that any odds can be overcome.

The battle would have ramifications to the wider conflict that was World War II. The Soviet Union's failure to quickly overcome tiny Finland was noticed by Adolf

Hitler. Up until that point, Hitler had no intention of embarking on a two front war and repeating the mistakes of World War I. With a non-aggression pact in hand with the Soviet Union, he had seemingly achieved that goal.

The pathetic performance of the Red Army during the Winter War, as a result of Stalin's purges, showed that the Red Army was a paper tiger. As a result, Germany invaded the Soviet Union on June 21st, 1941, in an attempt to exploit the Red Army's weakness. Finland's desperate fight for national survival changed the course of World War II.

Now close your eyes and imagine what World War II would have looked like if Nazi Germany never invaded the Soviet Union. Germany could have turned its full focus to subduing Britain. The three million German troops used for the initial invasion of the Soviet Union could have been used in North Africa and elsewhere. The end result being Germany taking the oil fields of the Middle East and perhaps not stopping until they came into contact with Imperial Japan. Maybe not even then.

With no further opponents on the continent, the Germany would have embarked on a crash shipbuilding program using both their own shipyards, and the yards of their conquered territories. With oil to spare the Italian Navy could have been joined to Germany's growing navy and used to support a resurrected Operation Sea Lion. An operation in which the Royal Navy would have had to fight through literal clouds of Luftwaffe planes to prevent a German landing in the United Kingdom.

Would the United States have been able to aid Britain in time to stave off a German invasion? Would the Soviet Union have been content to sit out or would they take advantage of Britain's isolation? Perhaps the Soviets would have betrayed the Germans by violating the non-aggression pact?

This sounds like a world where freedom dies. Fortunately, we weren't born into that world. I can't help but to think that fact may have been due to a small group of Finns fighting for their freedom in the forests of Central Finland against the might of the world's largest most modern Army in December of 1939.

About the Author

James Mullins holds three college degrees, a Master's and Bachelor's in Business Administration and an Associates in Acquisition and Contract Management. He lives with his beautifully intelligent wife Anna, two cats, and his son Tristan Alexander.

James served as an Avionics Attack System Specialist for the United States Air Force's 71st Fighter Squadron, known as the Ironmen. During several tours of duty in the Middle East, and Iceland James came to appreciate the beauty of two of the world's harshest environments. Next, he built upon his problem-solving skills as a Pest Control Department Manager for Patriot Pest Control. During this time, he happily slew millions of bugs for the betterment of humankind, or at least making the lives of many a little less gross.

After finishing college, he became a Production Controller for Newport News Shipbuilding (NNS). Over the course of thirteen years, James helped to build Nimitz, and Ford Class Aircraft Carriers. In addition, he participated in the construction of several Virginia Class Submarines. During his time as a shipbuilder, he spent six years in supply chain production control, four years creating the paint forecasting methodology used by NNS' Carrier Program's and two years as the Blast and Coat Facility's Carrier Overhaul Production Controller. In his last year with the only company that manufactures nuclear aircraft carriers in the Western Hemisphere, he used his writing skills to help fend off government auditors.

Today, he works for the United States Department of Transportation's Federal Highway Administration as the Finance Manager for Virginia. His team assists the Virginia Department of Transportation to unlock Federal Highway Funds. These funds are used to maintain and expand Virginia's circulatory system, its highways.

Outside of his professional career, his passion for history led to the creation of his own stories. He has a diverse interest in history in general and military history in particular with interests in Rome, the Medieval Roman Empire (Byzantium), the Middle Ages, World War II, and the American Civil War. The Raate Road is his eleventh novel.

Printed in Great Britain
by Amazon